OFF BALANCE SERIES

TWIST

LUCIA FRANCO

OTHER TITLES BY LUCIA FRANCO

<u>Standalone Titles</u>
You'll Think of Me
Hold On to Me
You're Mine Tonight
Tell Me What You Want
Irresistible Stranger

<u>Hush Hush Series</u>
Hush Hush
Say Yes
The Proposition

<u>Off Balance series</u>
Balance
Execution
Release
Twist
Dismount
Out of Bounds

Dear Reader,

The Off Balance series is a continuation series. The novels must be read in order to follow the story.

This story is purely fictional and does not reflect on real-life events.

Each novel in this five-part series follows a heavy May-December romance between a gymnast and a coach. If you consider this subject and any related content disturbing, then the Off Balance series is not for you.

Gymnastics is a hands-on sport that involves hours of close contact with a coach. My goal was to focus on the beauty of the sport in detail, show the emotional aspect of the dedication an athlete makes, and show how two people are able to cross forbidden boundaries and evolve together.

This story will push you, question you, and take you outside of your comfort zone.

The Off Balance series is intended only for readers 18 years of age and older. Reader discretion is advised.

—Lucia

To my devoted and passionate readers...

Please forgive me.

I love you,
and it's killing me.

—Anonymous

GLOSSARY

All-Around A category of gymnastics that includes all the events. The all-around champion of an event earns the highest total score from all events combined.

Amanar A Yurchenko-style vault, meaning the gymnast performs a round-off onto the board, a back handspring onto the vault with a two-and-a-half twisting layout backflip.

Cast A push off the bar with hips and lifts the body to straighten the shoulders and finish in handstand.

Deduction Points taken off a gymnast's score for errors. Most deductions are pre-determined, such as a 0.5 deduction for a fall from an apparatus or a 0.1 deduction for stepping out of bounds on the floor exercise.

Dismount The last skill in a gymnastics routine. For most events the method used to get off the event apparatus.

Elite International Elite, the highest level of gymnastics.

Execution The performance of a routine. Form, style, and technique used to complete the skills constitute the level of execution of an exercise. Bent knees, poor toe point and an arched or loose held body position are all examples of poor execution.

Giant Performed on bars, a swing in which the body is fully extended and moving through a 360-degree rotation around the bar.

Full-In A full-twisting double back tuck, with the twist happening in the first backflip. It can be done in a tucked, piked, or layout position and is used in both men's and women's gymnastics.

Free Hip Circle Performed on the uneven bars or high bar, the body circles around the bar without the body touching the bar. There are both front hip circles and back hip circles.

Handspring Springing off the hands by putting the weight on the arms and using a strong push from the shoulders. Can be done either forward or backward, and is usually a connecting movement. This skill can be performed on floor, vault, and beam.

Heel Drive A termed used by coaches to inform the gymnasts they want them to drive their heels harder up and over on the front side of a handspring vault or front handspring on floor. Stronger heel drives create more rotation and potential for block and power.

Hecht Mount A mount where the gymnast jumps off a spring board while keeping their arms straight, pushes off the low bar, and catches the high bar.

Hop Full A giant to handstand. Once toes are above the bar, a full 360-degree turn in a handstand on the high bar.

Inverted Cross Performed by men on the rings. It is an upside down cross.

Iron Cross A strength move performed by men on the rings. The gymnast holds the rings straight out on either side of their body while holding themselves up. Arms are perpendicular to the body.

Jaeger Performed on bars, a gymnast swings from a front giant and lets go of the bar, completes a front flip and catches the bar again. Jaeger can be done in the straddle, pike, and layout position, and is occasionally performed in a tucked position.

Kip The most commonly used mount for bars, the gymnast glides forward, pulls their feet to the bar, then pushes up to front support, resting their hips on the bar.

L-Grip One hand is in the reverse grip position. This is an awkward grip and difficult to use.

Layout A stretched body position.

Layout Timers A drill that simulates the feel of a skill, or the set for a skill without the risk of completing the skill.

Lines Straight, perfect lines of the body.

Overshoot, also known as Bail A transition from the high bar facing the low bar. The gymnast swings up and over the low bar with a half-turn to catch the low bar ending in a handstand.

Pike The body bent forward at the waist with the legs kept straight; an L position.

Pirouette Used in both gymnastics and dance to refer to a turn around the body's longitudinal axis. It is used to refer to a handstand turning moves on bars.

Rips In gymnastics, a rip occurs when a gymnast works so hard on the bars or rings that they tear off a flap of skin from their hand. The injury is like a blister that breaks open.

Release Leaving the bar to perform a skill before re-grasping it.

Relevé This is a dance term that is often used in gymnastics. In a relevé, the gymnast is standing on toes and has straight legs.

Reverse Grip A swing around the bar back-first with arms rotated inwards and hands facing upwards.

Round-off A turning movement, with a push-off on one leg, while swinging the legs upward in a fast cartwheel motion into a 90-degree turn where legs come together before landing on both feet. The lead-off to a number of skills used to perform on vault, beam, and floor.

Salto Flip or somersault, with the feet coming up over the head and the body rotating around the axis of the waist.

Sequence Two or more skills performed together, creating a different skill or activity.

Shaposhnikva A clear hip circle on the low bar then flying backward to the high bar.

Stalder Starts in handstand with the gymnast moving backward and circling the bar with legs straddled on either side of their arms or inside their arms.

Stick To land and remain standing without requiring a step. A proper stick position is with legs bent, shoulders above hips, arms forward.

Straddle Back An uneven bar transition done from a swing backwards on the high bar over low bar, while catching the low bar in a handstand.

Switch Ring Performed on floor and the balance beam. The gymnast jumps with both feet, lifting their legs into a 180-degree split with the back leg coming up to touch their head.

Tap Swing Performed on bars, an aggressive tap toward the ceiling in a swinging motion. This gives the gymnast the necessary momentum to swing around the bar to perform a giant or to go into a release move.

Toe On Swing around the bar with body piked so much the feet are on the bar.

Tour Jeté A dance leap where the dancer leaps on one foot, makes a full turn in the air, and lands on the other foot.

Tsavdaridou Performed on beam, a round-off back handspring with full twist to swing down.

Tuck The knees and hips are bent and drawn into the chest. The body is folded at the waist.

Twist The gymnast rotates around the body's longitudinal axis, defined by the spine. Performed on all apparatuses.

Yurchenko Round-off entry onto the board, back handspring onto the vaulting table and Salto off the vault table. The gymnast may twist on the way off.

CHAPTER 1

S tage 4 kidney disease.

There were five stages, and I was already at four. Like it was a *stage* of *cancer*.

Plus lupus.

My body ran cold and goose bumps broke out down my arms. The number four banged around inside my head, taunting me. I needed to start dialysis and get placed on a transplant list.

I knew better than to google anything, but I couldn't not. I needed to know what I was up against.

At first I started with the medications the doctors had prescribed. Antibiotics, steroids, blood pressure, and pain medication. Then curiosity got the best of me and I explored websites that led to other websites with normal to rare outcomes. Hours of researching how both diseases worked together consumed me. I read countless pages of life expectancy, threads on the side effects of treatments and both illnesses, threads on how my body could reject the transplant, chats on how difficult it would be to get pregnant and carry to full term, topics on how the disease escalated and ultimately had the power to take the life of a loved one.

The stress and anxiety of what could happen, and what most likely would, hammered through me at a pace I couldn't catch up to. I was sick to my stomach over everything. The truth was, I needed to start dialysis immediately, and I needed to find a match for a kidney transplant.

I stood in the kitchen of my condo staring at the row of medicine bottles with names I couldn't pronounce. Pills my life depended on.

My cell phone rang and I snatched it off the counter. Xavier's goofy face lit up the screen.

"Hey, big brother." I smiled, thankful for the distraction. "Long time no talk."

He groaned into the phone. "Yeah, I know I'm a flake, but I think of you all the time and it's the thought that counts, right?"

"Yeah, I guess so. To what do I owe this pleasure?"

"Dad called me." My smile disappeared and I grew quiet. "Ana?"

I hadn't heard that nickname in so long. "I'm here. What did he tell you?"

"Everything. I know everything. How are you handling it? Because I'll tell you what, it makes me sad and really fucking angry that you have to go through this," he said, his voice taking on an array of emotions. "If I could trade spots with you I would. I hate this for you."

I blinked, pushing back my emotions. I'd cried so much lately that I didn't want to start again, and I felt like I would from how sweet he was being.

I exhaled and reached into my refrigerator to pull out a carton of coconut water. I uncapped it and took a sip, eyeing the pill bottles with distain.

"Well, I'm currently standing in my kitchen with bottles of pills lined up and the warnings they print on the sides staring me in the face. May cause vomiting. Take with a meal. May be taken on an empty stomach. Take in the morning. May cause shakiness. Take as needed for pain. May cause drowsiness. Just about every symptom I have for lupus is the same listed for kidney disease. The headaches and hair loss, the pain in my chest, my drastic weight loss I attributed to training so hard. The brain fog and forgetfulness. Lupus has the power to kill people in their twenties due to a heart attack or a stroke, and often causes difficulty getting pregnant with half resulting in miscarriage. Kidney disease goes hand in hand with lupus. My immune system will attack my tissue, organs, and joints. Basically, I'm my own worst enemy."

I stopped when I realized I'd just repeated what I'd read online without taking a breath.

"I'm sorry," I said. "It's probably not what you wanted to hear."

"Don't apologize. And it's exactly what I wanted to hear. I just wasn't sure how to ask, you know?"

I swallowed. "Yeah, I guess."

"Are you scared?"

Fucking right I was. I didn't want to die. I had too much to experience first. And I wanted a family with two-point-five kids one day. And a dog. I wanted a dog, maybe two. Joy never let us have pets.

Kids.

Sadness consumed me. Kova and I had unprotected sex—a *lot*—and by some miracle, I hadn't gotten pregnant. Not that I wanted to right now. But the thought of not being able to ever have babies hit me hard with a force that took my breath away. I'd always wanted to be a mother someday. Dreamed of it.

Abortion…

Avery. God, my heart hurt, my chest feeling hollow for the way I shut her out. She'd gotten an abortion, and I treated her like shit.

"Ana? You still there?"

I shook away the melancholy. "No, I'm not scared."

Xavier chuckled and I did too. "I knew you'd say that. Always putting on a strong front. A Rossi gene that you're born with."

I let out a sigh. "Yeah, I am scared. Okay? It's a lot to take in, and it's really overwhelming reading all this crap online basically telling me how hard my life is going to be."

I walked over to the couch and plopped down. I leaned my head back and let out a tired sigh and stared at the ceiling, watching the fan move in a circular motion.

Xavier coughed. "It'll get easier in time." He paused. "Probably not what you wanted to hear. Probably don't believe it."

No, it wasn't. And I didn't.

I closed my eyes and drew in a lungful of air. I had to be up early for practice, against my doctor's better judgment. But I couldn't stop. Not after all I've ever dreamed of having was finally at the tips of my fingers. Gymnastics was the one thing I couldn't bear to have taken from my life. Gymnastics gave me life, it gave me freedom. I was nothing without it. I didn't know who I was outside of the sport, and having it erased completely from my life terrified me.

To be blunt, I don't see you making it into your twenties still competing and training at the rate that you are now. It's not impossible, just highly unlikely. My mind raced a mile a minute as Dr. Kozol's words added to the thoughts swirling around in my head, demanding to be heard.

My phone beeped and I pulled it away to look at the screen. *Dad's Cell.*

"Hey, Dad's calling me. I gotta take this."

"Oh, yeah it's cool, grab it. Just wanted to tell you I'm rooting for you. You're strong, Sis. You got this. I have an appointment to be tested to see if we're a match. Anything you need, even if it's just to talk or curse me out, hit me up. I'm your guy."

A sad giggle rolled off my lips. A tear slipped this time. "Thanks, Xavier. We'll talk later?"

"Later, little sis."

I clicked over.

"Hey, Dad."

"Sweetheart, why haven't I heard from you? I've been waiting all day."

"Because you already know," I responded quickly. Turns out he'd known before I did. He knew what I was walking into. "What else is there to talk about? You know everything."

Dad was silent for a moment. "You're upset with me."

"Yeah, a little. You should've told me. At least you could've prepared me. I've been in a state of shock ever since this afternoon."

"I wanted to, believe me, but I felt the doctors should be the ones to deliver the diagnosis so they could better explain." He paused, then said, "I was also worried you might panic and not show up."

I mused over his words. "I guess you have a point. I wouldn't have not shown up, but it would've been nice not to be blindsided either."

"I truly am sorry," he said, his voice full of regret. "Is that why I haven't heard from you?"

"Yes and no. I'm just all over the place right now with my thoughts, trying to figure out how I got to this point. Dad?" Emotion clogged my throat, making my voice sound shaky.

"Yes?"

Tears filled my eyes and I broke down faster than I could stop it. "I'm scared." The confession was a shattered whisper on my lips. My breathing deepened and I started crying. "I'm really scared. I don't want to die."

"Oh, sweetie." His voice broke, which only upset me further. "I'll be there first thing in the morning. Please don't cry. I promise everything will be okay."

"But that's the thing." I sniffled. "You don't know if it will be okay. No one knows. My life is in limbo now and it's terrifying. For the first time in my life, I'm seriously petrified of what's to come. I can taste the fear and it's suffocating me."

"Adrianna, I'll do everything in my power to help you." Dad drove his words home with absolution. I cried harder at the struggles I was facing. My future was now—and would forever be—an uphill battle. "You just have to be strong like you've always been. Keep pushing on. Don't let today affect tomorrow. Take your medicine and focus on gymnastics. I'll handle the rest. You will have everything you need. I can promise that."

"You're not going to tell me to give up the sport?"

"Sweetheart, I know how much it means to you, and I spoke in depth with Dr. Kozol. It's not unheard of for a pro athlete to still compete with illnesses like yours. It's rare, but not impossible. You'll have to work with him and his team. And you'll have to be completely open and honest about everything. No more pushing through the pain."

"I thought I was just overworked. It comes with the territory of training elite. I thought nothing of it."

I sniffled, trying to pull back my emotions. On top of everything, the pain I had been feeling, the nausea and blood, Dr. Kozol informed me was due to a kidney infection. It was causing one of my kidneys to swell. My body was failing me, and failing me fast.

"How could I be this sick and not know it?"

"Adrianna, you can live a healthy, full life. Yes, there will be complications, but there are also precautions you can take to prevent them, or at the very least, slow them down."

I exhaled a heavy breath, then let it all out and told my dad what I'd read.

"Don't read any of that garbage on the internet. I should have every form of cancer known to man if it were true. In fact, I should be six feet under rotting away." He paused. "You know, if you decide you want to come home for a little while to take a break, you can do that."

I shook my head as if he could see me. "No, that would only put me behind and I'm too close to risk that. Thanks, though."

"I'm not sure you're aware, but with your Amex Black Card, you have a personal concierge on call twenty-four seven. They're paid to do whatever you want and get whatever you need—as long as it's within legal parameters, of course."

I was aware of that, but I'd never used the service before.

I wiped away my lingering tears with the back of my hand.

"You don't have to come tomorrow. I'll be okay."

"I'll be there," he insisted.

I softened. "It's okay, Dad. You'll be bored. I have back-to-back practice the next few days anyway, and then I leave for competition. I'll hardly have time to see you or talk to you."

"I'll be at your competition, then. If that's the only time I can see you, then I'll be there."

Damn it. The tears started up again. "Okay." My voice sounded so small.

"Sweetie," he murmured, "don't cry. We'll get through this together."

"I love you, Dad."

"Love you too."

I drew in a deep breath and attempted to shelve my emotions again. "Dad? Please, don't tell anyone else. Family is one thing, but no one else."

"Adrianna, your coaches need to know."

I sat up straight. "No."

"Adri—"

"Dad, *no*. I don't want them to know. They'd make me change my training schedule again. I've come too far for that."

Dad was quiet for a long minute. "They need to know you're starting dialysis."

I gasped, my jaw hung open. "No, I'm not. I'm not doing dialysis right now." Anger dried up my tears. "The trials are right around the corner, and the Olympics only last like two months from start to finish after that. I'll begin treatment once it's over."

His voice hardened. "Use your brain, Adrianna. You don't have the time to wait to start treatment. I've already made the appointment for you. You're going."

My nostrils flared. "Dad!"

"Adrianna." He said my name with frustration. "I will *not* lose you. You'll be at that appointment whether you want to or not. How are you going to enjoy being a gymnast if you're dead?"

I slammed my mouth shut, my teeth grinding together.

That was heartless.

"Dad, please." My voice was low, broken, and the stupid tears were back. "It's only a few months. I can handle a few more months. After everything I read online, if I start now, I won't be able to compete. I'll lose everything I've worked for because I won't have the strength to continue. I'll be even sicker. Please, I'm begging you to just give me more time."

"Sweetie, you simply don't have the time."

I swallowed hard and clenched my eyes shut. I hated that he was right.

"Please." I cried softly. "I'll do anything you want as soon as I know about the Olympics." We were both quiet for a long moment. "Please, Dad, please give me a little more time."

His voice was low, grim. "Adrianna, I just can't allow you to wait."

Tears were streaming down my cheeks. "Dad, a few more months won't hurt. I'll go to the doctor every week if you want me to instead of every three weeks just for a checkup. I'll bring a doctor to meets with me. Please don't take my gymnastics dream away from me. In a couple of months I'll have to say goodbye forever. Don't make me say it now, because that's what you'd be doing if I start dialysis."

I was crying uncontrollably. All I needed was a few more months and then I would give myself up to the diseases and do whatever my dad and my new team of doctors wanted me to do. Until then, this was all that I was asking for. I would be fine until then. I knew I would.

Dad let out a heavy breath while I held mine. "I don't think this is a good idea."

"If I feel like I've taken a turn for the worse, I'll call you and tell you. I'll go to the doctor. Anything, just don't make me start treatment now." I paused when I thought about when the Olympic Trials were. "I just need a few more months, that's all I'm asking for. It won't make that big of a deal if I take my medicine and go to my checkups. Plus, by then, I'll know if I made the team or not. Just give me a little more time."

"Adrianna, sweetheart…" I could tell he was caving. "So much can happen in two months."

"Nothing is going to happen. We wouldn't even be having this conversation if I hadn't gone to the doctor."

"But you did go and it changes everything. Your health is at risk." I heard the sound of ice clinking against a glass like he was taking a sip of his drink—drifted across the line. "I know what gymnastics means to you and I don't want to take it away, but as your parent, I'm responsible for your well-being."

"Dad, please, I'm begging you."

He groaned like he was torn. "If anything changes, or you need to talk, you better call me. I don't care if it's the middle of the night or if you already called fifteen times, just call me."

Hope surged through me. I sniffled. "Does this mean you'll let me wait to start treatment?"

He hesitated. I could tell he wasn't happy about this. "I don't like this idea, but I'd do anything for you, Adrianna. I hope you know that. You have a long road ahead of you. I just want to see you get well and keep you happy." I smiled sadly to myself. "Keep your head held high," he said, but he didn't seem too sure of himself.

My head was a messy configuration of emotions that I couldn't compartmentalize like I typically was able to. It was too much at once, but he was right. I needed to keep my head held high and focused. I'd gotten my way but needed a subject change before he changed his mind.

"Thank you! Thank you! Thank you, Dad!" He chuckled and it loosened the tightness in my chest. "So, um, not to change the subject, but I have a question about Mom."

"Your mother isn't—"

"No. I mean my real mom. Sophia."

Clearing his throat, he seemed caught off guard. "Oh? What did you want to know?"

I'd have to start asking family if they were open and willing to match test for me, otherwise I would end up on a long list of hopefuls and possibly never get a donor.

"How did you meet her?"

He let out a sound somewhere between a huff and a scoff. "Are you sure you want to have this conversation right now?"

"Why not? My life is already shit. What's one more thing?"

He sighed deeply into the phone. I imagined he was rubbing his forehead. "She was my assistant."

"Was she legal?"

"She'd just turned eighteen when she had you."

So, no, she wasn't. I'd had a weird feeling she was young after I'd met her, but I hadn't expected her to be *that* young.

"Did you love her?"

"Love…it's a tricky thing."

I laughed under my breath. Didn't I know that.

"Do you still talk to her?"

Silence stretched for such a long moment to the point I thought he hung up. Just as I was about to call his name, he spoke. "Yes, I do."

"How often?"

"Quite often, actually."

I rubbed the ache in my chest. Judgment and distrust blackened my vision as all the lies I'd been told over the years flashed through my head.

"How did she end up in your office that day when I came to see you? Before that when I asked about her, you told me you didn't talk to her."

"It's a long story, but I'll sum it up for you. After you were born, I foolishly thought we all could work out joint custody since it'd be in the best interest for you, but I should've known better." Dad's voice trailed away like he was deep in memory. "Sophia was young and poor with nowhere to live, and Joy used that against her to keep her out of your life. Sophia begged me not to take you from her…and I couldn't. It takes a selfish person to deny someone their child. So, I worked with her as much as I could and lied to Joy about it. My arrangement with Sophia went on for years until Joy hired a private investigator to keep tabs on me. Joy built a fictitious case against her, insisting she was mentally unstable."

My brows rose. This shit just got better and better. To our rich, little island, we were the picture-perfect family. Behind closed doors, we were all living double lives.

CHAPTER 2

What?" I said. My voice elevated to a shocking level. "What was she trying to prove?"

"I tried to reason with Joy and asked her to put herself in Sophia's shoes and pretend it was Xavier. You know what she said? 'I feel no pity for the whore you cheated on me with.' That's when I knew it would never be easy. In order for Joy to stop the harassment, I gave her the one thing I knew would placate her. Money. Reluctantly, I gifted Joy for her *selflessness*, but also to act like a mother to you. I thought everything would be okay, but it was far from that."

Gifted. "You mean you paid her off." I scoffed to myself at the sheer ignorance of it. "You paid off your own wife."

"Sophia fell into a terrible state of postpartum depression after you were born. It lasted a long time." Dad ignored my comment. "I felt guilty, like it was all my doing. When I stopped seeing her, she became irrational, highly unstable, and on top of her sister's death, she threatened to run off with you and disappear. I knew she loved you dearly, but I couldn't chance that. I told her if she wanted to seek mental health treatment that I'd pay for it, which I did. I gave her a fully furnished condo once she was out of the inpatient facility, and money to live on so she didn't have to worry. She tried to refuse both and fought me over it because she saw it as payment for you. I assured her it wasn't like that." Dad was quiet for a moment. "During this time, I became a total disaster. My business took a huge hit, I was drinking heavily, and I had a child with someone who wasn't my wife but I was madly in love with. I wanted a divorce. Joy knew that and used whatever she could to her advantage. She insisted I file for full custody so we could give you a healthy and stable home with your brother. She was so sincere…and I believed her. I just never expected Joy to exploit my affair or to use my child for her gain."

I frowned, feeling so low inside. What a bittersweet tragedy my birth caused. It wasn't a happy occasion like the new life of a child should be. It was one full of misery and adultery. I was unwelcomed, and that only further solidified the isolation I fought deep inside throughout my childhood.

"Sophia and I started talking again once she was better." His voice was quiet.

"How long ago was that?"

"Oh, I'd say over ten years ago. At least."

My brows shot up. "What!" I yelled into the phone. "Over ten years ago? Is that why Joy is the way she is? I'm assuming she found out."

"She didn't find out until a couple of years ago actually. That's when things started to get really tense between us. She hired another private investigator."

"Sounds like she has them on standby."

"She does. It's her weapon of choice. She loves collecting evidence that would ruin someone." He took a sip of his drink again judging by the sound of the ice clinking against the glass. "Sophia and I, we've always had this connection that Joy could never break, no matter how hard she tried. I love Sophia and have loved her since the moment I met her. That will never change."

I grew quiet, feeling bad for my dad and Sophia. The longing in his voice for a love with my real mom curled around my heart like a wet piece of satin and saddened me. Joy may have been the only mother I've ever known, but now a lot of things that happened over the years made sense. She may be married to a multimillionaire and want for nothing, but she is still, and clearly will always be, the other woman. I'm sure that had to harden her heart.

Dad continued. "After living with Joy for so long and seeing her for who she really is, I needed to know what she was up to, so I hired a PI myself. I knew she wouldn't find much on me, other than being with Sophia."

"Did you find anything on her?" I clutched the phone in my hand, unblinking as I waited for his answer.

"I found out a plethora of things she was hiding, including offshore bank accounts."

"I can't believe I never knew any of this."

"You weren't supposed to know."

Fair enough. "I take it Joy won't bother being tested for me."

"She doesn't know about it yet."

I wasn't sure whether to be happy or sad about that.

"Maybe that's a good thing." I licked my dry lips. "I know I don't know her all that well, but do you think Sophia will be open to being tested?"

"It may not seem like it because you don't really know her, but Sophia will do anything for you. She's just a little sensitive right now after hearing about your illnesses. It brought back memories of her sister." He paused. "Sometimes when I look at you, all I see is Sophia," he admitted. "You guys could pass as sisters."

I choked back my emotion. Sophia once told me I looked like her sister. "Where does she live now?"

His voice dropped to a low, quiet tone after another long pause. "North. A few towns over."

My jaw took a dive, heart flailing into my stomach. My real mom lived a few towns over, and I never knew. I couldn't stop the questions from flying out of me.

"Does she ever ask about me?"

"All the time, sweetie. All the time."

I blinked long. "Does she still want to see me? Has she ever asked?" I held my shaky breath as I waited for his response, terrified of what he would say.

"She has asked about seeing you…" I could tell he was thinking carefully about his words before he spoke them. "I know Sophia would love to see you again one day, but I told her it would need to be up to you. She completely agreed."

I let out a long and heavy sigh, trying to wrap my mind around the last couple of days. From Kova saying I needed to start with my mother if I wanted answers, to being diagnosed with kidney disease and lupus, to effortlessly being able to talk to my dad about my real mom, I had so many questions left that I wasn't sure I'd ever get my thoughts in order to ask all of them.

"Does she have other children?"

"No. She didn't feel it was fair to bring other children into this world when she couldn't have you."

"Why didn't she fight to have me as I got older and she got better?"

"She didn't want to disrupt your life, so she stayed away thinking it was best for you. Looking back and realizing how Joy treated you, how I traveled a lot for work… You have to understand, Adrianna, I thought I was doing what was best for our family. I thought I was doing what was best for you. For that, I will forever be sorry."

Each word he spoke chipped away at my heart. He was filled with remorse, and I didn't want that for him. Up until Easter, I'd loved my life, even if I did feel like an outcast at times.

"Dad, don't dwell on it. I don't. I'm okay, and everything turned out just how it was supposed to. I've always been a firm believer that if something is meant to be, it will find its way. Things happen for a reason, and sometimes that reason makes no sense other than to just cause heartache and absolute destruction. Maybe this was how it was supposed to go."

"You are wise beyond your years, you know that?"

"Debatable." I laughed. "So, there's a reason why I was asking about her."

He chuckled. "Oh, really? I hadn't caught on."

I smiled sadly into the phone. "Does—" I didn't know what to call her. "Does Sophia have any other illnesses or diseases in her family history? Anything else I should be concerned with, aside from her sister having MCTD? I don't need any more surprises."

"Her father passed away from liver disease about ten years ago, and I think her mother is okay. I'd have to call Sophia and ask."

I perked up. "When do you think you'll do it?"

"I'll call her now. Once I talk to her, I'll get back to you."

Before we ended our conversation, we went over all my medications. Anything Dad wasn't sure about, he searched on the internet and we went over my symptoms, the importance of that specific medication, and which ones were crucial. He had me use Post-its to write down what they're used for and then stick them to the sides of the bottles. He knew I didn't want to use the pain medications, so those had different color sticky notes. It was much easier this way. The anxiousness that had filled my chest when I first got the prescriptions started to taper off. I was able to breathe again, but I was also too scatterbrained to handle it myself, too stressed and worried about everything I'd read, and where my future with this new diagnosis would lead.

My dad was there for me when I needed him the most, and for whatever reason, that made me emotional and tear up a bit.

"Dad? Remember, don't tell anyone. I don't want anyone to know except for our family, and well, Sophia since you have to talk to her. I have enough on my plate I have to deal with right now, and I don't want anyone to look at me any differently or feel bad or pity me." I paused. "I'd just rather not talk about it if I didn't have to."

"Sweetie, I'll do whatever you want, you know that, but we're all your family and we'll be there for you." Dad sighed when I yawned into the phone. "We'll talk tomorrow, sweetheart. Go get some rest. You've had a long day."

We ended the call and I curled up on my side, holding the phone close to my chest. My hands were shaking, and I had this void inside me that made me feel so cold. I needed someone to tell me it was going to be okay, to hold me tight and take this fear from my chest and make me promises they couldn't keep.

Instead, I was alone in a lavish condo on the beach with the world against me.

Reaching behind me, I pulled the throw blanket over my body and stared at nothing until I dozed off.

Pretending I was okay was easier than explaining why I wasn't.

CHAPTER 3

wanted to call Avery after I spoke to Dad last night, but I didn't have it in me after the lengthy and somewhat emotional conversation I'd had with him.

I knew talking to her would expend any energy I had left, and I needed every little bit I could muster.

I'd been a shitty and pretty selfish best friend for a few months now and that wasn't fair of me. I knew it was wrong and I needed to rectify that. I just wasn't sure how.

At the next light, I picked up my cell phone and swiped it open to find my favorite contacts. I pressed down on a name I hadn't dialed in many months. It didn't even ring twice before I heard her voice.

"Adrianna?"

Her hopeful tone seared off another piece of my broken heart.

"Hey, Avery." My words came out thick. The phone trembled in my hand. Whether it was from the new steroids I was on, or from finally calling Avery, I wasn't sure. I only knew that I wasn't safe to drive like this. Thank goodness I was about to pull into World Cup.

"Aid…" She said my name again, this time backed with her own emotion.

We didn't speak a word to each other while we sat on the phone and cried together.

Then…

"If you ever press that fuck you button on me again—even once—I swear I'm going to beat your ass. I don't care how much stronger you are than me, I can still bite and pull hair with the best of them. I will totally punch you in the vag."

A giant smile spread across my face and I laughed. I wiped the tears away with the back of my hand.

"Oh man, I needed that more than you could imagine."

"Same here. I've missed you so much."

"Avery?"

"Yeah?" Her soft voice burst with optimism.

"I'm so, so sorry for the way I acted, and for the way I've been treating you. It was wrong of me… I'm so ashamed of my actions. I feel terrible."

And I truly was. I just hoped she could hear the honesty of my words through the phone. Remorse pierced my chest and I tried to rub away the tightness.

"No, *I* was wrong," she insisted.

I shook my head to clear my thoughts as I parked my truck. I didn't want her to feel wrong. She had no reason to.

"I should've been upfront about everything from the beginning, and I wasn't." Avery continued. "I hid how I felt about Xavier from the one person I never should have. If I could rewind history and do it over again, I would tell you in a heartbeat. Nothing is worth losing my best friend over. Nothing."

My shoulders sagged from the cracking of her voice. I hated that she felt that way.

"Just stop, Ave. It's okay. You did nothing wrong, and you could never lose me. This is all my doing. I was hurt, dealing with so much shit at one time, and I lashed out at the one person who has always been there for me. It wasn't fair to you. On top of everything, it was the beginning of gymnastics season and the perfect excuse to avoid the situation since my schedule was just go, go, go. I'm a shitty friend. I honestly don't even know why you didn't give up on me and say fuck you and throw in the towel."

"Ah, newsflash, idiot, you're my best friend. No matter what, I'd never do that. I just think we both were dealing with a lot of shit and didn't confide in each other like we'd always done in the past," she said. "I mean, how could we? You with your sexy-as-fuck coach, and me with…your brother. Two relationships that should've never ever happened did, and we couldn't even talk about it. Look at you and Fish Lips." She laughed, and I giggled at her old nickname for Kova. I hadn't heard it in so long. "It took you a hot minute to tell me about that whole thing, and I get that. Now imagine if you were in my shoes and you were secretly dating one of my dumbass brothers. You probably would've done the same thing I did knowing all I'd want to do is to steer you away from him. So, I get it. I understand now. We both were stupid and we both reacted wrongly."

"You're right," I said. I stared through the windshield watching some of the gymnasts practice. "So…are you still with him? With Xavier?" I held my breath and braced myself for her answer. I wasn't sure why.

"No. There will never be an Avery and Xavier again. You can believe that."

"But I saw on your Insta you were with him on the Fourth of July."

"Ohhh look at you stalking me."

I laughed again. "Hush. And here I was finally getting used to the idea that we could actually be family. Hopefully I still have the receipt for your wedding gift."

Avery grew quiet and it troubled me. "We don't need a stupid piece of paper to tell us we're family. But I promise we're not together. We tried to work through things, but, well, it's complicated. All we end up doing is arguing."

I softened at her words, though still concerned. "You're right. It would've been cool, though. What happened?"

"Honestly, Aid, I'm not trying to avoid the subject, but that's a conversation we need to have in person. Trust me on this. There's too much to explain, and some things are better said face-to-face. You'll understand why, and hopefully forgive me. It's not pretty. It's downright hurtful, and I may need my best friend to get through it. I'm not over it and I don't know when I will be. The story is long and sad and full of ugly tears. And, I just put my mascara on."

I smiled. Avery and her makeup. "Are you okay, though?"

She was quiet for a moment. I had my answer before she spoke.

"I'm okay now…at least as okay as I can be."

I knew Avery, and I knew she wasn't okay. I could hear in her voice she was still going through the motions.

"Let me check my calendar to see when I have a break in between meets. I can drive down. I want to see you. I need to talk to you too."

I had no time to spare in between meets but I was going to try and make it work, even if it meant driving both ways in one day. Avery Heron was my best friend, and she needed me.

"About what?"

My heart started to beat a little harder. I wanted to tell her about the doctor visits, but I couldn't find the words.

"I can take off on a Sunday. I'll drive down straight after practice Saturday afternoon, that way we'll have half that day and a full Sunday to hang out. I'll have to leave that night, though. Does that sound good?"

"Would it be easier if I came to you? I know you're busy with camps or some shit. What is it exactly that you do at camp, anyway? Am I going to hear a story similar to what happens at band camp, except some kinky girl-on-girl action?"

I laughed loudly. "Oh my God. Not even close! It's not like that. I can barely walk when it's over."

"Adrianna…" She drew my name out, then chuckled. "What kind of shit goes on down there? Leave it to Kova. He should write a book on sex positions and how to thoroughly fuck someone while doing gymnastics."

"Get your mind out of the gutter, Avery! Kova doesn't go to the camps with me, but he's had to literally carry me out of the airport because they're so brutal."

"Are you still fornicating with him?"

Fornicating. I rolled my eyes and smiled. God, it felt good to talk to her.

"It's a long story, one that's done better face-to-face as well."

"Understood. But are you?" she pushed.

"Not fornicating, but we did mess around a time or two. It was the first time since Easter, but nothing since then."

"Holy shit! That long! Why?"

Heat bloomed under my cheeks. "I'll fill you in once we see each other. Wait—how did you know about the training camps I was doing?"

"I've been following your achievements, dumbass."

My heart swelled. "On TV?"

I knew the big meets were televised and an internet search was just a few clicks away, but camp wouldn't come up unless the coaches were conducting interviews and mentioned one of us.

She stayed silent and then it hit me.

"Xavier," I said quietly.

"Aid. Please don't hang up or be mad at me, I just wanted to know how you were doing!" she shouted in one long breath.

"I'm not. I'm…just surprised."

"Let me put it this way—he hates me, and he'll never forgive me for what I did, but that doesn't stop me from asking how you are. A little nagging goes a long way." Avery was persistent, that's for sure.

I couldn't even begin to imagine what transpired between her and my brother, but I hope whatever it was, it was something that could be mended. Our families would forever be bound together by business. They had no choice but to be a part of each other's lives, whether they were amicable or not.

"I'm so proud of you, girl. You're really doing this," she said, her voice sounding heartfelt and genuine. I wished she was in front of me so I could hug her until she yelled at me to let go. "You know what? I'll just drive up and hang out for like a week or whatever. It's still summer and school doesn't start for a couple more weeks, and I don't have anything to do anyway. I'll go to practices with you, hang around, maybe trip Reagan and drop some Visine into her water, go shopping in between."

I laughed, my shoulders bouncing. "My practices are really long, Ave. I have extra ones added in, and I'm still doing therapy for my Achilles. I'd love for you to come, but I'll feel bad because you'll have nothing to do. If you don't mind being bored out of your mind, I'm game."

"Then it's settled!" she announced. A huge smile spread across my face and excitement fluttered in my stomach. I couldn't wait to see my best friend. "Wait. What is it you wanted to talk to me about?" she asked.

I glanced at the clock. I needed to get a move on or Kova was going to blow a gasket. "Listen, Ave, it's really good to hear your voice. I've missed it, but I have to go. I'll call you tonight and tell you. What I need to tell you, it's going to take time."

She was quiet for a moment, then her tone turned serious. "Are you okay?"

"No, I'm not," I admitted, my voice low.

"What's wrong? What happened?"

"I just… I went to the doctor recently for some checkups and discovered that I'm sick." I paused and exhaled a deep breath. "I'm really sick, Ave."

Tears filled my eyes. I didn't want to cry, especially while I was at practice, but Avery was the first person I was going to talk to about it outside of my family, and it was hitting me much harder than I thought.

"Sick with what, bestie?"

Bestie.

A tear slipped from the corner of my eye, the words lodged in my throat. I covered my mouth to hold back my silent cry.

"Aid?"

I drew in a lungful of air and let it out. "Yeah, I'm here."

"Sick with what?"

"I… I have kidney disease. Stage four kidney disease."

"What does that mean?"

"There are five stages, and it means my kidneys are failing at a crazy fast rate. The doctor said advanced kidney damage. I have to start dialysis soon, and eventually I'm going to need a transplant. I'm holding off on the dialysis right now, though, and started with medication that will hopefully suppress symptoms. My dad said he's going to talk with family to see who will offer to be tested, but if I don't match with any of them, I'll have to be put on a waiting list and basically pray for a miracle."

She was quiet again. I was trying to stay strong, but I could hear her soft cries in the distance and it only made it harder for me.

"Ave?"

"I'm here," she said, but I could barely hear her.

"I'm scared. I don't want to die."

Her cries came in a little stronger this time, and so did mine. I felt empty inside, terrified of the unknown, because no matter what I could do, my body was going to do whatever it wanted.

"Get your head in the game for practice. Let's talk more about this later. I love you, and I promise everything is going to be okay."

We said our goodbyes and I hung up the phone. Climbing out of my truck, I grabbed my duffle bag and made my way inside the gym to the locker room. Drawing in air through my nose, I took a couple of deep breaths to steady myself.

I felt awful for opening up to Avery when I'd shut her out for so long. But I needed her, and I needed her support to go through with this, especially if I was going to go the route I planned.

I quickly undressed out of my sweats, balled them up and stuck them in my bag. A slight pang shot up my leg, but I ignored it. I'd ice my calf and ankle once I got home. I had enough pain already to deal with and I hadn't even started practice yet.

CHAPTER 4

There is no glory in practice. Sports reveal character. Games, meets—they reveal your true character. What would it say about you?" Kova asked the girls. He walked past me to grab some mats. "The way you practice is the way you compete. Give me everything you got today, ladies. I want it all. Show me what you are made of. Prove to me that you deserve this."

"Someone's a little too happy today," Holly said quietly with a small smirk. "I'm kinda scared for what he has in store for us. There's too much pep in his step."

I laughed, totally agreeing with her.

Lifting my gaze, I observed the way Kova moved in a shirt I'd detest on any other guy. It was the crew neck kind where someone took a pair of scissors and cut the sleeves off with their eyes closed and made giant, jagged holes that drooped down to their hips. The only saving grace was the fact that Kova was shredded and his god-awful shirt showcased the part of his body I loved the most—the left side of his ribs, exposing the black Olympic ring tattoo that looked like it was floating every time he took a breath.

Damn this man. Damn his eyes. Damn his fucking body.

"He must be getting laid a lot right now," Reagan chimed in. I glanced over at her and felt instant aggravation over her words. She reached down to grab her toes. "He's totally giving Katja that D and boning her hard. He can give it to me any day." She snickered.

"What would give you that impression?" Holly asked, arms extended above her head as she stretched out her shoulders.

Reagan gave her a knowing look. "It's obvious. You'd have to be blind as a bat not to notice, Hols."

We'd already ran two miles and completed a thirty-minute warmup. We were seated in a straddle position on the floor and I was about to spark conversation with the girls when Kova came up behind me and grabbed my ankle, lifting it.

Kova's freshly clean scent enveloped me like an invisible trail. The citrus and cinnamon pulsed through my nose and invigorated me. I tried to lay forward, but he placed a hand around my ribs and stopped me. The warmth of his fingers spread through my ribs.

"What would it say about you?" Kova asked again. His body was so close to mine his heat radiated onto my back.

I glanced at Reagan, and a smile spread across my face. "I'm not sure what it would say about me, but I know what it would say about you as a coach."

"What is that?" he asked too proudly.

"You love to coach because it gives you the power to control everything and everyone. You like to dominate, like having the final say."

Holly and Reagan giggled. I pressed my lips together. I couldn't help but laugh myself.

Kova pulled my leg higher, closer to my side. I winced from the pull in my hamstring. "Relax. Breathe through your stomach, Adrianna, and focus," he said in my ear just for me. "Grab your ankle."

I wrapped a hand around my foot, struggling a bit. "Control equals glory for you. You like having the upper hand because that's how you win," I said.

"Ah, you think you know me so well." Kova shifted closer, giving Holly and Reagan a friendly smile. They blushed ten shades of red.

Kova kneeled to the side of me, his thick thigh pressed to my back. I was off balance and placed a hand in front of me to steady myself. With the pressure of his hand slowly sliding to my stomach, Kova forced me to sit up straighter. Shifting my hips, I pulled my shoulders back…and felt him, hot and long tapping gently on my back. If he had worn boxers then I might not have felt anything. But of course, Kova didn't own any, so I felt *all* of him.

I sucked in a breath and watched to see if my teammates would think anything of his hand movement. I knew they couldn't see his penis touching me so provocatively from behind. Not once in front of anyone else had he so boldly touched me like this.

Easing my leg down, I released a quiet breath as my muscles loosened. I stretched well on my own, but with Kova's helping hand it was always more intense. He had the ability to manipulate my body to the extreme, and I really did love to stretch like this. Kova shifted to the other side and mimicked his stance, pressing his body closer than before. This time he was plastered against me, and the girls didn't even bat an eye.

He wanted me to feel him, to show me his control ran deeper than just gymnastics.

"Do you trust me?" Kova asked, and repeated the words louder for Holly and Reagan. They nodded, while I hesitated for a minute. "If you do not trust me, then we have a problem. This control you speak of so sweetly is for your benefit."

If it were even possible, their faces were as red as a fire hydrant.

"Lots to work on today. Do not waste my time."

Kova moved over to work on both Holly and Reagan, but didn't get as close to them as he did me. All the while, our eyes stayed glued to each other's. The intensity he bled into me was the distraction I'd desperately needed. He always gave me what I needed. Even when I didn't know what I was missing, he was just there, silently encouraging me on. He was my biggest cheerleader. He believed in me. He saw my dream when no one else could.

He was my salvation.

And in moments like this, when I could feel his passion, I forgot every negative thing he'd done and said to me. I smiled and appreciated all that he'd actually done to get me where I am today, because I hadn't been so innocent and naïve either. He'd gone out of his way to give me what I've asked for when he didn't have to. Kova may be controlling, but I was demanding.

Two negatives make a positive. And that's what we were. Two flaws. But when put together, we were amplified in the most dazzling, inconceivable way imaginable.

"Did you not sleep last night?" Reagan asked a handful of minutes later as we stood near the vault. "You look terrible."

I kept my focus on the floor and stomped my feet in the container of chalk. "It was just one of those long nights." I finally looked at her. "I tossed and turned, you know. Couldn't sleep."

She observed me a little too closely. I knew my eyelids were swollen and my eyes glossy. Another symptom of kidney disease, I had learned, but after all the tears I'd shed last night, I assumed the puffiness was from that.

"Yeah. And after this next meet is when it gets real for you. You know, that is, if you qualify at this one to go overseas where the big dogs compete. Then it's the Olympic Trials for you, if you're lucky."

"I'm pretty confident," I said. My lips were a tight smile. "If I made it this far, there's a reason for that."

"Ladies!" Kova yelled, and we both looked in his direction. "Stop the gossip and let us go."

I stomped my feet in the powder again, smiling at the floor. "Kova and his lack of contractions," I said. "I swear, those three words are his favorite."

"I know," Reagan responded. "*Let us go*," she mocked, and I chuckled. "Someone needs to tell him he sounds like a robot."

"I mentioned it to him once and suggested he take some classes. He said he wasn't doing his job if that was what I had on my mind."

Reagan glanced at me for a long moment, then burst out laughing. "That's such a Kova comment."

I smiled. "I know."

"You ladies want an extra hour of conditioning? Get your asses moving!"

"Go on," I said, my voice low, and got behind her.

We'd been practicing vault all morning and it was helping me keep my mind off yesterday. My focus had been solid and my training even better. Vault was one of two apparatuses I excelled at. It was my golden ticket.

Reagan landed and Kova gave her a few pointers, then he turned toward me and waved for me to go. I inhaled a deep breath then exhaled, and got in the zone.

Running toward the stationary object, I visualized what I needed to do, then I turned over my roundoff, backflipping onto the vault, and pushed off as hard as I could with my shoulders and hands. I soared through the air, euphoria bursting from me as I held on tight and twisted with force and drive.

I opened up and spotted the ground, then held my breath. With both feet together, I stuck my landing and fought not to hop.

I stuck it perfectly and smiled. Glancing over my shoulder, I looked for Kova. He stood parallel to the vault and stared at me, unblinking.

"Back in line."

My face fell. "What did I do wrong?"

"Nothing." He shrugged. "Absolutely nothing. That was flawless. Whatever you just did, you must do it every time. Wherever your mind was, go there again."

My heart began to bloom. I needed to hear that. Offering him a small smile in return, I nodded and jogged to the end of the white tape. When it was my turn again, I got right back into the frame of mind I'd been in just before and took off running.

"Incredible, Adrianna," Kova said, almost breathless and in awe. "A couple more and then we will move onto your second vault and practice that. I hope to see the same result for that one as well."

This time my smile was a little bigger. Hope burst inside of me and it was exactly what I needed after the night I'd had. He waved back in line, then signaled for Reagan. My second vault was a forward flip. It was much harder and took more energy out of me, but worth more points.

I could do it. I knew I could. I just had to keep my faith and my outlook positive.

I completed two good ones, but something happened on the third. Lethargy took over as I ran, and my vision danced with stars. As my hands met the leather horse, my sight turned blurry and pain shot through me.

Flipping forward onto the horse, I had too much momentum and panicked midflight. I lost control and stupidly focused on the throbbing pain in my back.

Kova noticed and swiftly reacted.

I descended like a block of weights, completely out of clean form. He reached out and tried to stop me from face-planting and belly flopping. Thankfully I caught my bearings just in the nick of time and tucked my arms and legs in as I flew out of the dismount and into a front roll.

I flopped open and stared at the roof of World Cup, out of breath and wheezing. Little silver spots danced in my vision. I closed my eyes and focused on breathing for a few seconds. My head was cloudy and dizzy. It took me a minute to regain myself.

"Are you okay? Does anything hurt?" Kova asked. When I didn't answer, he dropped to his knees and leaned over me with concern. I opened my eyes and locked onto his, but I wasn't looking at him. I didn't see him. It was more like I was looking right through him. Kova placed one hand on each side of my head and his brows bunched together. He knew better than to move me in case I'd seriously injured myself.

"Adrianna?" His voice rose with distress.

I wiggled my toes and fingers first, then I blinked a few times until I found my voice. "Yes." My response was a whisper on my lips. "I'm fine. I'm okay."

Kova released a breath and stood, offering me his hand. I slipped my palm into his and he held on. He didn't let go. He eyed me a little too long. My heart started to pound viciously against my ribs.

"Are you sure you are okay?" he asked again, his voice very low. "Do you need to take a break?"

My eyes shot around the gym nervously. A break? Since when was he okay with breaks? Maybe he *was* giving Katja the D like Reagan had said.

"I'm fine… I'm okay. I don't know what happened, but I'm fine," I responded, finally pulling my hand away. "I had a little too much power and I wasn't prepared, that's all. I'm just going to grab some water and I'll be back," I said.

Kova didn't respond. His gaze was on mine as he addressed the team. "Girls. Take a break. Meet me at bars in ten minutes."

I gave him the faintest smile, quietly showing him I was thankful. I knew he wouldn't miss it. Then I turned around and kept my eyes on the floor as I walked past Reagan like I was in my own world, despite her heavy gawking and ignored her silent will for me to look her way.

CHAPTER 5

walked back into the gym and took a deep breath, bracing myself, nervous that Kova would ask questions.

I shook out my fingers and stumbled when our eyes locked, not expecting him to be there. In fact, he looked annoyed more than anything else.

Damn paranoia was already getting to me.

"Two miles. Now." He lowered his voice. "Running will help you regain your focus."

Nodding, I quickly returned to the locker room and changed into running clothes and put on my sneakers, then I headed outside. Despite my earlier run this morning, I didn't grunt about it. I needed to breathe. I needed to let go of all the shit on my mind. I was so irritated with myself for slipping up. Kova was right, though, I needed to regain my focus.

The diagnosis was still so fresh. I knew that was the sole reason for my mistake. The moment I'd felt an inch of fatigue, my mind shut down and I'd allowed the thoughts to take over. I couldn't afford to let that happen again. I could do better, I knew I could. I just had to push past the weariness and body aches like I had in the past and everything would be how it used to be.

I focused on my feet hitting the pavement, keeping my gaze ahead of me. I ran my best time—a seven-minute mile, twice. I was shaking and edgy by the time I was done, but the exercise was exactly what I needed.

Sweat dripping down my temples and my cheeks flushed, I walked back into World Cup with purpose. My heart beat hard, faster than usual. I had so much adrenaline pumping through me I was wired and ready to get back in the gym. Kova spotted me immediately and I smiled. There was something in his gaze that just felt like home.

His forehead was creased, and I strode toward the locker room to wipe myself down and change.

"I said two miles."

I dug out some water from my bag. "I did do two miles."

"Not possible. You were gone for less than twenty minutes. You are usually running for at least thirty."

My back was still to him. Shrugging, I said, "I ran fast and regained my focus like you said."

"Get rid of that attitude you have. I will not put up with it."

I didn't have an attitude. *He* had an attitude. "Okay, *Coach.*"

I wasn't going to argue with him.

Exhaling a long breath, I turned around to face him. He was studying me a little too intensely and it bothered me, but only because I didn't want him to dig. It wasn't that I didn't want him to ever know about my illness, I just didn't want him to know right now. Once everything was all said and done, and I'd achieved my goal, then I would tell him. Until then, I had to be careful not to slip up.

"So we are back to that again? *Coach?*" he asked me, eyes narrowing.

I took a gulp of water and nodded, trying not to be aware of how much that disturbed him. How sterile it was for us. I wasn't just Adrianna, and he wasn't just Coach. We were Ria and Kova, and we both knew that.

"That is too bad. We are not taking a step back."

Staying quiet, I placed my bottle back in my locker and grabbed my leotard and a fresh sports bra. I pulled off my tank top and balled it up and threw it into my bag. I hooked my thumbs into my shorts and leaned forward, about to pull them down when I realized Kova was still standing there.

I glanced over my shoulder. Our eyes met. The heat in his stare stunned me.

"What?" When he didn't respond, I said, "I'm trying to get changed. You can't be in here, *Coach.*"

I smirked. His nostrils flared. I realized I liked to call him Coach when I was mad. This was how we roused each other. It was a game and I loved it, and I found I couldn't stop myself from doing it every single opportunity I was given. A perilous game that came with no winner or end in sight.

"What is going on with you today? Is something wrong?"

"Nothing is wrong with me. I'm just trying to get changed so I can return to practice."

Much to my surprise, Kova changed his tune. "When you are finished dressing, meet me by bars."

I nodded and quickly changed after he exited the locker room. Before I left, I checked my little white notecard Dad had wanted me to keep specifically in my gym bag. It had all the times I had to take medicine and which ones until I remembered them by heart. I read over it, then pushed my pill bag all the way to the back and locked up my locker.

Kova and I practiced hard together, him instructing me the whole way with any little tips of the trade he could offer. He barked out orders and I took them in silence like a good student. It was just like we'd done from the beginning and I craved that mentally. I'd completely forgotten about the dark cloud that hung over my head while I was in the zone.

"I think you are ready to move forward," he said, rubbing his hands together. The bold optimism in his eyes gave me the courage I was lacking today. There was no way he'd even consider this if he didn't think I'd thoroughly mastered the skill to move on to the next step—adding the full twist. This was huge for me right now.

Maybe I'd been too hard on myself.

"You feel like I'm ready to move on?"

He studied me. "I would never have you move on if I did not have complete confidence in you."

I smiled from ear to ear. If he felt I was ready, then I was ready.

"Okay…but will you spot me?" I asked, adjusting my grips. I needed him, wanted him there as cushion.

"Of course. I plan to be here until you are ready to do it on your own."

Stepping near the low bar, Kova moved to stand in front of me instead of behind me. I looked at him, a little trepidation riling me up. His eyes softened.

"It is only one more half turn. You can do this."

"I know I can, Coach. The first time is always the scariest, though."

One corner of his mouth turned up. "Adrianna, you do not have to keep calling me Coach. We both know I am much more than that."

I offered him the faintest smile, then pulled myself up onto the low bar before swinging to the high bar. A handstand and two full swings, I was letting go into the first layout, floating through the air into another straight body layout.

"Tight… Tight… Tight…" Kova said, his voice so close to me.

Right where I would twist, I pulled my arms to my chest, fists in snug balls and head tucked in, I cranked to the left and pulled a one-and-a-half twist. Spotting the ground, I drove my heels down, but my chest was too low and I felt my body leaning over.

Kova was there immediately. As a coach, he needed a sharp eye and quick reflexes. He needed to be a hero in that moment, and he was. His strong arm came out and coiled around my stomach to prevent me from falling farther. I took a step, and he pulled me back like it was nothing.

Breathing heavily, I grabbed his arm and dug my fingers into him. I was a little uneasy.

"Not too bad," he said, releasing me quickly. "There are a few things I could comment on, but seeing as it was your first time, I will refrain. Let us do it again."

Exhaling the anxiety, I chalked up, then I was back on the high bar. Another dismount, and Kova caught me again. I waited to be critiqued, but all he said was, "Again."

Gymnastics was all about repetition, repetition, repetition. Hours upon hours of the same thing over and over would seem daunting to most, but I loved it, because I still found it fun after all these years. Muscles needed to be trained to remember how to perform, and the only way to do that was to duplicate the exercise or skill hundreds and hundreds of times. It created a memory for the muscles and brain. And as much as I was hard on myself for not getting it right the first couple of times, I knew it was par for the course.

We were nonstop with no break in between. However, after two hours, a sudden sense of sheer exhaustion took hold of me just as I cast into a handstand on the high bar. I blinked a few times and breathed through my nose, gripping the bar as tight as I could.

"Squeeze," Kova ordered, drawing out the word. "Squeeze, Adrianna."

I tried so hard to fight it. My arms became weak and my elbows shook violently. I tightened my fingers around the bar and prayed I could hold on, but my heart was racing so fast and I felt winded.

Something wasn't right. And if I proceeded any further, I had a feeling it would be bad.

My hips dropped and I came down recklessly, slamming my pelvis onto the bar with an *oomph*. My arms bent and I let out a long grunt. I struggled to lock my elbows to pull myself up, but I just couldn't do it.

I released my hold, free falling to the floor.

And Kova watched me fall.

My knees crashed into the landing mat. Little specs of chalk floated in front of my vision. I closed my eyes, ashamed of how my body just gave out like that.

"What the hell was that!" Kova yelled. "Get back up! We are not done here!"

I got back up on the high bar, but lethargy was a pressure in my chest that consumed me. My hips rested on the bar. I couldn't lift myself into a handstand. I tried to swallow, but my mouth was dry. I blinked a few times trying to make the silver flashes of stars disappear. I didn't have the strength to hold myself up, and it scared me. My heart was pounding viciously. Had I always been this weak and I didn't know it, so I kept pushing until I could barely walk?

With his hands propped on his hips, Kova glared up at me. "Now, Adrianna. What are you waiting for?"

"Coach?" My quiet voice crackled with fear. I couldn't make eye contact.

He took a small step closer. "You have an hour of practice left, then conditioning. I was counting on you mastering this tonight so we could move on to the release skills tomorrow, and then connect it all for the meet coming up."

Letting Kova down—letting *myself* down—was the last thing I ever wanted to do, but there was no way I would be able to do any of that right now. Not with how I felt inside. There just wasn't. I simply didn't have the strength.

"Please…" My voice broke. "Please, help me down."

Without further question, Kova stepped right in front of my dangling legs and reached for my hips.

His gaze was painted with concern as he effortlessly lifted me and guided me down from the bar. Expelling a breath, I let go and wrapped my arms around his shoulders, but I couldn't tighten them. My head fell into the crook of his neck, and my toes tapped against his shins. I was so tired and felt like I could just fall asleep.

"Adrianna."

His voice was thick in my ear. He wrapped his strong arms around my back and held me to him. We were in a compromising position, but his warmth comforted me, and in this moment, I needed him.

"What is wrong? You are trembling."

CHAPTER 6

don't know what happened. I got really weak for a second," I
said, somewhere between the truth and a lie.

My forehead was pressed to his neck and I snuggled closer. I
inhaled his cinnamon and citrusy tobacco scent and my body
relaxed into his embrace. My eyes rolled shut.

"The only thing I do know is that I would've hurt myself if I
continued. I need a break for a second, Kova. Please. I'm so sorry."

I hoped by using his name he'd hear my desperation.

His hand splayed across my lower back, and I sighed. "Ria," he
said low enough so no one else would hear. "I have to put you down.
There are too many eyes looking our way, we cannot be seen like
this. *I* cannot be seen like this with anyone."

Pulling back, I shook my head and looked into his eyes. "Please,
I can't stand. I feel like I'm going to faint."

It was the truth. I didn't have the energy to stand. I needed to go
home, but I bit my tongue because I knew that wasn't an option.

With a frown, Kova curved an arm under my knees and brought
me up higher, cradling me to him.

"Take me to the therapy room, please," I said, and he nodded.

When we got there, he gently laid me on one of the tables. I curled
onto my side and allowed my eyes to close, lying there for a couple
of minutes. The room was icy cold and my teeth were chattering.
Kova stroked a gentle hand over the side of my face and pushed my
stray hair back.

"I knew I was pushing you too hard." A string of what I presumed
to be curse words in Russian flew from his lips. "I thought you could
handle it."

Talk about a bolt to the chest to wake my ass up. "I can handle it.
I've proved that already, haven't I?"

He cocked a brow, but his words were soft. "Then why did you have me bring you in here? It is clearly too much for you, Adrianna. I do not want to wear you down, but what happened out there? The way you were all over me could have raised quite a bit of questions. You know we cannot do that when people are here. Tell me what is going on."

"I almost fainted, Coach. I was *not* all over you."

Screw this. I pushed myself up to face him, my eyes blazing with anger. Kova's words filled me with resentment and I stared at him, letting him see just how I felt. How dare he. He made me feel guilty and I didn't like that one bit. Not when I'd proved myself time and time again. One mistake and it was suddenly the end of the world for me.

"*Nothing happened, Coach.* I just had a mental block and needed to stop for a second. I worked myself up, I guess. I didn't eat today either, and I got lightheaded, but I'm fine now. Let's go. I'm ready to get back out there."

"No. Lie back down."

Christ, this man was infuriating. "I'm fine. Excuse me for not being perfect like you."

Kova released a long sigh and looked away. He scrubbed a hand down his face. "No…no. I am just being, how do you say it? A dick?"

"Wow. Is that your way of apologizing?" I asked, and he regarded me with jaded eyes. I was fighting internally to hold myself together. "You aren't the type to admit when you're wrong."

"Just know I do not approve of this. You need to be out there practicing, earning your spot on the Olympic team."

"What is it exactly that you don't approve of? What did I do that was so wrong?"

"Taking time off from practice? Leaving early? Arriving late? *Taking a little break because you had a mental block?* We were not finished for the day, and we have a lot of work ahead of us with so little time."

My jaw dropped. "That's funny. I recall you insisting I sleep in the bed that you share with your *wife* so I could relax. What about the time when you had me miss practice so I could recover from camp when I didn't want to? That's on you, not me. I could've handled it. Or how about the time when you wouldn't let me come back to practice until I went to the doctor to make sure everything was all right when I told you it was—which it was!" My voice rose with each sentence, and I could feel the vein in my throat straining from yelling back at him. "So it's okay for me to skip out on your terms, but not mine? I wasn't even asking to leave early, just to take a small break, which I never, ever ask for. How is this fair?"

I was getting so angry that I wanted to cry. "Answer? It's not. You're a walking double standard. It's okay when you say it's okay but not when anyone else does. You want everything on your terms so you can hang on to control. Your way or the highway, right?"

Kova's nostrils flared and he stepped closer. He was just a few inches from my face. Pointing a finger downward, he clenched his teeth as he said, "Lower your voice. What happens outside of these walls bears no weight on what happens inside. Inside World Cup, I push you, you take it, and we both win. Just like we have always done. I am doing my job, one you require from me because I am the *only one* who can give it to you."

A sarcastic laugh broke from my throat. I shook my head incredulously. "You're a piece of work, Konstantin Kournakova. You should be thanking your lucky stars Katja puts up with you."

His eyes glowed with newfound anger. The vascular veins in his arms twirled up toward an astoundingly handsome face. Even mad he was too good-looking for his own good.

"I will get your stuff and take you home," he said.

My jaw dropped. "I'm not leaving."

"You are. Go home and sleep. End of discussion," he bit out stiffly, enunciating each word.

"No."

Kova turned to walk away, but I reached out and grasped his wrist. "Then get Hayden. I want him to take me home." A low growl sounded in the back of his throat, and he twisted his wrist out of my hold. "I want Hayden."

"Very well."

Moments later, far away voices drifted closer and Hayden stormed into the room.

"Jesus, Aid. Are you okay?"

I cracked open an eye. "I'm okay. I'm just freezing. Is your practice over? Can you take me home, please? I forgot to eat today and I'm a little lightheaded." I wanted to add that Kova was being a dickhead and making me go home, but I didn't.

He glanced up at the clock on the wall. "I have an hour left, but I'm sure Kova will understand." He turned to look at him over his shoulder. "Won't you, Coach?"

Kova nodded but I shook my head hastily. "I can wait," I said. "I don't mind."

"It's no issue—"

"I'll wait for you," I insisted, my voice firm. I wasn't going to take away from his practice because of my actions. I should've just taken my chances and completed the dismount to avoid all this.

"Okay…let me get some clothes for you, though."

Hayden came back seconds later. I glanced at his hands, confused by where he'd found clothes. I'd rather freeze to death than wear Reagan's stuff.

"Here, let me help you."

"Where did you get that?" I asked, and raised my arms above my head.

"It's mine." He placed his T-shirt over me.

Thank God. I glanced down. It had a big, golden yellow M on it. *Michigan.*

I eased back onto the table and Hayden moved to stand by my feet.

"Kova, lift her hips for me so I can get these on her."

"I got it," I said firmly. Hayden handed me a pair of navy blue sweatpants. I slipped them on and felt warmer already.

"You don't have a jacket here, do you?" Hayden asked Kova.

"No."

He nodded. Not many people carried a sweater around in the middle of summer in Georgia.

"That's okay. She should be good for now." Hayden looked at me. "I won't be long."

"Thank you."

Once Hayden stepped out of the room, Kova looked at me with concern. "I think you should see a doctor."

He couldn't be serious. I was in this state because of him. Kind of. I laughed sarcastically, unable to control myself.

"I almost think you're a hypochondriac. Why do you keep wanting me to see a doctor?"

"Do not make me call your father," he gritted out. He wasn't impressed, but I didn't care.

"Go ahead and do whatever you want, you always do anyway," I said in surrender. "Just leave me alone. At least allow me the luxury of sitting in silence while I stare at the wall for the next hour."

"I do not approve of this."

"There's a shocker," I said full of mockery and turned my back to him. Minutes later, as hard as I tried to fight it, sleep consumed me.

⚏⚏⚏

"AID…" I HEARD MY NAME in the distance. "Aid… Wake up."

My eyelids were too heavy to lift. The voice sounded much closer, but I was too tired to care. I muttered something unintelligible, a leave-me-alone moan, and curled up tighter into a ball.

"Adrianna." I heard my name again, this time in an exotic tongue with a heavy roll to the R.

My eyes burned as I willed them to open. I exhaled a sleepy sigh. There were two different people near me. People I couldn't place who they were, but more importantly, where was I?

Disoriented, I cracked open my eyes to a blurry vision. I couldn't focus. I tried to sit up, but I didn't have the strength and collapsed back down, but not before strong arms caught me.

"Adrianna." This time my name was much clearer. I recognized the voice, but a familiar scent roused me.

"Hayden?" I yawned, and rubbed my eyes. They felt so swollen. "How long did I sleep for?"

"Maybe an hour? I'm not sure."

"That's it? Felt like so much longer."

"Yeah. Come on, let's get you home."

I sat up slowly with the help of Hayden, but my focus was on Kova. A fleeting shadow of regret cast in his eyes. I grimaced. Good. I hoped he felt like shit. It was too soon to forget the way he had spoken to me and how he'd made me feel. People often said no one could make a person feel inferior to anyone, but that was total bullshit. When your heart cared deeply for someone, it was impossible not to feel the weight of their words no matter how strong the front was.

Kova extended a hand out to help me, but I tugged my arm from his reach. My relationship with Kova was the same song and dance. One day I'd learn. Just not today, and probably not until I left World Cup for good.

"I need to grab my bag," I said, standing up. Jesus, I was so tired. I felt like I could sleep for a week straight. Yawning, I walked to the locker room and retrieved my bag. I couldn't leave without my medication.

Turning to Kova, I asked a bit detached, "Is it okay to leave my car here overnight?"

"Yes. That will be fine."

Hayden extended an open palm, waving his fingers at me. Placing my hand into his, he laced our fingers together and guided me out of World Cup to his car. Kova was hot on my tail, nearly stepping on my feet, but I played it off like I hadn't noticed. It didn't matter, though, because Hayden did.

"Why don't you just piss on her?" he yelled over the hood of his car, his blue eyes intense.

"Hayden, be nice," I said, stifling a giggle. I actually felt bad.

Hayden glanced over at me, his feelings shifting in his gaze. "Aid, I'm sorry, but I refuse to hold back where that man is concerned."

"Just doing my job and making sure the others do not get the wrong idea when they see you guys leaving together," Kova replied with a twist of his lips, unfazed by Hayden's comment.

"Whatever you need to tell yourself."

At that, Hayden got into his car and I followed, putting on my seat belt then leaning back against the seat. I glanced through the tinted window toward Kova.

I was drawn to his confidence and strength. I was addicted to the way he pushed me and challenged me. I could push past an injury and keep practicing. I could train for hours on the same skill without a single complaint. But this was something that caught me completely off guard and terrified me. It was like all muscle mass had disappeared and a fifty-ton boulder had been placed on my chest. I crumbled.

Pulling out of World Cup, I spoke once we were on the main road. "Thanks for taking me home, Hayden."

"You know I'd do anything for you," he said, and I smiled. I did know that. "Do you need me to stop anywhere? Get you anything?"

"No, I'm good. I just want to go home and crash. Can you pick me up for practice tomorrow?"

He nodded. At a red light, he angled his body my way. "Are you okay, though? You look pale, Aid."

"I'm just a little overworked and lacking sleep. I'll be fine."

"I'm worried about you. It's unlike you to leave practice early. Who's going to look after you when I'm gone?" He smiled sweetly.

"Ugh. Don't remind me that you're leaving," I whined. I was going to miss Hayden dearly when he left for college. "I can't believe you're leaving me here with Reagan." I stuck my index finger in my mouth and pretended to gag myself.

"You aren't going to be stuck with her for much longer. She'll be leaving for Louisiana around the same time."

"I totally forgot about that." Reagan had accepted a partial scholarship from the University of Louisiana.

About ten minutes later, Hayden pulled into my complex, right up to the front sliding glass doors to drop me off. "Thanks again for being there for me. I'll see you tomorrow."

"Anytime. Want me to come up?"

I shook my head but offered a gracious smile. I didn't want him getting the wrong idea. I'd rather buy a rope and hang myself before that ever happened again.

CHAPTER 7

had only a handful of competitions left that I needed to attend—
and qualify for—in order to go to Worlds, which was an absolute
must if I wanted to make the Olympic team, God willing.

World Championships were typically held out of the country
and lasted for a week since there were so many qualifying rounds.
There were other ways to qualify, but this was the most logical way
and the least stressful.

Once I arrived at World Cup, I automatically ran two miles before
changing into my leotard. I was thirsty and drank almost a whole
bottle of water before I left the locker room. Yesterday was rough,
but it was behind me. I was determined to make today better.

I smiled to myself and stepped inside the gym, embracing the
chalky air and spirit around me. I was eager for practice to begin
so I could take my mind off the reality of my life and what I was
up against.

It was hard to wrap my mind around the fact that just as I was
starting to come back from heartbreak, my body decided to betray
me. This quietness that had taken over stuck to me like superglue.
I didn't want it. I wanted it to leave, only, I didn't know how to
make it go away. Instead, it grew with each passing second like an
impending sense of doom. I felt different inside, alone, a little par-
anoid and completely isolated. I decided the more I practiced, and
the more time I spent inside World Cup, that it would eventually
go away. It had to.

I just wanted to be myself again. Only now I feared the way the cells
in my body were destroying each other I would never reach my full
potential as a gymnast, and that was devastating to me. Gymnastics
was my life. I couldn't imagine not being able to do it.

I glanced around at everyone on the different events, looking for the one person who seemed to calm my worry without even knowing he did.

One look at Kova, and I could tell that he, too, looked like he hadn't slept all night. Dark circles lined his eyes and a thicker scruff dusted his chin. When he turned his head in my direction, I could see the anguish tormenting him. My heart clenched at the longing gaze in his eyes. He was staring back at me, asking for something he couldn't put into words. He didn't have to. I felt what he was saying, because I felt the same way.

I rubbed my eyes with the heels of my palms, then walked over to the balance beam where he stood.

"Adrianna, can we speak for a moment?" Kova asked.

Kova let his guard down for me to see and I studied him. There was no life in his eyes, no color at all. We were both numb. I was used to the empty feeling, but I didn't like seeing him like that. It bothered me immensely.

"Is it okay if we wait until after practice? I really just want to get to work."

He looked at me, brows bunched together, and gave one firm nod. Maybe he needed the release in the same manner I did that gymnastics gave me.

We practiced for hours on balance beam, breaking down my routine and working on connections, sequences, jumps, and leaps. Whatever Kova suggested, I did in silence, and I made sure I did it well. Each landing was soft, light and airy. Kova didn't commend me—it was rare he actually ever did—but I could tell I was practicing well be-cause he didn't ridicule me either. He almost seemed pleased. There wasn't one balance check. I didn't fall, and I stuck the majority of my dismounts on soft mats. Even my turns were nearly on point, though not all, because turning on your toes was actually harder than doing backflips on the four-inch wide beam. Go figure, but it was true.

I knew now that pushing myself wasn't the brightest idea I'd ever had, but I didn't have any another options. I was backed against a wall. I didn't want kidney disease to be what stole gymnastics from me. If I never achieved my dream, it was going to be because of me, not because a disease stronger than me took it.

I hardly spoke until Kova finally cornered me when we rotated to vault.

"What is wrong with you today?" he asked, his voice low and laced with curiosity.

I shrugged one shoulder and averted my gaze. I watched my teammates. "Nothing. I'm fine."

Kova shifted on his feet. "Listen, if this is about yesterday—"

I glanced up. "It's not. I have a lot on my mind right now and I'm just focusing on the skill at hand. I'm sorry for my attitude."

He observed me for a long moment. Probably surprised I apologized for once. "If something is wrong, you would come to me, right?"

A mixture between a laugh and a huff escaped me before I could stop it. "Yeah, I'll run right over," I said full of sarcasm.

He stepped closer to me and angled his head down. My heart beat a little harder. Lowering his voice, he said, "I am serious, Adrianna."

"So am I, Coach."

Kova exhaled through his nose like he was defeated. "Let us get started on vault. You practiced well on beam today. I am very impressed."

I was a little caught off guard by his praise. A timid smile tugged on one corner of my mouth, and he returned it.

Little actions like that, they were what pierced my heart more than words. They brightened my day.

Vault practice was different. I went light on my dismounts. Kova placed a three-inch-thick landing mat on top of the foam pit so my heels wouldn't slam into the floor each time. I had a forward flipping vault and a backward flipping vault to practice.

"Two hours. One hour for each vault."

I nodded and chalked up, rubbing the dry, white powder on the bottoms of my feet and behind my knees. Stepping behind the white tape, I visualized my skill.

Clapping his hands, Kova crouched at the knees so he was parallel to the apparatus, and yelled, "Go!"

I loved when he turned coach mode on. It helped snap me into place.

And so it began. After the first hour, I was thirsty and needed to use the bathroom. My bladder was going to explode if I didn't relieve myself soon.

"Grab a drink. Ten-minute break."

"Thanks," I said and jogged to the locker room. I took a swig of water, then checked my notecard to see which medicines and vitamins I was due for. I was so happy my dad had suggested this idea.

Glancing over my shoulder to make sure I was alone, my hands trembled as I poured out the necessary pills. Quickly, I swallowed them back, pushed the bottles deep into my bag, and grabbed an all-natural protein bar. I peeled back the wrapper and took a small bite, then another, and another. I didn't have an appetite, but I forced myself to eat at least half. I didn't want to get lightheaded. Not after yesterday. I threw the rest away and brushed my hands together. It was really all I could stomach. Sticking to a low-calorie diet was easier these days when my mind was twisted with worry.

I grabbed an extra bottle of water to bring back with me into the gym. Sports drinks of any kind were not allowed inside, only water.

Right before I went back to train for the second half of the day, I stepped into the restroom. Pulling off a leotard during practice was like taking off soaked jeans. The struggle was real. I squatted to pee and hoped the burning sensation in my bladder left once I relieved myself, but the strangest thing was, while I had the urge to go, hardly anything came out. Guess I didn't have to go to the bathroom after all.

Washing my hands, I glanced at my reflection and frowned. I looked like a hot mess. There were flyaways everywhere. I tried to smooth them back with a little water and then tightened my ponytail. I had dark circles under my eyes and I was a little pale, but the good news was the rash I'd been sporting for the past two weeks had come down a lot. It was hardly noticeable now. That was a huge positive in my eyes because that meant the medications were working.

Kova eyed my water bottle when I stepped back into the gym. "That better be water." He nodded his chin toward it.

I gave him a droll stare. "No. It's vodka."

My lips twitched, so did his. "Do not start with me."

"Like I would ever do such a thing and talk back."

Kova didn't respond but I caught a shadow of humor in his eyes. A small smile tugged at my lips. I needed that.

Slinging my bag over my shoulder, I snatched my car keys from the bench and turned around to leave just as Kova stepped into the room looking as cool as a cucumber. Most everyone had left by now since it was so late in the day, so I wasn't surprised to see him in here with just me.

I drew in a breath. Our eyes locked. He had his hands in the pockets of his netted shorts as he leaned casually against the door frame. He wore a loose black sleeveless shirt and his hat faced backwards so the flat bill was in the back. He didn't have a line of worry on his face and he looked totally kissable.

Damn it. Don't go there.

My shoulders loosened. I was a little jittery inside, but his presence soothed me. I hated when he wore that hat because he looked so damn sexy in it. Black was his color.

It was also the color of his heart.

"How was ballet class?" he asked.

"It was actually great."

His forehead creased. "It was great," he mimicked.

No, I'd fucking hated every second of it and planned his demise in the process.

"Yeah! The new dance teacher was pretty awesome, and I liked that she had us do some kind of yoga stretching things at the end. That was cool. She said we're going to do it once a week."

Kova stared quietly. He wasn't buying it.

"Well," I said when he didn't say anything, "I'm gonna go. I'm beat. I'll see you tomorrow, Coach."

Walking toward Kova, I could smell the scent of his cologne before I reached him. He stopped me by placing his hand on the inside of my elbow. His thumb gently rubbed back and forth on the crease of my arm.

It was then that I noticed just how deep the lines under his eyes were. "What's up?"

Kova looked down and studied me. His eyes shifted, brows lowering. "Are you okay?"

I drew in a silent breath. "I'm fine, why?"

He leisurely shrugged one shoulder. "Just asking. When women say they are fine, it usually means they are lying, and I am fairly certain you said that you are fine a few times today."

He'd paid too close attention.

"I'm fantastic. How's that?" I retorted sarcastically with a massive smile that caused him to tug me closer until I was against him. I drew in a quiet gasp when our bodies touched. Without realizing it, I leaned into him and embraced his warmth.

I missed that. I missed him.

I missed us. What we used to be, what we had.

We didn't move, save for his thumb still running circles on my arm. I couldn't tear my eyes from his and went with what I was feeling in my heart. Leaning my cheek on his chest, I wrapped my arms around his back and closed my eyes. Kova didn't hesitate and that made my stupid heart even weaker for him. We melted into each other like this was where we belonged, where we needed to be. He hugged me tighter, then leaned down and inhaled deeply before kissing the top of my head. I squeezed him, releasing all the negativity in my life. I wanted him to come home with me, where I could just sit in his arms and forget about my issues.

Looking up at him, I felt the longing in his green eyes that I knew was reflected in mine and almost asked if he wanted to come over. I noticed the tight lines around his mouth and creases between his brows. But I didn't ask. Instead, all I could do was offer him a sad smile. He returned it, but I wished he hadn't, because that gave me the clarification I needed.

"I'll see you tomorrow," I whispered, then stepped away.

Kova reached for me, his hand dragging down my arm until he reached my wrist. He gave my hand a little squeeze.

The emotion swirling in his green gaze was overriding my common sense. I didn't want to leave, and I knew he didn't want me to either.

But Kova let go, and I finally walked away.

"Adrianna," he called right before I reached the lobby. I glanced over my shoulder. He was standing where I'd left him, looking so lonely that I almost ran back to him.

"Yes?" I finally said after a long moment.

His brooding eyes held me in place. My heart skipped a beat as I waited.

"Nothing. It is nothing. I wanted to talk to you, but we can pick it up another day. Go rest. I will see you tomorrow."

Without waiting a beat longer, I quickly walked out and climbed into my truck. If I didn't hurry up, I was going to turn around and run into his arms.

I had less than a week until my next big meet. I couldn't afford to break, but with everything on my mind lately, I felt like it was coming.

CHAPTER 8

have been trying to get ahold of you all day, Adrianna," my father bellowed through the speaker.

I pulled the phone away from my ear. I'd missed a bunch of his calls this afternoon.

After I'd arrived home, I showered and then heated up something to eat so I could take my medicine with food. I'd skipped eating regular meals today since I didn't have much of an appetite. I'd only had half a protein bar and I gathered that could be the reason why I was so anxious and edgy. My hands couldn't stop shaking, my heart beat faster than normal, and I was a little nauseous.

"Couldn't you have sent a text at least? I was starting to worry. I almost called Konstantin."

I pressed the phone to my shoulder with my ear while I sat on a barstool. "I'm sorry, Dad. I was so busy with practice that I didn't have much time in between. I have a lot on my mind right now."

"I understand that, sweetheart, but we made a deal. I need to be able to reach you." He sighed, and I apologized again for worrying him. "I got your appointments scheduled for the day after tomorrow. Will that work for you?"

I swallowed a spoonful of bone broth. I loved this stuff since it was easy on my stomach. "Yes. I'll let Kova know tomorrow that I won't be in. Did you mention that if I need any tests done they'll have to be done the same day and to make arrangements for that?"

I hoped I hadn't come across as a diva, but desperate times called for desperate measures.

"Yes. Everything is taken care of."

My shoulders relaxed. "Perfect. Thank you so much for doing that for me. I was worried the receptionist would give me the go-around and make me come back for each issue if I'd called myself. I just don't have the time for that right now."

"It pays to know people in higher places. Anything for my daughter. I'll text you the info and times. Please keep me updated."

I smiled and thanked him again. After saying goodbye, I placed my phone down and forced myself to drink the rest of the broth. Between the acidic feeling high up in my stomach, and the awful metallic taste in my mouth, I knew eating was a must, even if I wasn't hungry. The broth usually helped settle that uneasy feeling.

I walked into the kitchen and reached into the refrigerator to pull out the carton of eggs, butter, bacon, shredded cheese, an onion, and some garlic. Then I grabbed an avocado and a lime I had in a bowl sitting on the counter. I had a feeling the medicines were messing with me and that I needed to create some kind of barrier to coat my stomach before I took them. The broth had helped a little, but I thought actually eating might do the trick.

I pulled out a plastic bag of whole wheat English muffins from the freezer. I hadn't had one in so long and decided I would make a breakfast sandwich for dinner, and an extra one for tomorrow morning.

I scrambled the eggs while standing barefoot in the kitchen, freezing from the icy tile under my feet. Goose bumps trickled down my arms. Quickly, I walked to my room and grabbed a sweater. I wasn't usually this cold and now I wondered if the chills had to do with some other underlying illness I may have now.

I was going to turn into a hypochondriac at this rate.

As the eggs cooked, I took out the necessary pills for the evening and placed them on the counter, then I took out the ones for the morning as well and placed them in a separate little bowl.

I was anxious about my appointment. With my Achilles injury, all I had to do was get out of bed the wrong way and I could pretty much snap it completely, but at least that was fixable. I had control of it, in a sense. But with the chronic illnesses I now faced, and all the family history I'd recently discovered, I had zero control over my body, and *that* terrified me. I wasn't in control of my thoughts anymore. They grabbed the reins and controlled me. Keeping my focus and emotions in place had been harder than I thought, and I was fighting blindly to take it back.

I wanted to call Avery and talk to her. I needed an outlet, and we'd always been each other's shoulder to lean on. No doubt she'd listen to me now—it was just who she was—but I still felt selfish for how I'd treated her when she'd wanted to come clean. I'd refused to allow her to and had shut her out for so long, yet here I was wanting to vent to her when I hadn't been there for her. She didn't deserve that. She didn't deserve to bear the burden of my thoughts and fears when I selfishly hadn't been there to hold hers.

I shook my head, disgusted with myself. I was a terrible person and regretted how I'd treated her. If I could go back and change how I'd behaved, I would.

Fifteen minutes later, I sat on a barstool with an egg and cheese sandwich piled high with bacon, slowly sautéed onions and garlic, and smashed avocado and lime. I took a bite and moaned. Thank goodness no one was around to hear the sounds coming out of me.

I took a few more bites, then I palmed my medicine and swallowed the handful of pills. I took another bite. And another. Halfway through I was full and wrapped what was left in foil.

I turned everything off and climbed into bed with my sweater still on. I was still too cold to take it off.

Exhaustion hit faster than I expected, my eyes heavy and trying to close. I yawned, pulling the blanket up to my chin and rolled onto my side. Now that I was sitting still for the first time today, my joints and muscles started to coil up and tighten. I swallowed, praying for sleep to take over so I didn't have to endure the pain I knew was about to hit any minute once my body had a chance to relax.

I BOLTED UPRIGHT AND RAN to the bathroom in the dark. Before I could stop it, projectile vomit flew from my mouth and splattered on the floor just as I reached the toilet. Crashing to my knees, my hair fell around my face, shielding me in even more darkness. The putrid smell assaulted my senses as more bile climbed up the back of my throat. Blindly, I crawled to flip on the light switch. *Oh God.* My stomach twisted with knots as my body rejected more of what I'd eaten for dinner into the ceramic bowl.

I closed my eyes and tried not to breathe in the smell, knowing it would only make it worse. Little beads of sweat bubbled on my upper lip when more vomit came up. Leaning over, I grabbed the edge of the seat as I spewed, the tips of my hair falling inside the rim. My eyes widened. Tears were free falling from vomiting so hard and I panicked at how thoroughly grossed out I was at seeing my hair mixed in there.

After what felt like ten minutes of throwing up that ended with dry heaving, I was crouched on my knees holding my cramping stomach. Heat spread throughout my lower back and I winced in pain. Using the wall, I stood, wobbling on my knees and walked toward the shower. I pulled off my sweater, then grabbed my shirt and used it to wipe my mouth and face before discarding it to the floor along with the rest of my clothes.

I stepped under the spray and sighed from the heat of the scalding water when another surge of pain attacked my back. I cried out and braced myself, placing one hand to the tiles and the other on my back. I took deep breaths, panting heavily as I cursed everything I knew and prayed for the pain to stop.

Curled up in a ball, I was back in my bed with relentless shivering. I glanced at the clock and blinked. It was 3 a.m. Two more hours before the alarm would go off.

Tomorrow would be rough, but I'd endure it. I clenched my eyes shut. Tears seeped from the corners and I wept in silent agony as I fell asleep to the sound of my muffled cries and the throbbing pain beating on my back.

⫷⫸⫷⫸⫷⫸

"COACH?" I SAID, TAPPING LIGHTLY on his door. Kova was in the middle of paperwork or something. His hand was moving quickly over the paper he was scribbling on.

Kova glanced up and did a double take. He almost looked as bad as I felt, and for a brief moment, I wondered if he'd even gone home last night.

"Why are you here so early?"

"That's why I wanted to talk to you. Tomorrow I have an appointment to see my orthopedic doc. Now before you think—"

He looked down without letting me finish and started writing again. "I am already aware."

My stomach dropped and clenched. Kova's words were clipped with underlying aggravation. I hoped he wasn't upset with me.

"How'd you know?"

Such a stupid question when I already knew the answer.

"Your father."

"Oh, yeah. What did he say?"

He glanced up again, pinning me to the spot with a riled stare. I truly didn't think my dad would go against me like that, but now I wasn't so sure.

"You tell me, Adrianna. Is there something I should know?"

My jaw bobbed wordlessly. His brashness caught me off guard. "No, I just didn't want you to think I was trying to get out early or miss practice or anything, so I had my dad make sure everything was done in one day. That's why I came in early, so I could make up for time—obviously not the whole time because that wouldn't be possible—but as much as I can." I said the words so fast I didn't take a breath. His long, quiet stare provoked me. I propped my hands on my hips and said, "Well?"

"Well, what, Adrianna?" He enunciated each word with a bite.

I swallowed hard. "Is that okay with you?"

"Why would it not be? It would be unwise of me to say no. I may do questionable things at times, but I am not stupid enough to hinder your performance."

"But you're mad."

"No, I am not mad."

"You're mad at me?" I pressed, a little timid.

Kova was most definitely mad, I just didn't know why. His clipped tone was like little needles poking my skin.

His shoulders turned lax and his voice softened. "I could never be mad at you, Ria."

Ria. He only used Ria to get his point across.

I bobbed my head subtly and tried to fight the smile on my lips. I didn't want him to be mad at me. I wouldn't be able to handle that on top of everything else.

"Okay, well, I'm going to condition now."

I turned to leave when the sight of his sofa caught my eyes. I paused to stare at it, thinking about the night we'd spent tangled in each other's arms and the words Kova had said to me. Crazy how that felt like years ago when it had happened. My cheeks bloomed with heat remembering the positions we were in, how he'd added pressure to my throat at just the right time before I orgasmed…

"Is there something you *need*?" he asked, his voice taking on a huskier tone. I didn't miss the double meaning in his question.

I swallowed before replying. "No."

"I did not think so."

CHAPTER 9

You look terrible," Kova said an hour later.

I'd just finished conditioning and I was sweating profusely. I shot a brief glance at my teammates, hoping they hadn't heard.

"Very…white," he added.

My nostrils flared, but I pretended his comment didn't bother me. Propping my hands on my hips, I shifted my gaze up to his.

"I think you mean pale. Sometimes your Russian gets the best of you," I said, and Holly chuckled.

Truth was, I was suffering inside. After I left his office, I climbed the rope ten times in pike position and did so many crunches I lost count, among other core workouts that left my muscles screaming in rebellion. That blooming pain in my lower back returned and it was all I could focus on for the last hour. It was growing stronger with each passing minute.

Kova didn't respond to me, but instead turned to the team. "Today we are doing jump conditioning, also known as plyos, which I am sure you know. It is used to increase speed strength. Your muscles will exert maximum force and you will thank me later for it."

Kova wore arrogance with pride. It worked for him.

"We are going to be doing quick switching of the feet, with bending and jumps. Lots of leg power here. Quick, quick, punch!"

Kova had us stand in a line on the floor with a folded mat that stood about ten inches tall in front of each of us. I jumped on and off, pin straight and as quickly as I could, making sure my body stayed tight.

"On and off the mat. You must jump way higher, quickly," Kova shouted. He was circling us like an animal eyeing its prey with his laser gaze trained on our feet. "Nice, extend those ankles and pop off. Off!"

I was afraid to extend too much in fear of worsening my injury.

"You can go a little lighter on your extension, Adrianna." I swear he'd read my mind. Strange. After a few minutes, he said, "Now do the same thing on one foot."

My thighs were on fire as we switched legs again and proceeded with the same technique. I looked at my teammates and we all wore the same pained expression.

"Okay. Enough. Get in line over here." He pointed to the white tape on the floor.

I stood with my hands on my hips and watched as Kova added two extra boxed mats that were waist high and chest high. I knew where he was going with this.

Kova instructed us to jump over the mats with our legs straight and tight together. Sounded simple enough, only it wasn't. Nothing that looked easy ever was, even if the floor had springs underneath and helped boost us.

One by one, we jumped over four spaced-out folded mats like we were little toothpicks bouncing around. As I neared the end, I dug deep and pulled my knees up to jump onto the taller boxed mat. Drawing in an audible breath, I shot up to reach the top of the last mat and crouched on it. *Finally!* Jumping down, I released a strenuous pant and got back in line, but not before I stole a quick glance at Kova to see if he'd caught how fatigued I was. His eyes were already on me.

"Extend, ladies. Reach and jump. Light and easy on your toes. This needs to be as clean as possible. If toddlers can do it at birthday parties, there is no reason you cannot."

I chuckled under my breath. World Cup hosted birthday parties like most gyms did. The youngest child he allowed for a party was four years old, and they weren't leaping over mats this high.

"Excellent, ladies. That is what I want to see."

We were all a little out of breath when we reached the sixth round. I looked at the clock and realized we had another two hours of this. I was already more winded than the rest of the girls.

A tickle in my dry throat caused me to cough. Covering my mouth, I fought back another cough as a choked, hoarse sound came from the back of my throat. Reagan watched me. Deep lines formed between her eyes like she was trying to figure something out, which only made me feel more insecure about my coughing fit. My stomach tightened as I fought a cough back again. I offered a smile like everything was okay and inhaled a deep breath and held it. Once I exhaled, I felt better.

"On the next set, squat and touch the floor with your hands on each jump. Like frog jumps over the mats."

Breathing through my nose, I watched Holly go first, then Reagan, then I went. I missed the last mat I had to jump on top of it, and tried again.

"Pull those knees up, Adrianna." My thighs were blazing hot and shaking. I almost kneed my mouth. "Good. Just like that," Kova added.

Since there were only a few of us, the sets went quickly, and each time it took longer and longer for me to catch my breath. I avoided Reagan's nosy eyes and looked ahead. Rubbing the side of my face into my bicep, I wiped away the sweat from my temples.

"Touch the floor, now jump! Again. Touch…touch…touch. Jump! That is it!"

I hopped over the mat to the next mat, overanalyzing over my reality. I was okay. I'd be okay.

Had I never worked out hard enough? I'd always used the extreme exhaustion I experienced as my motivation. Now that I knew about the kidney disease and lupus, it was my crutch, and I feared the possibility using it as an excuse to slow down. It would be so easy. But just like all those other times when I'd struggled, wrestling with my aching muscles and strength to keep going, I always got back up and pushed myself ten times harder.

I wondered if I was dealing with the repercussions of what I'd always done now.

Springing off the floor to the last box, I brought my knees up and crouched on top. I smiled a little to myself. It took a little more energy, but I did it.

My smile grew a little bigger. I just had to get my head clear, that's all I had to do. Then everything would be okay.

With the folded mats about seven feet across from each of us vertically, Kova said, "Large hop twice, front tuck onto mat, set. Turn around, hop off, front tuck. Let us go."

Taking a deep breath, I released it and got to work. Two hops and I was rotating forward into the air in a tight ball onto the mat. My feet punched the mat as I landed, and I stifled a low grunt in the back of my throat as pain shot up into my back. My body hardened, waiting for the pain to leave. When a gymnast performed a tumbling pass on the floor, the force of pressure was nine times greater than their weight. When doing conditioning skills like I was, the pressure was half that, but obviously enough to affect me.

I swallowed, almost afraid to land and exhaled through my nose, telling myself it would be okay. The thought of landing on my toes crossed my mind but I knew there was no way of getting it past Kova. He had eagle eyes and saw everything, which sometimes was a curse.

Blocking out the throbbing in my back, I traveled across the floor again, springing off my toes then front flipping to land flat on my feet. I held my breath and bared down, squeezing every muscle in my body. My abs were rock solid and burning from the stress of holding back the groaning pain.

On the next conditioning pass, this time, the pounding across my lower back intensified, and I clenched my eyes shut hard. My mouth fell open and I let out a gasp.

"I got this," I mumbled to myself.

There was no reason why I couldn't push past my thoughts or the pain and go on like I always had. I'd come this far not knowing I was sick. I had worked through the side effects the illnesses brought, on top of the Achilles injury, Kova's secret marriage, my torn friendship with Avery, my parents' impending divorce, and the discovery of my real mother. Even the sadistic camps I had endured. There was no reason not to continue just like I always had. If I got through all of that, I could get through anything. This was just another obstacle I had to overcome so I could move onto the next.

Only, it really wasn't. And that scared me. Because no matter how much I lied to myself, I still knew the truth and it messed with me.

I looked around. I needed to pull inspiration from my surroundings. I was grasping at straws, needing something, anything. My gaze skipped from each teammate until it landed on Kova.

I was already looking for him, but he always found me first. In this moment of self-doubt, with a sea of insecurities growing inside me with each breath I took, the pull was too strong to ignore. I could deny it all I wanted to, but the truth was, I needed Kova, and he knew that.

Chest rising and falling like there were resistance bands holding me back, every nerve in my body was reaching out for him to breathe life into me.

The pain taking over my body frightened me.

He could see that.

The gripping fear caged by my ribs consumed me.

He could see that too.

His eyes flickered with anguish and his body moved to take a step toward me, only for him to falter. Like it was in his nature to protect me.

My heart dropped.

I didn't want him to look at me like he had earlier. I didn't want him to think anything was wrong with me, because there wasn't. I was still the same old Adrianna, only now I came with a label.

No. Scratch that. I didn't want a label.

I didn't want to be known as *that sick girl*. Labels brought pity and sympathy and restraint from friends and loved ones. A label was a disappointment, and the thought of that was like a burning boulder in my gut. I couldn't bear it.

As much as I wanted to be wrapped in his arms, listening to his comforting words, I didn't want him to help me. I needed to do this for myself and prove that I could get past the mental block. I could do it, I knew I could.

"Stop daydreaming, Adrianna, and get your ass in gear."

I gave him a faux flat glare and playfully rolled my eyes. I knew he wasn't purposely trying to be a jerk. It was just his way of helping me, and I appreciated that.

Holly chuckled under her breath. Leaning into me, she whispered through a guiltless smile, "It's okay. We *all* daydream about him. Trust me."

I grinned. If she only knew.

I started up again. Each tuck I landed shot a new flame of pain up my back.

"Punch that ground, ladies. Stick that landing and make it tight," Kova said to all of us.

Another aching bolt shot through me the moment my feet hit the mat. I clenched my eyes shut for a split moment, forcing myself to block it out. And I went again.

"Quick! Quick! We want speed!"

"Yesss," he hissed happily. "Like that. Feet and knees together."

"A little cleaner, Reagan," he said. "You look like you are squatting to pee." Kova clapped obnoxiously. "We have five more rounds before we move on. Let us get it, girls!"

Bearing the pain, I bit the inside of my lip and completed the task. Five rounds felt like an eternity, but I smiled to myself, happy that I'd endured it.

We stood shoulder to shoulder waiting for our next assignment.

"Now we do handstand hops that we will add a back tuck to. What you are going to do is handstand onto the mat, whip your hips down and jump onto the floor, then onto the mat where you will jump backwards. When your feet hit the ground, whip them into another handstand. Let me show you."

Kova walked over to the mat and stood in front of it. He took his hat off and dropped it to the floor next to his feet. I rubbed my lower back with the heel of my hand trying to soothe the throbbing ache as I watched.

With his arms poised above his head, Kova flipped over into a handstand. His shirt fell down around his chest and revealed his toned, flat stomach with a peek of the rings tattoo. He snapped his hips down, feet pounding into the ground, then jumped right back onto the mat before jumping backwards into another handstand. At what I had to guess was two hundred and thirty pounds of solid muscle, the springs ricocheted loudly, and the vibration of the floor hit my feet. He did it twice, showing us exactly what we needed to do, and each time the fabric of his shirt bounced with him.

"Got it?" he asked us. We all nodded in unison. "Great. Get moving."

CHAPTER 10

stepped into a handstand and kept my palms flat on the mat and my fingers spread wide.

I breathed in through my nose and whipped my hips down in a pike position.

"Snap your legs under faster, Adrianna."

I made sure to next time.

"Flatten those hips," Kova said to me. "Snap. Snap! Same for you, Holly."

I followed his instructions and pushed harder, shoving the increasing pain out of my mind. It only got worse with each hit into the floor. The more I did and the faster I went, the more lightheaded I became.

"Four more sets, then we are adding a back tuck."

I groaned inwardly. Adding a back tuck would make the skill more demanding on my body. It wasn't anything new to me. I'd done this set so many times I could do it in my sleep.

More importantly, I'd done this before I even knew I was sick. There was no reason why I couldn't do it now.

I bit down on my lip, angry that I'd let myself get so deep in my thoughts.

I snapped my hips down hard then popped right into a handstand. Repeat. I moved faster than I had before, driven by aggravation. I was so mad I could cry.

"Good, Adrianna. That is what I want to see. Holly, see if you can keep up with Adrianna. You too, Reagan. Make it a competition. Who could complete the last round the fastest—but safest?"

Once my last four sets were done, I stood with my hands on my hips in front of the mat out of breath while I waited on my teammates. Kova walked toward me.

"Nice job, Adrianna. Now add the tuck. Do it off the mat and set it," Kova said, and looked into my eyes.

I nodded, but my stomach plummeted to the ground. I hoped he didn't see my worries. Adding the tuck required additional force, which instantly said additional pain in my head. I had to whip harder and use more stomach muscles.

This should be fun.

On the first one, I saw stars. True, sparkly, silver stars floated in my vision. I knew seeing stars was a sign of dehydration. My mouth was dry, I just didn't think it was that bad. I slowed down on the second one to gain my stance correctly and glanced at the other girls. I rubbed my back again. They were moving so fast without pausing in between. Like little machines.

"What is wrong with you?" Kova asked me quietly in the middle of my handstand. I folded down and looked at him.

"What do you mean?" I asked, out of breath.

"For one, you keep rubbing your back."

"Oh." My jaw bobbed. "I think I just pulled a muscle or slept wrong or something." He gave me a pensive stare but I continued. "It's fine. I'm fine. Everything is fine. I plan to stop at the store after practice and get some of that Icy Hot stuff since I can't take Motrin. It should do the trick. I'm fine, though."

"You are *fine*," he said, his voice low, only for me to hear. And I knew what that meant.

I threw a smile at Kova, hoping he wouldn't say anything else.

"Come by my office before you leave today."

My smile faltered.

Fuck. My. Life. Damn it.

He knew. He had to know.

I nodded, then he turned to face all of us.

"I want twenty handstand tucks," he ordered. "Once you are finished with those, after you land the first back tuck"—he used his finger and drew an imaginary circle—"add one more back tuck, jump, jump to a handstand, whip down to the two tucks. I want twenty of these. Go."

Reagan and I glanced at each other. We both had the same thought: He was totally trying to kill us.

Or maybe just me. Maybe he knew I'd lied and the only way he could get revenge was through his lunatic training methods.

"Come on, girls! Get moving!" Kova yelled, clapping his hands loud enough to draw attention. "We have hours of work ahead of us! This is just a walk in the park for what I have planned."

Bringing my legs down, I snapped my hips and rebounded hard by punching my feet into the ground into a standing back tuck.

Searing heat reverberated across my back and I almost lost my footing. I gasped and palmed myself just below my ribs where it was nearly all-consuming and past the point of excruciating. I paused to arch my back, and inhaled through my nose. Bile tossed around in my stomach and I blinked rapidly a few times to get my head straight. I thought I was going to throw up. Eyes were on me, but not just any pair. I knew Kova was watching me without even looking at him. I could feel it.

I turned around and spotted him. He observed me again with his head tilted and stared deep in concentration. Kova was a perceptive man and that only raised my guard even more. The way his chin dipped lower and to the side caused a fluttering in my chest.

Pulling out my ponytail, I pretended I had to fix it. I shook out my chalky mop and flipped my head over to gather my hair, thankfully breaking the gaze. I stumbled for a second from dizziness, then I retied my thick locks into a messy ball. My shaky fingers sought the loose flyaways around the sides of my face and I brushed them back behind my ears.

"Kick those legs down hard, girls," Kova demanded.

I lifted my eyes to him and found his reflective gaze was still on me. Only this time, he was spinning his dumb wedding ring.

My back teeth ground together. That little act prompted a swift change to sweep through me. Like he was provoking me, trying to goad me to show him what I was capable of. I wasn't weak, and I needed to stop acting like every little thing affected me. Because it didn't.

I was annoyed with myself and said fuck everything. I let it all go, and began.

With each punch into the spring floor, I focused on the pain and told myself it wouldn't win.

With each backflip, I shoved the unbearable backache away.

Never in my life had I ever felt anything remotely like this.

I pushed harder, faster. My stomach was a sore mess and I could swear vertigo was on the horizon.

Still, I didn't stop. Not even when it felt like nails three inches thick were being hammered into my backside, I persevered.

I would not be held down. I refused.

I flipped and punched and hopped, chewing on the anger and spitting it out with each handstand tuck set I completed. I drove myself to move quicker, in spite of it all, while I whipped my hips and drove my feet into the ground, cursing the pulsating boulders that were attached to me. I resented myself for feeling this way, but I refused to allow my emotions to control my practice time anymore. I never had in the past, and I sure as hell wasn't going to start now.

Tears threatened to fill my eyes, and I thought I was for sure going to throw up from the sheer agony I was in. I wasn't sure how much more I could handle, but I wouldn't break without giving my all first.

Every second was pure torture, but I kept going...and going...and going. I wouldn't finish early. Not even when I added the extra back tuck and the fiery hot throb was all I could hear and feel and see.

Not today, kidneys. Not today.

Just maybe when I got home.

"AH, ADRIANNA?"

Fuck. My hand was on the door ready to push it open. I was so close to leaving without having to talk to Kova.

All I wanted to do was go home and die.

"Yeah?" I said without turning around. I lowered my head and waited.

"I need to speak with you."

Shit.

I turned around to follow Kova, but he was already walking toward his office. Five minutes, I told myself. I would be in his office no more than five minutes, then I would leave.

He was seated on the front edge of his desk waiting for me when I stepped inside. Impassive, his face bore impatience. His arms were crossed in front of his chest, his beautiful biceps tight with irritation. I could feel his emotion without even touching him.

"Take a seat."

My eyes shifted between the chairs in front of him and the couch. I preferred not to sit on the couch for obvious reasons and salty memories, but I didn't want to sit in the chairs either. There would hardly be any breathing room between us.

So I sat on the sex couch.

I dropped my bag to the floor and plopped down very unladylike. I rested my head back on the cushion like I was at home and closed my eyes. I sighed as the little bit of energy I had floated away from me. It was my first time sitting for the day.

Yawning, I opened my eyes and looked at Kova. "What's up, Coach?"

"Rough workout?" One corner of his mouth tugged up.

"You could say that." My legs were so sore it took effort just to stand.

"So rough you forgot I wanted to speak to you, yes?"

I lowered my eyes. "I'm sorry. It won't happen again."

"What is on your mind?"

I looked up. His question was more intrusive than curious.

"Nothing. What do you mean?"

Kova stared at me. "Adrianna, I was not born yesterday, so do not take me for a fool. What is going on with you?"

Oh, God.

I sat up straighter. "Nothing is going on," I said. His jaw flexed but he remained silent. I tried to drive my answer home again, this time a little softer and more sincere. "Nothing is wrong with me, I just have a lot on my mind. That's all."

He pinched his bottom lip between his thumb and forefinger and turned his head to the side, then shook his head.

"*Chto-nepravil'no,*" he said under his breath. "*Chto-nepravil'no. Ya chuvstvuyu eto.*"

"What?"

"Something is not right. I can feel it." He paused. "You are lying to me."

I moved to stand. "Believe what you want, but that's the truth. Now if you'll excuse me, I need to leave."

"Sit down."

I didn't sit down. I toed the line. "I have a lot on my mind, okay? Think about when you were in my shoes and where your head was. How close you were to your damn goal and terrified that anything could go wrong at any given minute." I held my chest. "That's how I feel right now. We're so close to having it all. Don't tell me you were cool as a cucumber while under stress the entire time. You are not that perfect. No one is."

Kova's eyes widened and he stood.

"I almost ran to you today, Adrianna! In front of everyone!" he yelled. His voice echoed around the room and I reared back. "I saw the look on your face…in your eyes. I could feel it, feel you screaming for me to help you. Do you have any idea how hard it was for me to hold back? Any idea? What is going on with you and why will you not tell me?"

I glanced around in a panic. I was too ashamed to look him in the eyes.

"No one is here. Now, tell me what is wrong. Please. I cannot take it anymore."

CHAPTER 11

y chest rose and fell fast. "Nothing is wrong," I murmured. He leaned his head down toward mine. "You are lying to me." His voice was low and controlled. "You look sick, Adrianna. You are *pale*, you have dark circles under your eyes. Something is off. Give me your keys."

I scoffed. "We are not doing that again. And I could say the same for you, *Coach*. You look tired and have bags under your eyes. You haven't shaved in days and you're constantly lost in your thoughts. Most days you look absolutely miserable, but I don't push. I don't invade your personal space. I give you room to breathe."

"*I am miserable!* The only time I feel anything at all is when I am here, with you. And what I feel lately is detachment and sorrow. It is eating away at me." He shook his head. "You should push me, just like I push you. Outside these walls I feel numbness. I hate leaving here. You are the only light I have in my life, but right now, all I see is darkness in you and I do not like it."

My lips parted and my breathing deepened. He was getting too close to home and that terrified me. "Stop," I whispered. But he didn't. Kova stepped closer to me and I sucked in a breath. "Stop," I repeated.

"Sometimes we *need* people to push us, Adrianna. We want it. And I think you want me to push you. Just like I wish you would push me."

I shook my head and felt the tears climbing. He was right. I did want him to push me. I was unsteady, lost, scared. I needed someone to hold me.

I tried to step aside but Kova stopped me. "We were making progress, you and me. And then something changed in you and you woke up a different person."

"Yeah, I remembered you're married," I said defensively.

His vibrant green eyes darkened and his eyelids lowered to slits. Shifting on my feet, I deflected and glanced at the wall. That was a low blow. I didn't care that he was married. He knew that. His wedding band had never stopped me. It sure as hell had never stopped him either.

I turned and looked up at him. The turbulent look in his eyes pleaded with me to open up to him. "I'm sorry. My back hurts, okay? It's killing me and it's honestly the worst pain I've ever felt in my life. Since I can't take Motrin, I just have to deal with it. I thought that ointment shit would help it, so I was going to get it. That's all. Haven't you ever trained on a strained muscle? It's not that easy, you know."

Kova studied me. His eyes traced over my face, taking my features in. I stared back at him, hoping my words were enough to get him off me. It wasn't exactly a lie, but it wasn't the truth either. A pulled muscle didn't make someone this sick. It didn't cause persistent nausea or fever or dry mouth. A strained muscle didn't make me feel like I was actually dying. Or cause constant headaches. It wouldn't cause weakness everywhere.

"I know you are lying to me."

Letting go of my arm, he walked around his desk and opened one of the drawers. After shifting things around, he pulled out a tube of something and a box, then he was standing in front of me again.

I glanced down at the red, green, and white tube of ointment he was offering me. The box was the same thing, except they were in pad form.

"You just happen to have that in your desk?" I asked, my voice full of skepticism.

"Adrianna, I am a gymnastics coach. I am always prepared. I have a whole bunch of shit in that drawer. Take it."

I pursed my lips together and nodded my appreciation.

"Do you need me to apply it for you? I saw you grab your back a few times today. The gel may be hard for you to reach to rub in, but the medicated pads should be easy for you to apply. They just stick on."

"I think I can do it. Thanks, though."

I reached for the items, but he pulled them back. My eyes shot up.

"Let me do it for you, please. Let me help you."

There was nothing but genuine concern in his eyes. Sometimes I wish he wasn't so proactive about making sure I was okay.

A tired sigh rolled off my lips and I yawned. I just wanted to go home but I figured this might help get him off my case for a few days.

"I don't have anything to change into." Everything I had was damp with sweat from this morning's run. I refused to put that back on.

He shrugged like it wasn't an issue. "I will give you one of my shirts."

I frowned. "Do you happen to keep clothes here too?"

"Sometimes."

He was holding back. Now he wanted me to push. Whatever he wanted to say was on the tip of his tongue.

But I didn't…because I was scared to hear his answer.

"Will you let me help you?" he asked again.

I nodded. "Thank you," I said softly, and elation bloomed in his eyes.

"Let us go into the therapy room."

I glanced at his couch. "Can we just do it in here? That room is colder than an igloo."

He smiled, and I almost lost my breath. I hadn't seen Kova smile in what felt like ages and I missed it. I'd forgotten how much I loved seeing him like that.

"If you wish."

"I do."

He gestured with his hand. "Take a seat. Let me grab you a shirt."

I sat down and pulled at the straps of my leotard, sighing as I rolled the fabric down until it rested on my hips.

Kova glanced over his shoulder at me with a curious look on his face. His eyes dropped to my chest. I always wore a sports bra, so it was nothing he hadn't seen many times over.

"I love taking my leo off at the end of the day. It's like taking your bra off."

A chuckle rolled off his lips. "Well, I would not know how that feels, but I imagine good, yes?" He turned back to look through his things.

"It's sublime," I said. "The best feeling."

Kova pulled a duffle bag out of a drawer in his filing cabinet and ruffled through it. Without another word, he reached behind his head and cinched the fabric of his T-shirt in his hand and pulled it off. He shook his shirt out then handed it to me.

I looked away, but not before sneaking a peek of his abs. "Oh, no. I'm fine in my sports bra."

"Take it," he insisted.

"It's okay, really."

"Adrianna, take it." He waved the shirt in front of me.

I reached for it. "But what will you wear?" Slipping it over my head, I kept my arms under the shirt and removed my sports bra.

He shrugged like it was no big deal. "Nothing. I do not need a shirt."

Dropping my bra to the couch, I said, "But you can't go home without one."

He pulled back. His face twisted. "Why not? It is my home."

"Won't your wife say something?"

He gave me a dry, unamused look. I almost laughed at his expression. "Adrianna, please. You should know by now she will not say a damn word to me."

I always wondered why that was.

"She probably will not be home when I get home anyway."

He stared into my eyes, silently begging me to push. This was the second time he'd coaxed me to ask questions.

"How should we do this?" I ignored his unspoken request.

"Just turn around to face the couch and lean over. It will not take long. Just a few minutes."

Kova sat down behind me and lifted the back of the shirt. I gathered it in the front and held it just under my breastbone. Crossing my legs, I leaned into the couch and rested my head on the cushion in the corner of the couch.

"Point to your area of pain," he said, and I did. "Hmm. I thought it was much lower." His voice was full of concern.

"What do you mean?"

"Usually back pain is down here," he said, and dragged his finger just above my butt. "Not high up by your ribs."

"I probably didn't stretch out enough. I told you I could've slept wrong too. I'm just a little sore."

Kova didn't respond. I couldn't see what he was doing, but I could hear him rubbing the gel between his hands right before he applied it. His cool palms touched my back and he began massaging the peppermint scented stuff onto me.

I closed my eyes. I could fall asleep like this. The touch of his hands felt divine as he applied pressure to the sore points in my back.

"This feels amazing." I wasn't lying. It actually felt like it was starting to help. I'd feared the worst earlier, but maybe it truly was a pulled muscle or something.

"It should start to work pretty quickly. What did the pain feel like?"

"Just constant throbbing, but unlike anything I've ever felt before. I thought I was going to die when we were doing the tucks every time my feet hit the ground. It was taking my breath away and making me feel sick."

"You should have said something."

"It's nothing I can't handle."

After another minute or so, Kova pulled his hands away. "Okay. We are finished. This should work for a while. After you shower tonight, stick the pad where your back is hurting. It will be much easier than rubbing the gel on."

I protested. "No," I groaned, dragging the word out. I reached blindly behind me for Kova's hand. "That feels so good. Don't tell me it's over."

Kova chuckled and placed his hand in mine. My shoulders relaxed when his fingers wrapped around mine and I nestled further into his couch.

"It is. Unless you have any other areas of pain, you are free to go."

I should've gotten up and left. Instead, I placed his hand on my shoulder then tapped the top of his hand.

"Please, don't stop," I said, my face all but mushed into his couch. I smiled lazily. Kova laughed and obliged, but seconds later, his concern returned.

"You are all knotted up."

I grunted when he pushed on the curve of my shoulder. "I told you I slept wrong."

"If you want me to massage you, let us go into the therapy room where you can lay out. I have your table in there and I can give you a full massage. You need it."

"If I get up, I'm going home. I'm too tired for anything else. Plus, I'm really comfy right here. I like this couch." I made a little sound under my breath and wiggled for him to keep going.

Kova sighed. "I will never understand why I put up with your little demands the way I do," he said, but I could hear the smile and amusement in his voice, and that made me feel good.

"Because you love—"

CHAPTER 12

I froze.

My eyes flew open.

Fuck.

Fuck.

Fuck!

How could I be so stupid!

His fingers tensed. A solemn pause. I could feel the tension and electricity in the air, and the deep pull of oxygen into his lungs like it was my own. Sixty seconds of dead silence passed. My heart was going five hundred miles an hour.

Trembling to the bone, I sat up and rolled his shirt down. "I have to go." My voice came out shaky, but I didn't care. "I have to go. I have to go. I need to go." I kept repeating.

I was definitely going to be sick now. I leaned on the side of the couch to push myself up, but I wasn't quick enough.

Kova grabbed my hips. "Wait."

My entire body shook. Goddamn it! I couldn't believe I'd said what I did.

"No, I need to go."

I pulled away and slipped out of his grasp, but he grabbed me again and pulled me toward him.

"Adrianna, please, just wait."

The urgency in his voice did not go unnoticed. It was getting harder to breathe. My throat was closing up. How could I have been so stupid? Kova didn't love me. He didn't love anyone but himself.

"Why must you make me get rough with you?"

With one firm tug, he pulled back and I fell into his chest. A lungful of air gushed from me. Automatically I tried to spring forward and reach for the couch as leverage to pull myself away.

Embarrassment flooded me. I had to get out, but Kova refused and wrapped both his arms around me until I was securely in his lap. He enveloped me completely and brought his face to the curve of my neck.

My arms were stuck to my sides, my chest rising and falling fast. The warmth of his skin and the comfort of his body ignited my own. I struggled against his hold, but his thumbs began a soothing rub on my hip and shoulder while his fingers gripped me for dear life. The steady rhythm of Russian whispers against my ear calmed my rattled nerves.

"Kova…" My voice shook. "I didn't mean what I said. I didn't mean it."

"Ria." I squeezed my eyes shut.

"Please. I want to leave." And roll off a steep cliff and die.

But he surprised me. "Do you remember the first time I called you *malysh?*"

Flustered, my eyes bounced around the room. I swallowed as I thought back to that day shortly after I started training at World Cup.

"Yes." My answer came out in a broken whisper. "We were standing right outside your office in the hallway. You laid into me afterwards."

Kova tightened his embrace. "You had already begun to affect me." His breath tickled my skin. "I could not stop what I already felt for you and it fucked with my head every day, because every day my need for you grew. Calling you *malysh* felt so natural that it just slipped out. I was shocked and could not believe I'd said it, especially in public. I knew I had to fix it, even if you did not know the meaning, and what I said after came out harsher than I meant it to, but that was because I was so upset with myself for slipping."

"I'd always wondered why that happened, why you called me *malysh*, I mean."

"Truthfully," he said, "I could not believe it even came out of my mouth. I am always so controlled, meticulous with everything I do, but there has been something about you since day one that threw everything off balance for me. I am reckless when it comes to you. I do not think but instead move on feeling. I know when you need me, and I know when you are looking for me. Me and you… What you make me feel… What we have, it is maddening. Do not deny that it is not the same for you."

The same for me.

"You're one hundred percent right," I whispered, terrified to open up to him. Yet, the tension loosened from my limbs and I relaxed under his hold. I nestled into Kova's chest and brought my knees up, and he hugged me.

"So, *malysh*," he said, his voice thick with raw emotion. "You can see why I understand how that came out naturally for you, as it did for me. I want you to finish that sentence."

I turned my head to the side in shock and glanced up. Kova gave me a daring look. Our faces were so close. This man was certifiable. No chance in hell was I finishing my sentence.

"No."

"Finish it," he demanded. His heady stare pierced my heart.

I shook my head vehemently. "I can't."

"I will never understand why I put up with your little demands the way I do…" he repeated, initiating our conversation from just before.

I shook my head again. My heart raced so fast that every time I took a deep breath, Kova's forearm rose with my chest.

"Please don't," I said. My cheeks felt like they were swelling from the heat that had crept under my skin. If I said it, then it took us a step further. I wasn't sure if I could handle that.

"*Pozhaluysta,*" he said, and for once, I knew the meaning. *Please.*

"Why?" I asked.

"For reasons I cannot explain." He waited a few seconds, then said, "Why do I put up with your little demands?"

The same reason I put up with his, and he knew it.

I licked my lips nervously and found the courage I needed to get the words out. "Because…" I stammered. "Because…you…love me."

Kova's eyes flashed with emotion that took my breath away. His lips parted just subtly.

"Again," he rasped. Now it was his turn to breathe deeply. We moved together.

"Because you love me," I said softly.

Kova leaned down and slowly bridged the distance between our lips. I held my breath as he grew closer, until he gave me the softest kiss imaginable.

He hovered above me, the tangible air thick with unspoken words that would never see the light of day. They'd stay between us. He panted as he pressed his lips against mine. Even the simplest action made the world fade away, allowing the true chemistry between us to grow even more. When it was just me and Kova and not the outside world to influence us, he put himself out there to show me who he was. Even if it was just a simple look, the embrace of his arms, an action that expressed his secrets, I *saw* him, and I *understood* him. Just like he understood me. Saying he loved me was the equivalent to *malysh* for him.

Kova broke the kiss but he didn't pull away. Damn his eyes and the way he looked at me. The smoldering heat split my heart open.

"I should go," I whispered.

"No, stay." He pressed his fingers down into me. "We do not have to talk anymore, but at least let me work those knots out for you. You will sleep better because of it."

God, the urgency in his voice and the look of dread in his eyes were hard for me to deny. I had to wonder if admitting his love for me was as intimidating for him as it was for me.

"Okay."

"*Spasibo*," he said. "Let me do it right. I will go grab the salve from the other room. Take the shirt off and lay on your stomach. I will be right back."

Kova released me and I stood up. I watched him leave his office, his gait marked with determination, his shoulders reminiscent of a tiger.

I did as he asked, then held his shirt to my chest, questioning myself as to why I was staying in the first place. Leaving would be the wisest decision.

Lying face down on his couch, I sighed at the softness and realized just how tired I really was. I folded my arms and pulled them up to my ribs. Kova was back in a few short minutes. He positioned himself behind me, squatting with one knee on each side without lowering his weight.

The moment his hands touched my shoulders, my eyes closed. A heavenly breath rolled off my lips from the blissful touch of his skilled fingers. He knew exactly how to target the tension and knead it away precisely.

"We should do these more often," he suggested.

"I'll make sure to pencil you in." I joked. "I hardly have time to shower, you know." The thought of finding time for a massage was tiring in itself.

"The life of an athlete."

"Tell me about it."

Kova dug deep and pressed hard and I moaned from the pressure. I loved it so much.

"There is a lot of tension. Let me know if I am hurting you."

"You're not. I like it harder…" I hummed in pleasure. "It feels good. Like when you press slow but deep, it feels the best."

Kova's hands paused, and it caught my attention. I felt the telltale signs of concealed laughter.

"What?" I asked, trying to peer over my shoulder.

He stifled a chuckle. "You say my Russian is showing, but sometimes you do not even realize what you say."

I thought about what I'd said, and how it could be taken any other way when it finally hit me. Fuuucccckkkk. Talk about delayed reaction. God, I was so stupid today.

"Oh, hell." I laughed, mortified. I covered my face. *I like it harder… it feels good.* "I wasn't thinking."

"Obviously. Anything that is innocently spoken to a man is never taken that way at first. Remember that."

"Believe me, I will now."

The quiet solitude of the room ensued, and I smiled to myself, happy that my plans for the night changed. I knew the moment I walked into my empty condo I would break down and cry myself to sleep. I'd felt it during practice and I almost looked forward to it. But now I felt lighter, more optimistic. My chest didn't hurt, and I could breathe a little easier. I didn't feel like crying anymore, and I was so happy about that. I hated crying.

I felt like Kova had worked out my issues without even knowing he did.

Days like this got to me. Days when Kova knew what I needed without me having to say anything. When he saw the underlying issue, could feel it trying to burst from me, and then took measures into his own hands to help me. There'd been countless times this had happened. When he saw what I needed when no one else had, and he gave it to me fully.

To live in this outrageous, intense and hectic world of elite gymnastics, everyone needed a lifeline. Someone they could hang on to when times were tough, when life felt all-consuming or the future seemed bleak, they could see the crash coming before anyone else and be there. We all had that one go-to person who we relied on when nothing made sense to anyone except them. Who accepted all our flaws and imperfections.

Kova was my lifeline whether I wanted to admit it or not. I didn't want to drown. I wanted to stay afloat, and he was my ultimate salvation. I clung to him.

He was controlling, but I was selfish. Had I ever once given him what he needed? Even once?

I didn't want to think about my answer.

🤸

I OPENED MY EYES, TIRED and a little disoriented. Yawning, I glanced around the dim room trying to figure out where I was and why I was so stiff.

Across from me, Kova was asleep in his leather desk chair. His legs were spread wide with one leg straight and the other bent, his jaw was propped up on his fist, and still only in his netted shorts and nothing else. I watched him for a few moments, quietly taking him in. My gaze dipping to each feature of his handsome face when I noticed the tension knitted between his blackish brows. Unforgiving lines pulled at the corners of his eyes, his thick lashes laying in half moon crescents on his cheeks. Even while he slept, he had something on his mind.

Kova stirred, his eyes moving beneath his lids. He drew in a deep breath and exhaled. He must've felt me staring at him.

"Hey," I said. He gave me a lazy smile that was so damn hot. "I can't believe I fell asleep. You should've woken me up."

"You looked like you needed the rest. I did not want to wake you."

Early morning sleepy voice was sexy on Kova.

"But don't you need to go home?"

"Do not concern yourself with that. You looked like you were struggling yesterday with something. I wanted to be there for you, even if it was just for you to sleep."

I frowned, half grateful, half confused. What kind of wife was Katja for not tracking her husband down, let alone letting him sleep somewhere else? It made no sense to me.

"What time is it?" I asked.

Kova glanced at his wrist. I had the sudden urge to go to him and sit on his lap. I wanted to burrow myself into his warmth, feel our bare chests pressed together, and go back to sleep.

"It is almost five," he said.

Reaching above his head, he stretched his arms behind him. The Olympic rings tattoo I loved so much on his ribs contracted with each pull and shift of his fit body. He watched me watch him. I didn't think I'd ever grow tired of staring at him.

"How does your back feel?"

I thought about the agony I was in yesterday and if I felt the same this morning. I offered him a small smile. "It's okay. Not nearly as bad as before."

My bladder was about to burst as I sat up. "I need to get going… I have my appointment today that I can't be late for." I yawned again. "I can't believe how long I slept. I feel like I could sleep until tomorrow."

Kova nodded and stood, the cracking of his knees echoed throughout his office. He turned around and laced his fingers together behind his head and stretched once more. I lusted after his muscular back as it flexed with power, then I dropped my gaze to the two little dimples above his butt. Konstantin Kournakova was a walking, breathing Russian god. The urge to wrap myself around him was even stronger now, but I glanced away and slipped his shirt on.

"It's freezing in here. Aren't you cold?"

"No," he said through light laughter. "You do not know cold until you have been to Russia. It is bitter there."

A tired smile formed on my face. He was probably right. "Do you miss it?"

"Miss what?"

"Russia."

Looking into my eyes, he contemplated his answer. "Yes. I have not been back in a very long time. I would love to go back sometime in the near future, just not to live."

"Why not to live?" I asked, curious.

He rolled his bottom lip between his teeth before answering me. "There is nothing there for me anymore. Everything I want is right here."

My stomach sank to the floor, a sign to get moving.

Gymnastics. Katja. Me. Possibly in that order.

I felt like this was another one of those push questions, and I wasn't up for that, just like I hadn't been earlier. There were too many likelihoods and not enough energy left to handle them.

He must've sensed my indecision, because he continued.

"Let me rephrase. Everything I want is right here in this room."

All the air left my lungs. I blinked a few times then stood up with my duffle bag in hand. I shot a quick prayer up to God to slow down my pounding heart.

"I'll see you tomorrow. Thank you for everything," I said, and added a small smile to seal my words.

He nodded. "Hang on. Let me give you something."

My forehead furrowed in wonder as I watched Kova unlock his filing cabinet and reach all the way to the back behind all the folders.

My lips parted over what he produced.

"Read it later."

CHAPTER 13

Our notebook.

I'd forgotten all about it, but then it dawned on me. I walked over to him.

"Wait. Where did you get this? Last I remembered, I put it in my nightstand."

He relocked the cabinet and handed it to me. "I noticed it when I was at your place on my birthday. You did not seem too keen on giving it back to me any time soon, so I took it. I had some things I needed to get off of my chest."

I glanced down at the notebook, wondering what he'd written and when he'd done it. What he needed to get out.

"I don't even remember the last thing I wrote in this."

Kova grinned and his eyes flashed with amusement. "It was… colorful to say the least." His smile grew. "Go back and read it when you get a moment. I did not expect those words to come from your lips, that is for sure. Cannot say I did not deserve them either. I quite liked that side of you."

Oh man. My mind raced back to when I last had it in my possession and what the hell I wrote. I flipped the pages open but Kova stopped me.

He was right, I had to go. Nodding, I said, "I'll talk to you after my appointment?"

His head tilted to the side. Kova regarded me. I could hardly see the brilliant emerald color of his eyes. Finally, he nodded.

Clutching the spiral notebook to my chest, I readjusted the strap of my duffle bag, gripping it tight in my hand. I left his office and threw the bag and notebook in the back seat of my truck. I couldn't wait to see what he wrote.

LATE INTO THE AFTERNOON, I sat on the patient table listening to the doctor go over my results from the ultrasound she'd just done on my Achilles.

By some miracle, and much to my surprise, I hadn't had any new tears, just the same micro-tears as before that were a little deeper, along with some inflammation. I couldn't believe it. I thought for sure I'd torn it.

"You seem shocked," the doctor said.

"That's because I am. I thought I'd torn something more, or worse. It was really bad. I could hardly walk. I was prepared to put up a fight."

"Well, you aren't far from tearing your Achilles completely. All that tightness and burning you feel is due to overuse, which is completely normal for an athlete of your stature given the sport you play. Once the season is over, I highly suggest we schedule surgery to repair the tears and give your injury the proper time to heal. I don't see you lasting another season with this. It's better to repair it while we can, which means less healing time if you tear it completely."

I sat staring unblinking at the doctor. After this season, after the Olympics, if I made it that far, I was supposed to start dialysis. Somehow I needed to fit college into the mix too. I could feel the blood draining from my face, feel the cold seeping into my bones at what my future held. I didn't like it.

The doctor regarded me. "Is everything okay?"

My jaw bobbed. "Ah, yeah, it's fine. I just recently discovered I'll need dialysis after the season too, and I was thinking about how I'm supposed to fit in a surgery on top of that now. Eventually I'm going to need a transplant down the line," I said. Lines formed between her eyes. "I have stage four kidney disease."

This time the doctor's brows rose to her hairline and her eyes widened. "You have stage four kidney disease, and you're still competing?" I nodded and she whistled under her breath. "I wouldn't worry yourself about how you'll be able to fit it all in. Given the declining state of your health, I'd meet with your team of doctors and devise a plan. It's manageable."

My shoulders sagged. Relief coursed through me and I smiled. "Thank you."

"If you're not on dialysis yet, are you on medication? Steroids?"

"Oh, yes. I take a lot of pills a day just to get through it."

I reached into my purse and pulled out the notecard listing my medications. I handed it to the doctor and her eyes scanned over it. Dad had said the doctor might ask what I was taking and to bring the paper instead of having to carry the bottles. It was a good idea.

"Do you have an infection? You're on a few antibiotics."

I nodded. "I have a kidney infection. A bad one I was told." I blinked when it hit me. My jaw fell open. "I'm so stupid! I've had terrible pain in my back to the point that I've been sick to my stomach. I completely forgot I have a kidney infection. I thought it was a side effect of the medications or lack of appetite I've had." I shook my head to myself, feeling so dumb that I forgot about this. "I can't believe I forgot," I said out loud.

"It's natural for something to slip your mind given your situation, especially in your position. Don't beat yourself up over it. That being said, I would highly suggest you be in constant contact with your specialist and let the doctor know of the pain you're dealing with. If you're on medication, the infection should've started to clear up by now. Also, you can't take steroids a week before any platelet injection, should you need another, so we'll have to plan for that. You're on a few right now."

My teeth worried my bottom lip. I hadn't thought of that and now I felt even more stupid for not thinking about it beforehand. I just knew not to take the anti-inflammatory medications.

I was in over my head.

The doctor suggested I continue the blading sessions with Kova as needed, and the typical ice therapy I dreaded. She reminded me to stay away from Motrin, and I promised to make an appointment once the season was over should everything continue the way it was.

Easy-peasy.

Once I was back in my truck, I dialed up Dad to tell him about the pain in my kidneys and how bad it's been. I had promised him not to leave anything out. He called Dr. Kozol on another line while I waited. After three minutes, he came back and told me to go see him immediately.

An hour later I was sitting in front of the doctor. A kindness surrounded him that was very welcoming and made me feel at ease.

I'd already given a urine sample, had blood drawn, and had a new ultrasound done on my kidneys right when I came in. The technician took photos and measured the size of my kidneys and heart. I watched the screen as she moved the wand around, trying to see anything but all I saw were black and white masses everywhere that ballooned and then shrunk. I had no idea what I was looking at.

Dr. Kozol reviewed the tests, then he got right to the point.

"Adrianna. Tell me what's been going on and don't leave a thing out."

I smiled and eyed the folder in his hand, then proceeded to tell him everything—how I've been feeling since I left his office a few weeks ago, how I threw up, how terrible my back has been, the headaches and chest pain, and the fatigue that made me feel like a ninety-year-old brittle woman. I told him I thought the medicine was giving me the shakes and I had nights when I slept like the dead and other nights where my eyes twitched from lack of sleep.

"I bet it's been a rough few weeks for you… A rough couple of months, hasn't it?"

I laughed lightly. "Yeah, you could say that."

"How are you handling everything?"

I shrugged. "Honestly, I don't talk about it. I just keep it to myself. It's easier that way."

His head angled to the side and he eyed me. "It's also very unhealthy to bottle your emotions in."

"I train close to fifty hours a week with tons of conditioning. It helps."

"Are you taking any other medications I'm not aware of? Any over-the-counter or prescriptions? Anti-inflammatory?"

I shook my head and explained I couldn't take them anymore due to my Achilles and the blading. He eyed my leg.

"You're almost eighteen and you're falling apart."

This time I let out a deep belly laugh. "Tell me about it," I said, and smiled.

Dr. Kozol placed the folder on the counter and then turned to wash his hands. "Right now, your immune system is weak, which means your body is a free-for-all. Not getting the proper rest your body needs will set you back, which it's clearly doing." He dried his hands off and pulled on a pair of latex gloves. "While there are preventative measures we can take to help reduce your flare ups and discomfort, ultimately, you'll need more intensive treatment. Your urine results show a slight increase in protein, but nothing I'm too concerned about yet." He pulled the stethoscope from around his neck and put the buds into his ears. "Take a deep breath." He moved the instrument. "Another," he said, listening to my chest. He pulled away and looked at me. "Lupus is a workaholic. It can cause headaches and weight loss, sometimes a low-grade fever. Joint pain. Pretty much what you're experiencing now. But coupled with the kidney disease, I need to be aware of everything you're dealing with at all times. Even if you think it's small, it could mean more to me. I wish you'd contacted me earlier about the kidney infection. The ultrasound shows small stones, which is why you're experiencing the pain you are." He listened to my back. "Take a deep breath... Another... Another." He leaned in, his brows bunching together. "Do it one more time for me." He paused. "Again?"

"Kidney stones?" I replied quietly.

"They're small and easily passable, but large enough to cause pain. Manageable, too, so nothing to worry about. Up your water intake and I'll give you something for the pain that will help break them down."

Dr. Kozol pulled away and placed the stethoscope around his neck.

"Is something wrong?" I asked.

"You mentioned chest pain, which I'm sure at one point you probably figured was from overexerting yourself at practice." Of course I had. I nodded. "Lupus causes inflammation around your lungs, but right now, I can hear the faint sound of fluid grating around them."

My eyes widened. Kidney stones. More protein in my urine. Fluid in my lungs. This had to be a cruel joke. How many more shitty hands could I be dealt? Of course I'd get the highflyer of autoimmunes. That was just my life.

"I have pneumonia?"

"No. Sometimes fluid will build up between your lungs and your chest. It's called pleural effusion and typically goes away on its own."

I exhaled a heavy breath, feeling my heart picking up speed. I was panicking on the inside but trying to remain calm as Dr. Kozol continued to speak.

"It's not bad, but it's something we have to watch since I can hear it. We'll switch your medicine around and up your dose. At any time your chest hurts, you need to take a seat and breathe. You're pushing too hard, Adrianna. I'd order bed rest, but something tells me you wouldn't take the advice."

"Why do I feel a *but* coming?" I said.

Dr. Kozol's lips flattened. He eyed me carefully, and I took a deep breath.

"Your father said you'll start dialysis after this gymnastics season is over. I'm highly against that, as you know. A waiver had to be signed saying you're forgoing recommended medical treatment. There's too much risk involved, especially since we haven't been able to find a donor match yet."

I perked up. "A donor match? Wait a minute. Who was tested?" I didn't know anything about that.

Dr. Kozol picked up my file and scanned a few papers. He looked at me. "Your brother and biological mother. Neither one was a match. Your father is expected to be tested soon."

CHAPTER 14

I listened to my body—and doctor—and took one day off.

I'd called Kova after I left the doctor's office and told him the tears were deeper but not completely torn. I'd also told him how my back was still hurting and I wanted to rest it. Much to my surprise, he was quick to oblige. He also said I only get one day and expected to see me first thing the following morning. I laughed. Typical Kova, but I was cool with that.

Since I had stayed home, I took one of the pain pills before I fell asleep. I woke up feeling so much better. It was like I had a brand new body and I loved it. I slept nearly the entire day, only waking up to eat and take my medicine before falling asleep again. I'd been exhausted, not realizing how badly my body needed the rest. It was a blessing in disguise, really, because it prevented me from overthinking the fact that I'd yet to find a match for a kidney.

I also took the time to write in the notebook Kova and I shared. I'd planned on rereading what I had written, along with Kova's responses, but decided I wouldn't. I didn't want to relive the past I held so much hostility for, and since we were in a fairly good place, I didn't see the point in welcoming those areas of negativity back into my life. All it would do is awaken old emotions I had put to rest. So I took the pages and bound them together tightly with packaging tape. They'd have to be cut along the seams in order to be read. Then I flipped to a new page and wrote him an honest note I'd give him the next day.

I wish I knew why I'm slowly giving you another chance and letting you back in. All I know is this hatred was hardening my heart and would continue to take up every last inch of space the longer I went on if I didn't let it go. I realized it's not healthy, and I can't afford anything less right now.

I don't think you're a bad person. I just think you made questionable choices with the intent of meaning well only for them to backfire on you. You're a double-edged sword.

I just wish I knew why I want to be around you all the time.

I wish I could understand why I look for you when I'm alone.

I can't explain this feeling in my heart that only you give me. I probably sound so stupid and young, but I don't feel this for anyone.

Please, I'm asking you to not ever hurt me again. That brokenness I lived through was caused by you, and yet you're the one who's slowly placing the pieces back where they belong. I know you're trying, but so am I.

I walked into the café room the following day and went straight to the refrigerator for the plastic bag I'd brought with me this morning. My lunch was safe for my kidneys, and I had packed wheatgrass juice to drink to help break down the kidney stones.

I sat down and untied the plastic bag then grimaced when I looked inside. My red apple tumbled out and onto the floor as I shoved the bag away in annoyance. I dropped my head into my hands. I didn't have an appetite. I didn't want to eat. And I most definitely wasn't in the mood for this food.

I lifted my head and shivered, then remembered Kova had a hoodie in his office. I also realized this was the perfect time to place the notebook in his desk under the guise of getting his jacket.

My bare feet were ice cold against the tile as I stood and walked to grab the spiral bound book out of my duffle bag. I then made my way down the hall to Kova's office and pushed the door open. His scent permeated the room and I inhaled the dark cinnamon and citrusy tobacco smell. Sunshine flowed through the blinds as I walked around his desk. Bending down, I pulled open his bottom drawer and shoved the book under a bunch of files, making sure it was covered before closing the drawer.

I reached for the hoodie on the back of his chair and slipped it on, then left his office.

"What are you doing in my husband's office?"

"Oh!" I jumped and grabbed my chest. "Katja. I didn't see you there. You startled me. Hi."

She tilted her head and wore a superior expression on her face I pretended not to notice. Her eyes raked down my body then back up to mine. "And why are you wearing his jacket?" She scowled.

My chin bobbed, unprepared for her brash tone. I looked down. This definitely didn't look good, but it didn't look bad either. I tried to think of something quick to defuse her attitude. Kova's *jsah-hket*, as Katja had pronounced it, was nearly down to my knees and keeping me warm. I wasn't taking it off just because she stood in front of me.

"Ah, I was just—"

"I see you located my sweater, Adrianna. Good."

My eyes widened and locked with Katja's. She straightened, her back stiff as a board and shoulders pushed back.

I looked past her to see Kova striding toward us. I was stuck in my stance when I caught the go-with-it stare in his eyes.

"I did. Thank you," I responded softly, unsure where this was going. He stopped when he reached his wife's side and placed his hand on her lower back.

"Allo, Katja." He didn't smile.

She openly glared at him. "Konstantin. Why is she wearing your clothes?" she asked, flipping up her palm, fingers pointing toward me like little sharp knives.

I looked at him, waiting to hear his response myself.

"Adrianna was not feeling well and said she was cold. She was ill a few days ago, so I told her to grab my sweater and take a rest in the therapy room."

Interesting.

"Why not send her home if she is sick?" she asked. Her voice was high and pitchy, and flat out annoying. "She will contaminate everyone else, including you. And you know I cannot get sick right now."

I wasn't a walking disease, for fuck's sake.

Okay. Technically speaking I was, but they didn't know that. And I wasn't contagious.

Kova cocked his head to the side. His expression, the look in his eyes, it screamed common sense. I chewed back my smirk and eyed the floor. I knew that look and I almost felt bad for her.

"We have a very important week ahead of us, which I have mentioned to you. She has no time to rest."

I looked back up as Katja placed her hand over her heart. The glittering diamond was bigger than her knuckle. I wanted to bend that finger backwards.

"But what about me? About what we talked about?"

"What about you?" he retorted.

She glanced at me with bitterness in her steel gaze. My brows angled toward each other with deep creases.

"This is not what we agreed upon," Katja said, then looked at me again like she was trying to say something without saying it. Her gaze followed mine and she noticed I was back to staring at her enormous wedding ring and band.

I quickly glanced away, but it was too late. It wasn't even that nice. Just a dumb circle and thin band.

The air between all three of us thickened to an awkward silence. I was the third wheel. Hitching my thumb up, I took one step backward and said, "I'm going to go rest now…"

They both looked at me. I turned away. Katja's glare left me with an unsettling feeling and I didn't like it one bit.

"Ah, Adrianna?"

I stopped and looked over my shoulder. "Yes?"

"No more than an hour."

Damn it. "Yes, Coach."

I knew Kova was just trying to look out for me and I appreciated that, but Christ on a stick, I was going to die of hypothermia in the therapy room before kidney disease.

A little dramatic, but I really hated being cold. I despised it more than anything.

Curled up in a tight ball under Kova's *jsah-hket*, my teeth chattered while I counted down the seconds until my sentence was up. My toes were frozen solid and the only thing that gave me any kind of alleviation was the husky scent of Kova's smell imbedded into the fibers of his hoodie. I burrowed myself into his sweater.

I didn't last the full hour. Between the sterile room and the clipped Russian language that carried down the hall, I needed to get out of there and back into the gym.

I returned to the café to clean up what I'd left out on the table before making my way to the locker room. I took off Kova's sweater and folded it up, then placed it in my bag. There was no way I was knocking on his office door to return it now. Not since Kova and Katja had been going at it ever since they'd walked into his office. They seemed like they were at war with each other. At least that's what I'd gathered. Neither one was backing down. While Katja's voice rose and fell, Kova's stayed on the opposite spectrum.

I took a step to leave the locker room and hesitated at the sound of Kova's unrestrained voice. I held my breath and waited another beat longer until I thought the coast was clear.

I should've just hidden out.

A loud slap echoed down the hallway. I sucked in a breath and pressed my back to the wall, debating whether or not I should run for it. I assumed Kova had been slapped across the face. I didn't want to be there when it was all over.

Expelling a nervous breath, I made up my mind to run back into the gym when a shrill of Russian words sounded the same time the door flew open.

Jesus Christ, my heart. My back stiffened, feet rooted in place as Katja stormed out of the office. The door slammed into the wall behind her and bounced off. She halted to a standstill in her high heels when she saw me.

Our eyes locked. She looked downright murderous. My heart rate escalated to an unhealthy rate, pounding so viciously I could hear it in my ears. Her stunning, ethereal face contorted into a fury of abhorrence, twisting into something I never expected her to look like. She scowled down her nose at me before spewing something in Russian and marching off.

It all happened so fast.

I tried to replay the words in my head so I could look them up later, but my brain couldn't process them at the rate she had said them. Shed spoken too quickly. I don't think she even took a breath. It was like one giant run-on squeaky Russian sentence.

I watched in silence as she stormed out of the building. A muffled sound behind me drew my attention, and I glanced over my shoulder.

Kova stood stretching his jaw, cupping one side while he rubbed it. I caught sight of the red handprint on his skin.

Our eyes met and I was caught off guard by his reaction. He looked…sad, and it confused me. I felt pity looking at him when he didn't deserve pity.

Without thinking, I walked over to where he stood and gently dragged my knuckles down the side she'd slapped.

"I'm sorry," I said quietly.

His eyes softened. I thought he'd be angry that I heard and saw what I had, but he didn't appear that way at all.

Kova reached for my hand, his warm fingers pressing into my cold palm. My stomach dipped as he pulled me closer until we were just a few inches apart. He looked deep into my eyes.

For a moment we were suspended in time, forgetting where we were or that anyone could see us. I took note that this wasn't the first time this had happened. It'd been happening more so lately and neither one of us seemed to care. We were getting too comfortable and becoming reckless.

Kova brought my knuckles to his lips and gently kissed them. I swallowed hard, fighting to tear my gaze from his. My fingers curled around his before he dropped our hands.

"Trouble in paradise?" I asked, my tone good-natured.

And just like that, his shoulders relaxed and he fell into stride next to me.

"I probably deserved it," he said.

I nodded in agreement, and he chuckled.

Quietly, just for him to hear, I said, "I put the notebook in your desk under a bunch of green folders."

I looked up waiting for him to respond. Instead, he dipped his head once and I caught the faintest hint of a smile.

"Kova?" I said as we rounded the corner.

"Hmm…"

"Why'd you lie for me?"

Kova paused at the door to the gym and angled his body toward me. "Sometimes, Adrianna, we do things not for ourselves, but out of need for others."

CHAPTER 15

With wide eyes, I looked all around me.

There were photographers everywhere and not an empty seat in the house. Chaos and coaches. Gymnasts and anxiety. Kova squatted in front of me, the black material of his dress pants stretched over his knees. I looked at his opened palm.

"Give it to me," he insisted under his breath. I handed him my sports tape. "What is wrong with you? Why are your hands shaking?"

I glanced at my fingers. I'd been tempted a few times now to skip the medicine, but after being on it for a few weeks, I was too scared of the repercussions I'd face if I did. I didn't want to mess with it, but the trembling had gotten so bad over the last week and it was starting to drive me nuts. My entire body felt like it was on edge, uncontrollable shaking down to the bone. I learned it was a side effect of the steroids and there was nothing I could do about it unless I called my doctor and asked for something else. I hadn't. Instead, I attempted to adapt to it and tried to regulate it the best I could, balancing myself by taking deep breaths, and flexing my hands and making sure I kept moving.

"Answer me," he demanded, his eyes shooting all around us.

"Nothing... I'm just nervous."

He paused before tearing off a strip of tape with his teeth. "Anything else?" he asked, lifting his eyes to look at me. Kova was acting strange.

"N-no," I said. "This is just a big meet and I'm honestly a ball of nerves, Coach. I'm nervous."

It wasn't a far stretch from the truth. I *was* nervous. The medications were kicking in and making me a little jittery on top of the meet stress. Unfortunately, they weren't helping with the fatigue. I was already drained. We'd traveled across the country for this one. The National Championships was a two-day meet where the best of the best gymnasts around the world competed, not to mention the Olympic team coaches were in attendance too. Next up if I got lucky was Worlds.

Kova's eyes softened. Maybe it was all in my head. He applied the tape then ripped off another piece. "I understand. Just remember you are here because of the work you put in. You proved that you are worth it, that you can handle the pressure. You are now considered a valuable piece to the Olympic team. You have what it takes and deserve to be here."

I gave him an appreciative smile. "You're just trying to make me feel better."

"Whatever it takes, Adrianna. But you should know by now that I do not speak bullshit."

I chuckled. "I do not speak bullshit," I said in a low faux Russian accent. The corner of his mouth curved up and a sense of ease rolled over me.

"How does that feel?" he asked.

I flexed my foot and moved it around. "Good."

"What about here?" he asked and placed a hand to my calf. "We have not done blading in some time."

"I haven't really needed it, but it feels good. Thanks."

Kova stood and held his hand out. I took it and readjusted my leotard, pulling it to cover my butt. I glanced around the stadium once more, trying to see if I could spot my dad.

"Do you want to know where he is?" Kova asked.

I glanced at him. "How did you know I was looking for him?"

"Wild guess."

I knew it was against the rules to see or talk to family before a meet, but something inside my heart was reaching for the kind of comfort only a parent could give. With everything I was going through, I'd been more emotional lately. Sometimes a girl just needed her dad.

I chewed my lip and nodded my head. Kova turned around and pointed. My eyes searched as quickly as my heart beat for the familiar face.

It didn't take long. He was already waving before my eyes landed on him. Our eyes met and happiness burst through me. I smiled from ear to ear, waving frantically. I hadn't seen my dad in months, but I felt like I'd grown closer to him despite the distance between us.

"Thank you," I said softly. "I'm surprised you let me say hi." It wasn't meant maliciously, but honestly, and he knew that.

He shrugged one shoulder. "I just want you to be mentally prepared for today and tomorrow, and if saying good day to your father is necessary for that, then sometimes rules are meant to be broken."

We broke the rules every chance we got.

"Good day?" I laughed, and smiled. "See? You need to work on your English. No one says that. You sound like you're from the Stone Age."

"I say it." He played back. "And I am not old."

I was still smiling. "You're insufferable. At thirty-four, you're kinda old."

One brow peaked. "Kind of old?"

"When you start growing grays, isn't that when you're considered old?"

His brows shot up to his hairline. "I have grays?" He patted his head.

I stifled a chuckle and tried not to smile. "I saw one the other day."

"One?" His eyes twinkled with amusement. "How close to my head were you to see one lone hair?"

I bit down on my lip and propped my hands on my hips. "I saw it, okay?"

"If I have gray hair, it is because of you, you know."

"Right," I said, drawing the word out through a smile from ear to ear. "You should start looking into dyes. After one, they start growing like weeds."

"Adrianna," he warned, and I burst out laughing at his tone. "You need to understand now that I will never dye my hair."

This was too much fun. "I can dye it for you."

"You will not."

"I'll get you to drink a lot of vodka one night. You won't be able to say no."

"I already feel like that with you," he admitted, this time seriously. "I find it harder and harder to say no to you."

A shy smile tugged at my lips that grew into a full blown one. My cheeks heated. I liked this easy back and forth with Kova.

"So that's a yes? Cool. I'll start researching dyes for men, and while I'm at it, I'll look for hair regrowth."

Propping his hands on his hips, he smirked. "Nice try, but I am telling you right now that it will never happen. I do not need to color my hair to look young. You make me feel young, and that is all that matters."

Kova reached out but quickly pulled back. Recognition dawned in his eyes. Sometimes when it was just us being normal and playing around, we tended to forget the outside world. I felt his pull, his playful need to wrap his arms around me and tug me to him. I needed that too. My emotions had been an array of sadness and fear, and something as little as this interaction gave me life and a reprieve from my thoughts. People usually took the big moments in life as what spoke volumes, but for me, it was the little things.

"Thanks," I said softly. I brushed back a few strands of loose hair behind my ear. "For this." He knew what I meant without having to say it.

Kova nodded, regarding me with a heartfelt look in his eyes. The way my pulse beat for him wasn't normal. The way he looked at me wasn't normal. And what I felt deep in my bones for him most definitely wasn't normal.

"Okay." He clapped his hands. "Chalk up and let us get going, yes?"

I turned to walk away, feeling so much lighter on my toes.

"Adrianna?"

I looked at him over my shoulder.

"It is nice to see you smile again. Oh, and when you get a private moment, check your duffle bag." He gave me a knowing look.

The notebook.

I could feel a flutter of the wing that had been clipped desperately trying to fly. Kova didn't know it, but he was breathing life back into me. Each day he helped me find my inner strength so I could grow strong enough to hold myself up again.

What scared me about that was I had a feeling he was going to be the only one who would help me get there.

This time I gave him a real smile that showed exactly what I felt in my heart. And I didn't give a shit if anyone saw.

"Okay," Kova said, rubbing my shoulders a few hours later. He bent down to look me in the eyes and said, "Two events down, two to go. You ready?"

I nodded. I was more than ready. I had this. After two rotations, I was in first place with just four-tenths of a point separating me from second. Anything could happen from here until the last event, but I had a good feeling about it. A really good feeling.

Those two events were my best ones—vault and bars. I stuck both dismounts and received almost maximum points for my routines.

"It is like gravity does not apply to you. You flowed more smoothly on bars than I have ever seen you do before and with height that made even my heart drop. Your lines could not have been more perfect. Let us do the same for beam."

The only event I was truly worried about was beam because of how jittery I already was. It was subtle, but enough to throw me off balance. My bones shook, muscles rattled, and I didn't like it. I couldn't feel it on the other events, but I had a feeling I would on beam.

Kova grabbed my hands in his. He glanced down. "You are still shaking," he said more to himself.

I tightened my fingers around his. "I'll be fine," I said. "Just nerves." The flash of a camera caught my eyes and I pulled my hands from his.

"Nerves are a good thing if you channel them properly. Focus and control."

I nodded and applied powder to my feet and hands, then to my inner thighs. I stood to the side, letting the judges know I was ready. When they gave me the green light, I saluted first then stepped onto the memory foam mat and walked up to the balance beam and faced it.

Exhaling a calm breath, my hands hovered over the four-inch piece of wood and shook a little. Clearing my mind of everything except this moment and what I was about to try and attain, I mellowed my soul and mounted the beam.

I finished eighty seconds later, both feet stuck together with a small hop that would cost me. But I felt good. Really, really good that as I walked off the podium, I went straight into Kova's arms.

We broke apart and walked toward my chair. I was breathing heavier than normal and my chest was a little tight. I rubbed the ache, thankful the pain in my back from the kidney infection had reduced to a dull throb.

"I wobbled on my turns."

"You still finished with an unparalleled amount of ease."

I glanced up at him. "I had two balance checks, *Coach*…"

"Everyone does," he said. "Just little things we will work on before Worlds."

Worlds.

I nodded and took a few sips of water then dropped the bottle back into my bag. I stood up and adjusted the sleeves of my all black leotard that had an enormous amount of peridot rhinestones. It'd been my favorite to wear to date, and the colors were finally a good match for my auburn hair.

My knee bobbed.

"What's taking so long?" I said just for him to hear.

I took a deep breath again to regain my poise, hoping I would catch my breath too. Kova glanced at me, his brows bunched together, but I averted my gaze quickly and acted normal. I had a gut feeling the wobble would knock me down to second place. Or maybe the hop would. Or something they saw that I didn't feel. Maybe it was all three.

"Patience is a virtue."

I scoffed. "I hate that saying."

"Does not matter that you slipped up. You still had the highest amount of difficulty in your—"

I looked up to see what had interrupted him and followed his gaze. Chills wracked down my arms.

My score posted.

The only deduction I received had to be for the balance checks because my score wasn't far from the max. In fact, it was almost too good to be true for an event that was considered my weakest.

I stood in disbelief. Kova, on the other hand, was losing it.

He turned toward me and grabbed my shoulders. "You do not give yourself enough credit," he said, his voice much higher than usual. I gazed into his lively eyes. "Well, say something!"

"I… I'm speechless." I really was. "How the hell did I pull that off?"

Kova let out a loud good-natured laugh. "I knew you could do it! When you place your focus properly, you dig deep to do whatever it takes to get you there. I see it every time when you compete." He pulled me in for a bear hug. "I am so damn proud of you," he said then pulled back and grabbed my shoulders again and gave me a little shake.

A bashful smile splayed across my face. It wasn't over, but I could breathe a little easier knowing I only had floor left.

"Give yourself a pat on the back."

I literally patted my shoulder, and Kova smiled at me with more pride in his eyes than I'd ever seen before.

I was going to rock my floor routine.

CHAPTER 16

H ow does it feel to come in first place?" Dad asked, his voice full of cheer.

It'd been a couple of hours since we got back to the hotel room and the disbelief still hadn't worn off. Dad hadn't stopped smiling. Seeing my final score left me stunned with too many feelings to sift through. It was overwhelming in the greatest way. Today was my best meet to date, but it also required the most energy from me. Now my body was settling, and my muscles were crunching up into tight coils.

I couldn't believe I finished in first in prelims on the first day of nationals. On the airplane to the meet, I'd read a few articles that predicted I had a chance of finishing in the top three. The pros expected Sloan to take it because she was that good and finished in first place nine times out of ten. But I took it, while she fell to third.

I glanced at my dad, who was still smiling.

"I'm happy, but this is a really big meet. I still have another day, you know? I don't want to get ahead of myself, so I'm trying to remain calm and collected but prepare for the worst."

Today was surreal, but tomorrow was a new day with new possibilities. I could fall to third, and Sloan could take first. Anything was possible.

Dad's eyes glistened with pride. "My daughter is going to the Olympics." He took a sip from his crystal tumbler and grinned behind it.

I rolled my eyes and a little chuckle escaped me. "Don't get ahead of yourself. I'm not going to the Olympics just yet. There's still tomorrow, and then another competition after this. It really comes down to the committee and whether they think I can handle it or not."

"You're going all the way. I can feel it. Mark my words."

"I'm glad you can."

He tilted his head and a puzzled look crossed his face. "You don't?"

I glanced over his shoulder at the sheer curtains that hung from the ceiling to the floor in the penthouse suite of his hotel room. They reminded me of my current status: a foggy future that will be hard to wade through.

Anxiety filled my chest and a level of dejection settled in me. My life would forever have some sort of barrier to work through. Learning a new neck-breaking skill at practice didn't seem so terrifying anymore. Tomorrow seemed scary. Next week, next month, a year from now, it seemed impossible.

"I have hope."

"Okay." My dad placed his glass down and leveled a stare at me. "What's on your mind? You hardly ate dinner, and now you *have hope*? That's not you. Talk to me, sweetheart."

I squeezed my eyes tight, then I opened up about my insecurities.

"Today wore me out, both physically and mentally. I can barely keep my eyes open right now, and tomorrow is going to be even more exhausting. I ache *everywhere*," I said. "My bones actually hurt. It was hard today, Dad. Really hard. I was running on adrenaline and stubbornness but now I feel like I'm about to crash any second. I'm fighting it, honestly. Monday's practice will leave me crawling. Tuesday will be a fight to get out of bed. Wednesday will make me want to give up. It's been like this for months now and I never knew. I'm wondering when it'll all catch up to me—because it will. I selfishly ignored the signs for so long when I should've addressed them. Now they're stronger than me and pulling me down because I can't stop thinking about them. I pushed myself, which I can keep doing just like I've always done, but I'm worried I'm going to make everything worse and work against myself to the point that if I actually get handpicked for the Olympic team I physically won't be able to make it."

He regarded me with sympathy. Softly, he said, "You mean the kidney disease and lupus? I never would've guessed it's even been on your mind. You hold yourself together so well."

I nodded faintly. One corner of my mouth tugged miserably to the side. Even when I was sleeping it was on my mind because I'd wake thinking about it. I couldn't escape the way it was suffocating me.

"Today made me realize just how big this battle is. I don't want to make myself any sicker," I said quietly. "But I'm terrified I will with the way I keep pushing my body. That's why I don't want to get my hopes up."

"Listen, I've done some research and spoke to a couple of people. While there hasn't been a whole lot of athletes who've gone to the Olympics with an autoimmune disease *and* kidney disease, there have been a few with one or the other. With the right attitude and team of doctors, it can be done. You have both. You just have to have faith. Think positive and remember it can always be worse. Yes, the signs were there, but anyone would've mistaken them for overtraining. Don't beat yourself up over that. Try not to think about the things that can possibly hold you back, but look forward to this life you have and how lucky you are to have gotten this far when others haven't."

I finally looked at him. My emotions steadily climbed behind my eyes as I listened to his encouragement.

"There are so many more struggles now. So many more risks I'm taking that can hold me back. I'm worried I won't get there even if I have the aptitude. Like it's so close, but this fear, this voice in my head telling me it's hopeless and I won't make it because no matter how hard I fight I won't have the strength to keep going. It's so loud and always there. I hate it."

"You're the only one who thinks that way. You do have what it takes, you just can't see it yet because this is still very fresh for you, for us."

Harsh lines creased between my eyes. "What do you mean I'm the only one who thinks that way?"

Dad observed me for a long moment, unblinking. The silence grew thicker, dread curled its way into my stomach, one hefty bag of coal at a time.

No.

He wouldn't.

"Dad," I said, rattled. I sat up straighter. "Dad, you promised—"

He waved his hand through the air. "I just meant you're too deep in your head and reading too many what-ifs online. You put too much pressure on yourself and start thinking the worst. That's all."

"I had to read about the diseases so I could understand them."

I read all the good and the bad, even though it reduced me to ugly tears at times. Some of it was downright disheartening, but I couldn't live in denial. Being practical was smart. I needed to know. *I had to.* So I lost myself in article after article until I fell asleep most nights. It bothered me that he couldn't see it from my point of view and respect the fact I was studying up on it. I thought he, more than anyone, would want me to be informed.

His familiar eyes softened. "Your body is already used to this type of strenuous activity, sweetie, and has been for quite some time now. Nothing has changed except for up here," he said and tapped the side of his head.

I bit down on the inside of my lip and chewed it. I leaned back again as tears filled my eyes. "I'm not a mental case." My voice shook. "I'm just nervous."

"I never said you were. You're stressing yourself out when you have everything under control. Don't let yourself fall down a dark hole. It's not healthy."

A tear slid down my cheek. I wiped it away with the back of my hand.

"You have to keep your head up. Never look at the ground when you're walking. Your dreams, your views, your goals, all your aspirations, they'll come to a standstill because there's nothing to reach for when you're closed off. Instead, look forward with optimism and prospect. The path is wide open for you to take what you want." He paused like he was thinking about his next words. "Sweetheart, there's always going to be a mountain you'll want to move that'll make you question everything in you. You'll ask yourself how you can do it. That's how life works. And right now, you have it a little harder than others because you're surrounded by mountains with no view of the sky. Do me a favor."

I nodded, wiping more tears away and sniffled.

"Don't focus on the struggle of moving them because that's not what it's about it. It's about how much you put in when you decide it's your time. You can't move a mountain, and you certainly don't go around it. You climb that sucker and show yourself what you're capable of."

I burst into uncontrollable tears, my eyes heavy with strain and exhaustion.

Dad got off his chair and kneeled in front of me. He grabbed my hands and forced me to look at him. "Some days you're going to get knocked down. And you know what?"

"What?" I asked, my voice cracking. I attempted to sniffle back the tears but it didn't help.

"That's when you get back up and keep going to show yourself what you can do. I know it might sound impossible right now, but the battle will make it all worth it. One day you'll see."

He reached over to the table and plucked a few tissues from the box and handed them to me.

Between tearful breaths, I said, "I feel like I don't have the proper equipment to climb a jagged mountain in the dark."

I was surprised I came up with a good analogy to match his on the fly.

"You've always had it. You just lost your footing along the way. Look at it like you sprained your ankle."

I smiled through the tears. "Like little tears in my Achilles."

Dad pointed his index finger at me and gave me a look. I sniffled but my sad smile grew. "We get one life, Adrianna. You have to live it to the fullest and not let anything hold you back. I always thought I was until what happened at Easter. That day put things into perspective for me. I changed a lot after it, and very late into my life. I don't want you to have regrets and what-ifs plague you for the rest of *your* life. Be something now. And do it for you and no one else. Have no fear. Don't rest until you're about to drop."

I inhaled an audible breath, then exhaled the burden of the world I was carrying on my shoulders. A few more tears slipped down my cheeks. Talking to my dad was helping me cope with my thoughts. My chest didn't feel as constricted and I felt hopeful I could possibly take the reins of my life.

It wasn't that I didn't have the confidence, I did, but something shifted in me since I'd been diagnosed. I felt different. I felt like the world viewed me differently, like I was walking around with a stupid label. I felt like my time here had come to an end before I got to experience anything.

I lifted my eyes toward the ceiling and blinked a few times before responding. "My body is going to do what it wants whether I like it or not. On top of that, I've yet to find a match for a donor. That terrifies me and I think what stresses me out the most. What if I never find one?" My jaw trembled as I said it out loud for the first time. "I want it all so bad, Dad, so bad, and I don't want anything to hold me back. I'm scared knowing I have absolutely no control over that aspect of my life now. None. "

Dad glanced away, trying to hide his face falling, but I caught it. "That fear is normal for every single person in your shoes. Just don't let it scare you into a corner. Control isn't something I let go of so easily either. I'm a work in progress. It's probably a Rossi thing. Your brother is the same way. You'll get there. Just don't give up."

A smile spread across my face. Dad reached for me and pulled me into a hug. The comfort of his fatherly embrace eased my soul.

Maybe everything would be okay. Knowing that no amount of treatment could reverse the damage is what disturbed me daily. Knowing it could only grow worse from here on out is what taunted me.

I needed to find a way to accept that. I just hadn't figured out how yet.

"Am I making a huge mistake postponing the dialysis? Do you think I'm going to make myself sicker? Do you think I'll die sooner because of it?" My heart was frantic in my chest thinking I'd made a huge mistake.

My dad shook his head. "No, I don't think you're going to die because of it, don't ever say that. But you know where I stand on the issue. I'd rather you start treatment now, but after speaking in depth with your doctors, I understand that waiting a few months should be okay. That doesn't mean I don't think about it every day, because I do. I worry all the time, and if I thought for a second waiting would take you from me, then I would've put my foot down and pulled you immediately. You're going to have a lot of hurdles. I want you to have what you want while you can get it." Dad exhaled a heavy breath himself. "You've got this," he said, his voice thick with emotion. "You've got this, okay?"

I nodded and sniffled again as a knock sounded at the door.

"Who's that?"

Dad stood, his knees cracking. "I invited Konstantin and Katja for a drink."

Icy cold blasted through me at the mention of Katja. My heart sank. I hadn't even known she was here.

"Oh, that was nice of you."

His brows wrinkled. "Is that okay? You look pale."

I forced a smile. "Oh, of course it's okay. I just don't want anyone to see me crying and then ask why, you know? Once I get past the next few months with Worlds and the Trials, if I make it, then we'll tell people. Until then, no one. I'll get cleaned up while you let them in."

I quickly made my way to the bathroom and shut the door. Turning on the faucet, I didn't let it warm before I cupped the cold water and splashed it on my face. The last time I saw Katja, she'd given me dirty looks and mouthed off to me in Russian. I may not speak her language, but it didn't take a genius to see she clearly had an issue with me.

I frowned as I splashed more water on my face. I really didn't want to be in her presence right now. What would I even say with the three of them talking? Maybe I could excuse myself and go to bed early.

I patted my face with a towel, then leaned on the counter and stared at my reflection. I dabbed the puffy, dark circles under my eyes with my ring finger wishing I had some dumb cream my mom—Joy—insisted I use. My nose was red from crying, and my chapped lips were a little swollen too. I needed makeup…and about seventeen hours of sleep.

When I moved into the two-room suite earlier, I'd unpacked to prepare for tomorrow so I wasn't frantically looking for things at the last minute. Typically, gymnasts weren't allowed to stay with family during a meet, only afterward, but Dad had insisted I stay with him, stating Kova had approved it. I was secretly relived. Being the only gymnast at this meet from World Cup, I was glad to not be alone where I could stew on my thoughts.

I grabbed my Louis Vuitton makeup bag and applied just enough makeup until I looked halfway decent. I threw my hair up into a messy bun then glanced down at my attire. Yoga pants and an oversized sweater would have to do. I wasn't trying to impress anyone, anyway.

Expelling a heavy breath, I opened the door and smiled, preparing for an exhausting night.

CHAPTER 17

Kova was not his usual meet self on the second day, and I didn't like that one bit.

I fed off his energy. He gave me strength. Didn't he know that by now? He was what I needed to thrive. I was nothing in this sport without him. Nothing.

I had woken up feeling extremely emotional this morning. I hated when this happened, when these deep feelings hit, or when the littlest thing made me want to shed a bucket of tears. It wasn't often, but a few times a year I found myself more sensitive than usual, like I was due for a good purge to cleanse myself. I could definitely use one now, considering all things.

Sometimes being a girl sucked.

But Kova was broody and moody and walking around with a perpetual scowl since we got to the meet.

This wasn't him. He needed to get his shit together.

Last night after two hours of sitting in the same room with Dad, Kova, and Katja, I excused myself and went to bed. I'd sat with them, but mostly kept to myself reading a book on the chaise lounge. My eyes were on and off rolling shut and I couldn't take another minute. When the hardcover fell on my face and scared five years off my life, I knew I had to lay down or I wouldn't be fresh for today. They'd understood and wished me a good night, except for Katja. It wasn't like I'd participated in their conversation—I had no idea what they even talked about—but last night I got the memo quite clear. Girls always knew when another girl didn't like them, and for whatever reason, Katja seriously disliked me.

I glanced at Kova and watched him. Creases lined his forehead as he shot brief looks in my direction every few minutes. It made me wonder what he was thinking about, if it was about me, because every time our eyes met, I got the vibe his thoughts were of me.

That's it. I was going to ask him.

I sat on the floor with my duffle between my folded legs and rummaged through it for my tape and grips.

"Coach?" I said, and Kova looked at me. "Can you tape my wrists?"

He nodded without hesitation and squatted in front of me on one knee.

"Are you okay?" I asked only for his ears.

He nodded and wrapped the white tape around my wrist. "Yes. Why do you ask?"

"Because your mood is bothering me. You're not acting like you usually do when we're at meets together. I need the old Kova right now, more than ever."

He lifted his eyes but not his head. "What do you mean?"

"You're walking around like you're mad at the world. I don't like it. Did I do something wrong?"

"I am not mad."

"Then can you act a little more—"

"Adrianna, I am not mad. Okay? I just want today to be perfect for you. That is all."

I shut my mouth for a minute and watched as he wrapped my other wrist.

"Kova," I said, hoping he'd see I was serious. For the first time in a while, I was going to open up and tell him how I felt.

I dug deep for the bravado I needed to get my next few words out.

"I feed off your energy. *You* give me strength, and I need *you*. I feel like I'm nothing in this sport without you, but seeing you like this… It's messing with me. So, get whatever you have going on in your head straight and give me back my Coach Kova. Please." I paused, then added. "I need you, I need Coach Kova. I can't do this without him."

Ripping the last piece of tape with his teeth, he placed the roll back into my bag and stared at my hands. He picked up the cotton wristbands and slid one on to each wrist without a word. Tension rose in me like the building of a bass chorus.

I held my stomach in. My lungs felt constricted. I'd skipped all my medications this morning hoping the shaking would subside for the day, but my entire body trembled from head to toe. Kova noticed and took my hands in to his, comforting me.

He released a deep sigh and finally lifted his eyes to meet mine. A shadow of remorse cast in his gaze. Closing his eyes, he opened them to reveal his real emotion I was not privy to often. His steel green eyes pierced my heart and caused my lips to part.

"Did you read what I wrote you?"

I nodded and smiled timidly. I'd thought about talking to him about what he said, but I'd yet to bring it up.

Stop with the Coach bullshit.

I had laughed and turned the page, unprepared for his next entry.

When I saw you again after so many years had passed, I did not think you would become this important to me. I did not think you would be on my mind all the time, or that I would want so many things with you that I have never thought to have with anyone else. But you have, and now I cannot imagine you not here in my life. I will never hurt you again. You have my word. Hurting you inflicts pain upon me.

I'd tentatively turned the page again.

I have been thinking of calling you krasivaya instead of malysh. It suits you better.

I eyed him, and whispered, "I like *krasivaya.*"

If I didn't know Kova, or if I wasn't sitting so close to him, I would've missed the slight curl to the corners of his lips.

He shook his head, then looked down before meeting my gaze again. "I am so fucking proud of you and what you have become. I just want you to succeed. It is all that is on my mind. I promise. You have worked so hard to be here. I want today, the end result, to be everything you dreamed of. I apologize for making you feel any sort of way. I never meant to. I guess you can say I am stressed too."

My chest tightened. "Do you think yesterday was just pure luck and I can't place like that again?"

Kova pulled back, slighted by my words. "What? Why would you think that? Of course not. You know that."

I shrugged, then flinched when a photographer took a picture of us. The flash was nearly blinding and left stars dancing in my vision.

"I don't know. All I know is I don't like your energy right now. It's putting thoughts into my head and they're not good. I wasn't lying when I said I feed off you." I prepared to open up even more to him, show him I was being serious. "Some days when I'm really down and not feeling like myself, all I have to do is look for you and suddenly everything snaps back into place. I can't explain it, and I know this might sound cheesy, but you give me life. When I'm feeling weak and incapable or second-guessing myself, you breathe energy into me without even knowing it." I leaned forward and lowered my voice to almost a whisper. "But today, I don't see *my* Kova, the one who gives me strength. I see someone who is deep in his thoughts and confused and bitter."

His eyes glistened like my words were ones he longed to hear. Like they meant something to him. He was quiet for a moment.

"If I am being honest," he said lightly, his Adam's apple bobbing, "I had a very long night and did not sleep. There is nothing else on my mind but sleep, and you coming out on top. I promise, Ria. I just want the world to see what you are made of."

Ria. I knew the impact that nickname held.

One corner of my mouth tugged to the side. I felt a little shy now. "You and me both. My dad snores. Even with the door shut it's like a freight train coming through the room. At least you don't snore. I sleep like the dead when I'm with you."

My eyes widened, my cheeks blushing with embarrassment. Kova's head dropped and his back vibrated with silent laughter.

"You cannot say those things here, Adrianna." He looked up, his eyes flashing with amusement.

"I didn't mean to! It just came out." My voice was a high whisper.

"Come," he said, and stood with a grin. Kova placed his hand out and I took it. "Let us get going."

"Yes, let us." I mocked playfully.

He pulled me in for a side hug and glanced down. A real smile reached his eyes and his unspoken words poured out. I felt them. I saw them, and I let them comfort me.

"YOU ONLY HAVE FLOOR LEFT. You got this," Kova said bent over as he rubbed my upper arms.

I nodded frantically. My eyes lifted toward the scoreboard again but Kova stopped me.

"No. Only look into my eyes. Do not let the number throw you off. You hit bars, beam was rock solid, and vault is behind you. Now I want you to go out on floor and have fun out there. Be yourself and let your love for the sport shine."

I didn't have to look to know I was insanely close to dropping to second place, but I liked the reminder of knowing what I was up against. I was only 1.4 points away from slipping and I was a giant ball of nerves from it. The judges had been relentless today and stingy with the scores.

"Okay," I said.

I tightened my ponytail, then stepped onto the podium and made my way to the blue carpeted spring floor.

Within minutes I saluted the judges and took my position. The chime sounded before the music started, letting me know I was about to start.

A symphony of instruments echoed throughout the stadium and I knew all eyes were on me. Confidence radiated from me and I fell into pace with the music, knowing my personalized routine had to be in sync with the rhythm and beat or else I would face deductions. My routine was required to match the melody. The string of the violin shadowed the pounding keys of the piano, but it was the delicate harp that carried my heart as I floated across the floor from corner to corner in a series of dance skills and requirements.

With my first two tumbling passes completed, I stepped into the corner for my third pass. I brought my arms down and released a tight breath, then I started running. Halfway across the floor, I hurdled into a round-off, back handspring, double layout, and rebounded into a half-turn, wolf leap that we'd added into my routine for bonus points a few months ago. It was just one of the many revisions we'd made to my routine to up the difficulty. All my routines had been slightly modified for bonus skills, but the only way to receive the extra value was to execute it a specific way.

Only this time, I had so much power and momentum that I stepped out of bounds.

Fuck!

Recovering quickly, I sashayed across the floor, leaping and twisting along the way, flipping into handstands and practiced ballet skills until I reached the corner.

I've got this. Taking one last deep breath, I visualized my last tumbling pass and took off…

Only to step out of bounds. Again.

Oh God. That was twice now. I never, ever did it twice at a competition. Ever.

I finished my routine and saluted the judges, then immediately looked for Kova. He was already waiting for me near the stairs. I sprinted over to him with dread in my footsteps and unease in my throat.

"It is okay," he whispered as I stepped down and into his arms.

"I stepped out, twice!" My voice was hushed but heightened. I pulled back and we walked toward the chairs. There were cameras everywhere but I ignored them. "Who knows what other mistakes the judges caught. I knew it. I just knew yesterday was too good to be true. I just knew it."

Tears rose to my eyes but I pushed them back.

"Hey," he said, turning toward me. Catching my breath was a struggle. "Stay positive and take slow, deep breaths. There are still two more girls who need to compete, and from what I gather, they do not have the difficulty your routine does. Not even close."

I exhaled a deep breath. Blinking a few times, I stared at the scoreboard willing for my number to pop up. Without looking at Kova, I asked, "Did I step out with one foot or two?"

Inhale, exhale. I couldn't remember. Only that I knew for a fact I did on one.

"Two."

My chin quivered. "Both times?" I held my breath.

"Yes," he replied, voice grim.

"Seriously?" I asked, unable to hide the horror in my voice.

I saw Kova nod from the corner of my eye. Fuck. I blinked rapidly. No tears would fall today. I refused. But that was 0.6 of a point right there.

I turned to face Kova. My eyes shifted between both of his trying to gage his thoughts, but then the crowd erupted, and not the way I'd hoped. Both of our heads turned in the direction of the scores.

My blood ran cold as I stared at the numbers in disbelief.

I was going to have a heart attack.

This was worse than hearing my diagnosis. By far, much worse. I could control stepping out…and yet I hadn't.

"How?" I asked, covering my mouth. "How?" This made no sense. There was no way my score could be that low.

I looked to Kova for an explanation, but he was already sprinting in the other direction.

CHAPTER 18

I stood motionless and watched as my coach addressed the judging panel with poise.

He was submitting an inquiry. He was entitled to since he was an accredited coach.

Meanwhile, I did the math in my head and added up the difficulty and bonus points. I knew I'd stepped out of bounds, but I didn't deserve to drop to third place. That was a lot to lose. Usually I was very in sync with my body and movement, and trying to figure out where I had made errors was proving to be difficult. I replayed my routine in my head.

My gut told me I hadn't made them. But the judges said I had. I frowned. I was scored on both execution and difficulty. Had my execution been that poor?

No, a voice inside my head said. There was no way. I may have been beyond drained when I stepped out onto the floor, and my joints felt swollen and inflamed, but I did not lack when I competed. Ever. I gave everything I had to offer, and then some. Every struggle I faced, every risk forgotten. I didn't hesitate. I sucked it up and expelled it out to perform.

Four minutes. Kova had four minutes to file the appeal to contest my score.

I watched the judges hand him a sheet of paper. He checked his watch. Dipping his chin, he turned and our eyes locked. He strode toward me, his long legs eating up the space between us. Kova was pissed.

"I need a pen," he said.

Quickly I shuffled through my duffle bag. I knew I had one because I'd stashed our notebook in there. I planned to write in it after the meet.

Handing the pen to him, he said, "Turn around and bend over."

I flattened my back and Kova immediately started writing. He spoke to himself in Russian, the pen hurriedly moving across my back. He had to answer the questions and then calculate my routine.

I turned my head to the side, and said, "The numbers don't add up, Kova."

"I know," he snapped, but I knew it wasn't meant to be mean. He pressed down too hard and the pen poked me through the paper. I didn't flinch but Kova cursed. "What number did you come up with?" I told him. "Right. I did as well." Relief swept through me for the simple fact that I knew it wasn't just me who felt the numbers didn't add up.

Kova finished and I turned around. He blindly handed me the pen as he read. I watched as his eyes scanned over what he'd written, his lips moving. He glanced up. Eyes narrowing in thought as he recalculated the numbers one last time just to be sure. He glanced at his watch. Time was of the essence, so I kept my mouth shut and didn't tell him to hurry up. He knew.

Reaching into his pocket, he pulled out a silver clip of hundred-dollar bills and walked toward the judges. He had to pay a steep fine to challenge my score to make sure I received credit for the skills I'd performed. If Kova proved to be correct, he'd get his money back. If he was wrong and the judges didn't feel they'd deducted unfairly, he'd lose his money.

Without a word, Kova returned to the judge's panel and handed them the paper and cash, then walked back to me.

I let out a tense breath. That was it. All he could do.

I chewed the inside of my lip, and the familiar metallic taste slid over my tongue. I chewed again. Cameras flashed and clicked frantically. Everyone was on their feet in anticipation to see what the outcome would be. The next gymnast couldn't compete until they were done with my score, so all eyes were on us.

Kova stood patiently next to me while we waited. If he was nervous, I'd never guess it. I folded my arms across my chest and he pulled me tight to his side. I leaned against him, trying to soak in his composure. The screen turned on and the judges leaned in to begin reviewing my routine, replaying it on the small television on their table that was only used during times like this to see if the correct points were awarded. It wasn't like football where every little thing was reviewed.

I broke apart from him and paced back and forth. I stared at the floor. I propped my hands on my hips. I looked up at the ceiling. I looked back at the judges. I cracked my knuckles. I looked at the score screen. I wiped my clammy palms on my leo. I looked at the screen.

Tension balled on the side of my neck.

Too much time had passed. Something wasn't right.

"What's taking so long?" I asked.

"I do not know," he said under his breath. Kova glanced at his watch then back at the judges. His eyes were fixated on them.

Just then, one of the judges stood. I drew in a lungful of air and held it as she quickly walked up the stairs to the technical committee. She was running out of time.

Chills pebbled down my arms as I anxiously waited, and waited, and waited.

"What does this mean?" I asked Kova. He would know more than me. When he didn't respond, I glanced over my shoulder at him and paled.

His face grim, defeat marked his handsome features. The only time I'd ever seen that look on him was when he'd lacerated my heart with the news of his secret marriage.

His look said it all.

His gaze never left the new group of judges. Time moved so slowly. My heart plummeted to my stomach and I looked back up the stairs. There were three people. Two shook their heads and one nodded.

Hope was a distant dream and my faith was slipping through my fingers…until the crowd erupted.

I spun around to face the screen and searched for my score. Shock ricocheted through me and my lips parted.

I was one-tenth of a point ahead, and back in first place. One-freaking-tenth.

This couldn't be real.

I reached blindly for Kova, but he was already reaching for me. He tugged me to him and wrapped an arm around my shoulders, hoisting me up. He gave me the biggest hug as cameras flashed around us. I squeezed him tight, holding back the tears.

He put me down. Kova, like all coaches when something profound like this happened, alternated between pressing a kiss to the top of my head and congratulating me.

"How?" I asked, my voice muffled against his chest.

Kova reared back with a smile bigger than I'd ever seen before. "The judges made a huge mistake. I knew they did and acted quickly. It looks like you got the difficulty points, and possibly some for execution."

My brows rose, my vision blurred. I sniffled through a smile. Only by the skin of my teeth was I in first place. It was too bad reviewing routines via television weren't permitted in general.

"Really?"

"Yes. You are only leading by a small fraction of a point now, but I have a feeling it is enough. You deserve to have those points you killed yourself for."

I went in for another hug, squeezing Kova in appreciation.

He rubbed my back. "Well done, Adrianna."

"Thank you, Kova," I whispered.

He looked at me with such an intense affection, like I was the only person in the room who mattered to him, and it filled my heart.

I gave Kova a smile only for him before I broke apart and turned to look for my dad in the stands. He was much closer today.

For the first time since I could remember, he had tears in his eyes as he waved frantically…with Katja next to him.

𝄞 ✱ ✱ ✱ ✱ ✱ ✱

"I'M SO PROUD OF YOU. More than you could ever know," Dad said. "You amazed me today. I had so much pride watching you. I thought I was going to burst from it." He paused. "I regret not being at the other competitions, but that's going to change from here on out."

I smiled from ear to ear. "Thanks, Dad. You're here now and that's what matters."

We were in the airport, and I'd fallen asleep waiting for my plane to arrive. Dad wasn't flying back with me, but my plane was supposed to take off before his, so he'd stayed.

Sitting up higher, I winced from the stiffness in my joints. Everything hurt.

"You okay?" His voice conveyed concern.

I nodded. "I'm fine. Sometimes this happens once I finally sit down for the day. I swear I have the body of a ninety-year-old sometimes."

Dad chuckled. "I don't know about that. Where's your next meet?"

"I have to check with Kova. I can't remember where, but I think it's in a few weeks."

Thanks, kidney disease and lupus. Apparently brain fog was a gift from them.

With this meet, I'd victoriously secured a spot for Worlds since I'd placed first on both days and walked away with a few medals in the events for vault, floor, and bars. I'd just barely missed third place by a couple tenths for beam, but I was okay with that. I couldn't wait to get home to hang my medals on the wall. All of my medals held a special place in my heart, but these were more special. They were won after my diagnosis, and at my first big national competition. I really wanted to take them out of my bag and hold them right now, but I'd wait to do that in private when I got home. It was a little emotional for me, after all.

"I think it's in another country now that I think about it." I rubbed my head trying to remember which one. It was my first international meet—and another big one for me—I just couldn't remember where as there were a few meets that took place overseas.

Dad angled his head toward me. "Oh, yeah?" Then he looked in another direction.

I followed his gaze and masked my expression. Kova and Katja were walking toward us, both with drinks in their hands. Kova handed Dad a plastic cup of amber liquid and ice, and Katja extended her arm in my direction offering me a bottle of water. We three were on the same plane home. Hopefully in different sections.

"Thank you," I said, but she ignored it. I wasn't surprised. Katja had hardly looked in my direction. Normally it wouldn't bother me, but now it irked me. Her disdain was obvious.

Screw that. I was going to ask Kova when we got back.

"Adrianna tells me the next meet is in another country?" Dad said to Kova, stirring the ice with the little black straw.

I uncapped my water and looked the other way as they spoke, too tired and mentally drained to listen or participate. The icy water slid down my throat and I almost sighed. I drank half of it in one breath. No matter how much water I had to drink lately, I couldn't seem to quench my excessive thirst.

We had less than an hour before we had to board the plane. Bending down, I dug through my purse and pulled out our notebook. I rummaged for a pen then sat back and wrote.

> I'm writing this while sitting right in front of your lovely, perfect wife.
>
> She hates me.
>
> Don't tell me you don't notice the way she looks at me when I'm around. She acts like I'm a thorn in her side she wants to remove and throw away.
>
> I'm not crazy.
>
> I know when someone has it out for another person. She has it out for me. I can feel it in my bones.
>
> What scares me is that I think she knows everything. She knows what we have between us. I didn't want to face the facts, but I think it's time I do. It's the only thing I can think of. The only reason why she acts the way she does toward me.
>
> But my question is, why hasn't she done anything about it yet?
>
> Unless she has, and you just haven't told me.

I paused and looked up, thinking. My pen teetered between my fingers and my gaze shifted to Katja. She was staring at my lap, then lifted her eyes to mine. Placing my pen in the center of the notebook, I folded it shut and held it to me. This was the bluntest and riskiest

I'd ever gotten with our thoughts, but I had to get them out or I was going to burst.

She continued to glare at me with hateful eyes and a stone-cold expression on her face. It amazed me how someone so beautiful could look so ugly. An evil kind of ugly. Her eyes dropped to my lap again, then she leaned over and whispered something in Kova's ear. He turned his head toward her while she kept her eyes on me. I couldn't see what his gaze expressed but he grabbed her hand and placed their laced fingers on his thigh with a small smile. His knee bobbed.

Fatigue washed over me. My eyes grew heavy and warm. God, I hated this feeling. Like a heavy blanket of iron was draped over me, and I suddenly got so tired that all I wanted to do was sleep. Usually I had to push through it, but this time I didn't.

I turned my head in the other direction and rejoiced when the attendant announced the plane was finally boarding shortly after. Shoving my notebook and water bottle into my purse, I slung it over my shoulder and said goodbye to my dad, then got in line. It was a five-hour flight and I knew the moment my head hit that scratchy pillow I was going to pass out hard.

What I hadn't foreseen was that my notebook would vanish by the time I'd arrived home.

CHAPTER 19

ately, I felt like giving up.

Not because I didn't love gymnastics, but because my emotions caused by the reality of my life were too much to handle. My secrets were a burden. My very existence was a lie. I didn't know who I was anymore or what would become of my future. I was too lost in my head with no outlet to ease my soul. My skin crawled. I wasn't able to focus on one thing long enough except gymnastics, and when I was alone, my mind jumped from one topic to the next. I hated it.

I was so sick when I got home from the meet, but I wasn't going to let it hold me down. Exhaustion had taken over and my body cramped up. I had a small fever. Going to practice the next day was an absolute must and what anyone else would've done, so it's what I did too.

There was something about the powdery chalk and echoes of the apparatuses that helped calm my racing mind. For four days and four nights straight, I pushed myself and trained like a beast. No one questioned me. Madeline and Kova went along with it. To them, they probably assumed I was preparing for Worlds. And I was, but I was also just trying to keep my head above water the only way I knew how.

I kept telling myself that if I could do it before everything happened, then I could do it now. I ached more than ever, but I refused to rely on pain medicine at night. I knew it could have long-term effects and I wasn't going to go down the path of addiction.

Drained beyond comprehension, I kept to myself and didn't talk to anyone. There was success in silence, is what I told myself. Not even when I stayed later and only Kova was there. The walls of my life were slowly caving in, but being inside World Cup was the only way for me to breathe. I struggled to keep it together, yet this was the only way to remain whole. The only way I felt like me again, so I worked myself until I could barely stand.

But today… Today felt like more than I could handle. The pressure in my chest was mounting to capacity. I felt the break coming the moment I woke up, like a massive title wave forming in the distance, building up stronger and fiercer the closer it grew.

As I waited for my coffee to finish brewing, my phone dinged. Yawning, I opened the message from my dad and read it.

DAD CELL

Call me when you wake. It's important.

Frowning, I called him immediately. "Dad? Everything okay?"

"Sweetie. I didn't expect you to be up."

I glanced at the clock on my coffee pot and blinked. It was a quarter after four in the morning.

"I've been going into practice early, so I've been up at this time all week."

"Just like your father," he said proudly.

I was sure he only slept three hours a night at most just so he could work more.

He cleared his throat, then said, "Have you been watching the news?"

My brows bunched together. "No. Why? What's wrong?"

"A hurricane is headed your way. It's only a category two and nothing to worry about, but with the water still so warm and no land to slow it down, I want you to be prepared. A few early predictions say it could grow to a three. I want you to close the shutters even though the windows are double-paned. They should just slide shut easily. I'm going to have food and water delivered to your condo today just in case, along with flashlights and a radio."

"By who? Who has a key?"

"Thomas is already on the road and headed your way. He should be there in the next couple of hours. I figured you would be at practice, so I gave him a spare key."

My heart softened. "I'd love to see him."

"He'd love that too, sweetie, but I gave him strict instructions. I don't want him caught in traffic on the way back. You know how some people get when a hurricane nears, how the media hypes them up and creates chaos. I want him home and safe."

I laughed lightly. Being born and raised on the coast of Georgia, a Category 2 was nothing to blink about, but there were those who evacuated anyway.

"When is it supposed to make landfall?"

"The day after tomorrow, early morning and just slightly south of where you are. Turn the television on and watch. On your way to practice, fill up your gas tank just in case."

I smiled into the phone. "I know, Dad."

"Make sure all your medicine is filled and keep your phone charged."

I grabbed a mug and poured the coffee. "It already is."

"Wash any dirty clothes now. Don't open the fridge too much and turn the air down so it stays cool."

"Dad. It's just a two."

I was surprised he was worrying the way he was. He didn't typically worry until it crossed into a four.

"I know, but I'm not there to protect you this time. I just want to make sure you're okay. Anything could happen."

"Thank you," I said.

"I already spoke to Konstantin. He plans to close World Cup tomorrow as a precaution."

I froze midway of pouring the half and half. "What do you mean? It's only a two. Schools don't even close for that."

"He's playing it safe. I don't want you driving in that kind of rain anyway."

Oh God. A whole day alone, possibly more, to stew. My teeth dug into my bottom lip. I grew silent, wondering what I was going to do with my time. Maybe hang my medals and clean? I glanced around. I lived alone and I was rarely home. Who was I kidding? My condo was always clean. Maybe I should get a puzzle.

"Adrianna?" Dad said.

"Yeah?"

"Where'd you go?"

I thought swiftly. "I was thinking that I finally get a day off to rest. Thank you, hurricane!" I faked my enthusiasm.

He chuckled. "Just stay in the condo and don't make me worry. I have enough gray hair as it is."

"You can always dye it," I said, laughing to myself as I thought about how I'd said the same thing to Kova.

"Never in a million years. Listen, I gotta run. Call me and check in tomorrow."

"Thanks, Dad. Love you."

"Love you more, sweetie."

"Wait—" I paused. "Dad?"

"Yes?"

"I've been meaning to ask… Ah, have you gone and gotten tested yet?"

I tightened my grip on the phone. Testing could take weeks and I wanted to be prepared in case anything happened. He hadn't brought it up once to me and I figured I should.

"I actually began the process when you were diagnosed, I just didn't want to say anything until I knew for sure. The first blood test came back as a match." He paused, and my heart jumped so hard I had to clutch my chest. "But the following crossmatch tests ultimately showed we're incompatible and your body could reject the kidney." Dad's voice lowered. "I'm so sorry, sweetheart. I really thought it would happen. I was waiting to tell you after your gymnastics competitions. I didn't want it to mess with your head."

"Oh, okay," I said, my voice quiet. That's three people in my family with the highest possibility of being a match, and none of them were. I felt like the life had been sucked out of me once again.

"Don't lose hope. I've made some calls and am waiting to hear back from some people to see if they're willing to be tested. I didn't want to tell you yet until I had positive news to follow up with."

"It's okay," I said softly. "Back to square one again, I guess."

"It'll happen," Dad said. I could tell he was trying to pump encouraging words into me. "I know it will."

We said our goodbyes and I stood in my kitchen staring at nothing, wondering where I went from here, trying not to ask myself the one question I'd been avoiding since this shit started.

If I never found a match, would I die? Even with dialysis, would I die?

I knew the answer, though. Dialysis was not a way of life.

While sipping my coffee, I flipped through the weather app on my phone and read up on the impending storm. It was a good distraction to take my mind off what Dad had told me and to get my thoughts steered correctly. I really didn't want to stew on the fact I was back at square one again.

The storm was predicted to grow close to a category three. All the hurricane needed was a small shift and the eye would make landfall in Cape Coral. The feeder bands would last hours and do the most damage. However, I still wasn't too concerned. I had bigger pills to swallow.

I reached forward and picked up the medicine bottles. One by one, I poured out the necessary dose and took them, along with eating an apple. I'd been through countless hurricanes. I was in a secure cement building with shutters and having the proper necessities delivered.

What I did worry about was having no outlet to wear myself down to the bone the way practice allowed me to.

During all the research I'd done on lupus and kidney disease, many patients had reported their bodies aching more when there was a drastic change in the weather. I found it laughable someone would claim the weather affected their body, but then I thought about how I'd felt when I woke up this morning, and yesterday morning, and realized I had too felt it.

"EARTH TO ADRIANNA. YOU OKAY?" Madeline asked, eyeing me with concern.

"Yes," I answered, and yawned. "Why do you ask?"

Madeline took a bite of her banana and chewed slowly. I couldn't have those anymore, not unless I wanted to aggravate my kidneys.

"You're using the wall to hold you up. I thought you were about to fall asleep standing there."

"Oh." I smiled timidly, and shifted on my feet to stand straight. I'd been practicing with her all day. "I'm fine. Just taking a water break," I said, and gave the half full bottle a little shake. My throat was sore and my voice raspy when I answered.

"Alright… I'll meet you at vault. Don't keep me waiting too long. Use the bathroom, eat a protein bar, do what you gotta do, because we'll work for the next three hours or so straight."

"I won't," I said.

I perked up a little at the thought of getting worked to death. That meant no time to think about anything else.

Happy with my response, Madeline turned around. I watched her walk away, my gaze trailing her footsteps until she made an abrupt turn and my gaze latched onto Kova.

Rooted in place, I leaned back against the wall again and watched closely as Kova instructed the men's team. I hadn't trained with him today, or yesterday, and it felt strange. Foreign really, and I missed it more than I'd realized. I felt lost without him next to me.

A few days ago he'd paired me with Madeline to fine-tune skills she had a niche for, and we hadn't talked since. Not even when it was time to leave. All I got was a quick hello and goodbye. I'd hoped we would today, though. At least once before he closed World Cup for the storm. He was the only one I actually wanted to talk to, even if it was just for a few minutes. I'd take what I could get with him.

I couldn't take my eyes off him. He didn't know I was watching as his back was turned to me, but I stared. Even through the supportive way he coached the boys' team, I knew him well enough that I could sense something was on his mind. He appeared positive and reassuring, but then he turned around to pick up a thick landing mat, and I saw everything. I saw the dark circles under his eyes, the grim, firm line of his mouth. How the space between his brows was permanently creased with lines.

He looked much older than his thirty-four years.

Dragging the mat so it was centered beneath the rings, he dropped it with a loud smack and a cloud of chalk lifted around it. He scrubbed a hand down his scruffy jaw. His hair was a disheveled mess. The black hat he loved to wear was nowhere in sight. Kova looked as withdrawn as I felt.

He turned to the side and spoke to the men's team using his hands and giving examples of what he suggested they do.

I'd noticed he'd been at the gym longer than I had this week. He arrived before I did and left after. I frowned and drank the rest of my water. Had he even gone home?

Thunder cracked across the sky, the rumbling felt beneath my feet, and I jumped, grabbing my chest. I turned around and looked through the giant glass window at the thunderstorm rolling in. Large pellets of water came down hard and fast, the sound of the rain hitting the tin roof reminded me of a rainforest. It was oddly peaceful but then the sky darkened to a hazy gray and the world seemed to dim around me. My vision blurred and my lungs constricted. I loved the rain, but that impending feeling of doom curled through my chest again like it had early this morning. I was beginning to feel trapped inside myself. A tear leaked from the corner of my eye and I quickly wiped it away.

"Adrianna! Get moving!" Madeline shouted across the gym and clapped her hands obnoxiously. I looked at her, then shot a passing glance at Kova. I held my breath.

He was already watching me, which meant he saw me wipe the tear.

CHAPTER 20

My palms burned like hundreds of fire ants were chewing on my skin, and my inner thighs were chafed from the thick rope. I clenched my body, constricting every muscle I could to climb up and down the coarse rope. I'd alternated between crunches and rope climbing, utilizing every ounce of energy I had.

As my toes reached the floor, I let out a sigh of relief. I had thirty seconds until I was climbing back up. I was almost done with this round of conditioning I'd created for myself. The last thing I had to do was run, then I would be locked inside my condo for the next day or so. Hopefully sleeping the whole time.

"It is time for you to go home," Kova said, his voice flat. He was at the bottom of the rope waiting for me when I got down.

I glanced at him. His hands were propped on his hips and he wasn't smiling. Stern, he was trying to make a point, but I turned away and ignored him. I sat on the floor and laid on my back, then I placed my hands behind my head. Tightening my stomach, I pulled myself up to a sitting position.

One. Two. Three…

Kova dropped to his knees and held my feet down. "Adrianna."

"I'll go home when I'm ready," I said as I came up and faced him.

I was back down when he said, "I think you should go home now."

"No. I said I'll go home when I'm ready."

Kova hissed under his breath. "Adrianna—"

"I'll go home once I'm done. Okay?" I spat and focused on the ceiling.

"And when is that? When you cannot walk anymore?"

I ignored his cheap comment.

"Whenever I'm done. It's not like I'm in anyone's way. No one is even here. So what does it matter?" Everyone but Kova had left nearly two hours ago. "You don't need to be here anyway. I can handle myself."

His eyes bore into mine, one brow raised to a sharp point like he was holding back. "You are overdoing it, Adrianna."

That just irritated me. I was going to get plenty of rest for the whole damn day tomorrow and needed to exhaust myself enough so I could just sleep through it. Otherwise, I'd search things on the internet and feel bad about myself. I'd focus on the pain in my joints, and then they'd hurt even more. Pushing myself with extra conditioning until I could barely walk wasn't the brightest idea I'd ever had, but I was losing control of the situation and this was my way of grasping it and getting through. Especially after the conversation I'd had with my dad and the lack of donor match. I needed this more than ever. I needed to wear my thoughts out and shut my mind down. It's why I loved being at World Cup—it made me forget everything. I didn't want to be alone and stuck inside all day. God forbid the storm got any worse, then I would be stuck in there for days.

"Don't tell me what I need. I'm so sick of hearing what I need from everyone. Tell me, why did you push me off onto Madeline?"

"I did no such thing."

I sat up and faced him, hands still clasped behind my head. Sweat trickled down my temples. "Bullshit. You're lying to me."

"What is going on? Talk to me," he urged, his voice full of concern. "What is on your mind?"

Talk to me. I let out a haughty laugh and went back down. My heart was beating too hard while I tried to talk and work out at the same time.

"Tell me why you haven't spoken to me in days, *Coach*. Days. You barely even say hi, and now you want to talk?"

"Ah, *Coach*. You only use Coach when you are angry with me."

I wasn't really angry at him. I was just angry in general. He wasn't helping by telling me to leave.

"What happened between the meet and now for you to pretend I don't exist? I thought we were okay, for the most part anyway."

I hadn't deliberately sought anyone out, yet I wished he had at least tried to talk to me.

Then it hit me.

I'd gone many days ignoring him and now he was doing it to me. He'd only done it for less than a week and here I was turning into a cry baby over it.

"You're doing it on purpose, aren't you? Because I've been keeping you at arm's length since you married Katja, and you can't stand it anymore. This is your way of getting back at me."

"That is not true." Guilt laced his gentle tone and I felt myself breaking down, one stiff English word at a time. "Not true at all."

"So, I'm imagining it?"

"No. I mean, well…" He sounded remorseful and that was the opposite of what I wanted. "I felt like Madeline was better suited for what you needed. Is that why you are upset and forcing yourself to work out every day after practice now? Because you thought I was ignoring you? I would never do that to you. I am always here to talk if you need me."

I do need you, but I don't want to need you.

I sat up and breathed into his face, trying to catch my breath. My chest was so tight I fought back a flinch from the pain.

"I don't think anything. I know it. You're avoiding me."

Goddammit, I knew I was being irrational, only, I didn't know how to stop it.

Kova sat back on his heels and observed me. "I am not going to argue with you. Go home before the rain starts up and take time to rest. I will see you in a few days. Your attitude makes it clear you need the time off, and the *Coach* bullshit only solidifies it."

My eyes flared and I stood. Grabbing the rope, I fisted it and said, "I told you, I'll go home when I'm ready."

Gearing up, I held onto the rope above my head, but Kova grabbed my hips to stop me.

"No. You are finished," he said firmly and pulled me back. "You are going to kill yourself."

"I'm already dying anyway, so what does it matter?"

Kova's hands froze around my waist. I squeezed my eyes shut and dropped my head against the rope. Fuck! I couldn't believe that slipped out.

"What did you just say?" he whispered.

"Nothing. Just that everyone is dying the moment they're born. That's all I meant." I tried to wiggle out of his hold but had no luck. "Now let go of me so I can do my last round."

"I will do no such thing."

Blood simmering, I was fired up. Letting go of the rope, I spun around and slipped out of his hold. I glared up at Kova, expecting to see his anger, but I got the opposite.

"What's your damn issue? I'm just trying to stay focused and prepared for Worlds. Why are you holding me back?"

Kova stepped closer to me. "Do not put words into my mouth. I would never hold you back. I am concerned you are going to hurt yourself. Plus, with the storm coming, you need to prepare."

"I am prepared. This is my way of mentally preparing and dealing with shit."

His eyes lowered. "Every night this week I have held my breath watching you, trying to give you the space you so clearly need to deal with whatever it is you have going on in your head. But tonight, it stops. No more running yourself ragged."

I pursed my lips together. "Are you going to let me do my last one?"

"No chance in hell. I watched you enough tonight to know you are too weak to make it to the top. I thought you were going to fall the last time. That is why I came out here, to catch you if I had to."

Weak.

You are too weak.

Kova called me weak.

"You think I'm weak?" My voice trembled, and there was no concealing the hurt I felt. Calling me weak was by far the worst insult. It's what I'd been fearing, that I'd be too weak in the end to achieve anything. I'd rather him call me a bitch than weak.

Before I could stop it, tears filled my eyes as I replayed his words in my head. My jaw bobbed, my blood boiled with fury.

"Ria," he said softly, his brows angled with regret. Kova reached for me, but I stepped back. "I did not mean it like that. I just did not want you to hurt yourself."

I pushed my index finger into his chest, and whispered with a bite, "Fuck you, Coach."

I spun around and marched away from him. If I couldn't climb, then I'd go for my run.

"Come back here. Where are you going?"

Tears streamed down my cheeks as I threw the door open to the lobby. "To run," I shouted over my shoulder and rounded the corner. Kova was hot on my tail as I walked down the hallway. "You should know that by now since you've been here every night watching me like a freaking creeper."

"Like hell you are."

Oh, he was mad. Good. Now he knew how I felt.

I threw my locker open and reached for my workout shorts. I had a schedule and I needed to stick to it. I had to.

"You can't stop me. Why don't you go home and pick a fight with your wife and leave me alone."

I stepped into my shorts and pulled them up, then grabbed one shoe, but Kova stopped me. He spun me around and stepped up to me. I backed up until I was pressed against the locker. He pointed a finger at me. I had the urge to grab it and bend it backwards.

"Do not do this."

"Do what?" I yelled, my breathing heavy, eyes frantic. I shoved him away. I couldn't stop the tears from streaming down my flushed cheeks. My fingers trembled as I wiped them away with the back of my hand. "What am I doing that's so wrong?"

"You know exactly what you are doing. You had a long weekend, then you come in and train harder than usual by adding extra conditioning and hours to your schedule. You have a meet coming up."

"And? So? That's a bad thing?"

His eyes grew hard. "For you, yes."

Nostrils flaring, I said between clenched teeth, "Because you think I'm weak."

Kova stilled to stone. "Weak is the last thing I would ever call you."

"Then what is it?" I pleaded, my voice rising. "Why can't I finish like I've been doing?"

"Because I know you are sick and I cannot stomach to see what you are doing to yourself any longer!"

My lips parted in disbelief as air seized my lungs.

I stared at Kova, my jaw bobbing helplessly as I searched for words but came up short.

My mind had to be playing tricks on me.

I dug deeper, glaring at him, praying I hadn't heard those words.

The silence between us stiffened to a crashing sound, threatening me to an asphyxiating level.

"What?" I asked, breathless. I shook my head. There was no way.

Sympathy was in full effect and it made my heart crumble. He extended his hand, but I stepped out of his reach, as if I couldn't stand to be touched by him. Hurt showed in his eyes but I disregarded it.

"What did you say?"

"*I know*," he said softly. And in my heart, I knew what he meant. "I know everything, and I cannot handle seeing you torture yourself knowing what I know any longer."

I kept shaking my head and inhaling deep and slow. "You know nothing. Nothing." My voice was a whisper.

"Ria, *krasivaya,* I have known since the beginning."

I could barely breathe. The cage around my heart fractured down the center and opened up, spilling out my heart. I turned around to wrench my bag from my locker. My other shoe fell to the floor and I didn't bother to pick it up.

Fuck running. Fuck everyone. Fuck this life I was dealt.

"No," I said more to myself. No, my dad wouldn't do that. He wouldn't lie to me, not after everything. *Everything.* "You're lying. You're just trying to manipulate me."

Tears fell fast and hard and I was unable to stop them. Just as I was about to swing the bag over my shoulder, Kova placed a hand to my upper arm.

His fingers, his truth, his compassion, it was all felt in his touch and said everything I didn't want to know.

I lost it. The touch was so simple and enough to shatter me completely.

The strap slipped from my hand and my bag dropped to the floor. Turning around, my teeth gnashed together as I pushed Kova's chest with every ounce of strength I had in me. He was rock solid and I felt like I was pushing a brick wall, but I persisted. He stumbled back and tried to reach for me, but I pushed him again.

"You know nothing!" I screamed through the burning tears. "Nothing! My dad wouldn't do that to me! He wouldn't lie to me like that!"

"Ria," he said sadly, only trying to soothe me, but it triggered me even more.

One word, three letters, and it said everything I needed to know.

I shoved Kova again and he stepped back. I pushed him harder until he was against the wall. I couldn't stop. I couldn't process anything he was saying. I couldn't hear.

"Stop it. Shut up! You know nothing!"

He gently cupped my arm, his compassion all too consuming. His touch told me the truth again, and I revolted against it. He let me hit him, slap him, shove him.

This was too much. I hated it. I was going to be sick. He didn't know. He was lying.

Kova was lying just like he always did, but then his next set of words shattered me completely, forever changing us.

"I know about the lupus and kidney disease."

CHAPTER 21

snapped, and tears fell in thick streams down my cheeks to the corners of my mouth.

They seeped into me, fueling me with fierce resentment and hurt unlike I'd ever felt before.

"No one was supposed to know!"

Kova grabbed my upper arms and I reacted quickly by swinging myself out of his hold. He grabbed me again and this time I slapped his chest. He flinched but tightened his hold.

"Let go of me," I screamed, my hand connecting with his chest. "Get away from me. Everyone is a liar. Everyone! I hate it so much. All everyone does is just lie. No one was supposed to know, including you!"

I yanked away, but Kova was too strong. He pulled me to his chest and I fell into him. I let myself cry for a moment, whimpering against him as he held me, my back vibrating with sorrow. I let out an exhausted cry, but I didn't back down and continued to fight him.

"Your father was worried. He meant no harm."

I drew in an audible breath and pulled away. "So you knew this whole time?"

Kova stared down his nose, his eyes low and sober. "I have."

I blinked rapidly trying to get the tears to stop so I could see clearly. "How? How could you have known for so long?"

"Your father called me," he said unsympathetically. "He said the doctor's office had called him with the lupus results and wanted to do further testing but you had not shown up. This was months and months ago. He was concerned and knew you were under pressure but did not want to panic you, so he asked me to convince you to go. He also asked that I not tell you I knew." His eyes roamed my face. Lowering his voice, he said, "I cannot handle seeing you like this any longer. I am worried about you, Adrianna. You are fading away and wearing yourself out, and I know why. You want to avoid the problem and act like nothing is serious, that it cannot control your life, but you cannot do that. It will only hurt you more in the long run. That is what my mother did, and I refuse to see you do that. You should have come to me."

My lips parted in realization. "When you told me I couldn't come back to practice until I went to the doctor… That time I stayed at your house… That's how long you've known?"

"Before that. Your father and I have been in close contact regarding your health. I learned when you came back from the training camp that it was a high possibility there was something wrong. I found out shortly after."

Hot tears silently poured out of me. This whole time I thought I'd been fighting against myself to prove I could handle my training schedule, when in fact Kova was just allowing everything because he felt sorry for me. His tolerance made total sense now, and it offended me. His way of handling my sickness was pitying me.

My eyes searched his. I wasn't sure what I was looking for, something other than sympathy. Was he sad that my chance of achieving my Olympic dream had lessened dramatically? Or that I had an incurable disease that could strip me as a person? Did it change how he viewed me as just Ria?

Or even worse. Did he label me now?

"I have always admired your tenacity, but this madness ends now."

He admired me.

"I…I…" I swallowed, trying to find my voice. "I need to leave."

I couldn't be held responsible for my actions at this point. Between the blind rage and numbness, his touch, the sound of his deep voice enveloping me, the energy was too powerful in me to break free.

Turning away, I blindly located my bag, looking but not really looking. I bent down and reached inside to feel for my keys. Grabbing them, I stood up and quickly walked toward the door in a daze.

"Adrianna," Kova said, clucking his tongue behind me. "Where are you going? You cannot drive in this condition."

"Go away."

I gripped my keys tightly. No way was he going to steal them from me this time, but Kova was quick on his feet and trailed me to my car.

As soon as I stepped outside, the rain pelted me in the face, soaking me instantly. I was chilled to the bone with aches. Kova muttered a string of words in Russian, and for once I didn't care what he'd said.

"Let me drive you home."

"Go home to your wife."

I reached for the handle, but Kova placed his hand on the door and stopped me. I blew out a frustrated breath through my nose and grinded my back teeth together.

"Stop this. Talk to me," he demanded, pressing his chest to my back.

"I'm sure she's waiting on you."

"She is not home."

A mocking laugh escaped me. "How convenient. No wonder you're acting like this. You have no reason to rush home or anyone to answer to right now, so you talk to me because you won't get caught."

God forbid, he, or anyone, ever put me and my wishes first.

He stepped to the side and angled his body toward mine. "No, you misunderstand. She is here in Cape Coral but staying with a friend who has a generator. She did not want to lose power and she was concerned for the puppy. She is five minutes from here."

"You got a puppy?" My voice was small and far away. I turned to look up at him. He confirmed it with one nod of his head. The thought saddened me. "Lovely. Next comes kids because that's what *everyone* does. They get a stupid dog first before they have a kid."

Kova's nostrils flared. He stared, breathing down my neck, not caring he was soaking wet from the rain. His silence solidified my statement and a little whimper left my lips. My jaw trembled with emotion that was suffocating me.

"Adrianna, please. Let me drive you home," he offered.

Thunder sounded in the distance. "I want to be alone."

Kova stood close enough that I could feel him without touching me.

For a split second, I wanted him to reach out and pull me into his arms even though I said no.

I wanted him to fight me and tell me everything was going to be okay, to let me cry on him until I passed out.

I wanted him to say he would always be there for me.

It was a ridiculous thought, considering all things.

I didn't like that he had gotten a puppy, or that he knew my secret. His life wasn't thrown off its axis like mine had been. His life wasn't going to change for the worst the way mine had. No, Kova was busy planning a future, while I was struggling to hold on to what was left of mine.

My breathing labored. An eerie calmness settled in me, a slow current of endorphins rising through my blood. I fought it. I didn't want to let go. I knew it wouldn't be good if I did. I knew every single thing I'd been holding in would come to the surface and I'd break. I needed to be able to control my emotions, but what I really wanted to do was scream and shout and lose it and just cry ugly loud tears to get it all out.

"Adrianna. Answer me."

I slammed my hand against the door and turned toward Kova. Chills slithered down my arms, the rainy breeze pressed on my skin like little knives. Through gritted teeth, I bit out, "You already know everything! What more do you want?" He remained silent, a pensive look crossed his face. "What, Kova? What do you want from me?"

"I know you have not told anyone, and that is not healthy. You have to talk about it, otherwise it will eat away at you and you will lose everything."

"I don't have anything else to lose," I said, looking him directly in the eyes.

A melancholy loss plagued his beautiful eyes, making me almost crumble into his palm. "I want to hear you tell me through your words and your voice. Let me be there for you."

My chest ached from the beating my heart was getting. I didn't want anyone to be there for me, to make me talk. They were there because they felt bad and no other reason. Not because they cared or wanted to hear me complain. No one wanted to hear complaints.

Tears mingled with the rain and I hiccupped. He was right. I needed to get it all out, but there was no way I could do that without crying, without freaking out. Without looking like a total crazy person. I'd held so much in to stay strong. I was already on the edge and that's not what I needed right now, especially during a hurricane that would keep me trapped in the condo for a whole day, maybe more.

Thunder rumbled across the darkening sky again, this time louder. The hair on the back of my neck rose. The clouds illuminated from the bolt of lightning I caught in the distance.

Kova placed an arm around my shoulders. "Come. Let me take you home."

Digging deep, I reached for resolute determination and exhaled through my nose. I'd talk when I was ready, not because people were talking behind my back and they felt bad so they had to coax it out of me.

Hauling my car door open, I climbed in. "No," was all I said, then quickly closed the door in his face and locked it. No way was I letting my guard down again.

I threw my duffle onto the passenger seat and wiped my eyes. Thunder roared and bellowed, frightening me. Kova immediately pulled on the handle but had no luck. I pressed the start button, then slowly reversed my truck with Kova walking next to me yelling and pounding on the tinted window.

I ignored Kova over the rumble and roar closing in on us. I strapped on my seat belt and headed for the main road, soaking wet and freezing as I leaned forward trying to see the color of the road lights. My cell phone rang and I reached blindly in the cup holder where I always kept it. Empty. Shit. After a quick glance down, I realized it was in my duffle bag.

Forgetting about it, I focused on the road and carefully drove home. Tears poured from my eyes. Misery consumed me but vengeance filled my blood. I could barely see the road between the rain and the blur of my anguish. My fingers tightened around the steering wheel until the skin on my knuckles stretched white. I was angry. Why did everyone have to hurt each other? So many lies meant to protect but ultimately caused the most heartache. It was horrible and sad and I wanted it all to stop.

Bright lights flashed in my rearview mirror. I sat up higher and shot a brief look over my shoulder at the black car with the dark-as-night tint in disbelief.

I drew in a small breath.

My cell phone rang again but I ignored it. I pressed on the accelerator, gunning it, driving faster, a little too fast for the rain. Red lights flashed ahead at the bridge and the barricades lowered as the draw bridge went up. I should've slowed down, but I pushed the gas pedal to the floor. My truck jolted and I flew over the bridge. A rush of fear steamrolled through my heart and I gripped the wheel tighter, praying I didn't hurt myself.

A quick glance in the rearview mirror showed Kova flying over the bridge behind me. I guess I shouldn't have expected anything less considering he drove a sports car.

Within minutes, I pulled into my condo complex and parked my truck with a little too much gusto. I sniffled and grabbed my keys but left everything else. I ran through the rain to the entrance and toward the elevator as Kova pulled into a handicap spot.

The elevator dinged and I stepped inside. I pressed the number for my floor and tapped the close button incessantly so the door would close faster.

"Adrianna!"

I glanced up with wide eyes to see Kova running toward me. Heart racing, I pressed the button harder and faster and chanted to myself, "Hurry up! Hurry up!"

I sighed in relief when the door finally closed in his face. Silent tears fell and I wiped them away as I leaned against the cold glass wall of the elevator.

The doors opened on my floor and Kova was standing in front of me. My heart dropped and I stumbled, wondering how the second elevator got here faster than mine did.

CHAPTER 22

took the stairs," Kova answered my unasked question.

Of course he did.

We fell into step and walked side by side.

"Why are you even here?" I said.

"Because you are here."

"I want to be alone."

"I want to be with you."

I stuck my key into the lock and clenched my eyes shut. I tried not to feel his words or the gentle tone he used. Before I opened my door, I turned around and met his gaze.

"Listen, I know you're just trying to help me and be nice and all, but I'm not in the best of moods and can't be held responsible for my actions. You have no idea what I'm feeling inside right now. I'm hurt and upset and it's best if I'm left alone. So, please, go home," I pleaded with him.

"That is okay." He stepped closer, and the heat of his body made my heart skip a beat. "Take it out on me. Let me feel your rage. Give it all to me."

My jaw trembled. I didn't want him to be nice to me. Not right now.

"No," I whispered, and turned away to open the door.

"I know you are still angry with me and have been for a while now. I deserve it. I know what you are feeling has a lot to do with the secrets you hold inside. So, give me your worst. There is nothing you can do that I have not already felt anyway."

My breathing deepened, each breath lifting my emotions to the point of no return.

"You have no idea what you're talking about." I gritted my teeth. "I want to explode, okay? I want to punch things. I want to cry and scream and ask why me... *Why* me? What did I do to deserve this life? These odds? In the blink of an eye, my world changed overnight with things you have no idea about. I've been holding everything in for so long, on top of training and fighting against myself, and I just want to let go and do it alone. Why can't you understand that? Why can't anyone just let me be? Why does everyone have some sort of secret about me that just destroys my life?" I asked, my voice rising and tears climbing again. "Just go away, damn it."

A couple of hours ago I'd dreaded the thought of being isolated. Now that Kova was aware of my secret and had known about it for so long, I craved the seclusion. I felt weird inside. I didn't want him to see me any differently, but he already did.

He ran a hand down his face, then looked me directly in the eye. "I know about your mother. Frank told me what happened. I know everything, Adrianna."

All the air left my lungs again for the second time today. That was it. The tears fell again, harder, faster, and I couldn't stop them. I didn't want to. My head spun as my world spiraled away with one admission at a time.

"Why… Why did you not tell me?" Kova asked, the hurt in his voice did not go unnoticed. "You should have told me."

Prickles of resentment rolled down my arms. I bit the inside of my lip, trying to keep my composure, but knew there was very little to hold on to.

Any second I was going to burst. The dam was going to break and it was just going to come out.

"I should have told you? You have some nerve to tell me that after everything you've done. You know why I didn't tell you? Because it's none of your damn business, that's why. It has nothing to do with you! It doesn't affect your life."

He stepped closer and I pressed a hand to his chest. Inches from my face, he breathed down at me. "Like hell it does not. Everything you do has to do with me. Do you not see that by now?"

I scoffed and shoved at his chest but he didn't budge, and it only made me angrier.

"It's not, though. Not everything is about you. In fact, it has nothing to do with you! It's about me and my life, not yours. So, fuck off, Kova." I paused. "You know what? I'm done with this conversation.

Done with you in my face. Done with the lies. Just done with all the bullshit. I wish I could just disappear."

I turned around and opened my door to slip inside. I tried to shut it but Kova was quick and pushed himself in. His cell phone rang and the tone set me off.

Kova answered the phone and I used it to my advantage by pushing him out the door. I shoved and pushed and dug my heels into the floor to get him out, but he was stronger.

He positioned the phone between his shoulder and ear and used both of his hands to subdue me. He kicked the door shut and grabbed me by my upper arms and backed me up while he spoke Russian into the phone. I fought him but it wasn't enough. He walked forward until I was against the breakfast bar where I usually ate. I could have yelled but I really didn't need any more of Katja's wrath. Thunder cracked outside and I yelped. I looked over my shoulder toward the sliding glass door. I'd forgotten to shut the hurricane shutters.

Face pulled tight and twisted with irritation, Kova shook his head for me to stay quiet while he spoke over Katja's high-pitched Russian. I cringed. Her voice was like nails on a chalkboard. They were speaking at the same time and over each other. I gathered they were fighting, but I couldn't be sure. I didn't really care.

My back hit the marble and Kova stepped up to me. I drew in a quiet breath, lips parting as his body was flushed against mine. I resented him for how I felt when he touched me. I resented my body. I resented us and everything we'd become.

I swallowed hard and licked my lips. I felt us click together, just like we always did.

Kova's Russian slowed to a whisper. He frowned at me, gazing at my tear-stained cheeks until his eyes moved to my lips while Katja continued to scream. I felt his sadness, his longing. I felt *him*, and I didn't want to. I wanted to stay numb to the world. Life was easier that way, but with Kova by my side, it was nearly impossible. He was my light, my life, my protector, even when I didn't want him to be.

Kova shook his head and mumbled something, which only set Katja off again. I leaned back, fighting us as he leaned in closer. My heart raced. Using the heel of my hand, I pushed at his jaw, angling his head back, hoping he'd back off. A vein strained along the length of his neck and the days old black stubble scraped my palm, but he fought me by holding my wrist down. Kova's body hardened, heating against mine, willing it to life.

This is what we did. What we were good at.

I whimpered, missing the strength of his body against mine, the way he'd make me forget everything when it was just us. Kova was so strong. He had no idea how much I drew from him for weeks until that dreadful day at the doctor's office. Since then, I hadn't been myself, and now that it was just me and him, I felt myself awakening again. I felt that pull, that strength I needed only he could give me. My emotions simmered at the surface and that scared me. I wanted to fight him, to unleash everything I had in me on him. And I wanted him to fight me back.

Breathing heavily, our chests mimicked each other's as he descended again. I pushed him away and turned my head, giving him my cheek. Russian words not meant for me danced across my skin as he kissed where the tears had fallen. I squeezed my eyes shut and it broke me inside how gentle he was being. He wanted to help, but I didn't want the nice guy Kova. I wanted him to fume and walk away.

Kova inhaled deeply and dragged his nose through my hair. He continued to pepper little kisses all over my cheek, nuzzling me. His hot breath tickled my neck and I let out a small cry, cursing myself for it. Goose bumps broke out over my skin and I trembled against him, hating the need to feel every inch of him.

Gripping the phone in one hand, Kova pulled back just an inch to peer down at me. His piercing eyes held me captive, and for a moment there were no barriers between us. It was just the two of us. He breathed life into me and I inhaled it deeply into my lungs.

There were a lot of things I didn't understand in this crazy world. But the most peculiar thing was that of me and Kova. He had no morals and I had no dignity. We willingly stripped each other of everything except us. When I needed to be alone, when I felt lost and empty, he forced himself into my life. Just like the few times when he actually admitted to needing me, I gave him every inch and then some without reason. I was positive I'd never understand this savage push and pull we fed off of, but then again, some things were not meant to be explained.

But that look. I knew that look. It was the look that made my heart skip a beat. Kova was going to kiss me, and the thought provoked something inside my heart. Even when I didn't want him here, when I was so angry at the world for the cards I'd been dealt, and even while he spoke to his wife on the phone, he was going to kiss me.

He had no principles, but it was obvious I didn't either.

I reached up and took his bottom lip between my teeth and jerked him to me. His body stiffened but that didn't stop him. Whatever he was in the middle of saying to Katja was enough to enrage her and allow me to force my way in for a brief second. But I didn't need to. Kova was quicker and kissed me hard, plunging his tongue into my mouth. His thick tongue stroked mine and wrapped me around him. I melted against him and opened up to draw his essence into me as my body roused with desire. My free hand tangled in the hair at his damp nape, and I latched on, tugging and pulling it between clenched fingers.

Kova pushed his mouth harder into mine, growling and devouring my lips with precision, and elicited a moan from me. Letting go of my wrist, his hand moved to my throat and my nipples tightened as he applied pressure. Sensation took over. I let out a loud and satisfied moan, forgetting why I didn't want him here. He kissed me again, this time long and deep and slow. My body rolled into his, into the rigid length that hung between his hips. Shifting my feet apart, I hiked a leg over his waist and grinded myself on his hard cock. Kova pressed his thumb down on the center of my throat and wetness seeped from me. I cried out, craving more, when I heard the shrill of his wife's voice from the other end of his phone.

Cold water washed over me.

I snapped and broke the kiss. Not because I was mad at myself for how I was acting—I was a little—but because Kova played right into it with me. It was sick we both got off on fucking around. Kova had never admitted to finding joy in cheating, but he never stopped either. Not even after he was married. I had to wonder if he liked the rush as much as I did. I shouldn't, but the truth was, I did. I loved it, and that made me a terrible person. Now that I thought about it, I was certain that was the reason for the hand I was dealt. The diseases were Karma's way of getting back at me. They had to be.

Tears blurred my vision again. I'd gotten what I deserved.

Reaching up, I yanked his cell phone from his hand and slammed it onto the marble counter next to us. I wanted to silence her voice and get him out of my condo. I couldn't take hearing her anymore. The screen shattered and the phone turned black. And thank fucking God she was gone.

"You are fucking crazy. You know that?"

"All woman are. Now get the hell off me and get out."

But he didn't. Kova stared where the phone had slid from my hand on the counter. His eyes hardened to deadly points, and his body stiffened. I followed his gaze…

To Hayden's shirt.

It was sitting in a giant decorative bowl on the counter. He'd left it at my house after we had sex but I'd yet to return it to him. I'd just forgotten.

I smiled to myself, knowing this was the fuel I needed to make him mad.

"Was that another thing I should have told you?" I asked sarcastically. "Because I did. You just didn't believe me."

CHAPTER 23

Kova was off me like my body had come alive with flames.

I used his shock to quickly put distance between us.

There was no doubt the shirt was Hayden's, and Kova knew that. It had Michigan written across the chest; the college he was attending in the fall. The same college Kova helped him record a video to apply to the men's gymnastics team.

"Hayden came here," he said more to himself.

"Oh, he came all right." I wanted to hurt him the way he'd hurt me. I wanted to get it all out and not have any more secrets pressing on my chest.

Kova's eyes lit up as he glared at me. For a brief moment I stood frozen in place. Damn, his gaze was powerful. Dark and lethal, his eyes searched mine for the truth of my ambiguous words. I'd never seen him wear hatred this deep, or sorrow so profound like he was now.

As I looked him straight in the eye, a slow smile spread across my face from ear to ear.

"He came in my bed, in my shower, in my kitchen, in—"

I blinked and Kova was charging me, eating up the space I'd just put between us. My eyes widened with a little panic. I was nearly knocked over by the rage he emitted from across the room. I stepped back as fast as I could and hit a wall. Kova's hand flew out and grasped my neck. His thumb stroked over my pulse. I gasped and grabbed his wrist, trying to tug him off.

"You are lying." His eyes blazed so bright I was caught off guard by them. "Tell me the truth!"

My heart pounded so hard in my chest I thought I was going to have a heart attack. I knew he could feel it.

"Someone needed to take my mind off you, and Hayden did an amazing job at that."

"Did you fuck him?" His eyes were huge. I thought he was going to pop a blood vessel.

"Do you want me to spell it out for you? Better yet, I can describe his dick if you want me to. It's about five—"

A strangled sound erupted from Kova's throat. His face contorted like he was in agony. As he let go of my neck, he yelled out something in Russian. Kova picked up the delicate, sea-blue glass vase on the table next to us and slammed it down, shattering it into a million little pieces. I jumped and ran to the opposite side of the room, toward the sliding glass door, only to have him stalk me just as quickly, tracking me with his lethal glare. He was like a caged animal set free, ready to go in for the kill.

The tension between us simmered to a suffocating level.

Maybe now he knew how I'd felt when I'd found out he'd married Katja.

That dam I'd constructed to hold back the tears after the crippling and devastating moments that altered my life was cracking with each blink of my eyes. The flood of emotion in me was rising to a catastrophic level.

Could he feel it?

I felt it, and I couldn't stop it.

"Hurts, doesn't it?" I bit out with a sneer.

"Why would you do this to me? To us?" he said, sounding defeated.

I stopped moving.

My inner ticking time bomb just went off.

I. Fucking. Lost. It.

A maniacal laugh burst from my lungs. This time the tears didn't come because I was sad. No, they came because I felt rage pour out of me in ways I'd never experienced in my life. It inspired me and all I saw was blood.

Fingers trembling, I reached for the heavy candle next to me, and without thinking, I threw it, aiming for his head.

"How could I do this to us? Are you fucking kidding me?" I screamed, jaw quivering.

There was a pounding in my ears, and my chest burned with uncontrollable anger. The glass candle collided with the wall and broke. I would kill him. I would kill him for saying that.

"How dare you say such a thing to me. You're fucking married, Kova. That fucking ring on your finger is proof. You created this fucking mess," I said, moving my finger back and forth between us. "You broke me. You fucking broke us. How dare you try to turn this around on me. If it wasn't for the fact you got fucking married, none of this would even be happening!"

"I never cheated on you, though," he replied and then ducked when I threw another object at him. "Not like you think. I married her for you, not because I wanted to!"

Candles were missiles and I threw them one by one. I was determined to hit him. My breathing grew dense and thick with each intake of breath and all I wanted to do was inflict pain on him the way he had me. Why did my aim have to suck so bad?

I strode up to him with hate filling my veins. "Are you delusional? *You married her for me?*" He was breathing just as hard as I was. "That's what you're going with? No, you married her because it was a choice you made, then you came to me when you got married and fucked me on that couch." I pointed to my sofa, my voice cracking as I thought back to that night when I gave him every part of me. That night was the first and last time we ever made love, and it stayed with me ever since. "Another choice you made. How sick and demented are you to say you married another woman for me? How?"

"When did you fuck—" He scowled, the hurt prevalent in his eyes that I almost felt bad. He couldn't even say the word. Kova's eyes scanned the floor, he looked lost and tangled in his emotions. "I cannot believe you did this," he whispered, his accent thicker than usual.

My eyes widened at his ridiculousness. "When did I fuck Hayden? Is that what you're trying to ask me?"

He looked up. "Was it after the kidney disease? Or before?"

I broke inside.

"Don't say those words!" I yelled and offset his steps again with mine, crying so hard I could hardly catch my breath. Through blurry eyes, I grabbed the neck of the lamp and took a deep breath, struggling to hold on to the little sanity I had left. Kova's eyes dropped to my fisted hand then met my gaze.

"Was it after the lupus?"

"Stop it!" I cried. "Why are you doing this to me?"

Kova was pushing me, goading me, knowing I didn't want to talk about that. Anything but that. My face twisted with heartbreak and with all my might, I yanked the cord from the wall and swung my arm back to throw the lamp at him. An anguished cry left my throat as I hurled it through the air. I took off running to the kitchen, frantically looking for something to chuck at him if he uttered those words again. A wooden spoon would do, a glass, a pan, anything—my eyes landed on a knife.

I reached for the black handle when a heavy body flew into my back. Kova tackled me from behind. A gasp of air burst from my lungs as he spun me around.

"Get away from me—"

"Adrianna."

"Leave me alone. Why are you even here? Go home to your perfect house with your perfect wife and your perfect dog. Stop torturing me."

I shoved back at his chest with my free hand, trying to push him away, but he released all his weight and crushed himself to me. He was quick and pinned my hips to the counter with his strength. It was so easy for him. Air rushed from my lungs. Fuck. He was heavy. Given his height and frame, I estimated Kova to be around two hundred and thirty pounds of solid muscle.

My heart beat frantically against my ribs and hot tears blurred my vision. I thrashed against him, pushing at his neck with the palm of my hand to get him to move, but he only burrowed closer to me. He was such an asshole.

Kova yelled at me to stop, but I was too enraged and upset. He allowed this to happen.

"Aren't you ashamed of yourself?" I spat, trying to hit him. "Disgusted that you're married but here with me? What is she? Pregnant? Do you just unload your cum—yeah, I said cum, I use big girl words—in everyone and pray for the best? Do you have no integrity? No moral compass? How can you still fuck around with me while married to her?"

"Let me explain!"

"Let me explain," I mimicked in my best Russian accent. "You always need a reason to explain yourself, Kova."

I pinched his neck and his eyes blazed with fire. I dug my nails in deep hoping to draw blood. His skin broke under my fingernails, but he didn't flinch. Leaning in, I bit his arm and he grunted and yanked back. I moved my hips from side to side to show him my resistance but it only backfired. His cock hardened against me and I absolutely hated myself for reacting to it. The corner of his mouth pulled up into a smug grin. My arms broke out in goose bumps as a fire lit inside me.

It sickened me that I became hot against his dick. I was past the point of livid, but I needed to make him feel the weight of his words, I needed him to understand where I was coming from and how much he hurt me. He wasn't supposed to know about my secrets. I hated, hated, hated that he knew. Fighting him wasn't easy, especially when I was already so weak.

And yet I didn't stop, because the storm brewing inside me felt too good. The allure was too strong and it gave me a thrill to see him as hurt as I was. Provoking him only provoked me, which helped me breathe.

And that wasn't healthy for either of us.

"Once again, you've made me hate the sight of you. Here I was thinking you were my light helping me see past everything, but you really were just pulling my strings. You're a disgusting human being and I hate the things you make me feel. I'd rather be numb than live through what you've made me go through. I can't believe you would do this, come here and question me like you have some sort of right. And then to say how could I do this to you? The audacity. You are sick. This pulling me back and forth? I'm done with it. I'm done with you. Officially done with everything. I'm done with the medicine and the doctors and the needles. I want you out of my life and I never want you to touch me again. You're horrible!"

Kova let go of my wrist and surrendered. "Say what you need." He breathed heavily into me, almost as if he was struggling with me. "I know you do not mean any of it, but if it helps you, then take it out on me."

Gritting my teeth, I reared back, and with all my might, I slapped him across the face so hard his head snapped to the side and my palm stung from the connection.

An audible gasp escaped me. Tears filled my eyes over my cruel actions. The room grew jarringly quiet while it exploded with strain. Kova's entire body hardened to stone and I was nervous to see how he'd respond. I'd never hit another person before and I was surprised I did, but what shocked me the most was the lack of remorse I felt.

"You only ever give a shit about yourself. You're the most selfish man I've ever met."

The skin between his eyes crinkled together. *"Sumasshedshiy."*

Seething, I slapped him again because I knew what he said couldn't have been good. His cock hardened to a rock as wetness seeped from me.

"Your ethics are fucked up." I raged, my breathing weighted with untamed emotion. "How can you tell lie after lie and never feel bad about it? You use me. You use me when Katja isn't around, then make me feel guilty for fucking Hayden like you have some claim on me."

Chest tight as a fist, I gasped trying to catch my breath. My eyes were huge as I stared at him, wired and ready for war. I didn't care that I sounded like a lunatic, because everything I said was the truth and we both knew it.

"Do not ever fucking hit me again," he said through clenched teeth.

Eyes wild, I grabbed his hair and yanked it back. His neck strained with a row of veins as he fought my pull. Our bodies pressed into each other's. Kova's cock was thick and full, like a weapon pushing against my own arousal. I was stunned by how big and hard he was, considering the way I was acting toward him.

But then it clicked.

CHAPTER 24

All the screaming and arguing I was doing to make him see how I really felt was backfiring on me.

Kova was aroused, and oddly enough, I was too. My body flared with unshed desire that rocked me to my core, with emotion that I had buried. I was relentless, but I wouldn't cave.

"You've lost all control and you can't deal with it, so you're trying to use reverse psychology on me. It won't work."

"You do not know what you are talking about because you will not let me speak!"

"I don't want to hear your bullshit lies anymore! I can't believe you had the fucking nerve to say I did this to us." A mocking huff rolled off my lips.

Oh God. I couldn't take it. Why did he have to do this to me? I wanted him to feel the pain he had caused me. The lacerations of his actions and how they'd scarred me.

Whispering, I spoke slowly in a blind rage. He'd feel these words.

"You're nothing but a user and an abuser. I fucking hate you."

"You fucking hate me?" Kova yelled, his vibrant green eyes huge. Moving his hand to my hair, he grabbed a fist full of it and forced me to look at him.

Kova burned with a passion that made me question my statement. Did I hate him? Truly hate him?

I bobbed my head slowly, not holding back with a blanket stare.

"I never hated something more in my life," I repeated slowly.

Kova clenched my hair again and leaned down. I thought he was going to kiss me, so I swiped my hand between us. The tips of my fingers struck his nose and he flinched backwards.

"*Chyort poberi!!* I told you to stop fucking hitting me!"

He grabbed both my wrists and restrained them above my head to the cabinet.

"Fuck you, get off me!"

With his lips pressed to the shell of my ear, he spoke in his native tongue then translated it to English for me. "You could never fucking hate me." He was breathing harder, rougher, like he was struggling himself. "You cannot fucking hate me, because you love me. You. Love. Me."

I froze. My heart hitched into my throat, constricting with verity.

"What did you say?" I asked, my voice a whisper.

I angled my head toward him just in time for him to slant his mouth over mine. He devoured me with a savage kiss, a kiss I made him fight me for. I bit down and pulled his bottom lip between my teeth. Kova growled and delved his tongue around mine at the same time he rolled his hips into me. A groan vibrated deep in my throat. I softened, unable to not kiss him back.

"You love me," he demanded, pulling back. "Say it."

"I hate you."

He pressed his chest to mine, nearly suffocating me with his weight, and kissed my lips so viciously my heart ached for this untamed man who just so happened to be my coach.

Kova let go of my wrists. "You call me a liar, yet it is so easy for you to lie to my face. Tell me you love me."

I shook my head. "Never." I grit out. I'd never utter those words. I knew better.

"You have such a temper. Now tell me when you fucked Hayden."

My heart burned with fury and anger fueled tears filled my eyes. I was going to kill him.

Using every last ounce of power I had, I shoved at Kova's chest as hard as I could and turned around. My eyes landed on the black handle again.

Reaching for it, I grabbed it and took off, but I didn't get far. Kova grabbed my hair and yanked me back. I halted with a scream and he spun me around, pushing me onto the dinner table I never used. My feet couldn't reach the ground and I squirmed, trying to kick him. Kova stepped between my legs and locked me in. Without thinking, I lifted my arm with the knife but he grabbed my wrist to stop me. He wrestled me down until I was on my back.

"Tell me," he demanded, hovering over me. "I need to know."

"You're married." I paused, my eyes drifting over his irate features. "What difference does it make when I had sex with him? It doesn't. Just like my sickness has nothing to do with you."

His brows furrowed. "That is where you are wrong, Adrianna. Everything you do has to do with me."

I struggled in his hold, fighting against his power. I wanted to stab him, I wanted to hurt him. I wanted to make him bleed.

A devious smile spread across my face. My hand tightened around the base of the knife. I was going to make him feel the level of pain and destruction he had caused me.

"He came inside of me. All over me. And I loved it... I begged for it."

A tragic sound erupted from Kova's mouth that broke my heart. His hand shot out and clutched my throat. I strained against him. We both were breathing heavily and fighting the intoxicating desire streaming between us.

"You are a liar. You would never let him inside your body like that."

"I'm not a habitual liar like you. I let Hayden do whatever he wanted, however he wanted. Three glorious times," I said, drawing out the last three words with a sugary sweetness.

Kova released the hold on my wrist and lifted my leg. He turned me to the side and slapped my outer thigh painfully hard. I yelped, my hips jumping off the table.

"You want to know the best part?" I gave no fucks about hurting him, he deserved it.

"Adrianna," he warned. He looked so crazed, even his hands were trembling, but I knew I did too. Like we were both ready to kill each other. Kova wanted me to stop but I refused to this time. He was going to feel my wrath.

I continued, knowing this would set him off. His gaze dropped to my mouth. "He fucked me right where we're standing," I said, smacking the surface of the table. "Then he fucked me bare in the shower and I felt every incredible inch of him. He pulled my hair and bent me over until he was balls deep and then fucked me until I couldn't walk."

His face paled to a startling sheen of white. Frozen in place with only a deadly stare, I knew it would destroy him and I was glad it did. Only now would he be able to feel even an ounce of what he'd made me feel.

Without saying another word, Kova loosened his hand from my neck, but then he slammed his fist into the wood table three times insanely fast, right next to my head. I sat up and raised my arm with the knife held tight in my fist, and for a split second, I wondered if I could really stab him or not. That was how far Kova had pushed me.

Kova grabbed my wrist just as thunder struck outside. I could hear the rain pelting the balcony. Taking hold of my other hand, he placed them both behind my back and leaned into me. Our bodies flushed together in a bittersweet intimacy.

"Why? Why would you do this?" he growled and pressed his forehead to mine, then turned his head. His cheeks were red and he radiated with a heartbreaking emotion that I'd caused. Kova clenched his eyes shut and he pressed his lips to the side of my face, along my jaw, and down my neck, nipping and biting, sinking his teeth in and not caring. "Do you hate me that much you had to fuck someone else? Take it back," he pleaded, his hot breath trailed along the curve of my neck. "Tell me you are lying just to hurt me. Please, Adrianna, tell me you are making all of this up."

"Open your eyes and look into mine."

He did, and a sinful smile spread across my face, reaching my eyes. I pressed my chest into his and took joy in his revulsion.

"I had sex with Hayden," I said in a sultry voice purposely meant to taunt him. "I know it kills you to know another guy felt me come around his cock, just like it killed me to find out you married Katja. Even my diagnosis paled in comparison to that news. I don't think anything could equal that pain I felt. That's how much you destroyed me. Now you can feel what I've been feeling for months."

His eyes were a dark cavern of hatred. Lips a whisper above mine, he said, "I told you I would kill both of you."

"Do your worst. I'm already dead inside."

"You think you are the only one suffering? You think you are the only one dying inside?" His face was so close to mine. "Every day you have no idea what I am dealing with. Every day the darkness spreads to another piece of me. The numbness is unbearable. Now this with that little shit…" He shook his head and muttered in Russian. "The only time I ever feel anything is when I am near you, but now…” Kova trailed off and let go of my hands.

“I wanted him to make me forget you, what you feel like.”

Cupping my jaw, Kova rubbed his face against the side of mine and laughed under his breath. I gripped the knife handle tighter as a chill rolled down my spine.

“And how did that work out for you, hmm?”

I didn’t say anything.

“You know you will never be able to forget about me the same way I cannot stop thinking about you for even a fucking second of my miserable life. It is killing me.”

“He replaced you.”

Kova pulled back and eyed my hand with the steel blade. “You will never be able to replace me. Never. Just like I will never replace you.”

I let out a strangled whimper at the truth of his words.

“Could you live without me? Because I cannot live without you, and that is the God’s honest fucking truth.”

I whimpered again, overcome with emotion.

“Let go of the knife, Adrianna,” he pleaded, his voice so broken. I shook my head. “You cannot live without me, because I could not live without you.”

“Let go of me.”

“Why? So you can cut me?”

I nodded, breathing hard. I was worked up and running on adrenaline. “I want you to feel what you do to me. I want you to know what it feels like when I see you with Katja, when you called her and me both *malysh*, when you wear that fucking ring on your finger. Every time you’ve lied to me. I hate that you know my truth. I want you to feel it all and more.”

“Just tell me why.”

“Because I wanted to. Because I felt like it. Because I didn’t want you to be the last thing my body felt. I wanted—no, I needed— Hayden to make me forget, and guess what, Kova? For a time, it fucking worked.”

“But I have never intentionally hurt you, Adrianna. You did that to purposely hurt me. How can I hurt you like that when I love you so much?”

"Love?" I repeated, my jaw bobbing in horror.

Anger spewed through my veins. My eyes flicked back and forth between his. We both were breathing so hard the tension was stifling between us.

"You don't love me. You don't know what love is. You're incapable of love. What is wrong with you to say that to me? Why are you playing with my emotions like this?"

"Do not tell me I do not love you. I did not know love until I fucking met you! I love you! Everything I do is out of love for you."

My eyes bubbled with tears again. "Shut up! I'm so sick of all the lies. You don't marry one women, vow your love to her, then tell me you love me too!"

"Not once have I ever told Katja that I love her."

He was trying to give me a heart attack. "You're lying again!

"I told her before we were married, but never since."

"You always lie! You married her because you love her."

"She knows about us, Adrianna! *I had to fucking marry her*," he gritted out angrily. "I had no fucking choice in the matter. She was going to the police, and your father. She knows *everything*. She has our notebook, and even hired an investigator that your bitch of a mother suggested," he said, and I gasped in shock. "Backed up against a wall with no option, I did what I had to. I was not going to let her ruin you. She had been pushing for marriage because her visa was up. She knew I did not want to marry her, and that she would be going back to Russia. We just happened to be the fuel she needed to light her flame. I have been trying to figure out a way to divorce her, but I have nothing to hold over her head yet, so I was counting my days and giving you the space you needed."

He was trembling, breathing so heavily.

"But now I am done giving you space."

CHAPTER 25

W hat?" I asked breathlessly.

My mind raced through all the different scenarios. This was too much for me to process and just unreal.

"How? What?" I didn't even recognize my own voice. "So you were never going to marry her? And my… Joy…? Our notebook?"

"Do it," he demanded, pushing me. Kova's hand slid over the serrated edge of the knife and my heart rate kicked up to an abnormally excited level. "Cut me. If you want me to feel what you have been feeling, then cut me, but I promise you, *malysh*, a cut would never compare to the wound you just caused inside of me. You think you are the only one who is fucked up inside? Who is empty inside? You are wrong. Now you know what I have been going through. So put that knife to me and release me from the agony I deal with on a daily basis. Release both of us."

And I did. I didn't hesitate. Grinding my back teeth, I pressed the knife against his skin and sank it into his palm. I drew in a lungful of air. Kova's eyes widened for a moment in shock—he probably didn't expect me to actually do it, but I was so distraught over everything. The marriage. Joy. Sophia. Avery. The lupus and kidney disease. The lies and secrets. I didn't hold back.

Little by little all these life moments were annihilating who I was as a person that I couldn't take it anymore. It was too much, too intense for anyone. The worst was this feeling, this warped sense of love I had for Kova that made no sense. He was no good for me, we weren't any good for each other, but it didn't stop me from wanting him. I wanted to burn him to the ground, but I wanted him to take me with him. I wanted to hurt him with a passion I'd never felt before, but I wanted to hurt with him. He would let me, because maybe in the back of his convoluted mind, he really did love me, and I knew that. We both were guilty of having an unhealthy obsession of love for one another, but love was love, right?

Slowly, I pushed harder, drawing the knife down into his skin. Our eyes locked onto each other's, my tears finally drying.

Kova didn't flinch. He took the pain I gave him. To my shock, he wrapped his fingers around the steel and fisted it. He helped me cut him, pushing the blade into his palm. Warmth trickled over my hand, but I didn't stop. His lips parted and his eyes widened, and a euphoric rush of endorphins I wasn't expecting hit me. A little sigh rolled off my lips as a trail of dark red blood slid down his wrist and arm…when a thought hit me.

"Take your shirt off."

It wasn't a request, and he knew that. Reaching behind his head, Kova bunched the shirt and pulled it off with one hand, then dropped it to the floor. Warm blood seeped down the knife into my hand, into my palm, wetting the hold I had on the handle. A few drops hit my thigh.

A strange sensation took over that evoked feelings I'd never felt. Kova stepped between my legs again, igniting a darker edge of me. I welcomed it. My eyes lingered on the left side of his chest. I tried to block out the thoughts I had. Licking my lips, I dragged my teeth over my bottom lip and bit down. His tawny skin, too beautiful to mark yet I wanted to. Chest rising in falling, I didn't know where this urge came from to scar him, but it was compelling me to over his heart. To scar him the way he did me.

Tipping my head back with the tip of his finger, he looked deep into my eyes. "Every day when I look at myself in the mirror, this will be a reminder of the pain I caused you."

Chills danced down my arms. Kova was giving me the green light.

Our world came to a standstill. It was just us in this moment that only we controlled.

He grabbed my hand that held the knife and placed it to his chest. My chest rose and fell deep and slow. Eyes lingering for a moment, I hesitated as I took in his muscular shoulders and the honeyed curve of his neck, the vein trickling down. He was trying to steady his breathing like me.

I placed my palm to his chest and hesitated for a moment. Kova cupped my jaw, his blood coating my skin. I leaned into the slash on his palm, not understanding what was happening but for once not questioning it.

Instead, I let go and I felt him, this moment, us.

I felt his touch, the heat of his body, how his fingers threaded my hair. The way his lips danced seductively over mine, the desire building between us that we'd been fighting for so long. Little droplets of his blood fell to the top of my thigh. Tilting my head up, our gazes met and I held my breath. His green eyes were low and heavy, encased by thick, black lashes. Fingers grazing my cheeks, I sat up straighter.

"Do it. I want you to. I *need* you to." His voice was raw. "But just know the moment you put the knife down, I am going to fuck you senseless. Right here, on your table, and I will not hold back. I am going to spend hours inside your body to remind you of us. I have never in my life felt anything like this with anyone but you." He paused. "Tell me you feel it too, that it is not just me."

I nodded, admitting the truth. "I feel it…all the time."

Then, he kissed me.

Kova slanted his lips over mine and kissed me deep and hard, plunging his tongue into my mouth daringly slow and bruising at the same time. My body came alive, exploding with harbored cravings only he could satisfy. His tongue stroked mine, wrapping around it and rousing me the same way when he coached gymnastics. He was a ruthless kisser, one with unparalleled precision.

My hand vibrated from the rumbling in his chest, reminding me what I was supposed to do. Without another thought, I angled the knife and dragged the tip down, opening his flesh. The salty, metallic scent coated my nostrils and darkly curled through my stomach. Kova didn't flinch, he only kissed me harder, deeper, making me hotter than ever for him.

But I wasn't done.

Using my thumb to feel, I pressed into the bleeding, parted skin and felt for the top of the line I'd just made. I placed the blade right next to it and cut another angled line. Kova growled into my mouth and gripped my head in his palms. His erection pressed into my sex and I hooked my leg up to bring him closer. I wondered what it would be like for him to fuck me while I cut him. Wetness seeped from my pussy at the thought. His rich lips hadn't stopped, the thrilling silkiness of his tongue was overwhelming all my senses. Oh God. It was too erotic and my legs shook from the indulgence. I needed more. I needed to stop.

The wind howled outside as the storm grew closer. Locking my ankles around his back, I knew the next line would hurt and I wanted to trap him against me so he couldn't move. I pulled him closer and his erection pressed further into my pussy. I whimpered into his mouth. Reaching between us with my other hand, I stroked over his cock and felt his thickness. Kova growled again, then took his hand and guided mine into his shorts so I could feel his hot, thick flesh. I gripped him tight, feeling for my favorite vein.

"Kova," I whispered. My body was on another level of pleasure, like I was high even though I'd never done drugs in my life. "I need you." I found myself saying as I squeezed his dick.

"I know." He all but groaned out.

Feeling for the lines, my fingers smeared the blood and his tongue penetrated deeper, teeth nibbling and tugging. A moan erupted in my throat, my leotard wet with desire for him.

Turning my wrist, I pushed the knife into his chest one last time and made a horizontal line across the two I'd already created to form an A. I made sure I crossed over the open skin for further pain as I branded him. Kova's teeth sank into my swollen bottom lip. He thrusted his cock into my hand, releasing a wave of pleasure. I gasped a soft sigh and my body softened. I almost orgasmed from just this. I knew the last tear I made into his beautiful flesh hurt him. There was something exceedingly carnal when power was handed over and trust was given unconditionally. That's what he'd just done.

With one last caress around his kiss, Kova drew his tongue along the roof of my mouth and tugged my lip with him. Wetness seeped from me. Pulling back, our lips separated but he didn't go far. The heat of his breath drifted across my skin. The rain and wind had picked up outside while we'd created our own storm inside.

I opened my eyes and the first thing I looked for was the letter I carved into his skin. Fat, crimson droplets trickled down his chest, over his ribs. His cock was still hot in my hand, only now it was dripping with cum. My mouth watered at his tapered abdomen and the strong muscles beneath. He was a big man in pristine shape. Broad shoulders, a wide, thick waist. All I wanted to do was touch him.

My hand trembled slightly as I placed the knife on the table. I leaned in and dropped my forehead to his chest, and let out a gush of air. Kova's hand cupped the back of my neck, his other hand untied my ponytail. I touched the line of blood, spreading it over his obliques, the warmth stirring me. I lifted my head and looked at the mark I'd made. It wasn't small, about the size of the inside of my palm. One side of the letter was longer than the other. I'd done it blindly, but it didn't look bad either. There would be a scar for sure.

Something peculiar had taken over me. Something I'd never expected to do in a million years, or had ever considered doing until now.

Leaning in, I flatted my tongue and licked the blood, tracing the A and feeling the incisions I had just made. Kova's hand tightened behind me and his chest flexed as I tried to kiss the pain I had just inflicted away.

Slipping his hand under my hair, Kova twirled my locks around his palm then gripped my neck, angling my head back. His thumb pressed into the front of my neck and he tugged on my hair until our gazes met.

We'd been deprived for too long.

My lungs seized, desperate for air, and my lips parted against his. My expression mimicked his. The intoxicating stare in his eyes replaced the dark cavern of hatred, and I knew, that after tonight, after this moment, we would never, ever be the same.

"I am going to tear into you just like you did me," he said, his voice a rough whisper. And I was oddly excited.

Kova picked up the knife. He cut a tear into my leotard and sports bra, then into my shorts, and ripped everything off of me in the blink of an eye, along with his shorts. We were both naked and just as I thought he was going to slide into me, he picked me up and spun me around so I was lying face down.

"Put your knees on the table, *malysh*."

It was an awkward position at first, but my flexibility allowed me to lay on the table spread open with my hips pressing into the wood.

My pussy and ass hung off the table, but I wasn't going to fall because Kova was right behind me stroking his cock.

Kova gripped my hips then plunged right into me in one long, hard stroke that took my breath away. My hand came up and slapped the table. The entire lower half of my body quivered in rebellion. I couldn't even take a breath before he was pulling out and surging into me so hard that I saw stars. He was warm and thick, and he let out a strangled moan like he was in utter heaven. His hand roamed circles on my ass as he rolled his hips into mine.

"Fuck! Damn it, Kova, hang on."

"This is not for you, Adrianna. This is for me. Now, take a deep breath and stay down."

He was relentless, driving into me rough and hard and fast. His heavy sack tapped my clit, teasing me each time he surged into my pussy.

"Did Hayden fuck you like this?"

Oh, he was angry. I liked angry Kova.

My eyes were closed as I focused on how good he felt. "No, he fucked me better."

Kova's hand reached up to grip the back of my neck while the other pressed down on my lower back so I couldn't move. I gasped, drawing in a long moan as he squeezed me so tight that I was going to have a bruise. I was at his mercy and I found it utterly intoxicating.

"I am going to make you regret ever fucking that little boy." I giggled softly and that only excited him further. "Arch your back," he said, and he took me deeper. The giggles subsided and soft moans rolled off my lips as pleasure took control of my body. Kova didn't hold back and took me hard, painfully hard, but I was okay with that. I wanted it this way.

Fisting my hair, he yanked me upright and the wood dug into my knees. He wrapped an arm around my waist so I couldn't move, then placed his other hand around my neck and pulled me to his chest. My heartrate kicked up a notch.

"Did he squeeze you like this?" he said through clenched teeth near my ear. My pussy tightened around his cock, loving this angry side of him. "Go ahead and lie to me," he urged me on. "I already know the truth."

"Yes," I said breathlessly. He squeezed me so tight I could barely swallow. "I couldn't walk after."

Oh God. The sounds Kova made only heightened my pleasure. I liked hearing him like this and I began riding his cock.

"Did he make you bleed with his cock the way I do?"

My eyes opened and I glanced down. There were droplets of blood on the table and the top of my pussy was smeared with blood. Kova fucking tore me.

He chuckled in my ear when I noticed. "I can make you bleed too."

Kova held me immobile and increased his thrusts. I leaned against his chest and within seconds, I was coming on his cock with his hand around my throat. I reached up and had him choke me tighter. This angle was too good and I couldn't hold on any longer. My hips whipped back and forth as I rode his dick.

"Go ahead and lie to me again, tell me you came on his cock as hard as you just did mine," he said through clenched teeth, then he was unloading his hot cum inside of me, rolling his hips hard and slow into me like a crashing wave. He moaned in my ear and I wanted to tell him to keep making the sounds because they were so erotic and by far one of the sexiest sounds I'd ever heard in my life.

"I came all night with him." I taunted, out of breath.

"Fucking liar," he responded, then forced my head to the side so he could plunge his tongue into my mouth and kiss me good. "You better not ever fuck him again, or anyone else for that matter. You are mine and your pussy is mine."

I didn't argue with that. It was the truth and I knew it in my heart. He had ruined me in the best way possible.

Loosening his hold on my neck, Kova pulled out and turned me around. My legs felt like Jell-O. "Put your arms around me," he said, his voice scraping over me. Guttural.

I nodded. Kova picked me up, his hands under the back of my thighs as he carried me to my room. Our gazes never wavered, not even as he gently placed me on the bed and climbed onto the mattress. I scooted back until we were in the center and laid down. The softness against my back cooled me down as I opened my body to him. He hovered above me and placed his weight on his elbows, his heavy, wet length rested against my inner thigh. We looked at each other for a moment in silence as the whirlwind storm outside thrashed against the side of the building and my windows.

Reaching behind him, Kova grabbed the blanket and pulled it over him to encase us in a cozy tunnel. He reared his hips back and reached between us to grip his length. My gaze dropped to his lips in anticipation.

"Eyes on me, Adrianna. Now let me show you how much I love you," he said, his voice raspy.

Everything stopped.

Something inside my heart mended the tattered seams back together at the mention of those words again and the way he said them, like his life depended on them.

Nodding quietly, I widened my legs, knowing he was positioning himself. Heart racing, there was no foreplay was needed. His pleasure was still dripping out of me. Kova leaned down and whispered against my lips, his Russian like silk wrapping around my body. We both were ready and on the edge of something inconceivable to even understand.

Sliding his hands over my wrists, he laced his fingers through mine as he eased his way in. Our lips parted against each other's the same way our palms met. We both drew in an echo of breath at the feelings of our bodies uniting together again. Pure euphoria tangled us into a cluster of loops and ties. Kova's eyes darkened to a depth that sent chills down my spine and opened my heart to him.

We kept our eyes open as he slowly inched his way in, reaching a deeper intimacy. He pushed past every tender inch of my pussy, slowly, making sure we felt the other until he couldn't go any further. The pressure of him inside of me increased to an intoxicating level of bliss.

Our bodies locked together and we both inhaled. My heart pounded at our held breaths.

This was mind blowing.

This was how we were always meant to be.

One. Together. Whole.

CHAPTER 26

Heat flowed between us, Kova igniting me in ways I couldn't explain.

The weight of his body on mine, and the way he looked at me, was enough to make me remember where my home was, with him. It wasn't his length that tugged on every nerve in my body, it did, but his gaze was what held me immobile.

I released a breath of relief knowing this was how it should be when two people made love.

My thighs quivered, and I trembled beneath him as I readjusted to his size. Kova gazed into my eyes like he was lost inside of me. This was one of those rare moments where he was exposing himself, where he wanted me to look into his eyes and see what he felt. Because we both knew what he felt was wrong, and it pained him to say he loved me. When it came to Kova and our situation, it was all about touch, about actions when we were alone and in our own world, about looking deeper and feeling our emotions.

"Sometimes words are empty," he said. "Let me show you how I really feel about you."

Dragging his teeth over his bottom lip, Kova brushed his nose over mine, his mouth dancing seductively over my lips but never completely closing the distance. He looked down, then reared his hips back and created a desperate ache between my legs nice and slow, his gaze never flickering away from mine. A breathless rush of air escaped me and my back arched as he slid all the way in again. My fingers tightened around his, knuckles digging into his as he held them cushioned to the bed. Nipples pressing into his chest, Kova pulled out all the way to the tip and lingered. Without saying a word, I begged him with my eyes for more. He dropped a kiss to my lips, then he was sliding back in.

It was all too much to handle after not having him inside of me for so long. A sigh escaped my lips and I clenched around him. I sighed again and his jaw flexed in gratification. Pleasure blossomed as his sensual thrusts created a maelstrom within us. I hitched up my leg to hook around his back, trying to push him in faster, dying for more, but he stopped me.

He shook his head. "Let me take you slow this time, let me feel you," he said, and I nodded, licking my lips. "I have missed your body as much as I have missed you."

He was an earthquake shattering me with his passion.

Kova thrust in deep and my back arched, a pleasure-filled moan rolled off my lips. He decorated my jaw with rough kisses. His teeth nipping my skin only heightened the pleasure as he thrust into me with a sweet slowness that almost killed me. Sweat beaded on his chest, small drops of blood dripped from his wound, and I welcomed all of it onto me. It was raw and gritty and dirty, and I loved that he loved it with me. That we thought nothing of it. We accepted each other's lusts and fed our dark desires without question. He knew what I liked, and he gave it to me. Just like I did with him.

"Straighten your legs." Kova extended my arms above my head, his hands still in mine, and I looked at him in confusion. "Trust me, *malysh*."

So I did.

My body was stretched out beneath his, my nipples pressed to his chest. He made me feel so sexy like this, like I was all he'd ever need with the way he held me and looked at me.

With one of his knees on the side of my hip and the other leg straight next to mine, the pressure grew unbearably intoxicating as he plunged into my pussy with a degree of shameless finesse. The drag and pull of wetness echoed around us and it only added to the moment.

"Fuck me," he groaned from the tightness.

The pressure was building. It was so good and so addicting that I reached forward with my mouth and devoured him. I was so completely restrained and in a daze from the chemistry of our bodies fusing together that something unleashed inside my heart.

Kova kissed me back with the same ferocity. My toes curled as he pulled out then pushed back in with an unrestrained smoothness about him. My hips bucked and I whimpered as the pleasure reached new heights.

"I'm so close, Kova, please…" I begged, my heart racing.

The way my hips pushed forward and how my legs were closed brought the sweetest friction to my clit when he thrust in. My inner thighs shook, I couldn't wait any longer.

"So, let go."

"What about you?"

He laughed next to my ear. "Adrianna, I am only getting started. I told you, I am going to spend hours inside your body," he said, and pushed in until he hit my clit. "You are going to have to beg me to stop, and even then, I still might keep going."

My lips parted and he kissed me.

"Relax for me, *malysh*, and make love with me."

I nodded, my mind and body opening up completely to him.

"Think about what I am doing to you, how I feel in your tight, little pussy, and know that no one will ever make you feel the way I do."

He was right.

"Kiss me," I whispered, and he did.

Kova's body made love to mine, his lips matching the tenacity of his hips, so nice and slow until I was quivering and on the verge of release.

"Oh, just like that," I moaned, my eyes closing.

"Look at me. I want to see your face when you come around my cock."

That was all it took. I opened my eyes and searched for his, my orgasm taking complete hold of me while my body rippled with pleasure. I gasped, taking little breaths of air as euphoria took hold of my body. My hands squeezed his, and he returned the gesture. I was coming so hard I was on the verge of tears.

"Yes, like that, Adrianna. Just…like…that…" He drew out like he was proud and rocked into me. "I wish you could see your face when you come. How your eyes get glossy, feel how your pussy pulsates around my cock. You squeeze me so fucking hard I just want to tear into you harder."

My thighs were sticky with my pleasure, but I didn't care. Kova loved it, and so did I.

"Do it. Give me everything and don't hold back," I said.

Desire subsided and Kova loosened his grip on my hands and sat back on his knees to straddle me, still nestled deep inside. Breathless, I didn't move and stared at my ceiling in a state of astonishment. How could sex be this good? I was dazed and confused by how something like this could be felt. It wasn't normal. It couldn't be.

Palms skimming my stomach to my breasts, Kova cupped and tugged on my nipples. A zing shot to my core and I drew in a breath. I glanced at him and my eyes immediately dropped to the A on his chest. The blood had stopped and I could see the swollen outline of the letter. His eyes followed my gaze. The corners of his mouth curved into a sexy-as-fuck smile and he pinched my nipples harder as he looked at the mark—*my* mark—that would scar him forever. His cock jumped inside me and I exhaled from the tenderness.

Looking down at me, Kova's eyes were glittering with depraved thoughts, and it sent a shiver down to my toes. I bit the side of my lip and awareness sparked through him.

"You were wet when you cut into me. It made you feel good."

I nodded subtly. It was partially true. There were things that made me curious, I just never spoke about them because I thought it made me weird.

"I was also so over everything that I wanted to inflict pain on you because I wanted you to feel the pain that's consumed me for months. What I felt inside was because of you, and I wanted you to experience it. I wanted you to feel it more. But then the kidney diagnosis happened, and I feel like I'm constantly being lied to for my protection. I feel like I have to have this tight hold on my emotions for everybody else's sake and I just fucking snapped. Cutting into you felt like I was releasing all this pent-up emotion, like I was hitting this crazy high and it was all coming out of me. No one to fight me, no one to control me. No more lies. I was in control for once, and I was free of this fucking burden that couldn't hold me down anymore." I licked my lips. "I'm ashamed I used you like that. I'm so sorry."

"You wanted to keep going," he stated, thrusting into me.

I mused over his statement. "I don't know. Kind of. The feeling inside my chest scared me a little. I don't think you would've stopped me if I wanted to keep going."

Kova reached between my sex and felt for the sensitive little ball of nerves. Separating my swollen lips, he caressed my clit.

"No, not yet," I said through a sigh and softened.

I was trapped under him with his hard cock still inside me. The sheer pleasure felt so good the way he rubbed my clit that my hips took on a slow roll. My teeth dug into my bottom lip.

"Do not tell me to stop," he said. "I told you, all night." Kova glanced down and pulled my lips open to expose my clit. "You are correct, though. I would not have stopped you. If you needed to mark my entire body, I would have let you because I understand what you were feeling, you forget I also felt strongly too. Every day it was getting worse for me, but then you pressed the blade into me, and I knew it was something we both needed. I felt like I could breathe. We were both letting everything go and starting brand new."

Kova was exactly right. I had felt like I was being born again. All my sins were washed away with his blood, and my knife was freeing his demons.

"I am yours, however you want me," he said. Something wild entered his eyes as he watched himself pump little thrusts into me. "Always and forever."

I could watch him do this all day, the way he looked at my pussy, how he reached forward and gripped my hips fiercely and drove in harder. His head rolled back in pleasure and Kova seemed lost to the sensations taking over. He was growing closer. I could see the thick vein in his neck trailing down and over his collarbone.

"I love seeing you like this," I admitted. My voice was so husky, but I wanted to compliment him the way he did me. He needed it too. "So free and open to me when you're yourself. I could stare at your body for hours, feel your hands on me for days. I've never felt anything like this but with you."

"Oh, Ria..." he ground out, "it is taking more restraint than I ever knew I had to not relentlessly fuck you again. I love watching you fall apart under me."

Licking my lips, I said softly, "I'm yours. Take me however you want."

Kova didn't hesitate. Gripping my hips, his fingers dug into me, nails scoring my skin as he drove his cock in and out with skill. Thrusting sinfully hard three more times, he was coming. He held me so resolutely and shoved his way in so fucking deep that I felt a little tearing again, but I didn't tell him to stop. His warm cum leaked from me down my ass. It made me feel good, sexy and wanted, to see him aroused from me.

Chest blushing from ecstasy, he looked at me, and said, "I am sorry. I should not have finished inside of you, but I do not know what happens to me. With you, I do not think clearly. I am consumed with *us*. This obsession takes over and I lose control and make stupid decisions. Only with you, Ria. Only with you do you make me do and wish for things I should never." He panted like he was trying to catch his breath. "I will be better about that. No more after this. I will buy us condoms."

"It's okay. I do too." I swallowed hard. "I like when you come inside of me," I said honestly.

Tears instantly climbed the back of my eyes and I sniffled. I didn't want to cry, not after what we'd just shared but I couldn't stop it from happening either. Kova was worried about pregnancy. While I appreciated that, it also hurt because after what I'd discovered, having children one day seemed like another dream that I might not ever reach.

"Ria? What is wrong? Am I hurting you?" Kova pulled out and wrapped me in his arms, nestling me to his chest. We laid face to face on our sides with the blanket around us. Intimate. Like we'd done it every night of our lives.

"No, not at all."

He frowned, and a tear slipped from the corner of my eye from the reality of my situation.

I looked into his eyes and my jaw trembled. "It will be incredibly difficult to get pregnant with my illnesses. I think it's why I never did before. All those times we had sex, and when I took the Plan B, sometimes I took it late. Thank God I didn't get pregnant, but I should have." I paused and sadness cast in his eyes. "So you coming inside me doesn't worry me at all. Of course I'll get Plan B tomorrow just to be safe, but I'm not concerned like I used to be."

CHAPTER 27

His brows bunched together. "I do not understand. What do you mean?"

"I mean because I have both lupus and kidney disease. I'm stage four, Kova. Both mess with fertility, so it'll be a struggle to get pregnant. Everything I've read and learned so far tells me that, and it makes sense now, given our history." I glanced at his neck, my fingers moving over the plump vein and pressing on it softly. "I think I've been sick for a while, years, only I just didn't know it, so both illnesses went untreated and caused irreversible damage. That's what happens and what I've been reading about. Think about it. Why did I not get pregnant? Not that I wanted to—I would've had an abortion—but I should have. We never used condoms—"

Kova cut me off.

"You know what I think?" he asked soothingly. "I think things happen for a reason, the way they are meant to. Just because you did not get pregnant does not mean you never will. Maybe there is a bigger plan for you and that is why."

"A bigger plan… Like, God? I'm not sure I believe in God. Especially not after everything that's happened."

His frown deepened. "You would have had an abortion?" he said gently but seemed upset over it.

"Yes," I said without hesitating. I frowned. At least I thought I would. Now I wasn't sure. "Why do you seem bothered by that? I thought you would be relieved."

Kova rolled me onto my back and leaned over me. He kissed my tears away and brushed back the hair that was matted to my face.

"Do you want me to be honest?"

I nodded, and Kova sighed then exhaled.

"Do I want you to get pregnant and have a kid? That is a firm fuck no. A child would ruin our lives right now. However, I would never tell you to get an abortion. Yet hearing you say that you would have for some reason does not sit well with me. I know it does not make sense. It is your life and your choice. Your body is your body and I would never tell you what to do with it." Pressing a quick kiss to my lips, Kova continued. "Listen to me. You took those pills at the correct time, Ria. I made sure of it. That is why you did not get pregnant, not because of your illnesses. Did it worry me in the past that there was a chance you could get pregnant? Yes. I have never been so reckless with anyone in my life. I have used protection, so it did panic me a bit, especially given our situation and ages. But I do believe you will have a child one day, Ria. It would be a crime if you did not pass along all the amazing qualities you have."

My jaw trembled and before I could stop them, lone tears slid down my temples. I hoped one day that would happen.

"One day at a time," he said, and I nodded.

Cupping the side of my face, Kova leaned down and kissed me softly, taking it slow and spilling his passion into me. This was the last thing I'd expected to happen, and yet I wasn't mad at myself for caving after I'd sworn up and down I never would again. Had it been two months ago, it would've been a different story. But things changed. Maybe it was time I let go and accept what he said was the truth, that he had no choice in the marriage. I'd like to think Kova had more power in such a situation, but there were so many questions I wanted to ask before I jumped to any conclusions.

Pushing into him, I rolled Kova onto his back and straddled his hips. I sat up and without asking, I looked into his eyes and reached between us for his length and positioned him at my entrance. I sank down until my clit rested on his mound. Kova seemed pleased as our bodies infused together, a rush of heat flowed through me as I felt him swell. I didn't understand all these feelings hitting me other than I felt good for once and I didn't want it to end. Tonight, I would just let go and feel.

My teeth sank into my bottom lip and I moaned knowing it wouldn't be long. Hands skimming my thighs to my hips, Kova helped guide me. My hips rotated back, forcing my clit to drag back and forth over his pubic hair. Little sounds escaped me and I fell forward, bracing myself on his stomach to hold myself up. It already felt too good and I hadn't even shifted to slide up and down, I was just taking his length and indulging myself on him. I attempted to wait for Kova, but it was a struggle while I fell deeper into the decadence. Something that felt this intense was easily addicting.

"Am I hurting you?" I asked.

Kova let out a sexy chuckle. "Impossible," he said, then helped me reach the point of no return. He hardly pulled out, just little thrusts, as I rocked harder on him. "Let go on me," he said.

I shook my head, eyes closed as I tried to fight the orgasm off. "I want you to come with me."

"Do not worry about me. I am far from done with you."

Opening my eyes, I glanced down and took Kova's body in. The firm planks of abs, his pillowed pecs and dark nipples, and the A I'd carved into him was enough to make me see fireworks. I stared at the letter and released myself on him, teeth biting into my lip as I squeezed his shaft and came so hard it took my breath away.

My body weak, Kova sat up and cupped the back of my neck. I breathed into him, finally feeling like I'd been sated. Like a huge boulder had been lifted from my shoulders and I could find a moment of absolution.

He pressed his lips to my forehead, and said, "You know I can feel your pussy contracting around my cock?"

I blushed. "Really?"

He nodded, and I said, "That's kind of embarrassing."

"Why? I love knowing I can make you feel so good. It makes me even hotter for you. I have also noticed that you need to come at least twice each time."

"I do?" I hadn't realized.

Kova nodded.

Before I could say anything, he had me up and turned around so I was on my knees with my back to his chest. His arm was wrapped around my waist to hold me up, keeping us both on our knees as he reached between us and grabbed his shaft to position it at my entrance.

"Ease down," he said, kissing my neck as I took him again.

I tensed at the sensitivity, not sure I was built for more sex right now. I was already so tender as it was, but his kisses were luscious enough to make me soften to him. My head rolled to the side and a light moan vibrated in my chest as Kova thrust into me from behind like this was his talent. I quivered at the heightened ecstasy from this angle. God, he was good at this. Thighs pressed to the back of mine, we rode the same ride of rapture together in perfect harmony. The pleasure was already too much with the way his hands roamed my naked body like he couldn't stop touching me.

"Ohh," I sighed, bearing down on him.

He turned my face to his and stared at my mouth. "These lips"—he licked the top and tugged it into his mouth—"are mine."

I drew in a little gasp. Wetness seeped down my inner thigh at his seductive tone.

"This pussy," he said, pulling all the way out, "is mine," then he reared back in. Kova was so deep at this angle.

His hand found my throat and a little spark of anticipation swelled through me. Something cold touched my skin but it was quickly replaced with the hunger of Kova's words.

"Did he kiss you the way I do? Did he make you crazy and eager enough to make you come from just a kiss the way I can?" He kissed me the way he was making love to me.

Kova's tongue was everywhere in my mouth, stroking and tugging, working me up until I was pushing my hips back into his, meeting him thrust for thrust, whimpering into him to take me harder.

"Did he?" Kova asked again, and pushed all the way in until he was seated as deep as he could go.

I shuddered around him, feeling stretched to the max and almost afraid to move. His hand tightened around my neck and a shot of fire burst through me. I wasn't going to last much longer. His width was painful, but then again with Kova, pain and pleasure went hand in hand, and I welcomed it with open arms.

Lips puffy, I broke the kiss and shook my head. "I've only ever felt like this with you."

"Did he fuck you the way I do? Did you beg for more? Did you come for him the way you do for me? Did you fall apart in his arms the way you do mine?"

I didn't have to say it for him to know the truth. He knew I only burned for him.

"No," I said breathlessly. Looking into his eyes, I told him the truth. "I couldn't come every time. And when I finally did, I had to think about you. It was the only way I could finish, imagining you were fucking me. You have ruined me for all other men."

Kova's eyes flashed wildly. His hips pumped eagerly into me faster, crueler, demanding, like he was climbing into me. Air lodged in my throat, but I didn't panic. Not when I'd experienced this in the past with him and knew what was coming. It excited me.

Kova dropped his head to my neck. His hands were in my hair. Hot thick breaths tickled my damp, heated flesh. He grunted, the delicious vibration in his chest caused chills on my back with each thrust. I felt every inch of his thick cock down to the vein I loved to touch.

This wasn't just sex. This was making love. A deep, heart-tugging, animalistic form of lovemaking that no one would understand but us. I realized I didn't want anyone to understand us. Only we mattered.

Kova held me firmly in place and I found it insanely erotic. I knew he loved the fight, so I purposely struggled against him. The strength in him, the way his hips moved against mine, I wanted to grab him and hold him close and show him how much he meant to me too.

"That is where you are wrong. There will never be another man, Adrianna. Never," Kova stated, then sank his teeth into the curve of my neck.

Ecstasy shot through me, and I let out a long moan. Bliss exploded throughout my wanton body and ignited my veins with a pleasure only he knew how to give me. My pussy throbbed and my clit ached for his tongue. I wasn't going to last much longer. My eyes rolled shut and I moaned long and loud while he licked my heated flesh. Back arching wildly, I ached for him to bring me release already. I was close to yelling out the L word, but I refrained.

"You know why that is?" he asked, his voice heavy with desire. He turned my head again to look at him. Before I could answer, he did. "Because you are mine and will always be mine." Kova surged in deeper and I whimpered because it was the truth. I was forever his. "Just like I will always be yours," he added, then kissed me without remorse or guilt, like he worshiped the ground I walked on.

His hips rolled into me like a wave crashing, hitting so deep I gasped each time. My orgasm was climbing, and his cock twitched. We were reaching the pinnacle of ecstasy.

I'd never understood what lovemaking was until now.

As his hand tightened around my neck, I blindly found his other one and brought it to my clit. I helped him stroke myself and sighed breathlessly from the lust. Kova's body hardened and I took satisfaction in that. Reaching a little farther, I wrapped my thumb and forefinger around his girth at the base and helped guide his cock back and forth into me. Our pleasure covered my hand and I squeezed harder from the slippery mess we'd created. Kova bit down on my neck and chills scored my skin. He liked it, I loved it.

"Are you mine? Really mine?" I asked out of nowhere. If I was his, it was only fair he was mine.

"I have been yours since the day you walked into World Cup, *malysh*. The moment I saw you, I knew that was it and that I would have you one day."

He didn't need to say more. I knew why things had gone the route they had. Only this time, I actually believed him.

CHAPTER 28

My thighs shook.

I reached behind me and fisted his hair, pulling on the strands as I brought his free hand to rest on my mound.

"Feel that?" I pushed his hand down as he thrust his cock inside me. He growled against my jaw. He felt what I felt and it was hot as hell. "That's your cock fucking me. In and out, you can feel yourself taking me and how deep you are.

He shook his head. "This is not me fucking you, this is me making love to you, because, *Ya lyublyu tebya, malysh. Ya lyublyu tebya.*"

My lips parted and my breathing labored at his candor, but I couldn't say it back, even though my heart ached to.

I knew better.

"Come with me, *malysh*," he said, and I nodded. I was beyond ready. "Let me show you just how good it can be." Then he kissed me roughly, biting my lips, and I gave it right back, meeting his needs.

I placed my palm over our joined bodies to feel us orgasm together. I wanted to feel his cum leak from me, to know he felt just as good as I did. My lips, swollen and plump, were spread wide. There was something sexy about our bodies and how they moved and stretched to fit our carnal needs. Kova's fingers sped up on my tender clit, and the hold he had around my neck tightened to an asphyxiating level but I didn't fight it. I couldn't. Not when I was drowning in the pleasure he gave me.

Hips thrusting harder and faster, my nails scored his cock as our bodies trembled on the edge of desire. We were both there, and we both let go.

Kova released inside me, his cock pulsating as his warm semen filled me, seeping out the sides. He coated my fingers and my pussy softened around him to soak up what he gave me. His body shook behind me and a gratified smile tipped the corners of my mouth as

I bit down on his lip. I loved knowing he felt what I did. I quickly followed, coming on him. Reaching farther, I grabbed his sack and squeezed. The hand on my throat tightened to the point I couldn't breathe, but the pleasure was so intense that I didn't care. I wanted more, and more, and more, and to never come down from this high.

Little silver stars danced in my vision as the orgasm wracked through my body. My heart beat so hard and fast and an exhausted blissful sigh rolled off my lips. An out-of-body sensation prickled down my arms that ended with my toes curling in need. Kova was right. I didn't come apart in Hayden's arms the way I did his.

Kova was showing me who he was and what he had to give. His hips hadn't stopped moving, and I was too high on this intense thirst for more to realize the smoky black clouds crawling across my vision was partially from the sensuality and depraved passion only Kova could deliver, and from the grip he had on my throat.

I released a sigh just as the darkness closed in, and felt the plush softness of my bed against my back.

Opening my eyes, I took a deep breath and blinked a few times. I looked around. I was a little foggy, my head disoriented. Kova was leaning over me, his head propped on his palm and a sensual smile on his lips. His hand was between my legs, gently, softly, stroking me through his cum. This man never got tired.

"Did I fall asleep?" I asked. My throat was raw.

"Sometimes when the pleasure is so extreme, people will pass out. You passed out."

My brows rose. That couldn't be safe. "For how long?"

"Not very long. Just a few minutes or so."

"And so you took it upon yourself to touch me like that?" I joked.

His eyes flickered with wickedness. "I like the idea of my cum deep inside you," he said and gave me a little kiss as he inserted two orgasm-soaked fingers slowly into my sore pussy. The wet suction echoed in the confinement of my room. "It makes me utterly fucking hot for you."

My back bowed, lifting my breasts into the air. "No more, Kova," I said, breaking the kiss. "I'm too sore and I'm tired."

He shook his head. "I want to touch you."

I couldn't deny him. "Fine, but I'm going to sleep." I laughed and rolled into his chest with a smile.

I felt a million times lighter, like I was normal again. His fingers stroked me, teased me, but never penetrated again. A simmer of heat kindled in me as I fell asleep. I caught myself rolling over onto his hand and grinding down when a little pinch nipped at my skin, just hard enough to send me over the edge again and into oblivion.

I'D ONLY SLEPT FOR A few hours before I was rousing to the scent of spices wafting through my condo. I sat up and got out of bed to quickly grab a shirt and slip it on. I shivered as the material draped over me, a chill setting in my bones when I realized I'd forgotten to take my medication earlier. Shit.

I rubbed my eyes with the heel of my hand feeling so exhausted but less stressed at the same time. I knew Kova was the reason for that, but I didn't know if it was because we'd succumbed to our secrets, or the sex. Or both. I didn't feel a wedge between us anymore. I didn't feel like I was a foreign object trying to find its place in the world. There was still a lot to talk about, but the pent-up anger sitting on my chest wasn't there anymore.

The wind howled outside as I left my room, and I jumped from the sound of a bang on my wall. My patio furniture was sliding around. I should've brought it inside but it was too late for that now. Not with the hurricane on us the way it was.

I stepped into the living room and stopped short when I spotted Kova standing at the stove. His back was to me and he was in nothing but the shorts he'd had on earlier. They sat extremely low on his hips, revealing the two little dimples above his ass. They were so sexy. My hands ached to be on him, to touch him. I stared in a daze, my eyes traveling higher, dancing across his bare back while I took in every muscle as he cooked. I was salivating, and not from the delicious smell emanating from the kitchen.

Kova lifted a glass of water to his lips and I took note of the beautiful, sinewy curvature of his arms. I had no idea what he was cooking, and I didn't care. I just wanted to bite him.

I drew in a breath and he turned at the sound. Our eyes met and my lips parted. I'd forgotten about his Olympic ring tattoo inked in black lengthwise along his ribs. I loved it so much but it was only noticeable when he lifted his arm or moved it to the side. Like a little secret only privy to those who were fortunate enough to see it. I was drawn to it like a goddamn magnet.

I questioned if there would ever be a time when my stomach wouldn't flutter or my feelings wouldn't rush to the surface when he was around. I wasn't sure what one would call it, but the energy when he was near was exhilarating. I craved him, and I think he craved me too.

My feet carried me to him. I glanced at the stove and briefly wondered where this variety of food had come from when I re-membered Alfred had dropped it off. It smelled divine and looked restaurant quality.

Kova placed his glass down on the marble countertop then lowered the heat and looked back at me. A lazy, happy smile formed on his face and it made me feel good. He seemed free from the restraints of his world. Uninhibited, like me. I stood before him, my head coming just below his honey-colored pecs. Kova was larger than life in my eyes, and I was so small in comparison to him.

Going on basic necessity, I reached out to touch his stomach. I needed to feel him again. Just to feel and nothing more. My fingers pressed his taut skin. His abs dipped while my nails feathered across the little fine hair. My other hand came up to touch his hip, my thumb creating a continual swirl on the incredibly delectable oblique V that accentuated his physique. I liked when he let me touch him. His gaze darkened and his eyes lowered. Earlier I'd surrendered to exactly what I promised myself would never happen again, but now, now I was a different person with different desires, cravings, and temptations. Different limitations.

It was all there, ready to shatter the surface again. Taking one last step closer, my knuckles brushed his ribs to trace over the ink. Kova sucked in a breath. His ribs contracted from my delicate touch.

"Why do you like it so much?" he asked.

I subtly shook my head, unsure of myself. I didn't have a reason why I was drawn to it.

"Maybe one day you will have one."

My eyes lit up at the possibility but were quickly doused at a thought. I wasn't sure now I'd ever get a tattoo, or make it as far as he had, but I liked the idea of having one similar to his.

"I might never get the opportunity you had." I sketched all five circles with my nail, then, without thinking, I pressed my lips to his tattoo.

"Ria," he whispered. His stomach flexed beneath my kiss. "What are you doing?"

I shrugged. "Your body is so beautiful. I can never get enough of it."

I acted purely on wild, untamed desire. Both my palms moved slowly up his chest, and when my hands danced over his nipples, he moved fast and gripped the back of my head, fisting my hair and twisting it around his hand. He yanked me so I was flushed against his hard body. We both gasped, then exhaled. This felt so right. I was shocked my body wanted him again so soon. His fingers sensually massaged the back of my head and I reveled in it. Kova's nostrils flared, his jaw ticked, and I stared at his lips with a sudden need to suck on them. Desire swirled in Kova's gaze and I blinked, melting into this enigmatic man I should stay far away from.

"You should know none of what happened between us was any of my intention when I came here today."

Then he smashed his mouth to mine. Kova's tongue slid along the seam of my lips and I opened just enough for him to thrust inside.

CHAPTER 29

rose up on my tiptoes and wrapped my arms around his broad shoulders.

We kissed like starved animals, ravaging each other as if we were each other's last meal.

We consumed each other to an unhealthy degree, taking as much as possible.

He gripped my sore body, so mean, so rough, and lifted me up. My heart was beating so wildly for him that I almost told him I loved him. I slid along him, my legs automatically wounding around his waist as our tongues twirled erotically against each other's in a forbidden dance of life and death. Kova's hand cupped the crest of my ass and hip almost cruelly. I was beginning to think he was unaware of his strength and briefly wondered if I had marks on my neck, but his fingers slid dangerously close to my sex and every thought I had vanished.

It only took seconds for me to drip with desire from Kova's kiss, which wasn't surprising. The man's mouth was a gift.

"God, I have missed you," he said between kisses. "I thought you were going to wake up with regret and hate me," he said. My heart pounded viciously against my ribs and I felt bad he feared that. I needed to tell him. "I thought you were going to throw me out. I thought we were not going to be able to talk. I definitely did not expect this."

A tiny smile pulled at my face. I shook my head. "Quite the opposite. I feel alive again, thanks to you."

Kova slammed me into the refrigerator. His body rolled into mine and I felt his erection straining against his shorts. He tugged on my hair and I squeaked. I rocked my hips into his, silently begging for more. The budding bloom of an orgasm began to glow. I locked my ankles and squeezed so he was perfectly aligned with my pussy and rubbed myself on him.

I whimpered, a frenzied covet reverberating in my chest. I was wholly addicted to him and the sexuality he brought out in me. How amazing it was. There were no words for what he made me feel, only that I wanted it all the time.

"More," I begged breathlessly.

Kova growled, and I fucking loved the sound of it. The tips of his fingers teased my sex, prodding the seam, but I couldn't take it any longer. Reaching down, I moved his hand to where I wanted it and almost came.

"No. I think you should take a break," he said.

I shook my head. "I want you. I need you, Kova, so bad. You make me forget my reality, and I needed that more than anything."

He pulled back and grinned so sexy I wanted to jump him. "You just want my cock," he said. "Is that all I'm good for, Adrianna?"

Leaning forward, I bit his lip and tugged it into my mouth. I smiled and met his gaze. "I love your cock," I admitted, then sighed into him when his tongue met mine, but he swiftly moved his hand away.

With my back bowed and shoulders pressed to the refrigerator, my hips came off the cold appliance to get more of his cock. I moved his hand back to where I wanted it and he growled again, this time not liking my assertiveness because he pulled his hand away quickly.

He wanted to play like that. Fine, I could too.

I reached between us to palm his dick through his shorts, rubbing it to build friction, making sure to show attention to his sack too.

Kova exhaled a heavy breath and moaned, pressing his forehead to mine. "I love this untamed side of you." Then he bit my lip, tugging on it with his teeth.

I yelped and wetness seeped from my pussy. I slapped his bare back so he'd let up, but he didn't. Kova jerked on my lips, much harder this time, crueler than I'd expected. I felt a sharp pinch and gripped his cock, squeezing his swollen head in return. I was too delirious with pleasure and pain and undulated into him again. He grunted in satisfaction and slapped the door next to me. Kova thrust his hips harshly against my pelvis and shoved his tongue back into my mouth where I tasted blood. My blood. He'd bitten me to the point of bleeding.

I pulled back and he cupped my jaw with both his hands. Hair matted my face. I looked into his eyes and knew his glossiness mirrored mine.

"I made you bleed," he whispered, his gaze trained on my mouth. His hoarse tone was somewhat animalistic and it made my heart race. I felt a trickle of something slide down my jaw. "I made you bleed," he said again, as if needing to hear his own voice.

"It's only fair since I cut you."

"I love that you marked me. It took every ounce of self-control I had not to tear your clothes off and have you do it while I fucked you."

I gasped at the enticing thought.

"You want that," he stated. "You want to feel the knife press into my skin while you come on my cock."

My lips parted, cheeks flushing with embarrassment. I couldn't answer that honestly.

Kova flattened his tongue and pressed it to my chin, dragging it up where the drip was and licked it clean before kissing me deeply. I kissed him back with the same intensity, tasting the rich blood on my tongue. I was thoroughly spellbound by it and allowed him to lick my mouth all around, lapping at it before kissing me again.

"Kova." I panted. "Jesus…"

"I know," he said, reading my thoughts, knowing I wasn't asking for sex.

Reaching for his shorts, I tried to push them down. His pubic hair tickled my fingers, exciting me, but Kova pulled back and locked eyes with me.

"No," he said, stopping me.

"Yes."

"*Malysh*, no. You need rest."

I smirked and held still for a moment, but pushed the elastic waistband down farther. Per usual, Kova wasn't wearing boxers. His eyes glazed and his lips parted in pure erotic bliss. I smiled lazily. The back of my fingers grazed his cock and I slipped my hand inside his shorts, pushing them down his hips. I cupped his firm, round ass and pulled him to me. His skin was so soft and smooth and full of muscle.

"I just want to feel you," I begged softly. I stroked Kova, feeling the veins twirl down his length. "You know I love this the most," I said, and pressed on the vein.

His face was a mixture of confusion and smugness. I wanted to feel the flatness of his abs as my hands slid down to cup his balls, the thickness of his thighs as I held on to them. I loved Kova's body. Maybe not *him* at times, but his body, I could admit to loving that.

Kova shuddered as I caressed his length. He kissed me, softly, slowly, tenderly. As I brought my hand up, wetness hit my wrist. I glanced down at the swollen purple crown pressed against my pussy and saw a pearly white drop of liquid. Using my thumb and index finger, I rubbed it over his head, then an idea hit me. He moaned, guttural and hot, loving the attention I was focusing on his cock. His head rolled back and I pinched the tip. He sighed and clenched his jaw, releasing a breath. I pinched again and saw the vein in his neck pulse.

"Why do you do this to me?" he bit out. "Fuck."

My thighs trembled around his hips as he muttered something in Russian against my mouth, then he slowed his kissing.

"Let me down," I said against his mouth. Kova looked at me in confusion. "Let me down and turn off the stove."

His eyes widened. He'd forgotten he'd left it on, but I hadn't. As he lowered me to the floor, he reached over and switched the stove off. Still sandwiched between him and the refrigerator, I got on my knees and looked up at him. My body might have been sore, but my knees were okay, and I could—wanted—to give this to him.

His cock stood erect and thick against his toned stomach. Grabbing his hips, I gently slid his shorts down to his ankles. Kova was a sight at this angle, a beautiful virile sight. A man who made me ache for things I couldn't name or explain, something riskier that provoked an intensity between pain and pleasure. Much like gymnastics.

"What are you doing?" I asked as he pulled away. "Let me do this for you."

"No." He moved to pull away again, but I dug my nails into his thighs.

"I want to. Let me give this to you."

Before he could protest again, I took him into my mouth and wrapped my tongue around his length. I tasted myself on him and sucked hard. At least, I tried to. His body became lax. He brought his arms up and rested them against the refrigerator, laying his head on his forearms. Kova shuddered, releasing a moan so primal and unhindered I couldn't help but wonder what he had bottled up inside for that kind of relief to break free.

Taking him as deep as I could, which was only halfway or else I would've gagged, I suctioned my lips around him as much as possible and glanced up. His strength was more pronounced at this angle, and I could see every powerful, pliable curve and arc of muscle in his magnificent body. But his face was twisted in a blend of gratification and shame. The very two words that defined our illicit relationship.

Using my hand, I wrapped my fingers around the base and slid them up and down in sync with my mouth. Something told me he liked a tight squeeze, so I tightened my hold, digging my nails into his shaft. He drew in a breath when my tongue twirled around his heat and stroked it up and down.

"Ria…more."

"Tell me what to do. I don't know what I'm doing." I dug my nails in more and reached for his balls, mimicking the motion.

Kova let out a sexy growl and I smiled around his thick erection, knowing I was doing it right.

"Just like that," he whispered.

His hand came down and cupped the back of my head, pushing me into his painstakingly slow rocking pelvis. Kova groaned deep and low as he grew in my mouth, and a slight saltiness coated my tongue. His movement, high from pleasure, made me needy and hot for him.

"Suck harder."

The sucking was getting a little harder on my jaw and cheeks, but when I did what he asked, Kova released another moan and it made it worth the ache. The sounds escaping his lips were so incredibly erotic and I wanted to hear him do it again.

"Scrape your teeth *gently* down my cock and flatten your tongue." He slowly rocked into my mouth again. "Oh fuck… *Malysh*, what… Do not… Oh God." He drew the last word out with a slow roll of his hips. He couldn't formulate words and I basked in the glory that I was making him feel good.

His fingers gripped my hair and knotted it into a twist as he held my face pressed to his hips for a few seconds. I jerked my head to the side and flinched from the hair pulling and accidently bit down. I thought he'd be mad that I hurt him, but I tasted another gush of liquid on my tongue that told me he'd actually liked it.

I swallowed. Kova was a freak.

"Move your hands," he ordered.

"Where do I put them?" I asked with him still in my mouth. It came out garbled, but he knew what I'd asked.

Kova grabbed my wrists and wrapped them around until I was cupping his ass. Kova's dick was long. There was no way I could take his entire length into my mouth and not gag. The kind of vulnerability that came with this position worried me, but I let go and gave this to him.

Shifting his feet, he stepped closer and placed both hands on my jaw to hold my face. There wasn't much space left between me and the kitchen appliance pressed to my back, so I wasn't sure where he thought he was going.

"Relax your throat, *malysh*."

CHAPTER 30

Unsure of what that meant, I glanced up and met Kova's eyes. He saw my confusion and repeated what he'd said, then slid further into my mouth. My brows furrowed and my tongue automatically blocked him from proceeding. There was no room left for him to go deeper.

"See?" he said. "Loosen your shoulders."

Kova reached down and tenderly massaged my throat with his fingers. A shot of pleasure went straight to my pussy and my eyes rolled shut. I was ready to jump his bones. Puzzled wasn't a strong enough word to describe why I liked this so much—his hands on my neck coaxing me to learn a sexual act—but I did. A lot.

"Breathe through your nose and flatten your tongue so I can get to your throat."

I moved to pull away to compose myself a little better, but he pushed me back and kept me there. Clearing my mind, I focused on his words and did as he asked.

"Yes… Just like that, Adrianna. Just…like…that…" He slowly pushed in more, hitting the back of my throat.

I gagged and choked, my eyes filling with tears. He pulled away and I quickly inhaled before he was back at it again, my eyes watering now. His cocked tapped the inside of my throat with each thrust and guide of his hips, his hands threaded in my hair and massaged my neck at the same time.

"I want to feel the back of your throat. I need to get deeper…" He groaned. "Oh, the thoughts you give me, my girl, the things I want to do to you…"

That was the most bizarre thing I'd ever heard. Why the hell would he want to touch the back of my throat? I had no desire to ever touch the back of *his* throat.

"Have you ever swallowed?"

I shook my head no, and his eyes darkened. I hadn't. I'd never given a real blow job before.

I pulled back and quickly said, "I told you I didn't know what I was doing."

His mouth tugged into one of the sexiest grins I'd ever seen on him. Then he began a deep and hard roll with his hips, driving into my mouth so artfully.

"I am almost there… Oh, fuck. Just remember to breathe through your nose and loosen up, it will all slide down and you can swallow."

Okay. Sounded easy enough.

But it wasn't. Not even close.

Kova's cock slid over my tongue and past my throat into my neck. My fucking neck! The sounds that came out of him were not normal. They were carnal and sensuous and deeply hot. Something warm slid down my throat and his hand massaged the outside of my neck. I moved to pull back as panic set in me from the large obstruction in my esophagus, but my head hit the stainless steel refrigerator. My eyes watered profusely. It was like he knew my next move because he found my wrists and held them behind him. My nails scored his ass cheeks as he pushed farther into my mouth.

I was going to die from giving head. My family would be shamed for all eternity.

"Oh yes, take it all, take it all." He came…a lot.

His cock pulsated and stiffened. I wasn't prepared for the thickness of his semen or how awfully salty it was, but it filled my mouth, and if I didn't do as he said and gulp it back, I was going to throw up. I could bite down, but he'd probably like it.

I had to make a decision fast.

"Swallow it, Ria. Swallow every fucking drop."

My fingers dug into the seam of his cheeks, and it was in that moment I decided to do something no straight man would ever want. At least, I didn't think they'd want.

My throat contracted and I closed my eyes as I drank him down. It wasn't easy but I focused and managed so I could give him what he wanted. And I wanted to. I needed him to have this.

Kova yelled out in ecstasy while my fingers skimmed his round ass toward forbidden territory. Just when I thought he'd pull away, he did the opposite and trembled against me as I poked and prodded the puckered little hole with one finger. His butt cheeks clenched together, and I pushed deeper.

He fucking loved it.

Kova loved it so much, he let go of my wrists and cupped my jaw and the back of my head as he finished coming in my mouth. He shoved himself down and even though tears ran down my face, I kept sucking until I swallowed every single drop. He was sexy as fuck when he moaned.

"Never better," he slurred in a trance, and I pushed my finger in one last time. "Oh, fuck…I have never come so hard in my life."

He withdrew from my mouth before I could swallow the last drop and it dripped down my chin. Kova lifted me up. My legs automatically wound around his hips as he smashed his mouth to mine, not caring that I hadn't swallowed the last little bit of his cum, and he kissed me hard. I wrapped my arms around his neck and kissed him back with the same intensity. So much so my heart throbbed for this beast of a man who could be so cruel and passionate at the same time. Something forfeited inside me, something I was holding back. Something more than liking him, more than lusting after him.

His hand found the back of my hair and his tongue delved into my mouth, consuming me, not giving a fuck he that was tasting himself as he kissed the shit out of me. We pulled back at the same time, panting heavily into each other. His eyes exposed a collection of feelings, twisting my stomach with the impulse to listen.

There was that L word again.

I offered him a tender smile. He wiped my chin with his thumb and I grabbed it to suck it clean.

"Who are you?" he asked in sheer wonderment.

I laughed and shook my head, then slid down his body to stand.

Kova kissed my lips. He pulled his shorts up, but not all the way. I had a partial view of the width of his cock peeking out. I licked my lips. He was too sexy for his own good.

"I like this look on you," I said and rubbed his light mound of hair. With each passing moment I spent with Kova, I found I had a little less modesty.

He brushed my hand away, veiling a grin. "Now that we have worked up an appetite, let me finish cooking for us." He smirked, then slapped my ass as I walked away.

Before I sat down, I walked to where all my medicine bottles were lined up. I studied them, hating that I had to take so many pills and that I had to do so for the rest of my life. I wasn't sure what would happen since I'd missed a dose—hopefully nothing too extreme. I wasn't sure how much more I could handle.

"Don't watch me," I said quietly when I felt the weight of his gaze on me.

I uncapped a bottle and poured out two capsules.

Kova handed me his water glass, stirring the food on the stove with his other hand.

"Want to talk about it?"

I downed the first two capsules without looking at him, then I opened the next bottle.

"Not yet."

"I will take it. That is better than a no."

I stared straight ahead, trying to figure out a way to avoid this conversation. I took the next set of pills.

"You already know everything, Kova."

"But I did not hear it come from you."

I turned toward him, frustration simmering below the surface. Kova turned off the stove and looked my way.

"Why do you need to hear it from me?" I asked. "To hear that I'm scared? That I don't know when I'll be stage five and that terrifies me? I'm fragile right now, okay, Kova? Not talking about it is the only way I can deal with it."

Kova's voice softened. "I am asking so I can feel what you are feeling. So I can get inside your head and see where you are, what I can do to help you. I told you, we are a team. I exhale, you inhale. I want to hear from your lips what is going on in your head so I can get on the same level as you and understand. You do not have to do it alone."

My jaw trembled. I hadn't expected that or the compassion in his eyes or for it to wrap around my heart. It moved me to observe him with a little more kindness. He was trying, just like I was.

"Do you want to talk about Joy, your wife, and the way they blackmailed you into marriage?"

"I know it seems that way, but yes, I do want to talk about it. I am not ready to discuss the fact that both the women in our lives are dirty little serpents, but I do want you to know why I married Katja and that it was not something I wanted."

"But at one time you did. One time you wanted to marry her and planned to," I retorted, then cringed, wondering when I would let that go.

"Yes, I did. I even bought the ring for when the time was right."

My burning heart dropped into my stomach and I sighed, looking away. "I hadn't known that. I shouldn't have said anything, I'm sorry."

"Do not be sorry. I really want us to be open with each other," he said, and I narrowed my eyes at him. He chuckled. "I am a work in progress, but I promise I am trying. I just want to focus on you right now."

I chewed the inside of my lip in contemplation and finally nodded. "I feel like I'm taking another huge risk for you, Kova. One hand is saying trust you, the other is saying run far away. Please, do *not* lie to me ever again. I honestly don't know if I could handle it if you do."

Regret weathered him. "I am eternally sorry for what happened and the way I handled things. I did and said a lot of things I didn't mean. It was not right and I am not making excuses for my actions, but I was backed up against a wall. Once you know everything, then you will understand. At least, I hope you will."

Turning back toward the bottles lined up against the wall on the counter, I stared at them, hoping they would give me a sign or an answer to the questions in my head and the feelings in my heart that I tried to ignore.

Reaching for the third bottle, I uncapped it and dumped the pills into my hand, then threw them back and swallowed them. Only four more bottles to go. At this point, I didn't have much left to lose.

CHAPTER 31

Kova placed the large pasta bowl I didn't even know I had on the counter.

I glanced inside as he twirled the food around then spooned it into two bowls and placed one in front of me. My eyes widened. Grilled chicken and asparagus in an Alfredo sauce. The steamy delicious aroma filled the air and my stomach growled. I hadn't had this kind of meal in ages.

"Wow. I didn't know you could cook like this." I laughed.

Kova sat next to me. "I actually love to cook. Last time I did, you did not eat."

I definitely didn't know that about him.

"Thank you," I said.

My heart shifted, like a small piece that had broken was glued back in place. Kova was a good guy. Despite his outlandish ways, he had a good heart. Albeit a tarnished one, but nothing that couldn't be cleaned and wiped anew.

"I know we do not have a normal"—he looked at me in search of the right word, but typical Kova and his lack of English mixed it up—"relationship, but I am always here for you. And I do not mean that on a coach/gymnast level. I hope you know by now I sincerely more than care about you."

That was the thing. He had been there for me, and much more as of late. I didn't loathe it, but I didn't love it either. I needed to find a way to come to terms with it.

"Just please, don't baby me. I know you were probably careful with me since you found everything out, but don't be. In order for me to be the best, I have to train hard, and part of that is you treating me like any other person training under you. Otherwise it will mess with me."

He stared at me for a long moment and rubbed the back of his neck. I thought he was going to disagree, but he surprised me.

"I will promise to go hard on you the same way I used to, if you promise to tell me when you are not feeling well. It can be as simple as a headache, but I need to know. Deal?"

I lit up. "Deal."

Kova put his hand out to shake on it, but instead, I threw my arms around his shoulders and sealed the deal with a hug.

Twirling the pasta on my fork, I took a bite and the flavor exploded in my mouth.

"Oh, my God! This is amazing!" I said, then twirled more onto my fork.

Appreciation spread throughout his face. This was restaurant quality. I should've known better. Anything Kova sets out to do, he does well.

An easy calmness settled in the air while we ate. Rain drenched my patio and hit the sliding glass door, but there was something rather peaceful about this moment. There wasn't an awkward second between us and I loved that. Kova had seconds, but I was too full after the rather large portion he'd given me.

Once we were finished, Kova took our bowls to the sink. I watched as he cleaned up my kitchen and thanked him again.

"I can't remember the last time I ate something so delicious or was this full. I probably won't need to eat again until tomorrow."

He chuckled, and I loved how light and airy it sounded. Relaxed. It was surreal how this moment felt completely normal, like there was no huge age gap between us, no rules, no one to offer their two cents to us or look at us in disgust. Like we'd done this a million times. I wondered if this was what it was like to be in a full relationship with him.

"Oh, God," I said suddenly, clutching myself as cramps rocked my abdomen. My stomach quivered, little bubbles swaying and popping inside me.

"What is wrong, *malysh*?" he asked, turning off the sink and drying his hands with a cloth. He eyed me with concern.

I shook my head. Hunching over, a cramp tore through my stomach and bile climbed up my throat. Heat curled through me raking its claws across my lower abdomen. Kova came over to help me up, but I couldn't stand. My legs trembled, and I felt weaker than I'd been in years. My hand gripped the table for leverage just as Kova was there to catch me.

"My stomach. It hurts so bad. I need the bathroom. Now," I insisted, chewing my lip raw. Anything to not focus on the shredding of my stomach.

I tried to take a few steps, but my legs were of no use. My knees buckled and I almost fell to the floor in a heap, but Kova was quick and scooped me up, cradling me to his chest.

"I have you," he said, his lips pressed to my forehead.

I covered my mouth, and muttered, "Hurry, Kova. I'm gonna be sick." I felt the food I'd just eaten coming up and prayed it stayed down, trying desperately to not vomit all over him.

Kova flipped on the lights and then let go of my legs, keeping a hold on my chest to help me stand. My sluggish body slid down his tall frame.

The sight of the toilet triggered me. I gagged and covered my mouth, fighting the vomit, but it was of no use. My stomach clenched and cramped. I ran from Kova's hold and lunged for the toilet. My knees slammed down to the tile floor with a loud whack and I bent over. The pain didn't register in my head. I was just in time to expel everything I'd eaten. My fingers curled around the ledge and the smell of the water coated my nostrils. Everything came up.

Tears slid down my cheeks as every conceivable disgusting sound spewed from my lips. Embarrassment burned my cheeks. I wanted to die. This was not how I'd pictured tonight going.

Though I was pretty sure my stomach was empty, I couldn't stop hurling. My hair stuck to my face and snot dripped from my nose. I tried to shove at Kova's bare chest but I got nowhere. He wasn't budging.

"Go away," I choked out. I didn't want him to see me like this.

"Let me help you," he said sympathetically.

Thankfully, Kova did what he was good at and ignored my pleas.

He pulled my hair back, making sure to get the strands that were stuck to my damp face. Some of the tips had dipped into the vomit and I was instantly hot all over. Kova flushed the toilet, and a little mist hit my face. My teeth gnashed together as I tried to fight throwing up again, but it didn't help. Eyes clenched shut, I leaned deeper into the bowl, unavoidably inhaling the rancid water as my body trembled violently. The back of my neck burned. Little pebbles of moisture beaded my tepid skin as I broke out in a sweat. Slowly, I opened my eyes only to realize it was a huge mistake because I vomited one more time.

Kova held my hair back with one hand and rubbed my back with his other. He flushed the toilet, then handed me a washcloth. I wiped my face, gagging.

When I was positive there was nothing left in my stomach, I shut the lid and folded my arms over it to rest my head. I couldn't get up. Everything felt swollen—my eyes, my lips, my body, my feet. I felt like I had a fever. I was uncomfortably bloated and a little pulse thrummed under every square inch of my skin. I felt so incredibly weak down to my bones. I just wanted to crawl into bed and hibernate under the covers. Kova took the wash cloth from my hand and gently dabbed and wiped the side of my face and neck as I stared at the wall in a daze.

"Thank you," came out in a broken whisper. My throat burned. "There's nothing worse on this planet than throwing up in front of someone. I'm sorry."

"Nonsense. It is normal and does not bother me. But I think you may have spewed your pills."

My eyes fluttered. "I feel disgusting." I licked my parched lips and I became nauseated all over again. As if he read my mind, Kova stood and turned on the shower.

"I think you look beautiful as always."

I almost laughed.

Using every ounce of willpower left in me, I held onto the wall and used my thighs to stand. Despite all the muscle in my body, I was useless. A few steps and I was in front of the shower reaching to feel the warmth. The heat engulfed my face and I sighed in content, feeling a little better. I loved steaming hot showers.

Drained with barely any energy to stand, I looked at myself in the mirror right as I reached to pull my shirt off and caught sight of my face. Christ on a stick. Mascara streaked my face like a badly designed maze. My full lips were abnormally swollen and red, and my eyes were puffy and bloodshot.

Exhaling a sigh, I tugged on the seam of my shirt and attempted to pull it over my head, but I was too faint and didn't have the strength. Kova walked back in just in time to see my struggle and took over. I didn't object. He gently pulled the shirt off, then dropped it to the floor.

Steam filled the bathroom. I glanced down. My stomach was caved in, hollowed, with a steep slope toward my ghastly protruding hips. I knew I'd lost a ton of weight due to the illnesses, but it was something I'd learned to ignore.

A hiss flew from his lips with a subtle shake of his head. "Ria," Kova whispered in disbelief, the back of his hand grazing down my pelvis. "I did not notice before."

He was concerned at the sight, and quite frankly, I was too now that I finally let myself look in the mirror.

"I'm fine. Just help me, please," I said, reaching out for him.

"You are too small," he said more under his breath than to me. I pursed my lips together. I hated to hear the pity that was conveyed in his voice. "I do not like this, Ria. You are wearing yourself down too much."

"Kova, please," I said, shutting him down.

He wasn't wrong, but I didn't want to hear it. I knew I was wearing myself down too much, but I told myself this was what I wanted and what I needed to do. I didn't want to be treated any differently, especially not now. My dream had become an addiction, and I'd willingly done anything and everything to achieve that high, now more than ever. I may have destroyed myself in the process, but I wasn't going to stop. I was too close to the pinnacle of victory. There would be no change come tomorrow.

I stepped under the waterfall spray and closed my eyes. The heated water felt heavenly as it prickled down my skin. There was just something about a scorching hot shower that I loved. Squeezing a dollop of shampoo into my hand, I began washing my hair, but was suddenly overcome with fatigue. There was a rumbling in my stomach and the bubbles were popping again. I wasn't sure why was so sick, or why I felt the way I did now. It was a probably a culmination of things and I knew moving forward I'd have to make sure I was more careful about myself. My arms fell to my sides and I exhaled in a huff. I just wanted to go to sleep.

The glass door slid open and I looked over my shoulder. My heart soared as Kova stepped under the water until his chest was pressed to my back. I was so grateful.

He wrapped his arms around my shoulders, and I leaned back and took in a moment of harmony. He dropped a light kiss to the top of my head. Kova brought a sense of security that I soaked up each time and never questioned. A peace in me that I just rolled with that no one else ever gave me.

The water around our feet ran pink from the dried blood. I'd forgotten we both had it on us. We rinsed and lathered each other, and I made sure to be gentle around the A while I cleaned him. Kova washed me in the most affectionate way possible. He took care of me like he was devoted to me…and I let him. Because it felt right. Because it didn't occur to me to not let him. Because within these walls, it felt normal for us to be and feel what was natural between us, regardless of age.

CHAPTER 32

oach or not, Kova was the only person who gave me this soothing comfort, making me feel like everything was going to be okay.

I needed his strength right now. I didn't care that he had a wife or that there was a hurricane outside. Maybe that made me selfish, but when it came to Kova, my heart beat only for him. My accomplishments were for him just as much as they were for me.

God, I hated being so emotional. Everything was rising to the surface and I couldn't stop it.

Stepping out of the shower, Kova handed me a towel and said, "Dry your hair and wrap it up. I will take care of the rest."

He studied me, his eyes roaming over my face. I shot a fleeting glance in the mirror. I looked like death.

I put my hand up. "I know… I look like the ghost of Lucifer."

The corner of his eyes crinkled and Kova laughed. "I am pretty sure that is impossible," he said, hanging the towel up. "You could never resemble the devil. How do you feel?"

"Much better actually. I'm so tired, but I don't feel as sick anymore." I bit my lip. "I'm so sorry about that. I don't know what happened. I think I just need to rest a little."

I followed Kova out of the bathroom, my gaze on his perfectly round butt and the two little dimples above it as he walked toward my bed. I was infatuated with his body and could stare at it for hours.

The power flickered and my heart stopped for a second.

"Shit. The storm," I said.

"Where is your lighter?" Kova asked.

I pointed to my nightstand. He opened the drawer and shifted things around. He pulled out a tube and I drew in a mortified breath. Not the lighter he was searching for. He held it up and looked at me with one brow arched. Shit. I'd forgotten I'd thrown my lube in there for the times when it was just me and myself.

I reached for it but Kova pulled away. "Stop embarrassing me and put that away."

He grinned and I wanted to junk punch him for it. One by one, he lit every candle around my room just in time for the power to go out completely.

"Good thing we showered when we did." He joked. Handing me the lighter, he said, "But something tells me you do not mind being dirty."

I hid a smile and dropped it back into the drawer. Thank goodness he couldn't see the blush that crept up my cheeks.

"Get in the center of the bed and lie down," Kova ordered.

Once I did, Kova climbed on and lifted each ankle so my knees were bent, my body open to him. I watched him with unfazed curiosity. Little by little he stole my modesty and turned me into a vixen with loose morals.

He took my towel, and starting at my neck, he patted me dry, moving down each arm and breast. Kova was hard as a rock, his erection straining and the tip a deep purple, but he didn't try anything, knowing I wasn't feeling well. He made his way to my stomach and thighs, down my legs. Dropping the towel to the floor, he sat between my legs and pushed my knees apart. I widened them further for him until I was completely exposed.

"Kova, what are you doing," I whispered, lust filling my tone.

"You will sleep soundly after this. Let me give you what you want. You need this."

I nodded, hoping he was right. I couldn't remember the last time I 'd slept well.

Kova dipped a finger inside of me and curled it. My thighs quivered, and I clenched around him. He slipped another in. This wasn't what I'd expected, but I didn't protest. His rough thumb circled my throbbing clit and I bit down on my bottom lip. My hips rolled toward him in a slow, sensual wave, feeling the touch of him in the most delicious way.

Our eyes met. Neither one of us said a word. He continued to pleasure me slowly, in and out, in and out. Aside from the rain outside, our heavy breathing and the sensual suctioning were the only sounds in the room. It was erotic. Lips parted and knees leisurely widened on their own. I was too aroused to remember I wasn't feeling well.

It wasn't long until Kova's tongue found my center and licked me to the point of orgasm, only to pull back. I yelled out his name, begging for him to let me finish, but he told me to wait. I wanted so badly to hold his head down and smash his face between my legs. Kova was a bittersweet tease. I needed that pressure, that force, and all he did was hold it above my head and dangle it in front of me. His tongue caressed my sensitive clit while his fingers slid in and out, and just when I thought he was done, his teeth gently scraped over my swollen pussy lips…

And sank into the tender skin.

I yelled out and arched my back, twisting my body into him and clutching the sheets in my fists. He ignored me and bit my other side. A rush of desire seeped from me. I moaned, confused by how much I liked this. My eyes rolled to the back of my head and I was suddenly on cloud nine, floating in a beautiful bliss, high as my hips undulated in sweet desire and sexual frustration.

"You are very much like me in many ways, Ria." I looked at him, his face suctioned to my pussy. Deep down, I knew in many ways it was true. "You like a bite of pain with your sex, and I like to give it."

"How do I know I like it?" I asked hardly recognizing my voice.

Kova didn't reply, instead showing me by giving me one long stroke of his tongue, followed by a tight suck to my clit. I moaned in ecstasy, drowning in him.

"I know everything about you, *malysh*. I can tell by the way your body reacts. If you were not aroused this much by it, you would not be this wet."

With his eyes locked on mine, this time he bit my inner thigh, but then kissed it right after. I watched his tongue slip through his lips. Legs widening, I angled my pussy toward his face and rolled my hips up, praying he'd go back to it harder. His teeth tugged on my skin and desire leaked out of me.

"Oh, oh, oh," I moaned, my legs scissoring the sides of this face. "Kova… I can't hold on much longer." I was utterly aching to the point of pain for him and for release.

I leaned up and looked at the marks he'd made. I watched against the flickering candlelight as he flattened his tongue and licked the little crimson pearls. It pooled to new droplets and he licked again. But I couldn't formulate words because his thumb rubbed my throbbing clit in fast circles and I was too turned on watching him drink me in.

Without moving his head, Kova lifted his eyes to mine. He exhaled through his nose and the heated breath cascaded across my pussy. He was a wicked man. The corners of his delicious mouth curved up just slightly into a crooked grin before his head descended. The tip of his nose danced over my mound. My stomach swirled, this time in a good way, as he parted his lips and his teeth sank into my clit.

"I cannot get enough of you," he said, his voice hoarse.

A string of unexplainable sensations shot through me. My toes curled and I clenched around his pumping fingers on the edge of something amazing. I didn't scream or yell out. I couldn't. I panted, gasping for air. Kova rendered me breathless, certain he punctured the skin thoroughly by the way he pulled on my flush, his tongue sucking at the same time.

"Oh, Kova…" I whimpered, unable to tear my eyes from what he was doing. My nipples hardened to hard points. "I'm about to go… I need to…"

"Not yet," he said around my flesh.

He pulled his fingers out and licked them clean, then sat up on his knees. His cock was erect and bare, the tip purple as it strained between us.

He slid his hands under my lower back and lifted my hips, massaging them. Looking directly into my eyes, he said, "I made love to you last time, but this time, I need to fuck you until you remember who loves you."

I sighed under my breath, my heart clenching. I needed him just as much.

"Say it. Tell me, Adrianna."

"Kova." His name was a whisper on my lips.

In one swift motion, he slid all the way in. We both moaned in unison, our bodies fused together in the most deliciously illicit way. My thighs quivered to adjust to his size and there was a pinch from being stretched, but I loved it and reached for him.

Kova leaned over, his lips pressed to my neck, his breath hot. "Fuck, I do not know how I am going to do this." He pulled out then thrust back in hard and fast, my hips arched taking him deeper. "Be married to her but only want you."

No female in the world ever wanted to be the other woman. I never wanted to, never really thought about it until now, but when you're faced with losing in the situation like I was, you have a change of mind and heart and take whatever you can get.

"Then don't give me up," was all I could say. The thought of losing him physically hurt me. I was willing to be the other girl. "Don't leave me."

"I do not think I can," he said between thrusts. "I love being inside you. I love everything about you. I cannot keep going on like this without you by my side."

Kova pulled out and I cried in protest. "What are you doing?"

Naturally, he ignored me. Kova got off the bed and stood at the end of it. He grabbed my ankle and yanked me to the edge and flipped me over. He clutched both hips and hitched me up.

"Face on the bed. Arch your back."

I did as he said and turned my head to watch him. Breathing heavily, I thought he was going to slide back in, but I should've known better.

Pulling my butt cheeks apart, he bent over and dragged his flat tongue from the tip of my clit all the way up to my little puckered hole. I reached out and fisted the sheets, sighing as he circled the entrance.

"What is it with you and my ass?" I could barely say the words.

"One day you will beg me to take this ass."

"Never," I whispered as he devoured my pussy, his finger trying to penetrate the little hole. My eyes rolled shut in blissful agony. Why did it feel so much better at this angle? "I want to sit on your face," I admitted.

"Let me fuck you first, then you can," he said, then thrust in so hard and fast I wasn't expecting it.

This time I screamed. I shot up, but Kova pushed me down, making sure I took every inch of him at this angle. He rocked into me, forcing my hips into a roll and clutching my butt cheeks. He had a mean grip on my hips as he thrust so ruthlessly. His hips pounded my ass, slamming into me with brutal force, pulling me to him while he thrust into me at the same time. His cock hit deep and hard, penetrating without reserve. My bed slid across the floor from how hard he was driving into me. I clenched up and he pressed a hand to my back again forcing me to stay down.

"Ah, ah, ah." I moaned somewhere between pain and pleasure.

My stomach clenched, feeling a little more pain than usual, kind of hoping he would be done already. I wasn't sure I would be able to come like this myself. He was so deep inside of me that it hurt at this angle.

"Take it. Take all of me, please. Just take me as I am," he begged, then thrust faster than he ever had and came inside of me. "Let me have you like this." He grabbed my hips, helping me take his full length all the way. "Oh, Ria… Fuck…"

The pleasure was almost too much. I watched over my shoulder, fixated on him as his head rolled back and his sexy muscles flexed then contracted. He smashed into me hard, pumping, then holding me still as he orgasmed. He scooped an arm under my waist and held me tight, his other hand squeezing the back of my neck, his cock throbbing with virility and warmth as his seed spread through me. His damp chest was pressed to my back as he grunted and groaned and drove into me with the power of a hundred men.

Okay. Maybe I was exaggerating a little bit, but that's what it felt like.

"Do not move," he said, breathing heavily.

My thighs quivered relentlessly as he pulled out. I continued to watch over my shoulder, but Kova was engrossed with my sex.

"Push it out," he said, his voice hoarse.

I shook my head but gave it to him anyway. A little plop sounded, and I shifted to look between my legs. Kova's cum dripped out of me without even having to try.

"Do it. Push my cum out and let me watch it drip down your pussy and over your clit."

"You're such a dirty man," I said, then brazenly did exactly what he'd demanded.

The thick gooeyness did exactly what he said it would do, only it didn't drop onto the bed. Two of his fingers caught it and pushed it back into my aching pussy. My hips reared back and I moaned, riding his fingers, still needing the release. Kova's eyes glistened like he was in a trance while he shoved his cum back into me.

"Kova," I said in almost a whine. "This isn't fair."

In the blink of an eye, he was on his back with his head near my headboard. "Give me that pussy. Sit on my face, *malysh*, and do not hold back."

I was a little shy, but I didn't hesitate as I crawled up his body until I was up on my knees with my hands on the headboard. I looked between us. My nipples were hard and rosy, and he was staring right at them. We'd never done this before, and I was suddenly a little embarrassed. Kova sensed it and pulled me down to his mouth.

It was all over after that.

"Oh, fuck," I said, drawing out the word.

My hips took over of their own accord. I grinded on his face, hoping I wasn't hurting him but not really caring if I was. The pleasure felt too good and I didn't want it to stop. I guess he liked it because he pulled me harder to him. I rubbed myself on him, his stubble heightening the desire while I rolled my hips over him.

"Just like that," I said breathlessly. "This might be my favorite position."

Then, he stuck two fingers in me and bit down on my clit. His free hand pinched my nipple until I saw stars.

I. Was. Done.

My orgasm hit hard, exploding through my body. It prickled my skin and throttled me to high after high. A scream of ecstasy tore from my chest as I fucked his mouth with my pussy. I reached between us and fisted his hair to pull his head as tight as I could to my sex as I grinded down and came all over his mouth. Kova took me just like I took him. My thighs quivered and squeezed his face. I was probably hurting him. Hopefully he could breathe.

My heart slowing, the orgasm faded and I released my hold on his hair, hoping I didn't pull any out. God, that was amazing. Kova had me on my back in one breath hovering above me. He brushed my hair back. His mouth wet with my pleasure and his eyes a crazy intense kind of lust flaring with emotion.

"I fucking love you," he growled, then crashed his lips to mine.

I loved him, too.

CHAPTER 33

Adrianna… Adrianna."

I was sprawled out on my stomach with my head burrowed beneath a pillow. There was a chill in my bones but I felt so hot at the same time. A hand rubbed circles on my back as I slowly stirred awake. My eyes burned like I hadn't slept very long, but the deep slumber I was coming out of said otherwise.

"Adrianna." His thick Russian accent was a whisper that seemed so far away.

"Hmm…?"

I moved the pillow off my head and brushed my hair from my face, trying to look toward the sound of his voice. I opened my eyes but they felt like they were on fire. My entire body felt like it was swelling with heat. I attempted to sit up, but my elbows gave out. I felt horrible. Lethargic and dead tired. If I didn't know any better, I'd say I was having a flare up.

Rolling onto my back, I rubbed my forehead and a soft sigh escaped off my lips.

"I'm so lightheaded." The room spun and my head felt like an inflated balloon. "What time is it?"

Kova sat down on the edge of the mattress and looked down. It was still dark, but the light from the bathroom illuminated parts of the room.

"It is almost six in the morning. I need to get to the gym."

I frowned. "What about the hurricane?"

"It has passed us and luckily did not turn into a cat four. Your power is back on."

I nodded and tried to sit up again, but Kova didn't allow it.

"No, I have practice. I need to go. I have to be there." I struggled against him, but he was so much stronger and insisted I lay down. I wasn't sure how I'd do at practice feeling the way I did, but I needed to be there.

"Absolutely not. I want you to stay in bed. You have a fever and you look awfully pale. You need rest, Ria," he urged.

Last night I vomited, and now I felt like I had the flu. My body was completely worn down and I felt sluggish. I blinked my dry eyes rapidly. Fear consumed me.

"Kova?" My voice cracked, my throat tight and in need of water. "What's wrong with me?"

Was I having a flare up again?

He leaned down and kissed my forehead. Immediately I wrapped my arms around his neck and squeezed him. He pulled me to sit on his lap and I burrowed my face in his neck as he comforted me. I was still naked, but it didn't bother either one of us.

"Nothing is wrong with you, Adrianna. You are just extremely exhausted and need uninterrupted, deep sleep. You have a fever and your cheeks are red."

I nodded. "But I can't miss practice and you promised not to treat me any differently."

He pulled back and gave me a warm smile. "I was selfish and had you many times last night. You barely slept." He looked so pleased. "And"—he held up a finger—"I told you I would not treat you differently so long as you were feeling okay. You cannot push your body or your body will completely shut down. Missing practice will be out of our hands. Stay here and sleep. Hopefully that rash will go away. I will see you tonight."

Hope filled my chest. "You're coming back?"

He nodded.

"Take my keys so you can let yourself back in. What about Katja?"

Kova gave me a look that said don't go there. So I didn't. It was on the tip of my tongue to ask if he could bring me my medicine bottles and a glass of water, but when he kissed the top of my head and whispered, "*Ty ma-yo sak-ro-vee-sche*," it wasn't long until I was drifting off to sleep, forgetting about my pills.

IT WAS DÉJÀ VU ALL over again. Kova trying to rouse me. His hand on my back, his voice far away.

I sat up, swiping my hair from my face. I was certain I hadn't moved in hours.

"God… What time is it?" I asked, looking around in confusion. My eyes were swollen, my body aching even more.

Kova tilted his head, and his eyes narrowed. "Have you been sleeping all day?"

"I don't know?" I responded softly.

"It is eight o'clock…at night."

My brows shot up and my jaw dropped. "You're kidding me. I slept for fourteen hours straight?"

Kova reached out and pressed the back of his knuckles to my forehead. His palm cupped my jaw in concern. "Are you okay? You still feel warm."

"Yeah, I'm fine. At least I think I'm fine. Apparently, I was much more tired than I thought I was… Wow."

"Your body must have needed rest more than we both thought."

I agreed and moved to the edge of the bed, dropping my legs over the side to sit next to him. I needed to find some clothes.

"I don't think I moved at all after you left."

I was sure I could sleep another ten hours. I clenched my eyes shut then opened them, still feeling so tired.

"How do you feel?" he asked.

"Honestly? I hated that I missed practice, but I feel much better." I paused, my lips forming a thin, flat line. I didn't want to speak my next set of words, but he needed to hear them. "Thanks for making me skip today. You were right, I needed it badly. If you hadn't insisted, I would've been there and who knows what would've happened."

He shrugged shamelessly. "Good thing the gym is closed tomorrow, because I do expect you at the gym bright and early Monday morning."

My heart bloomed with happiness. He was sensitive yet stern. I kind of loved it.

"I'll be there with bells on."

"Coach knows best."

A chuckle escaped me. I laid back down and cuddled under the blanket. "Don't go getting cocky on me, *Coach*." I paused, somberness overtaking me. "Can you stay?"

Kova looked at me for a long moment like he was contemplating his answer, then nodded.

"Can you do me a favor? Can you get my medicine bottles and a glass of water for me?"

"Of course."

Kova came back and placed a glass on my nightstand then lined up the bottles so I could read the labels. "Your father called me."

I froze, panic heaving through me. I sat up. "What'd you say?"

"He was concerned about you and said your phone was off. I told him I would check on you and let him know."

"Shit. My phone is in the car. I forgot all about it." He must've been so worried he couldn't get ahold of me, especially during the hurricane.

Kova opened a can of ginger ale and placed it next to the water, then he reached into his bag and revealed a sleeve of crackers. One by one I poured the pills into a pile on the comforter. A groan vibrated in the back of my throat. I hated having to take so many a day.

"Do you have your phone? I'll call him now."

He grimaced. "You broke it."

My brows shot up, remorse staining my cheeks. "I did?"

"When you slammed it down, you cracked the screen. It still works, but be careful not to touch the glass. I do not want you cutting yourself."

"I'm sorry," I said, my voice low. I did get a little heated when he was talking to his wife on the phone.

One side of his mouth tugged up. He reached into his pocket and pulled the phone out. "It is okay. Nothing that cannot be replaced." He handed it to me.

I dialed my dad.

"Konstantin?"

"No, it's me, Dad."

"Adrianna? Are you okay? Of all times you don't answer, and during a hurricane?" he roared. I clenched my eyes shut, shame filling me that I'd worried him so badly.

"I'm so sorry, Dad. My phone died and I've just been so tired and sick that I came home and went right to sleep. I think I was having a bad flare up... I don't know. I didn't mean to make you panic."

His voice morphed from angry and panic stricken to distressed and concerned. "Sick? What's wrong?"

Kova stepped out of the room to give us privacy. I opened up to my dad about how I'd been feeling lately and what's been going on, and how I forgot to take my medicine. I even went as far as to say that I'd been working myself to the bone just to take my mind off the diseases.

"Sweetie, you can't be so hard on yourself. If you need someone to talk to, I can find you the best therapist on that side of the coast."

I contemplated it for a moment and glanced down at the pile of pills I hadn't swallowed yet. "It might not be a bad idea, but let me see if I can work on it first."

My front door closed and Kova walked back into my room. Holding his phone to the side, I asked him, "Where did you go?"

"To your car to get your phone." He held it up, waving it toward me. I smiled and mouthed thank you.

"What happened?" Dad asked. I relayed the events of last night, only telling him about Kova helping me during my vomit session and not the other fifty times we had sex. "He's such a good man. I don't know what I'd do without him being there for you. He's helped ease all my apprehensions I had about you going there in the first place."

I glanced at Kova. My stomach churned...

"Now that I know you're okay, put Konstantin back on the phone, please. I have something I want to ask him. Oh! And take your medicine now, young lady."

A sad smile tugged at the corner of my mouth. "Sorry to worry you, Dad. Love you."

I handed the phone back to Kova and he stepped out of the room.

Scooping up the assortment of pills into my palm, I stared at them with utter disdain. Taking Motrin was one thing, but these? I hated them with a passion I never knew one could have for medicine.

Reaching for the glass of water, I exhaled and then threw all of them back at once. Some of them were small, and some the size of horse tranquilizers. Of course that messed with my head. They lodged in my throat and I panicked for a split second, then I closed my eyes and forced them back. I drank half the contents of the glass.

Kova strode back in. He placed his hands on his hips and looked down at me. "I brought chicken noodle soup for you. I want you to eat it."

I grimaced. I knew I should eat, I just didn't want to. "I really don't want to eat after what happened yesterday. Can I just eat these crackers?"

"I really think you need to eat, Ria, even if you just sip it. How about we talk while you eat?"

I chewed the inside of my lip. Tempting, but I had a better idea.

"We as in you?" I suggested, hopeful.

"Fine. If that is what it takes, then yes."

I beamed up at him, happy he was making a compromise. I shifted the blankets off me and tried to stand, but Kova stopped me. I glanced up at him in confusion.

"What are you doing? I'm going to get the soup."

"Stay here. I will get it for you."

"I don't want to be babied, Kova. I can get it."

Kova's lowered his eyes like I'd insulted him. "I am not babying you, Adrianna. I just…" He paused. "Do you not know by now that I care for you deeply? This is for your own good. Please, let me take care of you," he pleaded.

I got the vibe he truly wanted to wait on me. I conceded and agreed, and his entire face lit up.

"Wait—What did my dad say?"

He shook his head, his eyes filled with pure shock and excitement. "You will never guess."

I tilted my head to the side. "What do you mean?"

"He asked if I could stay the night to watch over you. I almost told him I already was."

My jaw dropped. "You're kidding me."

"I wish I was."

My gaze wandered away, shame eating away at the lining in my stomach. I was going to give myself an ulcer at this rate. I placed the half-eaten cracker on my nightstand and then brushed away the imaginary crumbs on my blanket.

"Kova?" I asked softly, now picking lint.

"Yes?"

"What do you think would happen if my dad found out about us? We know Joy knows, and why she hasn't told my dad is beyond me. I feel like she's holding onto the information for some reason, I just don't know why. Katja is aware and knows everything. But my dad? He thinks you're staying here as a favor to watch over me, because you're his friend…"

My voice trailed off and the guilt I'd felt before multiplied by ten.

CHAPTER 34

honestly do not have an answer for you."

Kova sat on the edge of my bed. His face was drawn, and he appeared as horrible as I felt. "I wish I did, but I do not. Even if I was not Frank's friend, I do not believe it would go over well."

"How would you feel if the roles were reversed?"

His eyes sharpened. "I would be in jail. If I ever have a daughter, she will be on lockdown until she is thirty-five. No cell phone. No television. No friends." Kova raised a pointed brow, then said, "No friends who like to—how do you say—smush other friends."

A sad smile tugged at my lips and I laughed. "Did you just say smush?"

"I did. I am not too old to not know what that word means, and do not tell me a boy can fuck like a man at seventeen. They only just discovered their cock."

I smiled bigger. "You're terrible."

Kova shrugged without care. "I am who I am."

Reality faced me again. Guilt was chewing me up. "This is so wrong, Kova. I feel bad for my dad. I never realize how wrong it is until it's looking me in the face."

Kova sighed deeply. "Believe me. Every day when I look at you, when I think about us and the things I want, it will never be right. But here, Ria," he said and placed his hand over his heart, "I do not care what is right or wrong. All I care about is you. So if I have to sneak behind your father's back, then so be it."

"And you're okay with that?"

"What other choice do I have? Give you up? Never. I have tried and it did not work. Could you cut ties with me completely?"

I looked into his eyes. I knew the answer without having to say it. He did too.

Our love and pain were entwined, curling around us whenever we breathed the same air. We were stuck in a cycle. A painful, endless cycle that had no light at the end of the tunnel.

We were going to destroy so many relationships, but hopefully not ruin our own in the process.

I TOSSED AND TURNED ALL night.

Glancing at the clock, annoyance steamrolled through me. It had only been a few hours since I'd fallen back to sleep. So not really all night, but it sure felt like it. I turned on my side and watched Kova sleeping in the dark. The only light streamed in from the blinds. His arms were folded behind his head, the carved vascularity of his biceps accentuated at this angle. Kova was a brawny man, physically beautiful with immense strength and a surprising softness to him.

His naked chest expanded and contracted with each pull of air. I reached out, wanting so badly to touch him, to trace the tattoo on his ribs. But I didn't. I rolled over back onto my other side and closed my eyes, praying for sleep. After I'd had a large mug of soup, I curled up next to Kova with the intention of talking, but my eyes drifted shut before I could stop them and I fell back asleep, only to wake up every few hours or so.

"What are you thinking about," he asked softly, spooning me. Kova wrapped an arm around my waist and fitted me to him like a puzzle piece. His body was so warm and inviting. I sank back into him and sighed. My butt burrowed into his hips and I pulled up the covers over us.

My fingers laced his and I pulled them to my chest. "I didn't mean to wake you."

Kova kissed the back of my neck and asked me again as he cupped his legs to the back of mine. "What are you thinking about?"

"Nothing. Everything. I have a hard time staying asleep some nights. I'm so physically tired I can barely move, but my mind doesn't stop."

"Do you take anything to help you sleep?"

I shook my head. "No. I figured with all the other medications I take it wasn't a good idea to add more to the mix."

"Tell me something that is on your mind."

I picked a simple topic to start with. The darkness made it easy to expose myself without reservations.

"Remember my best friend, Avery, who you met when she came to watch me at practice? She's coming to visit me soon and I'm nervous about it. I've been friends with her since we were babies. Our fathers are business partners, our families live next door to each other. We tell each other everything, but she kept a huge secret and lied to me." I paused and thought about how Kova had done the same thing to me. I tried to not let that harden my heart again. "I've been so hurt over it. She was sleeping with my brother for well over a year and kept it from me. She got pregnant and had an abortion. I found out by accident, and I can't help but wonder if she ever planned to tell me."

Kova whistled. "What were her reasons for keeping it from you?"

"I don't know. She really didn't have a good one other than she thought I'd be mad. And I was. I was fuming. This was at the same time I found out other shit that just completely destroyed me. And then to hear she got pregnant? I kind of blew up on her. She cried hysterically, saying she needed me more than ever, that she was hurting in ways I couldn't fathom, but I just left her there." I shook my head. "I shouldn't have left her."

"If she told you from the beginning she was interested in your brother, would you still have objected to it?"

I pondered his question. "I probably would've tried to sway her from being with him."

"Why is that?"

"Because Xavier is a player. He's a one and done kind of guy. He doesn't care about girls, or feelings, or emotions. He cares about himself and money. How much he can drink in one night. Nothing else. I love Avery, and I wouldn't want her to be another notch on his bedpost, and I probably would've tried everything in my power to make sure that didn't happen."

"So, you would've objected regardless of what she wanted," he stated.

I chewed my lip. I hadn't thought of it like that, and putting it that way made me feel kind of bad.

"I guess so." I sighed. "God. That makes me such a shitty friend."

"Have you spoken to her?"

"I've only recently finally decided to talk to her and it almost broke me inside when I heard her voice. I felt so bad to hear how happy she was to talk to me and apologize. Before that, she'd called me numerous times, but I never picked up. I never responded to her texts."

Kova snuggled closer and sandwiched his leg between mine. The warmth of his body triggered me to fall deeper into him and absorb what he was giving me.

He kissed the back of my neck. "When did this happen?"

"Right before I found out you were married."

Kova groaned in the back of his throat. "We both did a number on you, yes?"

I ignored that because he knew he did.

"Does that make me a bad person that I shut her out? She never would've done that to me."

"No, you are young. It is normal to react that way. You were hurting so you reacted out of emotion, but I think you should talk to her. Explain where you are coming from and listen to her. Just listen. Do not shame her for her choices. No one is perfect."

I laughed lightly. "I know. I just don't even know how I'm going to start the conversation. I miss her so much. I miss her sarcastic humor, her laugh, the sound of her voice. I miss talking bullshit with her. I miss my friend. It's going to be that awkward silence and all because I'm an idiot and lashed out. I'm such a fool."

"You are not a fool. It will only be awkward if you make it awkward. If you guys are as close as you claim, the hardest part is the actual part where you admit you are sorry and apologize for your behavior the way she did to you. After that, it will go back to how it always was. Just have a little faith."

Slipping my hand from Kova's, I turned around so we were chest to chest and flung my leg over his hip. He nestled his thick thigh against my sex until our bodies were completely joined together. I released a sigh, wondering how I could ever live without him. Kova settled the anxieties in my heart and calmed my soul when it was just us. In moments like this, I wish it was always just us. We were in an extremely intimate position. Personal. The kind where two people held a link to salvation.

My hand searched for his and I laced our fingers together, bringing them to rest between our chests. I could fall asleep like this. There was a comfort and security I found in his touch that warmed me. I had to wonder if I did the same for him too.

The obscurity of my room made it difficult to see beyond the bed, but at this closeness our faces came into view. Kova's eyes glowed with vulnerability. In the darkness he was defenseless, but he still found a way to hold on to me.

"Now you tell me something," I said.

"Are you just going to skip over the lupus and kidney disease?"

I was quiet. "I was kind of hoping you'd forget. My dad told you everything anyway."

"I want to hear it come from your lips."

Exhaling a deep sigh, I gave Kova what he wanted.

"What do you want me to tell you? That I'm scared? That I want to live a long life and I'm terrified I won't? Because I am. I don't want to acknowledge how sick I am, so I do stupid things to keep my mind busy, like extra conditioning. I hate taking all that medication and sometimes I choke on it. I want to have a family one day but my chances are slim. I want to travel, I want to see the world. Right now I want to go to the Olympics. I'm so close but I'm scared something will happen and prevent me from making it all the way. That I'll get too sick. I don't want people to look at me with pity and feel bad, or look at me any differently. Will my kidney disease progress to the point I have to go on dialysis sooner than expected? Will I get so sick and worn out from it that I won't be able to do gymnastics any longer? When will I finally need a transplant? Can I even go to college or am I too sick? What happens if no one is a match? Because right now, no one is and the thought of never finding one terrifies me more than anything. Am I killing myself, literally killing myself for not starting dialysis now? What if the lupus causes me to have a flare up during a meet and I get so deep inside my head I become a basket case and ruin everything?" My voice shook and tears filled my eyes.

"I'm trying to stay positive, but my hope is slipping. Every day my window of optimism shuts a little more. The anxiety and fear is smothering me and all I do is cry about it. I'm too young to feel like this, but I don't know how not to think about it." Then, I went into a spew about all the medications and doctor visits and blood work and tests I have to do and how often. I let it all out without holding a thing back.

And it felt good. Really good.

Kova held me tighter. Dipping his chin, he lifted my face until our lips were just a breath apart. "If you were not scared then I would be worried. Yes, I knew all these things, but I needed to hear them from *you*. I needed to hear your voice speak them. Thank you for finally telling me." Kova paused and kissed the top of my hand. "I want to be that person for you, Ria. I want you to come to me, to talk to me whenever you are scared or worried. We both know I have not been great at that, but I have been working on it, which you have known. Our toxic moments are over, yes?"

I nodded.

"Good. We need to be there for each other at all times."

"I don't like talking about it though, because then it makes it real." I sniffled. "I don't want to make it real. I just want it all to go away."

Kova kissed my forehead. "Do not let lupus define you. Do not let kidney disease beat you. That is not what you are about. You are a fighter and why I love you so fucking much. Instead, look at it differently. Do not let it drown you. Let the diseases inspire you. Make them give you the life you have always wanted to live."

My voice hitched. "How do I do that? I don't know how. I feel so lost, so scared."

"You just live. You live like every day is your last. You live, and you let those who want to live with you, live too. Do not shut the world out because you are hurting. You are going to miss everything that is beautiful about this chaotic thing we call life. You have a reason to fight now more than ever."

A tear slipped from the corner of my eye and rolled down my temple.

"And you have me. You will *always* have me." Kova pressed a hard kiss to my lips. "Let me live with you."

I squeezed my eyes shut while Kova held me closer. His last words nearly broke my heart because they were honest to God so real and I felt them in every fiber of my body. Little whimpers left my vulnerable lips. I was petrified about my future. My heart burned with resentment for all the things I may never be able to do. But Kova's soothing words, the way his heart coated them with tenderness, meant more than saying I love you.

He was right. I needed to live, and let those who wanted to, live with me.

"I told you I love you, Adrianna. I have only ever truly loved you."

"You're only saying these things because I'm sick."

"Make no mistake, I have loved you since I saw you." He stared reflectively at me. "But when life flashes before your eyes, you take all the risks you can. I do not want you to second-guess me anymore. I want you to know how I feel." He licked his lips. "This is us, Ria. There is no going back after this. Only forward."

Nodding my head, I kissed him hard. I wasn't sure how this was going to work, but I wanted to do exactly what Kova had said.

I would live like every day was my last day. I *wanted* to live.

And I wanted to do that with Kova.

CHAPTER 35

Kova hadn't been at practice once I returned after the hurricane had passed.

It hurt my heart a little and I actually wondered if it had something to do with what we shared at my condo. About how he let me cut him and how he'd said he loved me, how he wanted to live with me. I tried not to focus on it too much, but when he didn't come in the following day, or the day after that, I really started to question everything. He'd been absent three full days, which again, was something completely unlike him. The last time he had done this he'd gotten married. My gut told me there wasn't a drastic reason this time, but I started to worry and contemplated texting him. I controlled myself, even though it was a struggle. I didn't want his absence to affect me, but he'd told me to live.

How could I live when he wasn't here to live with me?

Maybe he'd lost faith in me. Maybe what he'd said in my room a few days ago wasn't true. I'd shown more than just a moment of weakness. I'd let down my guard completely and welcomed him back in.

After practice I decided to take a drive by his house once the sun set to see if his car was there. I should've gone home to catch up on sleep I desperately wanted, but I knew my mind wouldn't rest not knowing.

Total stalker mode activated.

Much to my satisfaction, his car was parked in the driveway, but so was Katja's and a couple others I didn't recognize. Not that I would. The lights in his home were on and I could see shadows walking back and forth through the sheer drapes. If he didn't show up at the gym tomorrow, then I'd send him a text tomorrow night.

Thankfully, Kova did show up the following day, but he wasn't himself. He seemed restrained. His shoulders were rolled tight and his eyes were haunted. My heart felt lighter just from the sight of him. I smiled, but it vanished as he strode into his office without so much as a glance my way.

A knot formed in the pit of my stomach.

I inhaled, then exhaled. I had to let it go. I had a job to do, but the nagging feeling in my gut wouldn't go away now.

God. This sucked.

Madeline worked diligently with me for most of the day. Kova hardly looked in my direction. Usually when I looked for him, he was either already looking at me or would look because he felt me looking for him. But today he didn't acknowledge my presence. Not once. I didn't even feel the weight of his stare on me like usual. It was as if I didn't exist, and that hurt my heart so much.

Thankfully Avery would be here this week. I could vent to her and she could tell me what to do, and tell me if I was acting crazy or not.

When it came time to rotate to bars, Madeline said, "Great work today. You've shown so much improvement. It's like you're not the same person who arrived meek and afraid of her shadow on beam. All that hard work has paid off." She finished with a big smile. "Go over to bars. Don't keep Coach Kova waiting on you."

I nodded and smiled. During my day of doubt and questioning, I needed her praise more than I'd realized. "Thanks, Coach."

Taking a deep breath, I walked over to the uneven bars. I knew we were going to pick up where we left off with perfecting my dismount, but I also knew we had to start with the new release moves today too in order to stay on schedule.

"Hey," I said, walking right up to him.

Kova stood with his body angled away and his hands on his hips as he stared off into space. I glanced in his direction to see what he was staring at, but nothing caught my eye.

"How are you feeling?" he asked, still looking away.

"Much better…thanks for asking."

He nodded, his brows drawn together. "Let us get started."

"Kova…" I carefully and slowly drew out his name. "Are you okay? Is there something wrong? Did I do something wrong?"

He finally looked at me and his shoulders relaxed. Kova blinked rapidly a few times and the intense air surrounding him dissipated within seconds. He took a breath and I inhaled. Kova regarded me with a look of compassion that eased my doubts, then leaned in toward my face only to stop. He pulled back and I stared wide-eyed up at him.

His lips pursed together and he covered his mouth, smiling behind his hand. He'd been planning to kiss me as if it were normal for him to. I loved he had the instinctive urge to, just not here.

He cleared his throat. "Everything is fine. We do not have much time today with how much we need to accomplish, so let us get a move on. Wait—"

"Yes?"

"Are you feeling okay? Like really okay?"

One corner of my mouth pulled to the side. "I'm okay."

Kova nodded then walked over to the side to stand next to the bars. He retrieved his cell phone from his pocket and scrolled. I guess he'd gotten the screen fixed while he was away from the gym.

Chalking up, I watched him, his face scrunched up like he was reading something that bothered him. I picked up a small block of chalk and broke it, then sprayed water on my grips before applying more powder. Kova's fingers quickly moved over the screen and I knew I couldn't hold back. It still bugged me not knowing why he hadn't been at the gym.

Tightening the Velcro, I asked, "Where've you been?"

"Home."

I bobbed my head, knowing that was all I was going to get. I clapped my hands, then wiped the chalk on my thighs.

"Sorry I asked."

The next three hours of practice felt like the longest hours of my life. He kept his promise and worked me on bars the way he always had and not like he pitied me and needed to make sure I was okay every ten seconds. I was relieved and took every direction he gave, but it was his attitude that got under my skin. He seemed bothered, even though I was doing everything right.

Kova may not have been barking out orders, but he grilled me with every opportunity that arose. His eagle eyes didn't miss a beat, and there was an indignation to his words that poked at my already sensitive nature. Kova barely touched me. He purposely stayed away from me and instructed me from behind the wires of the bars, yet

I'd seen him earlier in the day work with other gymnasts at close range. There were times when I needed his guidance, his hands on me to show me how my body needed to be positioned, but he didn't budge. My frustration grew.

His engines were revved and poised for an argument, I could feel it. There was a storm brewing in Kova's eyes, I just wasn't sure if it had to do with me or not. I wanted to crawl under his skin and flush out what the issue was going on in his head. I wanted to give in, but I knew the only person who would suffer would be me. And that was upsetting for me because for some ridiculous reason I had no answer for, I wanted to help him like he had helped me.

At one point, I flat out yelled, "I don't understand! Show me how to do it!"

Still, he stayed back.

Even when tears coated my eyes from my inability to master a skill the way I wanted to, he stayed back. He saw my struggle. He was aware of how frustrated I had become. The distress in his torn eyes was clear, and so I resented him for making me open up. All I could think about was how dumb I was. How he could tell me he wanted to live with me only to put a ten-foot wall between us.

The clock struck seven and I clocked out mentally. Quickly, I gathered my things and rushed out to my locker, passing Reagan and Holly as they left. We said our goodbyes. The gym was nearly empty save for a few parents in the lobby. I needed to get home.

Stuffing my clothes and shoes into my duffle, I felt him before I even saw him.

"I'm sorry I let you down," I said through a broken, fragile voice. "I'm sorry I ever said anything to you." And I was. I wished I had never opened up now.

"Adrianna."

I didn't answer him. He called my name again.

Shaking my head, I ignored him. This wasn't fair. He didn't get to talk to me only on his terms.

I slammed my locker shut and turned around ready for a fight, only the Kova I saw wasn't the Kova I was expecting. I softened a bit, but I left my aggravated expression firmly in place to show him I wasn't accepting his cute little smile like he was finally happy to see me.

Kova stepped into the room and walked right up to me. He grabbed my elbows and tried to loosen me up. I spoke before he could.

"You don't get to tell me you love me one second and then the next second act like you don't give a shit about me. That's not fair, Kova." I paused, feeling myself get totally emotional over this. "You said you wanted to live with me," I whispered. "I took that to heart."

"I know, and I apologize. It had nothing to do with you. I promise."

I frowned, unprepared for that or for the absolute sorrow in his green eyes.

"Will you give me a few minutes for the rest of the people to leave so we can talk?"

His head tilted to the side and he gave me a lazy smile that was impossible to refuse. I nodded. I didn't want to stay mad at him, not after what we had shared in those few days, and I wanted to know what had happened.

"Wait in my office."

I nodded again. Kova glanced over his shoulder, then quickly dropped a kiss to the top of my head. Turning around, he strode out of the locker room only to stop at the threshold. He paused with his hand on the ledge of the doorframe and looked over his shoulder at me.

His gaze dropped to the floor for a moment then met mine. "Just… Just know you did not let me down. I have some issues with Katja right now and that is on my mind nonstop. Not you." Then he was gone.

I tugged my duffle bag onto my shoulder and left the locker room, heading for his office with a little smile on my face. I felt a smidge better.

Opening the door, I reared back in complete surprise. Blood drained from my cheeks.

"Oh. Hey, Katja."

CHAPTER 36

She knows. *Remember, she knows,* I told myself.

And she had my damn notebook.

"Adrianna," she said, rolling the R. She was seated in Kova's chair behind his desk, slowly swiveling side to side like she reigned supreme. "How is it you do?"

I plastered on an innocent smile and played it off. "I'm great. Just looking for my coach. I thought he was in here. I couldn't remember if we had a blading session tonight."

Eyes narrowing, she angled her head to the side. I had no reason not to like Katja. She'd been nothing but kind to me up to now, yet she was his wife and that was enough to make me hate her.

"But did you not have one just two nights ago?"

My brows bunched together. "Two nights ago?"

"Yes, Konstantin said he was here treating you."

Between her honeyed voice and devious grin, something told me she already knew the truth.

"Oh, yes," I said, covering for him. "I was here, we just didn't finish because it hurt too much. I asked if we could pick up another night."

The grin vanished from her flawless face and her eyes dropped. Katja had played me.

"Is that so?" she asked, and I nodded. "Because two nights ago Konstantin was not even in town. In fact, we just got back yesterday afternoon."

I nearly choked as I tried to swallow with a dry throat. Katja stared me down. The pounding rate of my heart was like a loud drum in my ears. I wasn't sure how I could get out of this one. I needed to remain calm and think of a casual response without muddling up the situation even more.

"Two nights ago? Oh, I thought you said a few nights ago. Or maybe it was last week. I can't remember. The practice hours are long and the days tend to blend together. The brain fog is real with lupus," I added with an airy smile, playing it off. I was a little upset with myself over using that as an excuse. "I never thought it was until recently."

"Ah, yes. Konstantin did tell me about your death sentence a couple of months ago."

I sucked in a quiet gasp and pulled back, hurt that anyone could stoop to such a cruel level. I adjusted the strap on my shoulder and held it a little tighter.

"I don't have a death sentence. I'm fine."

"Well, you will never get better now, will you? Just continue to deteriorate." Her sugary words prickled my skin. She spoke like a know-it-all. "And you will never know if tomorrow you will take a turn for the worse, or three years from now, yes? One day the medicine will not help."

Sadness crept into me like black grease. The small smile I wore slid into a frown. I stared at her, stunned by how she could attack anyone in such a horrible manner. I knew I deserved it a little bit—I was sleeping with her husband after all—but she'd stooped to a level that was off limits regardless. What she'd said was what I had feared the most and what I was trying to work through.

Katja was as heartless as Joy. For a fleeting moment I wondered if Kova knew how mean she really was. Tears threatened to well in my eyes and I swallowed what little saliva I had left. The tightness in my chest was holding me down and I needed to get out. Her words were harsh. She knew that, which was apparent by the satisfied smile on her face and the glistening satisfaction in her eyes.

My jaw quivered, and I knew if I spoke my voice would shake. Instead, I just bobbed my head and flattened my lips, exhaling through my nose. I glanced around his office, my eyes scanning the floor. The awkwardness reached a claustrophobic state and I needed to get out. I'd talk to Kova later, he'd understand. There was no way I could outswim a shark who was chasing the scent of blood. And that's what she was.

There was nothing left for me to say. I knew in my gut she'd come back ten times harder if I did. I couldn't handle that. Not when she went for the jugular.

Turning on my heels, I walked toward the door. Her snicker crawled over my delicate state, but I ignored it, reaching for the knob as the door flew open and Kova walked in.

I froze, anger replacing my heartache. Here he was in all his glory knowing his wife was in here. He'd sent me into the lion's den. I was strong, but I wasn't that strong. We all had our limits.

Troubled eyes scanned my face until he looked over my shoulder. His gaze lowered to slits and the glare he gave Katja said everything.

He had no idea she was here. And he sure as hell wasn't happy to see her.

I glanced at the floor. "I'll see you tomorrow," I said quietly.

I tried to step around him, but he put his hand on the crest of my elbow. "Wait."

My heart dropped. Kova was touching me in front of Katja.

I looked up at him and he dropped his hand. He was trying to convey something through his eyes, and even though I didn't want to listen because I was upset, I gave him a subtle nod.

Stay.

He had no plausible reason for me to stay here instead of his wife. I turned around and crossed my arms in front of my chest. Chewing the inside of my lip, I averted my gaze to the floor. This was uncomfortable.

"Katja." Kova said her name so differently than I did. "When did you get here?"

"A little while ago. I came in through the back entrance."

He placed his hands on his hips. Resentment flowed from him, circling around us.

"Is there something wrong? Are you okay?"

"Everything is just fantastic, my love. I missed you."

She stood and walked around his desk to stand in front of him. I could smell the perfume I once commented on only to learn it was her body wash Kova had shipped from Russia. It really did smell incredibly alluring, and I hated that she wore it.

"Why are you here?"

"Is that any way to greet your wife?"

Her seductive tone didn't go unnoticed. Katja leaned in to kiss Kova, but he stopped her. She pulled back and gave him an icy glare.

Hell hath no fury like a woman scorned. I couldn't stop staring at the heavy mascara that made her eyelashes resemble tarantula legs.

"I am busy with work and trying to finish up. Can this wait? Go home and I will see you there," he said firmly.

"If you are only doing a blading session, then I will wait for you. It will not take long," she said, a suggestive smile reaching her eyes. "I have a surprise for you that you are going to be so happy about. *We* are going to be happy. I wanted to give it to you here since this place is your second love."

"I'm… I'm gonna go," I said quietly.

"No," Kova barked with his eyes still on Katja, then switched to his native tongue.

Heat flushed through me and I clenched my eyes shut trying to swallow back the knot that was stuck in my throat. This wasn't good. The back of my neck was clammy from the embarrassment I felt being in this office. The tips of my fingers tingled and my palms were damp. I hated when they switched to Russian. Not because I was nosy—I most definitely was—but because it was uncomfortable and made me feel like they were speaking about me. Their voices were growing louder. I stood there feeling like the third wheel that I was.

I stepped backwards, thinking they wouldn't notice my departure, but I was wrong.

Kova reached behind him and latched on to me. My wide eyes dropped to his vice grip on my forearm. I held my breath and stood stone still.

Shit. Shit. Shit.

My heart was going to explode from my chest. I might as well just shoot myself to end the misery.

The intense argument reduced to an alarming silence. I looked at them. Katja scowled at Kova's hand on my arm before moving her focus up to my face. Her beautiful, crystal blue eyes were sharper than a knife and aiming for me. I had a feeling if she could choke me out right now, she would.

But then, then she stunned me.

Katja straightened her back and inhaled, collecting herself. I frowned, watching as she tugged the hem of her shirt straight down, then brushed a few loose platinum blonde strands of hair behind her ears adorned with massive diamond studs I'm sure Kova bought her.

She reached into her purse and pulled out a white envelope. She shoved it against his chest. Kova placed his fingers over hers, his brows bunched together as he glanced down then took it from her. Katja said something in Russian, then stalked out of his office, seemingly trying to remain dignified.

Kova frowned as he unfolded the sealed envelope and looked at it. There was a printed return address at the top, but the rest was left blank. He flipped it over between his fingers, looked at the back, then threw it onto his desk without a care. He dragged both his hands down his face, and for a split second I felt bad for the exhaustion he exposed when he dropped his hands.

"I should go, Kova. We can talk tomorrow."

"No," he said, his tone defeated, "please do not go yet."

I shifted on my feet. "But do you think it's a good idea that your wife, who knows about us, left instead of me? I'm worried she may do something stupid."

He shook his head. "Trust me. There is nothing else she can do that would be any worse than what she has already done."

Dropping his hips to the edge of his desk, Kova dragged his weary eyes up and down the length of my body. A small, needy smile curved on one side of his mouth. Reaching forward, he tugged the strap of my duffle bag toward him, pulling me with it. He removed it from my shoulder so it fell to the floor, then he grabbed my hips and pulled me between his spread thighs.

Kova wrapped his arms around me like I was his lifeline, sighing like he was finally home. I leaned into his chest and allowed him to soak up whatever he needed from me. He inhaled deep and held on to me like he was afraid to let go. His fingers pressed into me and I could feel in his touch, the way he leaned harder into me, the way his heart pounded against his chest, that he was sinking into a dark hole.

This was us. Everything that was wrong and everything that was right. It was like this subliminal feeling that couldn't be explained. When one of us needed the other, we were there. It could only be felt. We did what we had to do without question, because he loved me, and even though I never told him, I loved him too.

"I needed this," he said very quietly, breaking the silence.

"Needed what?"

"You. I just needed to hold you. I have missed you these few days. I never realized how much I do not like to go a day without seeing you."

Don't do it. Don't do it. Don't do it.

"Kova?" I said hesitantly, staring at his chest. "Where were you?"

"Dealing with Kat."

I lifted my gaze and waited for him to elaborate. Kova held a pensive stare as he looked at me like he was considering his words. He waited a good couple of minutes, then gave my hand a little squeeze and kissed my knuckles, leaving his lips pressed there for a moment.

"I suspect Katja is lying to me about something. She is not herself and has been too distant. I am not complaining that she is, but something is off, and I do not know what. It is bothering me. She used to fight me at night to be home, now she seems relieved when I have to stay in the gym, which I find peculiar given what she knows about us. I have a feeling she is trying to plan something big. I just do not know what it is yet."

CHAPTER 37

A deflated laugh escaped me.

He couldn't be serious. The thought provoked me with a pull of jealousy so deep it startled me. I wasn't typically a jealous girl, but I was glad his wife was refusing him. Jealously meant I was fragile, and I didn't like to think of myself like that. The last word I'd use to describe myself was envious. But when it came to Kova, that was a different story. I didn't want to share him. He was mine, just like I was his.

Still, I couldn't let it go.

I scoffed. "Wait a minute. You are *not* telling me you try to touch her, to have sex with her, and she isn't having it, are you?"

"I am trying to placate her so she does not go to the police, Adrianna." He sounded offended. "I have to use *my* body to protect *us*. I am disgusted, but that is the truth."

I ground my teeth so hard I heard the enamel crushing. Every time we took one step forward, we always took ten steps back. Always.

"Do you have any idea what would happen if we got out?" he continued. "I will go to jail, and you will not go to the Olympics. The committee would never allow it, you can count on that. I had to make deals with her to not speak to Frank, and for her to pacify Joy."

The committee would never allow it.

Breathe in, breathe out.

I hadn't even thought about that.

Kova was right. They wouldn't brush this under the rug. He'd be stripped and shoved behind bars, and I would be forced to retire due to an "injury," and that was that.

"I hadn't even thought of that," I whispered. I was scared now.

Was it crazy of me to tell him to keep placating her? Because if that was going to be what it took, then he should do whatever he needed to. I just didn't want to hear *how* he did it.

"She is arranging something. I just cannot figure out what it is."

"So what's your plan in the meantime? Fuck her into oblivion to silence her and then dig around when she's sleeping?" I stepped back and threw my hands up in the air. I was instantly angry again. "Why are men so stupid?"

Kova stood. Much to my surprise, he didn't jump down my throat. He remained calm. "I have to play her game for us to come out on top until I can find out what she is up to, then I can use it against her."

I exhaled a heavy sigh. This was so messed up. "For how long, Kova? How long do you have to play her game and pretend you love her?"

"For however long it takes until we are both in the clear."

My jaw dropped. "So that's where you were the last few days? Placating your wife when you were supposed to be coaching me? Listen, I'm all for you trying to make her happy for the time being since she's clearly a loose cannon, I just think I shouldn't hear about it anymore."

His face paled. The last thing I wanted to do was hurt him, but it physically hurt me to hear things like this even if I said I wanted to. I was not as strong as I thought I was, I guess.

"I had to be the doting husband and put her first to let her think she still had control over me. If I am going to play her game, I have to play it a few steps ahead of her."

Breathing heavily, I could feel tears climbing, but I forced them down. I pointed to my chest. "I tell you about my stupid disease and open up about the most heartbreaking moments of my life, and you respond with this stuff?" My voice broke. "You have to be kidding me. Why do you hate me? Do you get off on hurting me?"

Kova's face fell. He reached for me and I stepped back. His hand dropped helplessly to his side. "Do not do this, Adrianna, please. I am begging you. It is not like that, I swear on my life and everything I have to give it is not like that. I am just trying to talk to you and tell you what really has happened."

I exhaled a heavy breath trying to take control of the situation. "You're right. I did ask for this, and you're just telling me the truth. It doesn't mean I have to like it though." I paused, my jaw wobbling. "It just really hurts, Kova. Okay? I didn't mean to overreact. I'm sorry."

"Do you think I liked hearing you that had sex with Hayden multiple times? Or when you talk about your future that clearly does not involve me? We have to be able to talk about everything, is that not what you always say to me? Sometimes it sickens me to hear the things you say, but I try to not hold on to them and keep moving. We both do things we do not like right now, but think about it—if it were just me and you, would we do any of this crazy stupid shit we do? No."

He shook his head, his eyes so full of anguish it gripped my heart. He was right. I swallowed, surprised by how civil he was acting and not being defensive, and here I was letting my emotions get to me.

Softly, I said, "It's hardly the same thing and you know it."

He put his hands up and surrendered. "You are right. It is not. But I would never sleep with Kat, and you would have not been with Hayden. We would never have talked about this shit, and we would never fight because we are good together without any of that, and you know it is the truth. It would just be us and that would be it, but we are both stuck in situations we cannot get out of just yet, and probably not for a while. So we do what we have to and will continue doing it and talking shit out, whether we like it or not, because I never want there to be a secret between us again."

My heart pounded harder. "What do you mean?"

" Even if I divorced Katja tomorrow, we would still have to hide our relationship. I do not think the people around us would take lightly to it."

He was right again and here I was basically acting my age. That embarrassed me. I grimaced, wishing I thought ahead before I spoke. Here we were, just two people trying to find a way to each other only for real life—people and the law—to get in the way.

I looked at Kova, really looked at him. His eyes bore into mine like he was pleading with me to see his reasons, to agree with him that they made sense. I hated to admit they did. I was about to turn eighteen. What happened to us after that? Would I go to college? Would announce our relationship then? Would we have a long-distance relationship?

I shook my head and let go of the resentment I held and tried to focus on the now and not worry about the future.

"I'm sorry," I said again, my voice dropping. This was so hard.

"I am sorry too."

"This isn't normal," I stated softly. "I wish we didn't have to deal with this."

"As do I."

I'd give him that.

Propping my hands on my hips, I faked an attitude to lighten the dreary mood.

"You're needy and controlling and overbearing every day, but sometimes you're right and I don't like adding that to the mix. Your head gets big."

His eyes lit up. "I am always right."

I puckered my lips together to mask my smile. Kova reached for me again as he sat back on his desk. I stood between his legs and looked at him, then wrapped my arms around his shoulders.

"I like you," I said playfully.

"I love you," he said seriously.

Kova kissed my forehead and glided his palms up my thighs and over my butt. He scooped me up and I spread my knees to straddle him. I snuggled up closer to him, unable to ever get close enough, and basked in that feeling.

"Listen to me," he said, hardly moving his lips. "Only we matter to each other and that is that. Right now, things are not how we may want them, but I hope one day they will be. Until then…" He leaned in and dropped a kiss to my lips. "I want you, all of you. We are good together, Ria. I cannot help being addicted to you. We both feed each other what we desire, and that is what makes us *us*. Fuck what everyone else thinks. I know I am demanding and controlling, but I think you like that. Just how I like when you confront me and argue, going from sweet and innocent to angry and fired up and just want to fight in three seconds flat. I will always want you, Adrianna, always. I wake up in the morning thinking about you. I go to bed thinking about you. When I am buying groceries I am thinking about you. I make coffee, I think about you. I drink vodka, I think about you. I stroke my cock thinking about you. You are always on my mind because I only ever want you."

I shied away. "Kova…" I said, slightly embarrassed. My head dropped to his collarbone. "Why do you always have to find a way to be crude?"

"I am who I am. Now give me a kiss."

No thought needed, I kissed him with everything I had to give. We lost ourselves in the sensual tangle of our lips. Time stood still as our hearts beat against one another. There was no judgment, it was just us falling deeper and deeper in the seclusion of his office. If one paid attention, a kiss revealed truth, and his told me everything I worried he didn't feel but actually did. I wondered if he knew I felt the same way for him.

Kova cupped the back of my head and kissed me like he hadn't kissed me in months. Like I was his world and no matter what I would always be. His length hardened beneath me and I automatically circled my hips. I wound my arms tighter around his neck and nestled closer, returning that same affection, showing him just what he meant to me.

"Tell me what else is on your mind," I said, breaking the kiss. It was so natural for us to lose ourselves in the moment.

He kissed me one last time. "I am sorry for bringing her up. I never should have."

"No," I said, stopping him.

He was truly apologetic and making the effort I had asked of him. It wasn't fair of me to ridicule him for that. My heart beat faster for this man I never should've had the chance to be with. He'd been putting in the time these last couple of months and I had to not only show I respected that, but that I saw it too.

"I could tell something was on your mind when I asked you. I need to be asking you hard questions like this, and I shouldn't get upset when your response isn't the one I want to hear."

"I do not deserve you," he said.

I chuckled. I'd never heard anyone say that before. "I don't think it's about deserving someone. Does anyone deserve anyone? I think it's more about finding someone who understands you and accepts all your flaws but also helps you work through them. It's so easy to shut the door and keep walking, but it takes strength to hold it open, to see what that person is going to walk in with, and if it's worth it or not. The risk has to be greater than the chance, and I think you're worth it, Kova."

Kova's Adam's apple bobbed. His green eyes were rich with affection as they pierced the center of my chest. I held my breath from his deep stare.

"Bog, ya chertovski lyublyu tebya."

I waited on him to translate. When he didn't, I tilted my head to the side and smiled softly. "Tell me."

He shook his head. "You will not believe me, just like you never do every other time."

Ah. I knew. "It's that stupid word love again, isn't it?"

His eyes darkened like he was offended. "I do not find it stupid when I say it to you."

My heart bloomed even more for him. "Fair enough."

"God, I fucking love you. I really do."

CHAPTER 38

blushed, slightly embarrassed.

I'd thought he was going to say something mushy, but I wasn't expecting that.

"You're cute," I said.

Kova's head fell back and he barked out a laugh. "One day I hope you can find a way to love me the way I love you and actually say it."

I swallowed. He didn't know I already loved him, but something in my heart told me not to tell him just yet.

"What else? Tell me what happened with Katja."

Kova groaned. "I do not want to talk about it when I am hard for you. Talking about her is going to make my dick soft."

At that, I swiveled my hips down on him and smirked. "Tell me," I said, drawing out the words.

"Adrianna, I do not want to talk about my wife when all I can think about is sliding into your pussy right now."

"You know, I'm never ready for when you say that word."

"Pussy?" he repeated with a peaked brow, and I nodded. Kova smirked. "Let me bang you real quick. Then you can ask all the questions you want. I promise to answer them."

This time it was my turn to bark out a laugh. Bang sounded so foreign on his lips. "Did you just say bang?"

"Well I figured if pussy bothers you, bang might be a better word. I am too old to use smush sesh. Do not ask me to say that. I heard some boys saying it. I can say bang, but smush is where I draw the line. I said it once before but I cannot say it again. Unless you just want me to fuck you."

His eyes were alive with amusement. I couldn't hold back the giggles in my throat and burst out laughing.

"I can't even deal with how funny that is coming from you. It sounds so weird."

Rising up on my knees, I palmed his face and pressed my lips to his. Kova wrapped his arms around my lower back. I leaned into him and forced him to lay back on his desk. I hovered above him and kissed him again, my hand sliding down his stomach, over his rock-hard abs to cup his thick shaft over his sweat pants. I squeezed his cock and he twitched in my hand. Kova groaned, his back arched, and damn it all to hell, it was all so sexy the way the light from the moon shone between the shadows of the blinds over him.

There was something seductive and risky about us in his office like this—the thrill of getting caught loomed over me—and I fed off it. *We* fed off it.

"Adrianna," he moaned out my name. He gripped my hips roughly through the struggle of my hold on him.

I pressed my lips to his. "Tell me what happened and we can smush." I laughed. I could hardly say the word myself.

Kova chuckled darkly. His face lit up and it did stupid things to my heart. He looked so carefree and happy and I wanted to see more of that.

"You are so fucking not normal," he joked.

"You're right, but this is our normal, remember, and it's what I want. I like to ask about her when you tell me not to." Even though no sane person would ever ask about the other partner the way I did, I relished in reminding him he was still here with me. It was so wrong and for reasons I couldn't explain, I loved it. "So tell me about your wife while we bang."

He gripped my wrist to stop me. "You get off on it."

"Is that a bad thing?"

Kova loosened his grip on my wrist, flipped his hand over and cupped me over my shorts. My lips parted with a breath and I almost fell on him.

"Jesus Christ, you are wet. You do like it."

I nodded silently. A zing of desire shot down my back. I wish I understood why I loved the devious aspect of it all. And because he was still with me—mind, body, and soul—and not her.

Reaching into his sweats, I felt for his warm, swollen cock. I stroked him from tip to base, twisting my wrist around his length. I didn't bother hiding the moan in the back of my throat.

"You know, I have wanted to fuck you on my desk. Never did I think you would have me on my back like this."

A slow smile slid across my face. "I actually like being on top, so this is better for me."

"Whatever you want, however you want, just take it from me," Kova responded.

I shrugged off my zippered jacket and dropped it to the floor so all I was left in was a sports bra and tank top. Kova helped me remove my shorts and panties. In one swift move, he inserted two fingers into me. I sighed at the pressure and sank down on them, allowing the little bites of bliss to stream through me.

I rose up a little and placed one hand on his chest to slide up and down his fingers while I held onto his erection with the other. His thumb hit my clit at just the right spot and I let out a rushed breath.

"She is rarely home," he started. "Neither am I due to work, but I do not leave Georgia as often as she does."

The brittle sound of his voice tugged at my heart.

"Keep going," I said, and rose up to position his tip at my entrance. I was already hot and ready for him.

Before I could gently slide down, Kova thrust his hips up and slammed into me. He groaned, and I felt it deep inside me.

I slapped his chest. "You are such a bastard sometimes," I gritted out. "That fucking hurt, Kova."

"You make me this way."

"Sometimes I think you're too big for me," I moaned.

"I wish you could see what I see like this," he said barely above a whisper, like he was mesmerized.

I glanced down and angled myself so I could see, but I couldn't. "Stop deflecting."

"It is hard to focus when all I see is your pussy squeezing my cock."

I chuckled. "Kova…" I warned, my voice coming out raspy.

His head fell back and hit the desk. "You are the biggest pain and tease in my life. Fine," he said, swallowing hard, and I started to slowly ride him.

"She added a passcode to her phone. She has never had one before. She is cold, and I swear she has an attitude all the time. Her change in demeanor and secrecy raises too much curiosity in me. I know I should not question her, but with what she knows, anything is possible."

"So you're worried she's sneaking around behind your back."

"I used to be one step ahead of her and now I am not. She does not get to force me into marriage and then spread herself around and demand shit from me while holding you over my head."

I rode him harder, hating his words but taking them anyway. He breathed heavier each time I sank down and that only riled me up. I would never admit it to him, but I liked that she was behaving this way. She had blackmailed him, and while Kova was finally seeing her true colors, he'd only grow more distant with her. Our age difference may dangle between us, but our connection ran deep and the numbers were long forgotten when it was just us. Our conversations came naturally, and I didn't think anything truly did for him and Katja anymore. After what he'd told me about how they grew up together, I came to the conclusion they were convenient and just got comfortable. She may have found a way to hold on to him right now, but it wouldn't be forever. At least, I hoped not.

I took ease with my next set of words. I didn't want him to be offended by them, but it aggravated me that he was so concerned with her.

"Do you think it's a little hypocritical of you to be upset that she's lying about something when your cock is inside my pussy right now? That you're in bed with your gymnast any chance you get?"

Kova moaned, his back arching again. He looked at me with sensual eyes and a tight jaw through a sexy-as-hell smirk. I pushed up his shirt to look at his toned body.

"That is exactly why I try not to ever question her," he said, thrusting into me. "It *is* hypocritical of me. I try to not raise my voice because I am no better. I am a terrible human being. A terrible husband." He thrust hard again and grabbed my hips to hold me down so he could piston into me.

I inhaled and held my breath, my thighs quivered around his hips. I felt like I was stretched to the max and it hurt, like little tears were ripping in my tender flesh. Kova pulled back and I let out a gush of air.

"I thought since I brought her to the United States in the first place I should give her free reign to do as she pleases. I set her up nicely. There was a time when I wanted to make her happy, but she changed, and I saw a side of her that disgusted me. Then, I saw you."

Wanted. Kova said it in past tense. They were both going in different directions and playing the game with each other now.

"Did this start when I came to World Cup?"

My heart raced in anticipation. An orgasm was climbing but I wasn't ready to let go just yet. Once I had Kova in me, I always wanted more. I never wanted to stop feeling him or this intense pleasure he brought to the table each time. Kova was an addiction and he knew how to take me higher than anyone and anything. I was spellbound as I watched his hips roll into mine so slowly and sensually that I lost my train of thought for a moment. He was so fucking sexy with the way his body moved. I sighed a breath, feeling good, and allowed myself to just sink down into him. I was floating on a cloud, my entire body tingling and on the edge of desire.

"God, you feel so good," I said, biting my lip. "When?"

"It started before you came here," he said. His forehead scrunched together, almost as if it'd just dawned on him. Kova looked at our joined bodies again. "I would say about six months or so before that. You had nothing to do with it, but you did not help the situation either. It just showed me things I wanted more, things I was missing."

"Maybe she feels the same way about you and it's why she's acting the way she is. Have you tried speaking to her about it?"

"Adrianna?"

"Yeah?" I said breathlessly.

"Can we not talk about her anymore? I just want to watch my cock slide into your little pussy."

CHAPTER 39

y eyes rolled shut and a shot of bliss went down my back.
"I did say something to her." He answered my last question. "I am a very confrontational man if you have not noticed. She denies there is anything wrong." Kova was fixated on our bodies.

He carefully took my lips in his fingers and spread them. My jaw fell open and my head rolled back. I almost stopped moving from the passion of it. He pinched my clit and angled his hips so I hit his mound when I slid down.

Kova was good. Too fucking good.

"Oh, *malysh*, if you could see this…" His voice was rough like gravel and goose bumps danced down my arms. "Put your hands behind you on my legs and lean back."

I did as he said and almost orgasmed right then. I rolled my bottom lip between my teeth, trying to hold back. It was too much, too good every time at even the slightest angle.

I wanted his honesty, I wanted him to open up to me, and he had. The oddest feeling surged through me while we had sex. Like we both were free. I wasn't hurt. If anything, something reassuring settled in my stomach I couldn't name. Most people would refute the idea of a cheater talking to the other woman about his wife in this manner.

But we weren't most people. And I didn't consider myself the other woman. And, truth be told, we wallowed in the suspense of it.

It was sick. But I honestly didn't care. Kova told me it was okay to feel the way I did, and so I believed him.

"There is something else…" Kova gritted out, still staring at our joined bodies. "You are not going to like it."

Immediate panic ignited within me and I rode him faster and harder. I wanted to hear what he had to say, but I was too close to the edge of desire. I wasn't sure if I could handle it and changed the subject.

"Do you have a mirror?"

He looked at me like I had spoken Russian. I almost laughed.

"Why the hell would I have a mirror? And why do you need one now? I am about to come inside of you and you want to look at yourself?"

This time I smirked. "Close. I want to see what you see, how you see our bodies."

His eyes lit up and a shadow of hearty desire cast through them. Kova liked that I wanted to see too, and that excited me.

I thought quickly about what I could use so I could see before we finished. We both were close to the end. Spotting his cell phone on the desk, I reached for it and asked for his passcode. Funny how he didn't like that Katja had one even though he did. I unlocked his phone, then went for the camera icon and clicked on video. I angled the camera screen so it got our bodies and not my face.

Kova's cock slid effortlessly into my plump pussy, my lips suctioning around him with my tender clit showing. He stretched me wide and I wasn't sure how I fit him. He spread my lips again so I could see what he saw and my mouth parted, a breath rolling off my lips. I could see every fold and crease as his wet, rigid length pushed in and out. I caught a view of that sex vein I liked to play with and positioned the camera to get it on tape. I let out a sigh and moaned while I watched it disappear into my pussy. This was highly arousing and way more than I anticipated.

The sounds of sex infused with heavy breathing. Our panting and watching us on the camera is what got to me. Oh, God. It was all too much. I leaned back on one arm to get a better view and his cock pulsed inside me. My eyes locked with his. He was there, and so was I.

I glanced down. His cock looked massive from this angle. I couldn't tear my eyes from the screen. Now I knew what he meant and why he liked to watch us.

A few more voluptuous rolls of his hips, and Kova gripped my thigh, digging his fingers into my flesh. He moaned long and deep. I pulled back just enough to watch his thickness pulse as he came inside me. The veins on his stomach that led to his groin strained.

Kova gripped me harder, his decadence streaming into me as he let go. I let out a long sigh as his nails scored my thigh. I tightened my grip around his phone and we watched together as he filled me to the point where his cum oozed out of the sides, coating my pussy, my thighs, and his mound.

My lips parted in wonder. I was fixated on our pleasure. His orgasm had come out of me in the past, but I never actually saw it happen until now, and I found it insanely erotic to see. His cock twitched. My teeth dug into my bottom lip and I shuddered above him. Kova was still hard, and I was still beyond turned on by this.

Turning the camera off, I placed the phone face down and reached for him. I fisted the center of his shirt and pulled, forcing him to sit up. Kova's arms wound around my back as he slammed his mouth over mine. I kissed him deeply, only to have him return my hunger with more passion as I rocked into him.

"Tell me you love me. Say it," he demanded, his voice a husky whisper.

"I hate you."

Kova thrust into me without reservation and held himself deep inside. I groaned, biting down and pulling on his lip with my teeth. I wouldn't say the words he wanted to hear because then he'd have every part of me, and I needed to reserve something for myself.

He pressed his chest to mine, nearly suffocating me with his strength, and kissed my lips so fiercely my heart ached for this untamed man. I couldn't control the sounds erupting from my throat as he devoured me with a savage kiss, a kiss I made him fight me for.

Kova's nose nestled into the curve of my neck. He held me tighter and ran his hands up and down my body. I could feel him smiling against me and that made me happy.

"I know you are not done, and neither am I."

A throaty sigh escaped me. "You're right."

"You always need at least two rounds."

"You know, it's a good thing we don't live together. All we'd be doing is having sex."

Kova chuckled, his hot breath tickled my collarbone, and I shivered.

"And that is a bad thing?"

"What were you going to say that I wasn't going to like?"

"She wants a baby."

The silence was a thunderous beating of my heart. It was all around me. His words were a whisper and enough to reduce me to a speechless state. His cock was still hard and hot inside of me, and I wasn't sure how to feel about such a thing.

No, I knew how to feel, I knew exactly what I was feeling, and I was trying, trying so damn hard to be rational and listen. But this…

There was no way, and he knew that.

Kova bit down on my neck and held me immobile. I tried to pull away but he latched on firmer. First the puppy, now a baby. I knew it. I fucking knew that was coming. My gut said it was but I'd pushed it away and ignored it.

She wants a baby.

Chest tight from the four words that nearly broke me inside, I was struck with bone-deep hurt. A baby. Him being blackmailed made me think he was going to go through with it.

Kova let go of my neck and stood, holding me in his arms. He probably knew I was going to try and pull away. He walked to his office door and pressed my back to it. He adjusted us so we were still joined, then he pulled out and my back bowed when he glided me down his shaft until I couldn't go any further.

"Adrianna," he said, his voice filled with distress. "Look at me. Look into my eyes and listen to me, really listen to me." When I did, his face was blurry. "She has been asking me for a while. I told her it will never happen, just like I have each time she has asked."

I raked my nails harder down his arms, leaving red trails that made me feel good to see. I hoped it hurt. "You really know how to make me a fiend for you and then hate you." Kova held my hips down and drove into me without remorse. "When you fuck your wife, do you come inside her the way you do me?" I couldn't hold back. The images in my head of him screwing Katja were too strong and elicited a rage so deep I felt it creeping through my blood. "Does she let you lick her the way you do me? And I mean *all* parts of me? Does she know how nasty you can be?"

I couldn't say the words, but he knew exactly what I was talking about. He knew I liked those nasty sides of him, but did she?

"Does it leak out of her, and do you watch it? Do you bite her hard enough to make her bleed and then lick it up?"

Oh God. My heart could only handle so much.

"Adrianna…" He groaned, thrusting deep enough to make sure he caressed my clit.

My eyes rolled shut and I melted in his hold. I locked my ankles around his back and his mouth tickled my neck. His sweat pants were still on, only partially pulled down.

"Just shut the fuck up and stop talking," he said.

I struggled in his hold, trying to push him away. He was harder than ever, and the sad part was that I was so wet he was sliding in without resistance.

"You do, don't you," I said, grabbing his hair and pulling it. Such a girl thing to do, but I needed *something*. "You just unload your dick whenever you please. A drop and run kind of thing."

"No," he said below a whisper, and for a second, I thought he sounded hurt. But then I realized who I was talking about and that he didn't get hurt very often.

Grabbing my wrists, he stretched them above my head and pinned them to the door. His cock jerked inside of me and hit just the right spot. A delicious spot. My chest pushed out and I exhaled a breath. He knew the game he was playing, and I was ready to fight. But then he looked at me and his gaze surprisingly upset me, because he actually appeared hurt. I frowned.

I was seething and yet he was still thrusting into me. "I bet you fuck her bare because the perfect amazing Kova can't be bothered with condoms."

He drew in a long breath. "Never. I wear a condom every time."

A dark laugh escaped my throat. "Yeah, right. You actually think I believe you?"

"I bought them when I bought your Plan B."

Oh, he didn't. He did not just say that.

I resisted in his hold, struggling. My thighs squeezed around his hips, and I clenched his length. Kova's pupils dilated and he surged into me. We both held our breaths, our mouths open and mimicking each other's ecstasy. It made me want to taunt him just so I could feel that divine rush through me.

"This weekend? That's when you started?" I all about screamed my response.

What a joke. This fucked-up conversation was putting me through the ringer of emotions.

"No, it was the first time I bought your Plan B, you foolish girl."

My nostrils flared and I held back my emotions. I swallowed hard, almost believing him.

"Let go of me."

"Never. Have you not realized by now I can never let you go?"

CHAPTER 40

gasped and clenched my thighs around him.

Our hips smashed into each other and I allowed myself to bask in the warmth of the paradise our fused bodies were deeply in. A slow roll of my pelvis at just the right angle, and it was an overwhelming sensation for both of us. I sighed, not caring for a moment. It felt too good. *We* felt too good. Kova shuddered against me, feeling us. We both were close to the peak again and I softened around him.

Lacing our fingers together, his voice was a mixture of pain and fact. "I fuck her from behind so I do not have to look at her."

Kova surged into me, taking me like the animal that he was. I gasped, then released a breathless sigh veiled by rage with the news he'd just dropped on me. My skin prickled with heat, both ready for a fight and the pleasure that was about to tear through me.

"You would screw your wife like that because you're a beast."

"You have never been more wrong," he insisted. "I do it because I only want to see your face when I fuck. I put her face down and do not let her touch me. I even turn out the lights. The amount of vodka I drink is borderline dangerous, but it is what I do to get it over with. She does not get my cock hard. Only you ever get this part of me now. I swear it. If you never believe anything, believe this."

My jaw trembled. "You're going to give her babies, aren't you?" Giving Katja children would bound her to him forever.

He shook his head vehemently and drove into me. "No. Never," he whispered. "She will never get kids from me."

"I don't believe you. You'll do anything she wants right now."

"I have my limits, Adrianna."

"Sometimes you fuck me from behind."

His eyes dropped and he smirked. "That is only so I can look at your ass and spread your cheeks while I do. Do you have any idea how sexy you are from that angle? I told you your ass will be mine one day."

His raspy words coated every inch of my heated skin, almost making me wish he would take it now. I was too embarrassed to admit I liked when he touched me there.

As if he read my mind, his large palm slid to cup my ass. My lips parted in anticipation and I took a deep breath, tensing up when one of his fingers found my tiny, little hole and pressed on it. I drew in a blissful sigh, chest pushing out, and undulated on him.

"Kova," I said, swallowing hard, wondering if what I was about to ask was a waste of breath. "Please, don't hurt me anymore."

"Never again, my love. Never again."

The way he kissed me left me with no choice but to believe him. He released my arms and I wrapped them around his shoulders. My tongue delved around his and the movement of our bodies were one and the same.

It was scary how we couldn't get enough of each other.

Kova lifted me and took us to the couch. He pulled out and sat down, then turned me around so my back was to him and I straddled his lap.

"Reach forward so you are on your hands and knees."

I did as he asked, feeling very exposed. Grabbing my hips, Kova shoved me down harder and I released a gasping breath. This was a new angle for me, and by far the best one yet. I glanced over my shoulder as Kova brought his fingers to his mouth, then penetrated my tight hole.

"This is what I love to see," he said, spreading my cheeks. His eyes were fixated on our sex and my ass. I clenched up, and he whispered, "Relax for me, *malysh*." The tender ring of nerves he penetrated burned, and he said again, "*Malysh*, relax for me."

He demanded, I listened.

I nodded and did as he asked, rubbing my clit over his full sack. His finger slipped in my hole and I tried to breathe calmly.

"Fucking hell. You know I can feel my cock sliding in and out of your pussy like this." He all but moaned.

Kova's sexy, husky words took me to another level. The sensations flowing through me were all too much and I couldn't stop wiggling on him or rearing back, absolutely loving the ecstasy of both the pain and pleasure from both sides. My thighs quivered and my toes flexed and curled from the stimulation of his skilled fingers and dirty mouth.

"I want you to stop having sex with your wife." The words spilled from my lips.

"You know that is not possible," he responded and thrust so hard into me I lost my breath.

My lungs ached for air. Kova pushed deep and held me down. I became insatiable for this orgasm and started grinding myself on him.

"You can."

A whimper escaped my lips as I tried to shift because I was pretty sure he tore me again.

"Ria, I have to play the game, but I will make a deal with you."

I hesitated. Another instant that most definitely wasn't normal relationship talk, and yet it was ours. I couldn't think straight when an orgasm was about to shatter me, but I nodded anyway.

"She will never get my cock the way you do. I will never look at her face when I fuck her."

Kova groaned, and I got the feeling he wasn't finished. His fingers picked up the pace and so did his hips. He was close, just like I was.

"Kova…" I dug my teeth into my bottom lip. "I can't hold off any longer, and there is nothing you can say that will make it okay for you to be with me and your wife at the same time."

His seductive chuckle challenged my words. "I will never fuck her raw, and I will never, ever come inside her again. The last thing we need is for you to get pregnant, but the thought of my cum inside your pussy makes me so fucking hard it is painful."

My clit throbbed and I felt his dick swell inside me, enlarging to a thickness that said he was telling the truth. We both let out a guttural moan, our flesh slippery with lust and illicit desires.

"Ria…" he said, his finger still carefully working my ass. I actually found myself rearing back for more. "Do that thing with your pussy where you squeeze my cock." I thought about what he said and I tried it. "Yes…" he moaned, thrusting so slow and hard I knew I wasn't going to be able to walk. The tip of his cock hit deep. I ground my pussy on him and squeezed again. "Just…like…that…" Kova whimpered, and it was by far the sexiest sound he'd ever made. I wanted to make him do it over and over. "Harder," he begged, and I squeezed as tight as I could.

"She never gets your cum," I said. "Only I do." His hips picked up speed and for once I felt like I was in control. "Not even in her mouth will you come," I said, shocked by my own words. "Only mine."

"You cannot talk to me like that." He sounded like he was suffering.

"I don't even want you to come in your condom when you fuck her. You can use your hand or rip that condom off and come on top of her, but never inside of her."

His breathing deepened, and it excited me. "Keep talking to me like that."

"Want to know a secret?" I asked, pushing back so my ass was nearly in his face. "I love when you come inside my pussy. I love how wrong it is, that it should never happen. I get wet thinking about how you're my coach and I'm your gymnast and I can feel your dick pulsing inside. It's so fucking risky, and even though you have a wife, you're still here with *me*, coming in *me,* and I love that."

His body trembled and I made a mental note that Kova loved dirty talk.

"Do you hear me? You only ever come inside my pussy," I said, breathing heavily. "My young, little pussy that you broke and took for yourself." I was about to orgasm any second. How I'd held on this long was beyond me.

"You like that your coach is fucking you?" he asked, almost surprised by his question.

I moaned. "I think about it when I touch myself."

"You… You touch yourself? Fuck…"

"All the time," I admitted.

"With what?" he asked, breathless.

"My fingers, but you want to know another secret?" He nodded. "I just bought my first vibrator and I came on it three times in a row thinking it was your cock."

It was a lie. I hadn't bought anything, but it felt like something he'd want to hear.

Kova's rhythm slowed down. His breathing was rough and ragged as he pulled his finger out, but then he poked at my entrance again with two fingers this time.

"I want to fuck you until you cannot walk. Pound you so hard you are too bruised to sit down for a week."

A gasp rolled off my lips. My eyes widened and I tensed, then remembered him telling me to relax. I tried but my heart was hammering in my chest. I knew he wouldn't hurt me but it still made me a little apprehensive. Heart racing, my ass felt like it was on fire but not enough to ruin what we had between us. My thighs weakened and I could barely hold myself up anymore from the onslaught of pleasure taking over my body. Kova noticed and sat up so I could lean back against him.

"I… I can't hold on any longer. I need to come," I said, then turned my head around to kiss him. "But I will only come if you come with me."

"I will do whatever you want, anything, if you tell me you love me."

"No," I said, my voice below a whisper. "Why are you asking me this right now?"

His hips surged into me faster. A routine of perfect harmony enough to seduce me to a wild mess of passion.

"Tell me," he begged and I almost caved, but I stood strong and shook my head. "I want to hear you say you love me like I love you."

"No," I said again. He wouldn't get that from me.

"Tell me," he begged, placing his hand on my throat. "Please, so I know I am not the only crazy one."

"Oh God, it's right there," I said and reared back so I was riding his cock at the same time. My heart was fluttering and once again he took me to a new level I knew I would crave again after this.

"Tell me," he said one last time, and I partially gave him what he wanted to hear.

"I love the way we make love."

That was all he was getting.

Kova reached between us and pinched my clit so hard I screamed as he drove into me from behind. He used his strength to shove me down on his dick as loud moans purred from my throat. The pleasure was too much and I closed my eyes and let myself fall. Silver stars danced behind my eyelids as he tightened his grip. My breathing took on a sound of its own, and my body rode his wave until the pleasure subsided and we slowed down.

Our heavy breathing was the only sound in the room. Kova pulled his cock out with a little pop and leaned back against the arm rest of the couch, taking me with him. I glanced down between us, his length semi-hard and glossy with our abandoned cravings. A thin white line oozed from his tip and stuck to my inner thigh. His hand flattened against my entrance and I looked over my shoulder at him quizzically.

"Squeeze. I can feel my cum trying to leak out of you." He covered my tender vagina with his hand to hold it in. He was so filthy, but I loved that about him. "Leave it where it belongs." I nodded, trying to catch my breath, feeling it trying to pour out of me.

Turning over, I got up to face him and sank down on his lap. Kova grabbed my face and kissed me passionately and tenderly, something I'd noticed he did each time after we had sex. This was his way of showing me affection, I thought. He pulled back and I smiled. We both looked between us. His penis hung over his elastic waistband looking completely used, and I could see my clit as his cum leaked out of me onto his shaft. My teeth dug into my bottom lip as I moved my pussy over his length, rubbing his thick white pleasure on his cock. I lifted my eyes to study Kova. He was watching us intently.

I leaned forward to push his head back so I could press my lips to his neck, I slid my tender pussy over him. Kova growled and I felt it against my lips.

"Go ahead and come on me like this, Ria, I know you want to."

And I did. I rubbed our desires all over him until I was trying to squeeze his dick with my pussy lips and came again.

"God," I said breathless once I was done. I sat up feeling a little light-headed. My eyes were wide with surprise. "I don't know what comes over me when I'm with you. I feel like I turn into another person and all I can focus on is sex."

Kova grinned then kissed me hard. He stuffed his penis back into his pants and then dropped to his knees. Grabbing my hips, he placed a soft kiss to my mound and lifted one leg and placed it over his shoulder. I watched, curious to see what he was going to do when his bottom teeth gradually danced over my clit. I shuddered, a current of euphoria slaying through me. My fingers threaded his tousled locks and I raised my hips, rocking into his face while he teased me some more. If he wanted to give me more, fine by me. Kova flattened his tongue and pressed it against my sex and I almost came again. It was raw and dirty, but truth be told, I loved that he was tasting us.

"I love your pussy," he said like he was on cloud nine.

I felt a thick, slippery gooeyness trail down my ass onto the couch. I looked down and watched two of Kova's fingers wipe it up then push it back into me. He stroked the tender walls of my pussy with a softness that didn't quite match his rough exterior, massaging his semen into me. Kova's carnal desires resonated within me. I understood where he was coming from because I was just like him.

Kova looked up at me. Our eyes connected and something in my heart shifted into place. Each day he was mending what he broke inside of me. His vulnerability was back, defenses were down, and I saw the love he had for me. Not from the orgasms he gave, but from the way his distressed eyes stared into mine, the way his face contorted with agony and yearning. He dropped his forehead to my stomach and his shoulders bunched tight. He expelled a breath and then wrapped his arms around my waist and held me, releasing whatever pent-up emotion he had.

And I took it. I took all of it all, feeling the weight of his body and absorbing it deep into my bones. It was strange how I felt him more through touch than his words. I understood him. But sometimes when he looked at me, and how his body sank into mine, how he trembled beneath the surface, it was the only answer I needed.

Moving to my knees, I embraced this man who was so tormented by his feelings and actions. I wanted to tell him I loved him. I had too much empathy for him, and I didn't know how to close that gate to make it stop from happening, because the reality was, I'd unlocked the door and held it open for him to begin with.

"Promise me," I said softly. He nodded.

Kova was right. This wasn't normal, but it was our normal…and I was okay with that.

CHAPTER 41

Kova molded back into his old self with each passing day, and within weeks I was greeted daily with his cocky brashness I'd come to know and love.

I never realized how much my mental health relied on his coaching and what we accomplished in the gym, because despite the fatigue and bone aches, I was doing better than ever. I took all my medicine, I didn't miss my scheduled blood work, and I actually slept. I was even eating a little better. I hadn't gained weight, but I felt alive and I knew it was because I had rekindled my relationship with Kova.

I still didn't have a donor match. That was one thing he couldn't do for me.

We were both trying so hard to find the right medium to make things work. Inside the gym, we picked up where we left off and practiced my routines for hours each day, breaking down the skills and practicing to perfection. Wash, rinse, repeat. We were completely civil to one another and back to business. I ate up his words. My first, huge international meet was coming up, then one more competition a couple of weeks after that where the selection for the Olympic team took place.

This was it. The moments I'd been waiting for were finally here.

As the day drew to an end and practice was just about over, I caught a flutter of neon pink in the corner of my eye. I glanced over at a face I hadn't seen in many long months. Bright blue globes for eyes, a giant smile from ear to ear that I felt down to my soul, and platinum blonde hair and pinks tips she'd dyed.

Avery Heron. My best friend. Was at World Cup.

Excitement I hadn't felt in ages whooshed through me. My face lit up and I bounced on my toes eagerly. I wanted to run to her, throw my arms around her neck, but I couldn't just leave in the middle of practice, not even to take a break—I needed permission.

I searched for Kova, and he saw my silent plea. He nodded his head with a kind smile. I ran. Maybe opening up about Avery to him had been a blessing in disguise.

Within seconds I was in the lobby throwing myself into my best friend's open arms. She caught me and I wrapped my legs around her like I was a damn spider monkey. She stumbled back but luckily for both of us regained her footing.

"Adrianna!" she squealed in my ear. I almost cried hearing her voice in person. "Oh my God, you're squeezing me to death. Let go." She feigned a choking sound.

I chuckled as she released me. Our hands joined together and we stood inches from each other.

"I can't believe you're here! I figured not for a few more days!" I said.

"I wanted to surprise you, so I came early!"

I was so happy, tears filled my eyes. I hugged her again and squeezed. "You don't know how much I've missed you. How long are you here for?"

"For however long I want to be. I don't have a schedule."

"I'm so excited!" I nodded with a stupid grin on my face.

The door chimed and in walked the definition of a perfect woman. Katja.

She looked directly at me and I mused to myself that I didn't even know her last name. Not that it mattered anymore since she was now a Kournakova.

"Adrianna."

Her Russian accent was thicker than Kova's. She looked at Avery with questionable eyes, raking a bitter glance down her body. I swallowed nervously, thinking about how the last time I saw her Kova had kicked her out of his office for me.

"Hi, Katja," I said quietly just to be nice.

"Does Konstantin know you are out here?"

An odd question, and I decided not to answer her. She didn't need to know he gave me permission.

Katja made a little sound under her breath and squinted toward the windows that led to the gym. I looked at Avery, who wore the same baffled expression as I did. We both shrugged at the same time and laughed.

"You're so tan," I said to her. "Just like Ba—"

She pointed her index finger at me and raised one brow. "Don't you dare say Barbie, bitch. You know I hate that fucking shit."

I laughed as she scolded me. But she did. She was a life-like version of Barbie but with deep sun-kissed skin I envied. Aside from my Italian roots that blessed me with a Mediterranean tone, I was pale in comparison to her, and now I would always be because of the reaction the sun caused in conjunction with lupus.

"Fine. You look like Paris Hilton."

Her face scrunched up. "Ewww. A walking disease?"

I laughed. "Taylor Swift?"

Her eyes sparkled. "Much better."

"I have to finish up. I have about two hours left. Do you want to wait or go straight to my condo?"

"I'll wait. I don't mind."

"Sweet. I was hoping you'd say that." I smiled from ear to ear. "Ah! I'm so happy you're here!"

I opened the door that led to the gym, and for the second time today, something caught my attention. But it wasn't a color this time. It was Katja's hushed words drifting through the air, and I frowned. Her giddiness caused me to stall with my hand on the knob.

I fought with myself. I didn't want to turn around to see what she was doing, but I did anyway. I learned from Kova that everything she did had a motive, so her presence at World Cup meant something. I watched Katja hold her stomach as she spoke to a parent from one of the teams and I caught the faint purr of broken English that nipped my mended heart. I saw smiles and I swear I heard blessings of some sort.

"Hey," Avery said softly. Her brows were bunched together as she glanced over my shoulder. "Ignore that dirty gnat and whatever you heard. I have a feeling not everything is what it seems with her."

A sad chuckle rolled from my lips. "Did you just say gnat?"

One side of her mouth pulled to the side. She shrugged her shoulder. "Yeah, I heard it in a new rap song and I loved it. So everyone I find annoying is a gnat."

"Which is everyone since you hate the world."

"Except for you." Her smiled reached her ears. "Finish up and we'll talk later. It seems we both need to have a long girl talk."

I walked back into the gym trying to forget what I saw. I wanted so bad to ask him why she was here, but I couldn't bring myself to. He knew where I stood and how I felt. I wouldn't stoop to that level and lose respect for myself completely.

Inhale the chalk, exhale the bullshit.

For the next two hours, I pretended like I didn't have a care in the world except for gymnastics.

Kova didn't speak to me except when he was coaching, but then again, I didn't expect anything else since his scheming wife was here to watch her husband.

"Adrianna?" Kova said low, and only for me.

I pulled back the Velcro from my grips to loosen the straps. "Yes?" I said without looking up. Taking off my grips felt as good as taking off my sports bra at the end of the day.

"Look at me."

Hesitant, I raised my eyes. Kova rubbed the back of his neck, his face twisting in distress.

"Do not go there. I know what you think you heard, but it is not true."

I swallowed hard, praying what he said was the truth.

"I told you she wants one, not that she has one."

My stomach tightened, stunned that he was risking such a conversation in public.

Kova muttered under his breath in Russian. "I am asking you to please believe me. Please."

CHAPTER 42

He wants you to believe him?" she retorted, her voice surprised. "Did you tell him to go fucking kick rocks?"

I gave Avery a knowing look. "You know I didn't."

She sighed. "Sometimes I wish you would grow a spine and tell him to eat shit, then walk away." Avery's eyes widened and she looked a little worried and tried to retract her words. "Not to say that you don't have a spine, ah, I just that I wish you wouldn't let him walk all over you."

We were sitting on my bed having a powwow while we drank freshly squeezed lemonade Avery had made. We'd been talking for hours and it felt so good. It was the long-awaited girl talk we should've had a long time ago.

I left no stone unturned. I told her every single thing that had happened with Kova, leaving nothing out. I opened up about Joy, and Avery cursed her to seven different hells. She'd never liked Joy. I told her about my real mom and how I met her, the illness in her family and how it was genetic. Avery encouraged me to meet with her again one day when I was ready. I was honest and told her I was afraid of dying young.

She listened to me. She cried with me. She didn't judge, didn't criticize my choices. She was the ideal best friend who just sat and heard me. Sometimes just listening can be more powerful than anything.

I sighed in understanding. "I know what you mean, it's just hard. I guess I want to give him the benefit of the doubt since we don't have a normal relationship."

"But is it that? A relationship?" She posed her question carefully.

I picked at the imaginary lint on my comforter. "I honestly don't know what to call it." And I didn't.

"Maybe it doesn't need a label. Sometimes that can ruin a good thing," she offered.

I smiled at her, appreciating her effort. "Yeah, I guess so." I paused. "Does it make me stupid? Be honest."

"It doesn't make you stupid. Love makes people do things they wouldn't typically do, but it doesn't make you, or anyone, stupid. Maybe in that moment it was right and that's really all that matters." She eyed me with a challenge. "And don't even deny you love him. It's obvious you do."

I chuckled sadly. "To you? Or to everyone?"

"I mean, I didn't see you look at him with hearts in your eyes today. I'm sure you're careful not to in public, but when you talk about him, you get this cheesy ass dreamy look in your eyes that embarrasses the shit out of me, but yeah, I can see it. I also know you, so you're asking the wrong chick."

"I'm scared he's going to hurt me again," I said quietly. "I don't want to be hurt again, Ave. I don't think I have the heart for it."

"Aid?"

I looked up.

"He's done a lot to hurt you, there's no denying that. Call me crazy, I can't even believe I'm going to side with Fish Lips, but I don't think all of it was intentional. Your situation isn't a usual one, and you both did things you wouldn't normally do. Do I think you should tread lightly? Fuck yeah, I do, for more reasons than one. Love is risky, and even though they say love shouldn't hurt, it always does because no one has a perfect love. It's all trial and error. If you allow yourself to love someone, you're giving them power over you. To me, that hurts. I don't want anyone to have any kind of power over me ever again. Yes, there are a ton of reasons why you should walk away and let it go, but can you think of at least one reason that makes you want to stay and chance it?"

I nodded immediately. I didn't hesitate.

"What is it?" she asked, her eyes soft.

"It sounds so stupid—"

"No, it doesn't. If it makes sense to you, then that's all that matters."

"He encourages me. I want to be a better person, a better gymnast, because of him. I can feel his energy and I love it. It gives me life. He's made me strong, even at my weakest point when I shut the world out, I could look for him and he would always just be right there.

He doesn't even have to say anything, Avery, it's just like he knows, and I'm suddenly okay. Like a peace settles within me. I'm sure what I'm saying doesn't make sense. I know he does things backwards all the time, says all the wrong things, and he doesn't always make sense in that moment, but eventually, it does." I paused and shook my head. Nothing I said out loud made sense. "You know what he said to me when I felt hopeless? When I was terrified and sinking into a deep depression? That I should use my sickness as inspiration, that I should live for it instead of allowing it to kill me." My voice dropped. "He said he wanted to live with me."

I glanced up and Avery had tears in her eyes.

"You should marry that stupid Russian."

I burst out laughing. "Too late. He's already got a ring on his finger. Not that I could marry him now anyway."

"It won't last, Aid. Trust me, it won't. Not after everything you told me about the blackmail, Cuntja, the way—"

"Cuntja?" I asked, finding a comical flare to the sound of it.

"Yeah, Katja and cunt. Cuntja," she said like it was obvious.

A burst of laughter erupted from me and I giggled hysterically.

"Oh my god! That's the best!" I said between fits of laughter. It was the perfect name to describe his wife. Sobering up, I asked, "Do you think it's fair, though? I mean, she's probably the way she is because of me."

"You said Kova told you the issues between them started before you got here, so no. She's just a bitch because she was born with it in her blood, and because Joy also gave her the ammo to be a vindictive bitch at that."

I nodded, agreeing with her. Still, I was sure I didn't help their situation.

Avery continued. "What I was saying was, the way he is with you when it's just you guys is not the same guy you see out in the public. And who cares? What matters is how he is with you. He has to deflect right now and be a dick. I think it probably bothers him that he's banging a gymnast who is still a teen. At least, I hope it would." She laughed nervously. "Think about it. If it were you, like if you were in Kova's shoes, what would you do? Right now is the wrong time, yes, and some days he needs an attitude adjustment, but one day everything will be right in the world, and it will be for you guys too."

I smiled appreciatively at her. I loved my best friend. She sorted out my muddled thoughts.

"You never knew about any of this? About the lupus and kidneys? Xavier never told you?"

She shook her head and looked down with a sad expression on her face. I was genuinely surprised.

"No." Her voice was low. "I honestly never knew."

"Wow. I figured he would have."

"We haven't done much talking since everything happened…" she said quietly, like it hurt it to utter those words.

"But I saw you guys together on Instagram on the Fourth of July."

She shook her head and looked down. The sadness on her face told me everything I needed to know.

"It's not like that. I promise. We tried to hang out, but he can't get over what I did."

"You mean the abortion?"

She nodded silently. "It's not what you think… I didn't have an abortion."

CHAPTER 43

W hat? What are you talking about?"

Avery exhaled a large breath and eyed her glass of lemonade. A few seconds ago she'd been my rock, giving me inspiring words. Now she seemed broken inside, her face paling. Her thumb rimmed the lip of the glass as she blinked, like she was lost in her thoughts.

"Are you sure you want to hear this?" she asked me, her voice low. "It's not all rainbows and butterflies, and you have to make me a promise to never tell your brother, no matter what I tell you."

I reached for her hand and her fingers wrapped around mine. I didn't say anything. I didn't need to. She knew I'd never do that. We both positioned ourselves against my headboard and sat back.

"There's a lot you don't know about your brother," she said quietly.

Didn't surprise me. Most siblings were like that.

"Tell me when you started to date him."

She looked at me with guarded eyes. "We never dated. We were together but we never dated officially."

"I kind of gathered that. I just don't know how you guys made it work when he was in school."

"He came home on the weekends a lot to see me and then we hid out in the guest house together or went to parties. Or I'd go visit him. It wasn't hard to sneak around, honestly, and no one thought anything of it because my brothers were there too. I just looked like the little sister that tagged along, you know?"

I nodded. Made sense. Anything was possible with enough courage.

Avery released a breath like she just let the weight of her world go.

"Don't hold back from me, okay? No more."

She glanced in my direction and smiled softly.

"It sucks because I still want him, even after everything. He's a different person when it's just me and him. Kind of like with you and

Kova, I guess." She paused to swallow, then chewed on her bottom lip like she was nervous to tell me. "We started up about two years ago. We teased each other like siblings do, but then something somehow morphed into something else and we became more. He was like a best friend with benefits in a way. Once we started hooking up, we fell hard for each other. I loved him… I think I still love him."

My brows shot up. "I can't believe I never knew. How did I not I see it? I feel like everything is so obvious now, but at the time… Like New Year's… I should've seen it."

"You wouldn't have. No one would have. Our parents were never around. You were doing gymnastics morning, noon, and night, and we were good at hiding it. It was so easy."

I nodded my head back and forth. She had a point. Sneaking around is easy when you want something bad enough.

"The parties, though…that's where all of our issues stem from. There's so much drugs and aggression and testosterone at them. At the time, we didn't think anything of it. We were living our best life, but hindsight is a bitch. We'd drink and smoke some weed, then go back to his house and smush like rabbits. But it wasn't just like any hookup. It was way more for both of us. I can't explain it, like it just was, and he knew that."

Avery exhaled another big breath like it was hard for her to get into the nitty-gritty of the story. I felt bad.

"If it's too hard to talk about, we don't have to," I said gently.

She shook her head. "No, I need to tell you everything."

Scooting closer to her, I rested my head on her shoulder, hoping to give her the courage to keep going. "Go on."

She waited a long moment.

"So I'm not sure if you know, but Xavier's into fighting. Like MMA shit, but it's underground. He's good at it too, undefeated… or at least he was." Her voice trailed off like she was saddened by the memory. "Xavier said I was his lucky charm and he had me in his corner at every fight. He didn't lose a match, until we stopped being together. He hasn't won since."

"I had a feeling he was into something reckless, but I didn't know it was that." I thought back to one of the times I went home and he had some cuts and bruises on his face and how he had played it off. I just assumed he was being an idiot with his friends and left it alone. "How cliché of him. Rich punk into underground fighting." I rolled my eyes.

"He makes money, girl. Good money. Well, he did."

I shook my head, puzzled. "Why, though? He doesn't need it."

She shrugged one shoulder. "Because he's good at it and can. Why does anyone do stupid things like that? It was a rush to watch him, and he'd tell me that's what it was like for him too when he was fighting. He was high all the time, so I'm sure the adrenaline and coke were making him feel twenty feet tall."

"He was doing cocaine?" I asked, my voice low, as if someone might hear me. Cocaine and fighting couldn't be a good combination on the heart. Dread began to cultivate in my stomach like black smoke and I started to fear the worst possible scenario.

"Oh, he was doing more than that. Coke, Ex, Oxy, Vicodin, Xanax, anything he could get his hands on, however he could take it, he did. Snorting, shooting, chewing pills, he did it all. He'd get so high he didn't want to come down, so he'd move on to something stronger."

I was going to be sick. Instant worry for my dumb ass brother and his recklessness struck me when something else dawned on me. I lifted my head up and turned toward Avery.

"You were doing drugs with him, weren't you?"

She looked away. Embarrassment flushed her cheeks and she nodded.

My lips turned downward. "Ave, is he still doing this?"

"To an extent, yes." She struggled to admit. "It's one of the reasons I walked away. Every minute of every day, he was high and gearing up for a fight."

I frowned. I couldn't believe I didn't see any of this. "I'm so confused."

"We broke up and got back together so many times. Like we weren't together, but we were. When I walked away the last time, he said he was done playing with me. I was hurt and thought he was lying, but I said fine by me and gave him the finger. When he talked shit to me, I gave it back ten times harder. Xavier shut me out, and man, is he good at it. But that's what we did, you know? We fought then apologized and then went back to being how we were. I figured that's what would happen, but then we didn't talk for over a month until I saw him again."

"What did he say when he found out you were pregnant?"

"He was not what I expected at all. I thought he was going to flip the fuck out, but he was oddly excited about it."

My brows shot up. "What? That doesn't make any sense."

"Yeah, I know. It was weird. He was beaming like a fool and touching my stomach any chance he got. Here I was crying and panicking inside because, hello, I was only seventeen and pregnant. *Teen Mom*, here I come. But Xavier was jumping up and down and kissing me and hugging me nonstop. I'd never seen him so happy, Aid. I remember this feeling of relief, like okay, one down, ten more to go and then everything would be okay. My love for him developed into something more during that time. I also remember thinking we would actually get to be family like we always talked about."

I shook my head, unsure what to feel anymore. Xavier's reaction about the pregnancy was odd and it messed with my mind. They both were so young and shouldn't want a baby, yet he did.

"That doesn't make any sense," I told her. "He wasn't thinking clearly. No one wants a baby at that age. It had to be the drugs. Had to be." I paused, deciding to tell her what I was thinking. "Unless he really loved you…?"

Her shoulders dropped. "I don't know anymore. Honestly. I think maybe he did love me and we both didn't know it, but he sure as shit doesn't now. Not after what I did," she said, her voice cracking a little. "All I could think about was your ratchet mother—well, Joy—and how my parents were going to react to the news. Telling Xavier made my hands shake and my heart pound. Our parents? My stomach cramped and I was a sweaty mess. I mean, I'm in high school. I can't have a baby. But I was. I was gonna have a kid."

I rested my head back against the wood and put myself in her shoes. I couldn't imagine having a child at our age, let alone going through such heavy emotions with no one to lean on. We both had dealt with situations where we'd needed each other's support during a critical time, and we hadn't had it. I had to deal with the fact that Joy wasn't my mom, Kova secretly got married, and a stupid sickness was wearing me down. Meanwhile, my bestie was pregnant by my brother and had an abortion—only she hadn't.

God, I wished we both had had the strength to talk to each other. I couldn't help but wonder if we'd had each other to lean on if she would be here holding a baby now. But the past is the past and now that we were talking it through, I was going to make sure this never happened again. I couldn't reverse time, but I could try and prevent the same mistake from happening twice.

I lowered my eyes, regret spilling through me. I was the definition of a shit friend. Absorbed in gymnastics and Kova, Avery had to deal with this on her own. I'd make it up to her, though. Somehow, some way, I would.

"Keep going," I said softly. I knew there was more.

Avery took a sip of her lemonade. "I wasn't worried about needing financial support. I knew eventually our families would come together and our child wouldn't want for anything, but I was scared. God, I was so scared, and I had to tell our parents. I had to tell you. That was the worst part. I was more afraid to tell you than our parents. I didn't want you to hate me or to never talk to me again. I went back and forth about how to say something, but I could never find the courage to. I didn't want to lose you and I was so scared I would." Her voice shook. Avery pulled her knees up and wrapped her arms around them. "Not only was I hooking up with my best friend's brother, I gotten knocked up by him too." Avery burst into tears, and I knew why. She did lose me for a little while.

And it was my fault.

CHAPTER 44

I reached over and took her glass and placed it on my nightstand, along with mine, then I wrapped my arm around her shoulder and pulled her into a hug.

She hugged me back and cried softly while my heart broke for her and us. I couldn't imagine having to tell her something like that, and it made sense now why she hadn't. Opening up to her about Kova was a hard pill to swallow. But if I had to tell her I'd gotten pregnant by one of her brothers, I don't think it would've gone over well either. I probably would've done the same thing she had.

"I'm so sorry for the way I acted," I said honestly. "I wish I would've known. I wish I would've been there for you. I wish I would've given you the opportunity to explain. I wish I wasn't such a bitch toward you."

Avery hugged me back tighter. "It's not your fault. I was such a mess and so were you. I couldn't talk about it when I needed to. I kept to myself and ran through all these different scenarios in my head, thinking they had positive outcomes, but they really didn't. I was lying to myself and I knew I was."

Pulling back, I made her look at me. Her usually stunning blue eyes were bloodshot and screaming with shame. I wanted to take that from her so she never felt it again.

"Before you say anything else, let's make a pact. From here on out, we promise to never hold back, no matter how scared we are to tell each other something, okay? I never want to go through this again with you, because the truth is, we need each other."

She nodded and sniffled. "Never again."

"Never."

"There's more." She sounded scared, but I nodded anyway, and she began to tell me about the life of Xavier I never knew he had.

"Xavier was doing all these underground fights, and he was killing it. Right before each fight, he'd kiss me in front of everyone and tell me I was his, and afterward we would celebrate at a party with drinks and whatever we were in the mood for. I did them with him, I wanted to. He never left my side, couldn't take his hands off me, and if any other guy spoke to me, he got possessive and totally alpha. At first I loved it. I thought it was hot, you know? We were glued to each other and I know you don't want to hear this, but we had the best sex when we were like that after a fight. He had so much adrenaline in him." She smiled sadly. "Well, one night he was banged up pretty badly and almost lost a fight. The guy he fought knew about your brother's winning streak and prepared for Xavier's left hook. He was determined to take your brother out."

Chills zipped down my spine, a sense of fear curling in my stomach. I had a feeling this was going to be bad. Underground fighting was probably one of the dumbest things I'd ever heard of.

"Xavier was so hyped up from the fight and the drugs, that right before he almost went down, he looked at me one last time and gave me a naughty ass grin. It was so fucking sexy, Aid. God, I can remember it like it was yesterday. Anyway, this guy thought he would antagonize Xavier by using me."

"Oh shit. What did he do?"

"Oh shit is fucking right." Avery shook her head like she was there again living it. "He told Xavier he was going to fuck me raw after he won." She paused, and shuddered. "I thought Xavier was going to kill him. I really thought he was gonna go to jail for murder."

I'd never seen my brother enraged except during Easter when he'd pushed our dad up against the wall. This was all news to me.

"Even though blood dripped from one corner of his lip, and his eyes were swollen and already bruising, Xavier went to town on the guy. I don't know where his energy came from. He was hyped and beat the shit out of him *bad*. I mean, like, he pulverized him to the point it took a few people to pull Xavier off him. It was horrible. The guy was barely moving. He laid on the floor in a pool of blood with teeth missing. Xavier spit on him, said some shit, and then turned toward me. I thought he was gonna give me a celebratory kiss like he usually did, but he was angry, and it scared me. There was a blank look in his eyes."

I sat in utter silence listening to this side of Xavier I never knew existed. The thought of him like this scared me. Reckless and wild was one thing, but this was asking for a death wish. Hearing him take so many drugs and fight? That was a deadly combination. Someone needed to talk some sense into him. I wanted to do that, but I didn't want to betray Avery's trust either. Sighing inwardly, I didn't know what to say. I couldn't give advice because it was already said and done, so all I could do was listen.

"At the party afterward, he barely said two words to me but wouldn't let me leave his side either. He was strung out, but I sat on his lap like I always did while he drank whatever was handed to him. He wouldn't let me ice his face or help put anything on it to reduce the swelling. I tried to kiss him, tried to have sex with him like we usually did after a win, but nothing worked. All he would let me do was hold his hand. His fingers shook after he laced them through mine and his grip was so strong, almost like he was afraid I was going to leave. We did lines of coke together, probably shared an eightball that night, but then he took it further and took a Xanax and popped some Ex. I didn't, though, not even when he begged me to roll with him. I didn't like mixing uppers with downers because that's like asking for a death wish. But he did. I remember having this weird feeling in my stomach that night. He wasn't acting like himself, he'd had so much to drink, taking shot after shot of tequila. I begged him to stop but he wouldn't listen and got angrier by the second. He was like a ticking time bomb. Still, I stayed by his side." Avery's voice drew quiet and she lowered her gaze. Tears filled her eyes. "Around three in the morning, he fucking overdosed," she whispered. Her shoulders shook and she started to cry again.

I drew in an audible breath and my stomach dropped. Cupping my mouth, I stared, unblinking as I replayed the words in my head, not sure I'd heard her right.

"What? He overdosed?" I whispered, my jaw trembling. I blinked a few times trying to put everything together. My vision blurred imagining my brother like this.

Clenching her eyes shut, she nodded her head and wiped the tears from her cheeks. "We had to use Narcan to bring him back."

I frowned, brows deepening. "You just happened to carry that?"

She sniffled and took a deep breath before exhaling slowly. She could hardly look me in the eyes.

"No, one of the guys he was chilling with had it, but after that happened I carried it because I had to use it on him again another time. During the time I was with him, he overdosed a total of three times." She let out a sob that broke my heart. Now I was terrified for my brother. "Every night Xavier pushed the envelope. He turned into a completely different person, so mean when he was fucked up. I knew he wouldn't lay a hand on me, but his rage was a side of him that scared me. He became so volatile."

Red-hot fear sliced through me. "Avery," I whispered. My heart thundered in my chest at the thought of losing my brother. I wasn't supposed to say anything to him, but this was a matter of life and death and I wasn't going to risk it.

"We have to do something about this. Is he still like that?"

She shook her head. "From what I hear, all he does is drink now and take Xanax. Still a dangerous combo but better than what he was doing. I tried to help him at first, but he wasn't having it. That's when our fighting got bad. He was spiraling out of control and I couldn't stop him. He wouldn't let me. The first time I walked out on him was when he OD'd the second time. I thought it'd wake him up. But the third time it happened was the last straw. He didn't even give himself time to recover from the overdose when he was back at it again. Being that I was pregnant by that point, I was sober, so I saw just how far gone he was. I know I was just as bad at first—I don't claim to be a saint—but he was toeing the line to see how far he could go every night. I told him if he didn't get help I was leaving for good. He was so mad that night. We literally screamed at the top of our lungs at each other. He told me he'd take care of his kid, but he was done playing with me because all bitches are the fucking same and only good for one thing. I didn't believe it because it's what we did, you know, but I guess he was serious. For weeks he shut me out and wouldn't see me, wouldn't talk to me. Unfollowed me on all social media sites and blocked me. It was horrible. I was pregnant and so alone. I'd heard he was hooking up with new girls every night but then losing every fight too. When I finally did get to see him, it was at a charity event. He was with a girl your mom had set him up with." Avery's face scrunched up and she looked absolutely sick. "God, it killed me to see him like that. Xavier was all over her. He'd look at me then kiss her. It killed me inside. There I was wearing his favorite dress hoping to sway him, pregnant with his child that I was still hiding pretty well, and he was loving up on someone else."

"Ave," I said. I had a bad feeling about this. "Don't tell me you had an abortion because of that."

She looked away. "Yes and no… The cramping started that night, only I didn't realize they were cramps. I just thought my belly was stretching. The next day I went to the pool house to try and talk some sense into him. I could barely walk to my car, let alone drive to your house and walk to the pool house. The pain was unbearable, but I missed him so fucking much and wanted to fix things. I was willing to do anything, only when I opened the door, I found him tangled in the sheets totally naked with the same chick. Seeing him like that sucked the air from my lungs. It was the proof I needed to truly be done with him. I thought I was going to be sick and I held my stomach and leaned on the doorframe. Xavier got up when he saw me and walked over to me. He told me to get the fuck out. The weird thing was I could see his pain when he was yelling at me, I could feel it, how much it hurt to look at me because I knew he still wanted me just like I did him. His eyes were bloodshot, his hands shook, he had bruises everywhere. It was like he let himself get beat up. He gave me a little shove on my shoulder, but it wasn't bad or anything. I begged him to come back to me. I let myself cry in front of him. I told him my stomach was hurting but he brushed it off saying I was using the pregnancy as a way to keep him."

Avery took a deep breath and lowered her voice. "I didn't know stress could cause a miscarriage, but that's what happened. I never had an abortion, Aid. I had a fucking miscarriage. I lied to Xavier. I lied to everyone."

"How far along were you by then?"

"I was about five months when I had the miscarriage. You'd never know it, though. I hardly showed and hid it well."

Avery let go and her tears really started to fall. I reached over and pulled her into a bear hug. She softly cried on my shoulder, shaking. I cried with her over the loss of everything at once. She held me tight as she sobbed, her tears coming in fast and hard. My heart broke as she relived this moment I was sure she wanted to forget for the rest of her life. This whole time she was living a lie with no outlet. I knew that feeling and how it could consume someone, how the pressure mounted into something more, how you're stuck with these depressing thoughts.

But this was different. She had carried a life inside of her. Her child. A child she lost.

And I had missed out on being an aunt.

CHAPTER 45

I don't know what to say, Ave. I'm so, so sorry. God, I'm so sorry," I said again through my tears.

My issues felt so small in comparison to hers. Now I knew why she wanted to tell me in person. This wasn't a conversation to have over the phone.

Avery sniffled and drew in a deep breath. Pulling back, she used her shirt to wipe her eyes.

"I asked him to feel my belly that day because our son was kicking. I wasn't far along enough to feel kicks all the time, but they did start. Small ones, but I felt them. I thought if he wouldn't talk to me, then at least that could work. I remember feeling a sliver of hope, like my heart was going to pop out of my chest because he stopped yelling at me and looked down at my belly. His eyes changed, his demeanor changed, and I saw the old Xavier for a split second. Even though he claimed he didn't want me, he wanted our baby. His hand reached out only to pull back just as quickly. His wall slid back into place and he kicked me out, slamming the door shut. I cried for him to take me back. I didn't make it far inside your house when I fell to the floor in pain. Joy found me."

My entire body tensed over Joy being the one to find her. Then all at once everything clicked into place, and my mind flashed back to Easter when shit had hit the fan. Joy had said she'd cleaned up their mess and helped with Avery's miscarriage like she was proud of it. I clenched the back of my teeth while I tried not to relive that day.

"What happened next?" I asked, dreading to know exactly how Joy had helped.

"She took me to a private clinic," Avery said, her low drawl a hint deeper.

"Did she know it was a miscarriage?"

Avery hesitated. "She did. She said it would be better if I said I had an abortion. She knew about Xavier's partying and said he wouldn't take it as hard, so I did. Call me crazy but I agreed with her. I never knew when his next high was going to kill him and I didn't want him to take any of the blame at all, so I agreed and lied to him."

My jaw dropped and a splinter of heat zipped down my spine. "You're kidding me. Did she encourage it? I swear, Avery, I will kill her."

God. I was starting to seriously hate that woman.

Avery sobered up a little. "No, not really. I mean the doctor said I was in the early stages of having a miscarriage and that's when Joy suggested I just do the procedure to get it over with to move it along faster." She sat quietly for a moment. Her jaw quivered. "So I did. I killed my baby. I didn't know stress would do it. I didn't know how easy it was to miscarry," she stated, breathing heavily. "I didn't know anything," she cried out. "Now I'll never get to hold him, and Xavier will never get to call him Rocky."

"Rocky?"

She shrugged one shoulder dejectedly. "He joked that he was going to name him Rocky."

We were both quiet for a little while, letting everything sink in. I held my best friend's hand, trying to breathe spirit into her. It physically hurt me to see her like this and I wanted to take away her pain as much as I could. I wasn't naïve. I knew she'd never forget something like this, but if I could help make her a little happy, then I wanted to.

"Why not just tell him the truth?"

"I'd rather him hate me than think he caused the miscarriage and hate himself. If we were together and never fought, then I'd be sitting here with a baby with you. I don't blame him for anything, but I knew he'd blame himself. He went on a bender and pushed the partying the furthest I'd seen yet."

Avery burst out with more tears. "I'm so sorry," she sobbed. I told her to stop and to just to get it out. She shouldn't be apologizing. This was what I was here for.

"If he knew he was the source of the miscarriage, it scares me to think what he'd do."

"I bet he lost it when you told him." Not only was I sad for my bestie, but for my brother too. Just when I thought my problems were bad, there was always someone who had it worse.

Avery raised her head, eyes as wide as the moon. "It was the first time I ever saw him cry. He trashed the pool house, put holes in the wall with his fists and head, got wrecked every night for weeks. Joy had to hire people to redo the whole thing. I thought he was going to overdose again, and for good this time. Thank God he didn't."

"So what happened with the Fourth of July?"

She licked her lips and glanced down. "I wasn't sure when I got pregnant, and my period was irregular, so I was given two due dates. The doctors said that only time would tell as the fetus grew." She paused. "July fourth was in the middle of my due dates. I got pregnant sometime in October, but I didn't know until December."

"Wait a minute. You were pregnant on New Year's Eve and drinking?"

She shook her head. "I didn't actually drink. I pretended to sip it and when no one was looking, Xavier took it."

"I can't believe I didn't know." I was in shock.

"No one knew. We hid it well and I hardly showed. Once I had a small bump, I switched to more Boho style clothing."

"Okay, keep going."

"Before the Instagram post, we hadn't spoken to each other since the day I told him about the abortion, so when he asked to see me, I ran. It was the fourth." Avery grew quiet and I feared more heartache was coming from her. "We tried to be together on that day, but we barely lasted through the fireworks. I hurt too much. Xavier told me he would always look at me as the mother who'd killed his child. He wasn't mean about it, just hurting like I was. I don't blame him for saying it." Her eyes lowered to the bed. "He looked horrible, Aid. So bad. He unblocked me from social media after that day. Of course I'm always stalking him. While he looks happy, I know the look in his eyes is anything but that."

This time, it was my turn to cry. I couldn't stop the tears from pouring out of me and I cried so deeply for them and what they would never have again.

I wiped my eyes with the back of my hands. "I never would've guessed any of this happened. I didn't expect it at all. I don't know what to say to help you. I feel useless."

She regarded me with love. Avery shook her head. "There's nothing you need to say. Just telling you is all I need."

"What happens after this? Like with you guys?"

She glanced away with longing in her eyes. "Nothing. We go on like it never happened, I guess." She waited a long minute before she spoke again. "We'll never be the same."

My heart broke for the both of them. "You don't think telling him the truth would be better?"

She shook her head rapidly. "No. It won't do anything to bring the baby back, and honestly, the damage is already done. Like I said, I'd rather him hate me than think he had anything to do with the miscarriage. It's better that way."

⟡⟡⟡⟡⟡⟡⟡

AFTER TALKING AND SHEDDING MORE tears, we ate popcorn and watched *Cruel Intentions*.

Avery and I agreed that coming clean to each other was cathartic. We were way past overdue for it and promised each other again to never let it happen.

She said she wasn't going to contact Xavier again, even though I wished she would. I encouraged it, but after she told me she was going to cut my hair in my sleep if I didn't stop, I shut up. My hair loss had increased the last few months, so I needed all I had left.

I felt awful knowing how bad both Avery and Xavier were hurting, but more importantly longing for each other. And as much as I initially hated the idea of them together, from what I gathered, it seemed like they really were into each other. Crazy to think of them like that, but I had no room to talk anymore.

Hello, Kova.

Thinking of Kova…shit. I realized I forgot to tell him I had an appointment tomorrow.

"Hand me my phone, Ave. I forgot to tell Kova I have blood work tomorrow."

Avery paused our favorite movie before grabbing my cell phone off the nightstand and handing it to me.

"Thanks. I forgot all about my appointment. You don't have to come…it'll be boring. I have practice after, so if you wanna shop or sightsee or something, you can."

"You're so wrapped up in gymnastics that you forgot what tomorrow is."

I quickly shot a text to Kova then frowned at her. "What's tomorrow?"

Her eyes widened. "Your birthday, dummy."

I paused and stared at her. Holy shit.

"Oh, my God. How did I forget?"

Tomorrow I would turn eighteen. I'd been so wrapped up in my life and focused that I'd forgotten my own birthday.

"Why do you think I'm here?" she asked with a smile on her face.

It felt good to see her smile after our long-winded conversation. I couldn't take all the credit for it, though. She was a bit obsessed with Ryan Phillipe and swore one day she was going to move to Hollywood and marry him.

"Since I missed it last year, I came to celebrate your big day. I have an awesome surprise planned for you that no one will ever be able to top."

I continued to stare, dumbfounded. "I can't believe I forgot!"

"We'll just blame it on the lupus."

For once I could laugh about being sick.

"So I'm coming with you tomorrow to your doctor's and then I'm taking you out."

My happiness faded a little. The thought, though it sounded like loads of fun, was short-lived.

"I can't. I have practice after."

Avery shook her head, her blonde locks swaying across her face. "You don't," she said proudly, and popped a piece of popcorn into her mouth. "I cleared it with Kova. You're mine for the entire day."

Brows scrunched together. "What? How?"

She looked extremely proud as she wiggled her shoulders from side to side. "I have my ways."

I felt a smile tug at the corner of my mouth. My lips twitched. "For real?" I chuckled.

"Yes! I have the whole day planned. I've been looking forward to this, you have no idea. You're going to love it! Just trust me on this one, okay?"

I threw my arms around her shoulders and squeezed her as tight as I could. "I haven't taken a day just to hang out in ages; I usually just sleep on my day off. You're seriously the bestest friend ever!"

"I know I am." She joked, pretending to flip her hair even though it's tied up. "Now let me get back to my future ex-husband."

Then she said her next set of words so quickly I don't think she took a breath.

"Oh, you'll have to be at practice at six the following morning and take an extra ballet class, but don't worry, it'll be worth it."

CHAPTER 46

D o you want the good news or the bad news?" Dr. Kozol asked me.

I gave him a bland stare.

"I don't know, Doc, how much worse can it possibly get? I'm basically on my last leg."

"At least you haven't lost your sense of humor." Avery snickered next to me, and I grinned at her.

Dr. Kozol flipped open my file, his merry expression not going unnoticed. It was good to see my doctor had a sense of humor too. It helped me a little, mentally.

I'd already given blood and had done the usual physical. Now we were sitting in his office with the door shut reviewing my treatment plan and making sure the medicine was helping maintain my symptoms. I'd gotten to the point I knew this was par for the course every time I came in.

"The bad news is, while I'm going to send out your urine sample along with your blood work, your protein is still rising. Not by much, but enough to have me concerned. Have you been sticking to your new diet plan?"

"Yes, I have."

"That's good. And your medications? How are they working out for you?"

I hesitated. There were some side effects I'd gone through, but overall, they weren't too bad. I really didn't want to test out new medications.

"It took some time to adjust to them, but now I think they're okay. Like if I don't eat with two of them, I get really sick to the point of vomiting. I learned to follow the rules on the side of the bottle. I don't take any of the pain medications, though. I try my best to push through it. For the most part, the meds seem to be working, I guess."

He nodded and scribbled a few things down. "It's really all trial and error, as no two patients are the same," he said, reviewing my patient chart. Dr. Kozol paused to level a stare at me. "And none of them usually forgo treatment either."

Grimacing, I flattened my lips. I knew the risks I was taking, and I also knew if I didn't take them that I would regret it. Under normal circumstances I wouldn't have prolonged dialysis. I would've gone to the hospital for further testing like he originally suggested. It was just hard to grasp that after coming so far I would stop everything now. A few more months wouldn't kill me. Hopefully.

"I'm not forgoing treatment, per say, I'm just delaying it."

Dr. Kozol studied me, his pen wavering back and forth between his thumb and index finger. "You do know time is of the essence, right?"

I nodded. "I do. Trust me, it's on my mind all the time. What about my lungs? Last time I was here you said there were sounds you didn't like." I couldn't remember his exact words, just that he was concerned about them. "You heard liquid I think, right?"

He nodded. "They're better. I can still hear it, but it's definitely improved."

My face lit up. "At least I have one good thing going for myself, right?"

Dr. Kozol offered me a kind smile. "You're a week late to see me, you know. When I spoke with your father and we went over your new plan, I expected you to keep to the promise."

I averted my gaze and crossed one leg over the other. He was right. I was supposed to come in last week but never made it. I had pushed it back. He probably thought I didn't care or take my illness seriously, but that wasn't the case.

Sitting up a little straighter, I looked my doctor directly in the eye.

"I know the last thing you want to hear is an apology, but I really am sorry. It won't happen again. I promise. Last week…" My voice trailed off as I debated telling him the truth. "I've just been deep in my emotions, struggling since everything happened. I only just started telling people. I know it's not an excuse and I'm not trying to make it one, I'm just telling you why I wasn't here. It's a lot to handle and it scares me. I know I need to start dialysis, and the fact I'm not is on my mind all the time. I'm honestly just trying to not let the illnesses get the best of me." I paused, swallowing. "Sometimes they do. I'm slowly accepting it, even though I don't want to."

His face softened with empathy. "Understandable, but Adrianna, I hope you're aware of the risk you're taking. I don't like reminding you how sick you are every time I see you, but…"

I smile. "I know, I know. It's not a matter of if I will die, but when."

Morbid, but it was the truth.

"I'll let it slide this one time, but please don't do it again." Dr. Kozol glanced down at my file and started writing again. "Alright, when the blood work comes back, if anything is amiss, I'll let you know. Are you ready for the good news?"

I nodded vehemently. I couldn't imagine what it was.

Dr. Kozol exhaled a deep breath. "I'm happy to tell you we've found a kidney match."

I froze.

I couldn't move.

I didn't breathe.

"What?" I said, my voice a little raspy. "What did you say?"

Avery reached out to grab my hand, offering me support. My fingers were cold, her palm hot to the touch and she gave me a little squeeze. I glanced over and met her gaze. My smile was weak, but I tried to show her I was thankful she was here with me.

I blinked so many times trying to hold back my tears while her eyes glittered with profound happiness and love.

My breathing grew dense. "How? Who? When…" I had so many questions running through my mind. I couldn't think straight.

I was scared this was a dream and I was going to wake up to the nightmare I'd been stuck living inside of for the last couple of months. I prayed it wasn't a sick joke.

"You found a match," I said, and he nodded. "But who? My dad told me he, my brother, and biological mom were not matches. Did he find a distant cousin or aunt or something?" I wasn't going to get my hopes up that Joy was tested, but crazier things had happened.

"We have a match, Adrianna," he said again gently. "In fact, she's sitting right next to you."

Tears blurred my vision and my body broke out in a cold sweat. Wide-eyed, I turned to look at my best friend.

"What?"

I could barely get the word out without my voice shaking. My heart was racing. Before I could stop them, a few tears slipped down my cheek. I knew I wasn't the only person in the world looking for a kidney and the chances of finding someone to donate were slim. That's why my doctor was so adamant that I start treatment. My faith in finding a match had been a bit shaken, but I'd held out hope. But this…my mind wasn't processing everything.

"Avery?" I said, my voice shaking.

Her eyes were glossy with tears, and she was biting into her bottom lip. Her jaw trembled and I could see the truth in her gaze.

"It's true. We're a match."

My head shook at the sound of her raspy voice. A tear slipped out from her crystal-blue eyes and she quickly wiped it away.

"We really are a match." Avery sniffled.

Heart pounding viciously against my ribs, I was in complete shock. "I don't understand. How?"

"When you told me about everything, I went to your dad the next day and said I was willing to be tested." Her head angled to the side. "Frank then went to my dad and they talked about it. Eventually they reached out to him," she said, pointing to Dr. Kozol. "After a couple of days, they both gave me the green light and I got tested. I'm not big on praying, but I prayed like crazy and pretty much swore to every god there was that I'd do anything just to be your match." She stopped to regain herself. "I figured there wasn't a better time to tell you this than on your birthday."

I blinked a few times, making sure I'd heard everything correctly. Avery Heron, my best friend, was going to give me one of her kidneys.

When I didn't say anything, she chuckled. "We were all in shock, trust me."

An airy laugh rolled off my lips. "It's just… I don't know what to say, what to think. Are you sure you want to do this?"

"You're my best friend. I'd do anything for you. When you're ready, my kidney is your kidney. No more kidney failure for you. Not on my watch."

We both giggled over her cheesy lines, smiling at each other. I stared at her in utter awe that she would do this for me. We weren't talking about borrowing a shirt or a pair of earrings—she was giving me an organ that she could never take back.

I let out a huff and wiped away the fresh tears that clouded my vision.

"I don't know what to say other than thank you, Avery." Emotion clogged my throat again. "Thank you."

She squeezed my hand again. "Kidney besties for life."

CHAPTER 47

After spending another hour at the doctor's office going over the finer details and plans, we returned to my condo and shed more tears before calling our families.

I still couldn't believe it. I was going to get a kidney. Not right now, but eventually.

We sat on the couch drinking hot chocolate Avery had made from scratch. My cheeks ached from being unable to stop smiling, and I'd been crying on and off. Being an organ donor was a selfless act and took a huge heart on someone's part. I was extremely close to having renal failure, and Avery was willingly giving me a part of herself to help me live a longer life. She was changing the ending of my story by offering me the ultimate gift, something I could never, ever repay her for.

"I'm forever indebted to you, you know," I said quietly. Shit. Tears filled my eyes again.

She wrinkled her nose at me. "It's a good thing I know where you live."

"No takebacks." I joked. I licked my lips and drew in a deep breath.

Avery gave me a droll stare. "Like I'd ever do that. Oh! I have something for you," she said and jumped up from the couch. She placed her hot chocolate down on the coffee table, then ran to my room. A minute later, she was back and handing me a gift bag.

From the corner of my eye, I caught the glittery design on her shirt. I stared at what looked like lima beans. She must've chanced when she went to grab my gift. I frowned as I read the words and finally recognized the images. My jaw dropped and my eyes widened with laughter.

"Oh my God. I just realized what's on your shirt!" I said.

Two kidneys with the words underneath, "We're a match! Who wouldn't want a piece of this?"

I laughed out loud. "Where did you find that?"

"I got connections." She nodded her chin toward the gift bag she handed me. "Open it, but don't read the inside of the card right now. I got a little fucking mushy and I'm so embarrassed. Just read the front." My eyes drifted down as I opened the card.

I heard urine need of a kidney. Want mine?

"Oh man." I laughed.

"I know. I had a blast picking stuff out for you."

I placed the card back in the envelope and placed it to the side. "You didn't need to give me anything, you know. You're giving me a freaking organ."

"Yeah, but I wanted to."

I smiled, feeling grateful.

"This is for when surgery is over," Avery said as I pulled out the first gift wrapped in tissue paper. "You have to wear it."

"Promise," I said without even looking at it.

I unfolded the shirt and read the bold block letters. STRAIGHT OUTTA TRANSPLANT SURGERY. It had two little kidneys next to the wording.

I let out a belly laugh, and grinned from ear to ear. This was the first time in months I felt like I could breathe again, like there was a light at the end of the tunnel, and I owed it to my bestie. It was surreal.

"I love it! Leave it to you to find a shirt like this."

I reached into the bag again and pulled out another tissue wrapped gift. I held up the green shirt, the color associated with kidney disease, and read the white lettering. KIDNEY THIEF.

Avery poked her head around the side. She beamed with happiness. I loved that I could see her like this again but felt bad that it was only from being a match. But that was Avery. Always going above and beyond to make someone else happy.

As I pulled out yet another shirt, she said, "And this one is for now. There's two. One for you and one for me."

KIDNEY BESTIES FOR LIFE.

My lips parted. "This is what you said to me at the doctor's office today."

"I know. You didn't catch on to anything," she joked.

I couldn't laugh, though, not when I was crying again. My head fell into my hands and I burst into tears at her thoughtfulness. Avery reached over and pulled me into a hug, holding me tight as I cried softly on her shoulder.

"I love you, girl," she said, sniffling. "I know we had our first—*and last*—most epic fight ever, but that doesn't change a thing between us. I would do anything for you, like I know you would for me."

Damn it all to hell, she wasn't helping, but she was right. If the roles were reversed, I would do whatever I could to help her.

"Thank you, Avery," I said, pulling back. "Two words just don't seem adequate enough for what you're giving me."

"Stop," she said and wiped away the tear underneath her lash line. "If I didn't want to do this, then I wouldn't have been tested." She grabbed my hands in hers and scooted closer. "I want to do this for you, okay? I don't want you to feel like you have to say thank you all the time or that you have to try and find something to give me in return. That's not what this is about. I love you and I want to help you."

I nodded and dug my teeth into my bottom lip as I struggled to fight the tears. One day I would repay her, I just wasn't sure how yet. I'd find a way, though.

Reaching into the bag, Avery handed me something a little heavier. "This is the last one."

I unwrapped a mug and turned it around.

I got 99 problems but my new kidney ain't one.

"Oh, my God." I laughed again. "You really went to town with the kidney stuff." I smiled again, loving each gift so much. I had no idea where she'd found any of it, but it was so thoughtful and funny, and I'd cherish it forever. "I can't wait to use it."

She shrugged like it wasn't a big deal. But it was. It was a very big deal.

"Figured it was better to try and turn it into something fun rather than depressing. This is a good thing and we shouldn't be crying or sad about it." She handed me one of the matching shirts. "Put it on."

As I pulled the shirt over my head, there was a knock on the door.

"Are you expecting someone?" Avery turned to me.

I shook my head. "No."

I walked to the door and opened it.

"Kova," I said, a little surprised. "Hey. What are you doing here?"

His eyes softened. "Ria, may I come in?"

"Is that Kova?" Avery yelled, and ran up behind me. Placing her hands on my shoulders, she leaned over me. "Hey, handsome. You're looking mighty fine."

Kova shot an uneasy glance at me. My cheeks flushed and I mouthed sorry. While Avery knew everything about Kova and me, Kova didn't know that. I imagined he was panicking inside.

"Come in," I said.

He ran his hand through his hair and I shut the door. He seemed anxious.

"I will not stay long. I just wanted to bring you this," Kova said, then lifted his hand to reveal an iconic teal-colored gift bag.

"Oh-em-gee," Avery drawled, rubbing her hands together impatiently. We both looked at her, and she looked back at us. "Ah, I can step out to give you guys some time," she said, then turned and walked to my room. I heard her plop down on my bed.

"Don't worry," I said when I noticed the unease written on his face. "Avery is like a vault. I swear on my life she'll never say anything to anyone about us. I promise."

"Does she know…?"

I nodded. I wouldn't lie. "She does."

He expelled a deep breath. "If you say so, then I believe you. I will not take too much of your time since you do not see her often. I just wanted to bring you a birthday gift."

My eyes widened as he handed me the bag. "You knew it was my birthday?"

"Yes, of course."

"Really?"

Kova nodded and my heart beat a little faster for him. I wasn't one to broadcast my birthday, so the fact he knew without having to tell him moved me inside when my family forgot half the time. Stupid, I know, but I guess it's the little things in life.

"You didn't have to get me anything."

Kova stepped closer to me and I could smell his cologne. His tantalizing scent swirled deliciously around my head. He brushed a few strands of hair behind my ear and cupped my jaw. Tipping my chin back, he gazed into my eyes something fierce.

"You mean the world to me, Ria. I wanted to give you something special to show you that." He leaned in and his lips brushed the shell of my ear. "I really want to kiss you, but I will not with your friend here."

Turning my face toward his, I tenderly kissed his cheek without a sound.

"Thank you for stopping by," I whispered.

As he turned his face, I pressed my lips to his and snuck him a quick kiss. Kova swiftly grabbed the back of my head and pressed his lips harder to mine, inhaling through his nose like he was breathing me in.

"Please," he said against my mouth, "open your gift."

Pulling back, my cheeks heated as I grinned up at him. He moved to stand behind me and watched as I removed the square box from the bag. I placed the bag on the counter, then pulled the white satin bow loose. Kova played with my hair, moving it to the side to drape over my shoulder. I leaned back against him, falling into the heat of his body as he wrapped his arms around my stomach. My heartbeat rocketed but everything shifted into place in his arms. Inside the velvet box was a soft rose gold bracelet. It was double chained with an infinity symbol.

Lips parting, I removed it from the box and placed it in my palm. I drew in a gasp. My finger grazed over the thin chain to the charm in the center. Kova didn't say anything without thinking it through. He was terrible at exposing his feelings. But when he actually did both, they meant something, and something told me he'd put thought into this specific gift. I knew the meaning behind an infinity symbol. All I could do was focus on the delicate piece of jewelry and feel the tears well in my eyes. Damn it, I cried so much these days.

"It's so beautiful," I said under my breath. I lifted it to him. "Put it on me, please?"

Kova clasped it under my wrist. He laced his fingers through mine and lifted our joined hands to his mouth to press a kiss to mine. The outside world had no idea how sweet he could actually be.

"There is one more thing."

My brows angled toward each other. I didn't realize there was another box in the bag. Letting go of his hand, I reached inside and pulled it out, then opened it.

I stared unblinking at the dainty matching necklace. It was stunning and delicate and so damn pretty.

"Kova, you gave me too much. This is…it's beautiful. Thank you so, so much."

"There is no such thing as too much when it comes to you."

CHAPTER 48

His words tickled my neck.

I was very close to telling him I loved him.

Kova placed the necklace around my neck. Turning around, I grabbed his jaw and pulled it to mine. Inhaling, I kissed him. Kova's strong arms wound around my back. He lifted me up and placed me on the counter and stepped between my legs, kissing me back with the same intensity. I loved when he did that. I loved when he gave back ten times harder. Like we were proving who loved each other more.

"I love you, Ria," he admitted only for me to hear.

I licked my lips. "Ever since my secret came out and we talked about it, you tell me you love me all the time."

"Life is too precious. We take it for granted. I realized that when I found out how sick you were. I told you I do not want to hold back from you anymore. I want you to know how I feel all the time."

I smiled softly at him. "Thank you," I whispered. My fingers twirled the hair around his neck as we stared at each other.

"Can I come out now?" Avery yelled from my bedroom.

My smile widened, and Kova and I started laughing together.

"I love seeing you laugh," I told him. Then I angled my head and yelled, "Yes!" to Avery.

Avery showed no shame and came bouncing out of my bedroom. "Show me the goods."

Shaking my head, I lifted my wrist and picked up the necklace to show her. She came up next to us and Kova scooted a little closer to me.

"Oh, you did good, Coach," she said as she examined the jewelry, then turned to Kova. "Do you have a brother?"

I chuckled and Kova side-eyed me in confusion. Avery was a whole lot of personality to handle if you didn't know her.

She patted his arm. "I'm just playing. I don't do brothers anymore," she said, then walked into the kitchen to grab a bottle of water.

My cheeks flamed, but God, did I love my best friend.

"So I have heard," Kova responded.

My gaze snapped back to him and I took note of his face. My lips twitched. He wrapped an arm around me again, laughter highlighting his eyes.

"You told him!" she yelled at me, lifting her arm. Her gaze was accusatory but I knew she wasn't truly mad.

My jaw bobbed. "Sorry?"

"You're lucky it's your birthday and you're my bestie." She took a sip of water. "It's cool. I'm over it."

Kova let go of me and stepped back. He looked from me to Avery. I followed his gaze, trying to figure out what he was looking at.

"Why are you two wearing the same shirt? Is that a bestie thing?"

I burst out laughing over him saying bestie. It sounded like he'd eaten something sour.

Then he read the words. And he looked back and forth between us again.

"You didn't hear?" Avery said.

"Did not hear what?" Kova's eyes snapped up to mine.

"Tell him, Aid."

I bit into my lip as he stared at me. His chest rose higher and faster, and I swear I could feel his heart pumping. Kova watched me, waiting, looking hopeful.

"Ria?" he asked slowly.

I averted my gaze and hopped down from the counter.

"Well…" I began, and walked over to Avery. "I haven't really had a chance to tell you and honestly, I wasn't sure how I would." I wrapped my arm around the back of her neck and tugged her to me. She hugged me back, dropping her head to my shoulder and hooking her arms around my waist. I could see from the corner of my eye she was smiling softly at Kova.

"This birthday has been the best birthday of my life. Not only did you surprise me with a meaningful gift, but Avery, well, she…"

Shoot. Emotion hit me faster than I could stop it from happening. Tears filled my eyes and my jaw trembled. Trying to say I had a kidney match proved to be harder than I thought.

Avery lifted her head off my shoulder and looked at me. A tear slipped out of my eye and down my cheek. I still couldn't believe what she was going to do for me.

"For Adrianna's birthday, I surprised her too." She looked toward Kova. "I'm her match. Well, we already knew that." She joked with a playful roll of her eyes. "I'm a kidney match. When the time comes, because I know she's stubborn and won't do it now, I'll be giving her a kidney. I got these shirts for us since we're kidney besties for life now."

I watched Kova's face shift through a handful of emotions. The color in his cheeks drained and he stood stone still, like he was in shock and didn't know what to say. His Adam's apple bobbed. Lifting his hand, he ran it over his mouth and looked at the floor. Then, he walked toward us and surprised us both.

I thought he was going to pull me into his arms, but he didn't. Instead, he pulled Avery into his arms and hugged her.

My jaw dropped and my eyes widened as I watched his face twist into a blend of heartache and relief. Squinting, I caught the subtle shaking in his arms.

Avery looked to me for guidance. All I could do was shrug my shoulders because other than when we were alone, or he was with Katja, I never saw Kova show an ounce of emotion, let alone touch anyone. Right now, he was pouring himself into her.

Eyes twinkling, Avery went with it. She wrapped her arms around Kova's back and ran her flat palms ever so slowly up and down from his shoulders to his hips. Her eyes floated shut and she smiled from ear to ear.

"My, Kova, what a strong back you have," she said.

I laughed.

Kova pulled back, his lips twitching. "Thank you, Avery," he said. His voice was hoarse.

He turned and looked at me, almost making my heart stop. Raw love and affection filled his eyes. I knew he loved me, he told me often, but this time it was different. His love rendered me speechless. This was a side of Kova he never exposed to the outside world, for obvious reasons, yet he was allowing Avery to see it. It made me fall for him even harder.

"From the bottom of my heart, thank you, Avery," he said again, blowing out a heavy breath. He was struggling with the news the same way I had. "I cannot imagine my life without Adrianna."

We both stared at him in astonishment. Kova followed up with a few things in Russian, though I didn't ask him what they meant. Something in my gut told me to just give him a minute.

Avery recovered and pretended to dust her shoulders off. "Now that I made it so you guys can fornicate for the rest of your lives, show me her mark." Kova looked confused. I didn't know what she was talking about until she said, "Adrianna told me about the A, and I want to see it. Take your shirt off."

I covered my mouth. "Ave," I said, trying not to laugh. She was so unpredictable.

She looked at me like it wasn't a crazy request. "What? It's the least he can do for me. I want to see it. I think it's so sexy and sweet." Avery had a wistful look on her face that made me laugh even harder.

"No," he said, shutting her down.

Her jaw plummeted to the floor. She looked at Kova like she was offended. "What? Why not?"

"No."

"Okay. Fine. Don't take your shirt off, just lift it so I can see."

Kova turned to me for help. All I could do was offer him an apologetic look.

"No."

"What?" She huffed and looked at me. "Help a sister out."

"Just one peek?" I asked him, hesitantly.

He shook his head. "That is for Ria and I only."

"Aww, that's so adorable." Avery leaned into me and cupped her mouth next to my ear while looking at Kova. "Get a picture while he's sleeping," she whispered loudly for him to hear. "Don't be afraid to take a few and send them to me. I promise not to tell anyone."

Shaking his head, Kova's sexy smile curled around my heart. I shot a glance at Avery, and I could see she felt his charisma too by the way she watched him with a twinkle in her eyes. I wanted to kiss those lips again but I held back.

Walking up to me, Kova pulled me against his body. *"Ya lyubuyu tebya navsegda,"* he said, then kissed the top of my head. "I must go. Happy birthday, *malysh.*"

"Just one look," Avery pushed as Kova walked toward the door and opened it.

"It will never happen. I am just as stubborn as Ria. Ask her." Kova paused right as he was about to leave and looked over his shoulder at me. "I expect to see you bright and early tomorrow."

I nodded and he left. Turning to Avery, she looked like she was going to liquefy into a pile on the floor. I chuckled. She was finally starting to see what I saw.

"I hope you marry that stupid Russian one day," she said dreamily.

CHAPTER 49

S hit," I whispered under my breath.

I blinked, hoping the pink tinted toilet water was something I was imagining.

It wasn't.

Ever since I'd started training at the rate I was over a year ago, my period had been inconsistent. Sometimes I got it in four weeks, other times almost seven weeks would go by with no sign of it. Sometimes I had heavy periods, other times I would spot for three days. My body underwent a tremendous amount of strain, which caused it to mess with my cycle. With everything going on lately, it slipped my mind, so I hadn't been thinking about it.

I closed my eyes and took a deep breath. This would happen to me. Not only did I wake up with a raging headache and my stomach tossing around from nerves, I was in Scotland preparing to compete at an international competition, and now I needed tampons.

Quickly, I pulled down my leotard and wrapped a towel around my body. I opened the door and stepped into the room I shared with Holly. Reagan declined the meet due to not having the funds for it, so it was just us this time around.

"Holly?"

She looked at me from where she sat on her bed texting on her cell phone.

"Do you happen to have any tampons with you? I just got my period and I don't have anything."

She gawked and immediately stood. "You don't bring them as backup? I always just leave them in my suitcase."

"I wasn't thinking, I guess."

Holly handed me a bunch of tampons and I looked at them in horror. "What size is this?"

"Ultra. My flow is always really bad and heavy. Sorry, I don't have anything else."

"No worries. I'm just grateful you have them. Thanks," I said.

I went back into the bathroom and took care of business. I hated having my period during a gymnastics meet. I was always afraid it would show somehow. Luckily my leotard was a hunter green with encrusted hot pink Swarovski crystals. If I did leak, it wouldn't show.

"Girl, you always should have them on you," Holly said when I emerged from the bathroom dressed and ready to go.

I offered her a smile and nodded, then walked over to my suitcase to pull out my scarf and coat. My nerves were a little wired, but overall, I felt confident. After this meet, there was one more in Italy, the Olympic Trials, and then the team would be selected.

"I usually do but I don't know what I was thinking to not bring them. I guess I just have a lot on my mind. That's all." I would never forget after this, that was for sure.

She eyed me curiously. "Yeah, Hayden's mentioned you've had it rough lately. I know he's been worried."

I hesitated for split moment, then wrapped the headscarf over my ears. There were so many things he could've told her.

"What do you mean?"

She brushed it off and zipped her coat up. "Nothing we can't talk about tonight if you want." She smiled but it wasn't enough to smooth out my feathers. "It's not bad or anything, he's just been worried about you for a while. We both were."

I stared at her, wondering which direction this conversation would go in when she pointed to my makeup bag. I turned and found I hadn't zipped it closed, and the tops of my medicine bottles were showing.

"You don't need to explain anything to me, I just hope you're okay," she said gently.

Shit. I'd been good at hiding my illnesses for the most part, but with my head focused on my routines and the two-day meet we were at, I'd left the bottles out in the open. Taking the medicine had become second nature to me these days, and I'd been coming to terms with it. Kind of.

Holly walked over and hugged me. "I know we haven't known each other all that long, but I'm always here for you. I love you like a sister."

I smiled and thanked her. "Those are prescriptions from my doctors. I have an autoimmune disease and I have no choice but to take them. I'm fine, Holly. Honestly. I'm better than I've been actually, but we can exchange war stories tonight if you want to."

That was all I was giving her. I wouldn't add I that had kidney disease, or that I'd ultimately need a transplant. I wouldn't add I that was better because of Kova and the words he'd said to me.

I want to live with you.

But it was the first time I had spoken positive about my future, and surprisingly, it made me feel good.

RUBBING MY SHOULDERS, KOVA LOOKED down at me. I was freezing, and he was trying to help keep my joints warm before I stepped onto the podium for my first routine. I was a little jealous that he was wearing a thick turtle neck. Combined with his business slacks, Kova looked fine as hell dressed in all black. The color accented his alluring green eyes perfectly.

I shivered and rubbed the side of my head. The headache I woke up with hadn't subsided.

"You are ready," he stated.

Tight-lipped, I nodded as my eyes skirted around trying to take in everything at once. I chewed the inside of my lip. Nerves and a nauseous stomach were a terrible combo. Not only were the best athletes in the world here, but there were sports agents, news stations to televise the competition, college coaches trying to recruit gymnasts, and the Olympic committee too.

"Hey. Look at me," Kova said, and my eyes snapped to his. "Focus on me. Do not look anywhere else and do not watch the other gymnasts. Keep your head in the game."

He tipped his head down and his eyes bore deeper into mine. He was quiet for a moment, helping me find my ground, giving me comfort. I released a breath I hadn't realized I was holding.

"You got this. You have never been more prepared than this moment, yes?" he said, and I bobbed my head. "Remember why you are here, think about how you got here. You did it because of your perseverance when the world was against you and because of your hard work and determination. You got this, Adrianna. Do not let that voice in your head get to you."

"I'm working on it."

He leaned in and lowered his voice. "Two of your routines have the most points in difficulty than all the girls here. That is huge. It already puts you one step ahead. Even with everything you have been up against these last six months, you kept going when everyone else would have folded. You got this. Just get your head right. Think only about your routine, and smile. Have fun out there. You earned this."

He had a point. Even if the other competitors were able to maximize all their points, I could still take the lead in vault and bars—taking the World Champion titles. The only way that wouldn't happen would be for me to make a mistake. But I wouldn't. I'd worked too hard for this to let anyone take it from me. Especially now. Floor was my favorite and my routine always got the crowd and judges on their feet, so to speak. And beam, well, that was a whole other story, but I wasn't worried.

As usual, Kova was right.

"Adrianna?" he said, and I glanced into his eyes. "It is you against yourself. Some people thrive under pressure while others concede. You flourish more than anyone I have ever seen. And I am not saying that to fill your head with empty words just to encourage you or give you a little pep talk. It is how I truly feel and what I see. It is the truth. Remember, let *it* inspire you to live *your* dream. You came to win. Nothing else."

Exhaling a ragged breath, the tension in my neck loosened. I knew the "it" he was referring to was the kidney disease. He was trying to be as discrete as he could because he knew I didn't want anyone to know about it. My face softened. I knew Kova meant what he said, he wouldn't waste his breath on useless words. He was honest to a fault and I guess I liked that about him.

"Thanks," I said quietly. He was always right.

"Now go chalk up. I am sure you could use more."

I forced back a smile and walked over to the chalk bowl. I plunged my hands into the powder and it puffed up in a cloud in front of me. I could taste it in my mouth.

"I'm so nervous," I said to Holly, who was standing next to me. "Why am I so freaking nervous? Maybe I should've eaten something before I left. My stomach is in knots and I'm overanalyzing."

She chuckled. "Ah, because you have a lot more riding at the moment than I do? I'm just hoping I can gain the attention of a college coach. You want the freaking Olympic coaches to notice you."

"You haven't heard back from Alabama yet?"

"No, but it's still early. I'm just stressed and wished I had applied to other schools as a backup now.

Holly placed her hand over mine and took it in hers. I looked at her and she frowned.

"It's the medicine," I whispered. "Sometimes it gives me the shakes and makes me jittery."

"Nerves are good. They're what keep us going, make us feel alive. If you didn't have nerves, then you kind of lose the fun of the sport. Am I right?"

My heart pumped the adrenaline through my veins at a high speed, like a build up to the climax of a movie. I could feel it coming and I couldn't wait to feel the beat drop only to replay it over and over again.

"Yeah, you're right. It's just, gymnastics is so unpredictable, you know? And there are so many incredible gymnasts here and we all pretty much want the same thing. We're all fighting for a chance to prove ourselves."

I sighed, my shoulders heavy with the weight of the world.

Before Holly could respond, the bell rang over the intercom. A signal to let us know the meet was about to start. I brushed the excess chalk from my hands and wiped it on my thighs.

Go time.

Looking for my coach one last time, our eyes locked for a brief moment. With his hands propped on his hips, I felt like he was giving me the courage I needed to be brave.

Putting one foot in front of the other, I walked up the stairs.

CHAPTER 50

W hat is wrong?" Kova asked, squatting in front of me.

I was sitting on the floor stretching my foot out before I applied sports tape.

And I was annoyed as hell.

Gritting my teeth, I said, "First of all. I've had a headache since I woke up and it just won't go away. Second, there's a stupid Russian girl who's name I can't even pronounce just trailing my ass on every rotation. She's so close that if I blink she'll pass me."

Kova grinned proudly and took my foot in his hands to carefully flex it. He held my heel and pressed on the center of my arch with his thumb. I leaned back on my hands.

"Damn those Russians and their skills," he said, and I raised a brow. "Taina Mstislav." His accent was so thick as he said her name, I couldn't even mimic it. "It means glorious defender."

"Not what I wanted to hear."

He shrugged. "Russians have always dominated the sport. They view it a little differently. Most girls are plucked from small towns with nothing on their back and the family is poor. They are given a roof and food and all the training they need, but they have to pay it back by winning. It does not matter which Russian girl wins, only that Russia must win. You do it for the love of your country."

My forehead bunched together. "What happens if they don't win?"

"Russia breaks girls." He was silent for a moment, then said almost painfully, "You do not want to know."

I glanced at Taina, who was right behind me in the standings. She didn't know I was watching her.

"Is that her coach?" I asked Kova.

He followed my gaze. "Yes." He said her name.

"You know her?"

"I know of her."

I watched the way Taina's shoulders fell, how her back went ram-rod straight, the way she nodded quickly as she received instruction from her coach. The coach's eyes nearly bulged from her head. Taina's hands were cupped behind her back and she twisted and turned her fingers until the tips were purple.

Kova finished taping my Achilles and watched them for a moment with me.

"I will always have love for my country," he said, "but I do not agree with how Russia handles things. It is cruelty."

"Kova?" I waited until he looked at me before continuing. "I'm going to beat her," I said with resolute determination.

The corner of his mouth tugged to one side and he cupped the side of my face. "You better."

Standing, Kova held his hand out for me. I stood and fixed my leotard so my butt wasn't showing.

"Did you drink enough water today? I can get you some Gatorade if you'd like."

I shook my head. I didn't care for sugary drinks. "I'll be fine. The caffeine withdrawal is real," I joked. "I'm going to get the biggest cup I can find after the meet." All I had was the balance beam and floor left, and then I was free.

Kova studied me. The lights made his eyes sparkle, though I would never tell him that. "Are you feeling okay? Overall?"

"Actually, yes. I'm a little tired but nothing I can't handle. I think when I changed the way I viewed things, it changed a lot for me in general. It just took me a minute to get there."

Holly walked over. "Hey. Do you want to warm up with me?" she asked, then eyed Kova.

"Go," he said, playfully clapping my back. "You ladies have a few minutes until it is time to start."

Kova walked away and we sat down to stretch. After a few minutes, Holly spoke.

"Adrianna?"

"Yeah," I said, reaching for my feet and feeling the burn in my hamstrings. I loved the way my muscles pulled. I stood and turned over into handstand pirouettes.

Holly stood closer to me. Quietly, so only I could hear, she said, "You should really be careful with the way you look at our coach."

I froze. The back of my neck burned with guilt but I quickly recovered and pretended like I didn't know what she was talking about.

"I don't understand." But she knew I did. I could see it in her eyes. My heart was about to pump out of my chest. "There's nothing going on," I stated under my breath.

She gave me a knowing smile and tipped her head to the side. "If that's what you want to go with, I get it. It's one thing at World Cup, but at a meet, let alone an international one, you can't let it happen. Not with so many people and cameras around."

I struggled not to panic. "I didn't let anything happen, though."

"You may not have, but he sure did." Holly paused and chose her next words carefully. "Whatever is going on between you two, he's making it very obvious. It's why I asked you to stretch. I was worried someone would see."

I blinked, then blinked again. I didn't know what to say to that.

"When do you ever see a coach look at a gymnast with the intensity that he looked at you? Never. Usually we're all getting yelled at."

She had a point, and I worked on remaining cool and collected. "Holly, but nothing is happening."

Leaning in, she lowered her voice to a whisper. "I had a coach once… but he wasn't like Kova," she said and shivered like it was a bad memory. "If it wasn't for Kova, I don't know what I'd have done."

I frowned. "What does that mean?"

She licked her lips. "Tonight? We'll talk tonight. Just stop looking at each other like no one else is in the room."

Holly walked away while I stood there silently panicking inside unsure of what to do. I picked at my nails and stared in a daze, trying to think about what could have given us away just now. If she saw something, then someone else probably did too.

Shit.

"CONGRATULATIONS, ADRIANNA," MY DAD SAID, giving me a big hug. The meet was finally over and I got to see him. It would only be for a couple of hours because of the rules, but I'd take it.

"Thanks, Dad." He pulled back and wore a huge smile. "You know, it's kind of funny that I rarely see you in Georgia, yet you fly to Scotland to watch me?"

"This is a big moment. Of course I had to be here and I'm so glad I was. How many medals did you walk away with?"

I smiled bigger, still shocked I'd won even one medal despite everything. "Four. Three gold and one bronze." Naturally the bronze was in beam, but I didn't care. At this point in my life, any medal was better than no medal at all.

Kova walked up to us and placed a cup in front of me. "Coffee," was all he said, and I took it, smiling up at him, so thankful he'd remembered. I sipped it immediately and sighed.

"Konstantin."

I paused mid-sip at the enunciation of his name. I thought I caught a stiffness in my dad's tone.

"Frank. It is good to see you, my friend."

"Likewise."

"Adrianna did magnificent today," Kova said proudly. He was positively beaming, and for a second, I wondered if this was what Holly had been talking about.

"She did. I'm very proud."

"A few university coaches pulled me aside to ask about her future, if she had plans to compete in college. I was not sure if you guys had spoken about that yet or not."

My eyes widened in excitement. I'd been so busy with life that I hadn't had much of a chance to look into colleges the way I should have.

"Really? Who?"

He glanced down. "I cannot say, but there is interest. Do you remember when we talked about prizes and I did not recommend accepting them?" he asked, and I nodded, gripping my cup. The heat felt good in my hand. "If you had accepted, I would not have been approached and there would be no interest."

"Is there interest from anyone I should be concerned about?" Dad asked stiffly. His eyes were fixated on Kova like he was trying to get a psychic reading on him. All three of us stood in awkward silence for a moment.

"Well, I was not going to say anything just yet, but I did overhear the committee speaking and Adrianna's name was mentioned."

Now, I knew this was a lie. He wouldn't have heard them talking freely, because it never would have happened. The committee was very private and spoke behind closed doors, not out in the public. Kova was trying to cover up and brush off Dad's question like he was totally oblivious. I knew instantly to play along.

I gasped obnoxiously loud and bounced on my toes. "No way! You heard my name?" I said, and Kova nodded. I looked at my dad to gauge his reaction. "Dad! This is so exciting! I wish Xavier was here with us now," I said eagerly then leaned into his side for a half hug.

He wrapped an arm around my back and pulled me tight to him in an overprotective manner. My heart thumped against my ribs so hard it was beginning to feel painful.

Clearing his throat, Dad said, "This is fantastic news. Thank you, Konstantin. If it is okay with you, I'd like to have dinner with my daughter. I won't keep her late. I know she has to compete again tomorrow. In fact, after dinner when Adrianna goes back to her room, you can stop by for a drink."

I almost choked on my coffee. That was no invitation, but a demand. Kova had to be dense to miss it.

"Of course," Kova said with a pleasant smile on his face. "I look forward to catching up with you. We have a lot to discuss actually.."

My chest couldn't take anymore tension. I jumped in. "Dad, if we're going to dinner, let's get going. I'm frozen and I haven't eaten all day."

Kova stopped me. "Why have you not eaten?" he asked, looking at me with apprehension.

"I can't train, let alone compete on a full stomach. It has to be completely empty."

"You did not eat one thing today?" Kova glanced at his watch then at Frank before he looked at me again. "We have been here for seven hours, not counting the time since you woke up, and you had nothing at all?"

"No. Just a little water this morning."

Now that I thought about it, the medicine was probably what messed with my stomach this morning and why I felt so nauseous. Some of the pills were supposed to be taken with food and they hadn't been.

"That is very dangerous, Adrianna. That is why you had a headache all day. You need to eat something before you step foot on the floor tomorrow."

"You had a headache?" Dad added, his voice panic-stricken. Color drained from his face. "What else? Anything else bothering you?"

I knew where he was going with this, so I smiled sweetly at him and tried to ease his worries.

"I'm okay, Dad, really. Nothing else is wrong and my headache is long gone. I just hate to eat and work out. I'm sure your room has a fruit basket. I'll take it with me when I go back to my room and I'll eat before I leave the hotel tomorrow."

Dad expelled a breath and I saw the light reenter his eyes. I felt bad for worrying him, but in that moment I finally understood the meaning behind a little white lie.

People lied to protect those they cared about despite was the size of the lie may be. There wasn't much afterthought that went into the future if the lie was ever reveled, instead the conscious decision was made to shield another from the painful reality so they didn't endure the truth.

And I got it because truth was, my body ached angrily, and I fought back the vomit that had been climbing the back of my throat all day. I ignored the cramps and parched lips. I ignored the pain slashing through my chest.

I ignored it all and lied to myself and said everything was all right, when in fact, it really wasn't.

CHAPTER 51

eyed my dad as he sipped his amber liquid he often had with dinner.

He was reading over some documents he'd brought with him, scanning the papers and flipping them over. Dad never sat still, but was always working.

"What's happening with you and Mom?" I blurted out.

It wasn't often we got to speak, let alone about her. I figured I'd sway the conversation the best I could because I felt like something was on the tip of his tongue about me and I needed to avoid that, especially after how he'd acted with Kova.

"Joy or Sophia?"

That was the first time he'd responded like that.

"Joy."

"We're trying to work things out."

"What does that mean?"

Dad eyed my plate. "Why are you not eating?"

Diversion.

I glanced down. "I ate a little bit. When my nerves are shot, it's hard to eat."

He removed his glasses and pushed the stack of papers away from him.

"Why are your nerves shot?"

I glared and wondered how he couldn't figure it out.

"Dad, this meet is huge, and tomorrow is another full day of competition," I said like it was obvious, because it was.

"Is there anything else going on I need to know about?"

Heat spread through my chest. "Like what? I'm taking all my medicine and I feel fine. I'm going to the doctor as scheduled. I'm just stressed, that's all. What's going on with Joy? I feel like if she never heard from me again, she'd be okay with that. And, Dad, despite everything, she raised me. How can she just let me go like last season's dress she wore once?"

He leaned back and eyed me peculiarly. Whiskey in his hand, he asked, "Why do you not ask about Sophia?"

My jaw bobbed. I hadn't expected that, but it seemed we both had some things to discuss.

"It's not that I'm not curious about her, because I am, I just have a lot on my plate at the moment. Adding another mom to it is not something I feel I should do right now. I figured I'd reach out once the season was over. Before that would just mess with my head and it's not a good idea, considering I have so much going on as it is. Just remembering to take my pills on time is worrisome to me. Making time to see my biological mother is a lot of pressure, physically, as well as emotionally. Not to mention, a little awkward too."

His eyes softened. "I'm sorry, sweetie. You're right. I shouldn't have asked that. When you're ready to talk to her, you can."

"Does she ask why I don't want to?"

"She does, but I'll explain to her next time that you need to get through these next few months first before you do."

"I hope you tell Sophia it's me, not her."

Dad chuckled and the tension in the room relaxed.

"So…about Joy? What does working it out mean? I thought you guys were getting divorced."

"We are. She's just being extremely difficult."

"Why?"

"She married into money and signed a prenuptial agreement. Now she's attempting extortion to get whatever she wants. I've already purchased a home for her, a summer home in the Hamptons, agreed to a monthly stipend, on top of a nice settlement, but nothing more. We had an agreement when you were born, which she's broken countless times that I have record of. I've let a lot slide. I'm not proud of it and it's something I deal with every day, but enough is enough. I'm done letting her get away with whatever she wants because I feel bad."

"She probably hates me," I said quietly. "She probably blames me for everything, for ruining her lifestyle."

"She hates herself more and hides behind it every day with riches. It's why she acts the way she does. Joy is a very insecure woman, so she belittles those around her to build herself up. What she doesn't realize is when she washes that shit off her face every night and hangs up her hideous Hermes scarf, she's still the same person she's always been. I've been patient. I know I've made mistakes, but this latest stunt was the icing on the cake."

I contemplated my next move. With Dad mentioning blackmail, I felt like I could mention what Kova said to me. I just wasn't sure how without it looking obvious.

I pushed my plate away and stuffed my icy hands into the front pocket of my hoodie.

"Dad, I have a question… Some things have been said around the gym for a few months now. Is it true Joy helped Katja blackmail Kova into marrying him?"

Bringing the crystal tumbler to his lips, he took a long sip with an unnerving look in his eyes. His shifted back and forth between mine, and it was in that simple action that I had clarity.

My obvious response was that I needed to remain unaffected and completely blasé to the conversation. I wouldn't let him hear the anxiety in my voice or see my fingers shaking. The truth was, I was a ball of paranoia.

Dad placed the glass down on the matching coaster. His fingers remained wrapped around it before answering. "Supposedly."

"How?" I groaned inwardly.

"Why do you care?"

"I don't. It's just gym gossip." I responded too fast and now I needed to fix it. I sat back and casually crossed my legs. "I didn't know Joy and Katja were even friends. I always got the impression she didn't like her."

"She doesn't."

I blinked. "I'm confused."

"Joy has never liked Katja. Joy doesn't like anyone more attractive than her, or someone who has the potential to have more than her."

Mean girls were pretty on the outside but ultimately the ugliest of the bunch. The more I learned about Joy, the more I saw just how hideous she was inside.

"So it's true, then? She basically forced Kova to marry her."

"If I was Kova, I'd have married her too."

I tilted my head to the side, unsure how to take that. I studied him back.

"What do you mean?"

His eyes didn't leave mine. "He hasn't been inappropriate with you, has he?" he asked, testing the waters.

I blinked rapidly.

Keep calm.

Don't over react.

Keep calm.

Breathe.

Keep calm.

Fuck!

That was the last thing I thought he'd ask and it rendered me speechless. I should've known better than to even poke at this conversation.

So I gave him a confused look, trying to not let the question fluster me, when in reality my heart was pumping so loud it drowned out any other sound in the room.

"Inappropriate how? Who?"

His eyes were still locked on mine. "Kova. Joy insists Kova has dirty fingers that I should be concerned about. Is he a little more than hands on? Apparently Joy or Katja, I'm not sure which one, found some interesting things out about Kova that's somehow linking to you. Joy refuses to show me anything, but is using it against me for more money. She swears it will give me a heart attack and it's why she's withholding, but she also said if I don't comply that she'll go to the police and the media."

"Dad, that's ridiculous. Please tell me you don't believe her?"

An overconfident smirk slid across his face that rattled my nerves. I held my breath, waiting on his answer, wondering if I should've even asked now.

"Joy would *never* do anything that would taint her image. If what she said was the truth, which I highly doubt it is, she'd still never do it regardless. She wears the Rossi name. She'll always be attached to Rossi Enterprises, whether she wants to or not. If she plays dirty, it would come back to her to haunt her and she knows that." He sipped his drink. "She's being dramatic and most likely exaggerating about what she has. She's trying to intimidate me, but unless she supplies evidence, I have no reason to believe her."

Dad paused, his face slightly softening but his shoulders were bunched tight. "You're my daughter, Adrianna, and I'm always going to side with you first. Vindictiveness is in her blood. I used to think she was a woman with a goal. Now I know she's just malicious and I saw this as another one of her schemes to get what she wants."

"But why didn't you just ask Kova about what Joy said?"

"It's not worth mentioning to him."

"What do you mean?"

"It goes without saying that you're my daughter and if he ever hurt you, I'd break his fucking neck."

I tasted the not so subtle undertone in his words. The way my dad calmly uttered that statement jarred me. I got the feeling he'd do more than that.

Angling his head to the side, an air of superiority surrounded him as he continued. "Adrianna, a man is never going to admit when he lost his sense of pride and was forced into something he doesn't want to be in. A man will also never go to another man with his woes—that's for women."

Reaching for my glass, I took a sip of my water. Tension pulsed on the side of my neck. He had a point, but this was far worse than I could have ever fathomed. Uncomfortable silence filled our table as we looked at each other. Goose bumps broke out over my arms and my teeth clamped down on the inside of my lip.

I chose my words carefully.

"Dad, he's been a good coach to me. There's nothing bad or inappropriate going on with anyone. He's just very dedicated to the sport."

He swirled the ice cubes in his glass. "I think it also goes without saying that I'd ruin him if he did. Money comes with power, always remember that."

I didn't respond. I knew very well how much money could buy. I was out of words and wasn't sure if anything would help the situation.

"Joy put some thoughts into my head that I had always shut down," he said. My brows deepened in confusion. "I didn't believe them, but after today, and the way he touched you, the way you *both* looked at each other, it made me think otherwise for a minute."

My eyes softened. I felt so guilty inside. "It's not like that, Dad, I promise. Take a minute to look at all the coaches and gymnasts tomorrow. What you saw today between Kova and me is a normal occurrence between a coach and a gymnast. You'll see it tomorrow with everyone else. Joy is just crazy."

Dad finished off his whiskey, and once he paid the check, he walked me back to my hotel room. He wished me good luck tomorrow and said he'd be watching.

As I laid down to sleep that night, it dawned on me that he never flat out asked me to confirm anything. Either he was truly on my side and he believed me, or he had a better poker face than I thought.

CHAPTER 52

Congratulations, Adrianna!" Holly said, squeezing me in a tight hug.

"Thanks! Congrats to you too!" I responded and pulled back, smiling through the fatigue. "Girl, you rocked it! No doubt Kova's phone will be ringing soon with interest about you."

The window to recruit was extremely small and the rules set by the national committee must be followed. During an off period, college coaches could not reach out and speak with any athlete, and they were not allowed to watch competitions. I knew she had the academic requirements—an absolute must since sophomore year—but no one had introduced themselves to her yet, and if they were going to, now was the time to. That's all she needed—an introduction and that was showing interest.

Her eyes were full of hope. "I didn't medal, though."

"It doesn't matter. You made it this far and that's huge. You still have time left, you'll see."

I had a good feeling she'd get recruited, and if not, she could always apply. While Holly hadn't medaled in any of the events, she'd taken fifth place overall, and no coach worth anything would overlook that. It was just the waiting period that sucked in between because a week felt like a month and it made you second-guess yourself. I wouldn't be surprised if interest came from both Division I and II schools.

"You know, we didn't get to talk last night," she said, eyeing me.

When I'd returned to the room last night, she was already asleep, and when we woke up, we were too focused to talk.

"Tonight?"

Even though I would have dinner with my dad again, and I was technically allowed to stay with him, I had opted to stay with Holly since she was here alone. Her parents attended many competitions in the States, but none outside. They simply couldn't afford it. Being a competitive gymnast required a lot more money than people realized.

"Yes," she said, then leaned in and lowered her voice to a whisper. "You guys looked normal today, by the way."

I remained neutral and just smiled. We had a lot to talk about, and if I was going to reveal any secret, then she would too. And I knew just the one I was going to ask.

Before I went to bed last night, I made sure I would be on point today, but that was because I sent Kova a text last night and told him to get his shit together too.

"Adrianna?"

My name was a distant call, an echo faraway.

Someone nudged my arm a few times until I rolled onto my side and opened my eyes.

I squinted at Holly. "What time is it?" My throat was parched. "Do you have water?" I asked before she could reply with the time. "I feel like I have knives in my throat."

I sat up and my head spun. I knew without checking I had a fever. Fuck my life. I really hoped I wasn't having another flare up.

"You don't look so hot," Holly said, concern coated her words the way parents sound. She handed me a bottle from the mini fridge.

I thanked her. "I feel like shit."

"When did you get back here?"

Taking another sip, I winced as the icy water went down like shards. I recapped the bottle and blinked my swollen eyes a few times.

"We had an early dinner because my dad had a phone meeting." I picked up my phone and glanced at the time. My brows rose. "I've been sleeping for over three hours?"

Holly raised her shoulders. "Don't ask me," she joked. "I just got back and you were dead to the world."

I looked around, so confused. Loud bubbly sounds erupted in my stomach. We eyed each other for a split second before I was up and running to the bathroom. I dropped to my knees and unleashed everything I had for dinner into the toilet.

"Aid?" she said softly.

"I'll be out in a minute," I said before vomit came up again.

God, I hated throwing up more than anything in the world. I'd rather have my period for a month straight than vomit. Luckily it didn't last long and I was soon washing up and stepping out of the bathroom.

Holly's eyes were on me. Without saying a word, I walked over to my luggage and retrieved the small makeup case I used to carry all my medicine. I took it to the bed where Holly was sitting and pulled out the bottles, laying them in front of her crossed legs.

Frowning, she hesitantly reached to pick up one bottle, then another, and another, reading each label.

"What are these?" she asked, her voice soft.

"Not to be dramatic, but they're what's keeping me alive." Holly's head lifted, her pretty blue eyes filled with alarm. "I have lupus, which led to me having kidney disease." When she didn't say anything, I continued. "I have stage four kidney disease."

Her lips parted and she turned sheen white. "Out of how many stages?" she asked, barely audible

"Five," I answered her, and tears instantly filled her eyes. "Don't cry. I'm okay. I'm better than okay, actually. Some days are harder than others. Like today. The back-to-back meets wear me down big time and take a lot of energy out of me. Sometimes I get a little sick. I'm still adjusting."

"How did you find out? Like when?"

I sat down next to her. "Well, I don't know how long I've had either one for, but from what the doctors told me, if both illnesses aren't treated early, it causes long-term issues and the stages get worse. They gather that's what happened with me. I only found out a couple of months ago."

Her brows rose as her hands held two of the bottles. "You take all these?"

"Multiple times a day."

"Wow," she said softly. "Why didn't you tell me? Does Hayden know?"

"No, no one knows. I don't want anyone to know, to be honest. So please don't mention anything to Hayden. Only my family, Avery, and Kova are aware," I said, and she eyed me like she was waiting for more. "My dad told him."

Holly averted her gaze like she was guilty. "And here I thought there was something else going on when he was just trying to help you."

"What do you mean?"

"I thought for sure there was something more than a coach and gymnast relationship happening. All the signs were there."

I swallowed and smiled softly. "He helps me out a lot, and he looks out for me…"

I left out one major detail, but it wasn't something she needed to know. I wasn't going divulge anything that could be used against us.

"But…" She continued.

"He's my dad's friend, you know?"

"Wait. How does this affect gymnastics for you?"

Taking a deep breath, I went into detail, telling her all about the illnesses and how they affected me. I told her Avery's a donor match and that I'd eventually need a transplant.

"I can't believe you never told anyone," she said, her voice a little broken when I was done. Disbelief carved her face and I empathized with her. I'd feel the same as her.

"I considered it. I mean, it would be nice to talk about it, but if I did, what would that change? I'll still have the diseases. People don't want to hear someone always complaining, and I definitely didn't want pity or for anyone treat me differently, so I just keep it to myself. Maybe one day I'll be more open about it."

She nodded, accepting what I said. "Yeah, I guess I could see it from your point of view." She paused. "You're only telling me because I saw the bottles, aren't you?"

"Kind of," I said with a partial smile. "Trust me, I complain a lot to myself. I'm sick of hearing it." Holly laughed, but it was a sad one. "Don't feel bad," I said, "I'd rather deal with it on my own, to be honest. The last thing I want is for someone to worry about it, like baby me, you know?"

"Yeah, I get that. It just sucks."

This time I really laughed. "Just a little bit."

Holly was quiet for a little while. "I just can't believe it. You train harder than most of us, you attend more meets than we do, and you have your eyes set on the Olympics. All while dealing with this?"

"I'm more focused than ever now. When I got the diagnosis, I felt like I had a timer on my life. I was so scared I wouldn't get to live and experience life. I kind of fell into a little bit of a depression because of it and lost my sight, so to stay busy I would just train and keep pushing to take my mind off things."

"You did?"

I nodded. I met her gaze with a pained looked in my eyes. She knew I had a story to tell but I was deciding if I should go the whole mile. I opened my mouth, but she spoke first.

"So before you came to World Cup, there was another coach who Kova ended up firing once he bought the gym. He'd been there for years. We all grew up with him, but we all didn't like him."

Holly shivered, her face twisting in repugnance. I had a feeling what she was trying to tell me was more difficult for her to say than for me to hear.

"Every once in a while I'll see him at a meet and it's as fresh as if it had happened yesterday."

"Who's him? The coach?"

She nodded. "There's a reason why I said what I did to you yesterday about Kova. I know you denied it and all, but I was worried and didn't want you to go through what I did."

My chest deflated. "Holly? If you don't want to tell me anything, you don't have to."

"I want to," she said, still unable to look at me. So I closed my mouth and let her speak. "He was a coach I grew up with, someone my family was friends with, and someone we all put trust into."

She shook her head and mumbled to herself but I caught it.

It's always the ones you never suspect.

Holly took a deep breath and continued. "There was something about him that felt off. He was so mean, but he got results, so I never questioned what he was doing. None of us did. He was the coach and that was that, you know?

"But then...something changed. I can't pinpoint when, or why, but...he...there was this time, no, a bunch of times..." She sighed. I knew where this was going without her saying it, so I did.

Softly, with compassion, I said, "He touched you."

Her uneasy eyes lingered on mine for a moment before she blinked, and said, "Yeah. A lot. I didn't know that he shouldn't. I mean, that's not true. I know now it was wrong, but at the same time he was someone more than a coach, and I thought it was okay because why else would I think it was wrong? We're so isolated, people could never understand this sort of lifestyle is normal for us. Being close with our coaches, traveling alone with them, looking at them almost like a parent. We idolize them. I'm not stupid. I know no parent would ever touch me the way he did, but I didn't think it was wrong either. I know I'm not making any sense, you probably don't know what I mean." She sighed again, resigned, and I was saddened by this news.

I knew exactly what she meant. I'd heard it all before. It was something that happened all the time in the gym world. Now I knew why she was worried about me.

"You don't have to explain it. I know."

Her chest fell. "I spiraled out of control and I went on this crazy boy train. I skipped practice, hooked up with guys from school, snuck out at night, talked back to my parents. I was a mess. All the while my *amazing* coach," she said sarcastically and rolled her eyes, "kept molesting me and making me feel so disgusting. I thought if I went out with boys I actually liked, that it would be okay."

"If he made you feel that way, why'd you keep going back?"

She shrugged helplessly. "Sometimes I felt like I didn't have a choice. I was becoming a really good gymnast. I guess I thought I owed it to him. He was so manipulating, though. I never saw him for who he truly was until it was too late." She paused, her voice dropping like she was embarrassed. "I had to go to therapy for it."

I frowned. "How old were you when this happened."

A tear slipped from the corner of her eye. She quickly wiped it away.

"I was nine when the touching began. It stopped when Kova bought the gym. I was almost fifteen then."

My brows shot up. This was more recent than I was aware. I recalled Kova telling me a story about how he'd fired a coach the day he purchased World Cup for his abusive treatment. I didn't realize it was Holly's coach.

"Can you believe I cried on Kova's shoulder and thanked him? I was mortified, but I was so happy too. Kova threatened him and he never came back." Holly was quiet for a moment, like she was deep in her thoughts. "I wish Kova had come to the gym sooner. He saved me. I don't know what I would've done without him."

CHAPTER 53

I stared at Holly, wishing there was something I could say or do to help her, but I knew there were no words that would bring her comfort.

"Kova didn't call the police?"

"He called my parents. Kova wanted to call the police, but my parents begged him not to. He swore he wouldn't. If that wasn't enough, like any parent when they hear their daughter is being sexually abused, they wanted to pull me and my brother from World Cup and basically lock us in our home. They put complete trust and faith into that coach and he took advantage. They didn't want it to happen again. I was devastated. God, I was so upset. I apologized thinking, it was my fault, but looking back, I don't blame them. If it were my daughter, I'd react the same way."

Dread ran through me. I'd heard this story one too many times. "So he got away with it," I said, and she nodded. "And you thought the same thing was happening with me."

She looked up and wrapped her arms around herself. "I have thought that for a little while now. It was strange though, like you didn't look at him the way I did when I looked at my old coach. And Kova doesn't have those creepy eyes when he looks at you," she said, surprise lacing her tone. "I thought something was going on, I just didn't know what, but after what I went through and after all the therapy, I felt strongly about speaking up to you. I didn't want you to go through what I did."

I contemplated how far I should take this conversation, whether or not to reveal a secret that could jeopardize more than one life, or watch her drown in her memories and imagine the worst. I wanted to tell her, my gut said to risk it, but the less anyone knew the better. However, the need to soothe her damaged heart consumed me.

Holly continued, her voice splintered with each word. She reminded me of a crystal vase—the slightest tap would permanently break it.

"You know how there's a strict dating rule?" she said, voice low. I nodded. "It's because of me. There's things you don't know… that no one knows about."

"One time Hayden mentioned something about the dating rule and you, but he refused to say anything more. I tried to pry it out of him. That boy is solid as a rock. He wouldn't budge."

Despair layered her words. "Hayden is protective. I'm kinda glad he never told you. It's embarrassing."

I smiled to myself. Her twin was a giant teddy bear who wanted to comfort and guard everyone. A lot made sense now. Hayden would never accept Kova no matter how much I pleaded my case to him, because of what had happened to Holly. She had been easily manipulated by her old coach, and he assumed I'd been too. It was easy to say I wasn't, but the words were empty when his sister had actually experienced it.

"He's been worried about you, you know."

"I don't think Hayden is capable of not worrying about anyone," I said, and she agreed. "Why is there a dating rule in effect?" I asked.

She glanced at me, then let go of the comforter she was picking at, like she'd finally let go of the shame she carried with her. She dried her cheeks with the back of her hand.

"Before the coach was fired, I spiraled out of control. I skipped practices so I wouldn't have to see him. And like I said, I hooked up with kids from school just to feel normal. I had a terrible attitude. It was too late before I realized that my actions had backfired on me because my coach noticed too. He'd gotten worse than ever with me, and I ended up confessing to Hayden one night. I couldn't take anymore and I broke down. I told him I needed to take an STD test because I had a bump on me that I freaked out over. It ended up being nothing, but Hayden was furious and got involved trying to help. By that point Kova threatened to expel me from World Cup for my behavior." She paused, taking a deep breath. "Hayden went to Kova and pleaded with him, telling him everything that had been going on and how I needed to take an STD test. That's when Kova called my parents. When they wanted to pull us from World Cup,

Kova went to bat for us. He told them of his plans to fire my coach the moment he bought the building so we could stay. Unfortunately around the same time, my dad took a job in Ohio. It was an offer he couldn't refuse, but I didn't want to leave and neither did Hayden. They couldn't afford to keep us training here, let alone in a rented apartment, and they sure as hell wouldn't trust another coach so soon. That was when Kova suddenly had a scholarship program no one knew about."

My face scrunched up. That was news to me. "What scholarship program?"

"Exactly."

"The program would pay for me and Hayden to train full time and the meet costs. The only thing my parents had to pay for were the travel, leos, and other needs outside of the gym. Kova said he saw our true potential and that we could live with him and Katja until we got our own place so they could watch over us. It wasn't easy for my parents. They had to come to an agreement, like Kova agreeing not to go to the cops. It took time and money."

It was easily over two grand a month just for both of them to train full-time elite, not to mention the leotards could run as high as five hundred dollars for one. Training at the Olympic level often created financial strain on families, some going as far as to file bankruptcy. Elite was almost as heavy with expenses. With Kova footing the bill, it alleviated the burden on the family with the possibility of securing a future for Hayden and Holly. The whole reason Holly was still competing at an elite level was to hopefully gain a full-ride scholarship to college. Hayden had received one, and Holly was praying she would too.

"In return, we had to sign a no-dating agreement. Kova said his time was valuable and we had to respect it. He was giving us one chance, and one chance only. "

I laughed. "I'm sorry for laughing, it's just so Kova."

"I know. I think he felt guilty he hadn't caught on sooner with my coach, so this was his way of giving back. I don't have to tell you how often this happens or how most coaches get away with it. My parents said he even offered to pay for the therapy, but they declined and said he was doing enough for us already. Ultimately, my mom stayed back for a few months until she put us in the trust and care of Kova. We tell everyone that we've lived on our own since sixteen, but it's a lie. My parents were running out of money with the move to Ohio, so we lived with Kova and Katja for a little while. Once the coach was fired, we got our own apartment. That gave my parents the time they needed to get our place situated. Kova knew how much gymnastics meant to me and my brother and he wanted us to have it without worry, but with security. And we did."

My eyes were focused on Holly, my chest aching for the time that was stolen from her. She was the all-American girl on the outside, but on the inside, she was suffering and in a state of anxiety thinking I was being abused like she had been. There was so much I didn't know about the people I spent fifty hours a week with. I knew them, yet they were virtual strangers.

Quietly, she said, "Kova was the one to pull me out of it. He worked with me at my pace until I was ready to train elite. He said if I was never ready then that would be okay, but that we had to try. I owe him so much."

Tears immediately filled my eyes. I blinked them away. He'd done the same for me and it was something I could never repay him for. It was hard to wrap my head around Kova and this story. His generosity, his compassion, why he never told me. It made a lot of sense now. Kova had struggled growing up. The thought occurred to me that he was trying to make a change, possibly trying to give to those who might not have the chance. It placed him in a light that was riveting and took me by complete surprise. It made my heart beat for him and who he was underneath, the layer he kept hidden to the world. After all our ups and downs, I knew there was a man with a big heart there, I just didn't know how big it really was.

Swallowing, I exhaled the worry of telling a secret, and opened up the way she had.

"Kova was the one to pull me out of the dark hole I'd been stuck in too. When the diagnoses came, I shut down and didn't tell anyone. On top of that, I'd been dealing with so many personal things at home I was trying to not let get to me too. I had so much weight I was carrying around every day that I tried to channel into gymnastics. I'd wake up and think, what else could go wrong?" I paused for a moment, thinking. "It took some time, but you know how when you just hold it all in and then you explode and it's usually on the wrong person?" She nodded. "That's what happened. I blew up, and I blew up on him. He let me." Her brows shot up. "Kova knew about it—my dad told him, even though he promised me he wouldn't—and so he'd been trying all along to help me. I just didn't know it because I didn't see it from shutting everyone out."

Holly chewed on her lip for a long moment. "Was there something going on before this? You and him?" Her question was soft and without judgment.

"Yes."

Her shoulders fell. Her reaction part shocked part sad. "I knew it. I had a feeling, but I wasn't sure either."

"It's not like what you and your coach went through. I know it sounds like I'm defending him, but I'm not. I promise. If anything, I pushed him."

"I believe you, it's just hard to accept, you know? There's always a shadow of doubt. I know Kova and I would never put him in the same category of that other coach. It's just…" She let out a sigh. "Yeah, I get it."

I nodded. It made sense. "Do you think the others know?" I asked, praying for two little letters. Holly shook her head and I exhaled in relief.

"If they knew, they'd talk about it."

"Reagan kind of knows." Her eyes widened. "I didn't speak to her about it and I never will, but she caught on the day Katja came to the gym and told everyone about the wedding."

She blinked like she was thinking back to that day. "Yeah, that was a surprise."

"How so?"

"They just never seemed totally in love, you know? I knew they loved each other—like I love you, but not like I love you like that."

The knots in my stomach tightened just thinking about that dreadful day and how I wished I could erase it from my memory.

"He'd been married for months, Holly."

"Yeah, another shock. Especially with the way he always looked at you."

Air seized my lungs. "It's been that obvious since then?"

"No, I really don't think so. After what I've been through and given the fact I know him a little better than others, I can see it."

"How does he look at me?"

"With admiration, almost like he loves you. He sure doesn't look at his wife in the same way." She paused. "I take that back. He does seem like he loves her but it's just different. I can't explain it. Like he tries so hard not to look at you but when he does it's like awe in his eyes. It's kind of funny since he's a man. Usually it's the woman acting like that."

"No way. He doesn't look at me like that."

"It's the truth. Hayden sees it too. Kova looks at you differently. He definitely doesn't look at me like he does you, which I'm glad about." She laughed half-heartedly. "If he did, it might trigger PTSD."

I laughed, and covered my mouth. I giggled way harder than I should have at that comment.

"I'm serious," she said.

"I know it may seem hard to believe, but he didn't force me into anything. It was the opposite, actually. He tried not to but I just kept pushing and pushing until I got what I wanted."

"Even though you knew he had a girlfriend?"

My cheeks heated with embarrassment. I blinked hard, ashamed to open my eyes.

"Yes. I know it makes me a bad person. This might sound cheesy, but he's my other half. I can't imagine a future that he's not in." I inhaled and expelled a weighted breath, then got real with her. "The thing is, I don't know how to stop loving him. My heart beats for him, Holly, every single day. I know it's wrong and I'm not supposed to, but I love him. I don't know how to stop it."

She sucked in a quiet gasp. "Knowing he has a wife doesn't bother you?"

I looked her directly in the eyes and told her the truth. "No, it doesn't."

Her brows shot up, she was taken aback. I didn't blame her. "That's kind of... " Holly didn't finish her sentence.

"Shitty?"

She nodded regrettably. I knew I should feel remorse for what I've done, but the truth was, I didn't. I don't know if I ever did.

"I don't know what I'm going to do. I know the right thing would be to sever ties with him, but I just can't because deep down, I don't want to. My mind gives me warnings but my heart plows them down with nothing but love for him. And love always wins, right? Isn't it supposed to?"

Holly was quiet for a moment. "But he has a wife."

"I know."

"Is he going to divorce her?"

Quietly, I said, "No, not that I'm aware of. But I'd never ask for that either."

"Then what are you going to do?"

I thought about it for a moment before I said, "I can only love him in the dark."

CHAPTER 54

I vomited until I dry heaved.

The back of my throat burned like someone was scraping hot coal down it and my stomach was hollow.

I knew better than to eat airplane food. My stomach revolted just looking at it, but I'd already been feeling sick for most of the flight and figured it was due to hunger and my medications messing with my stomach.

Unfortunately, I couldn't get cleaned up because we had to rush to the next flight. But once we were on the plane, and the seat belt sign turned off, I used the god awful, putrid-smelling bathroom to brush my teeth.

The odor got to me and I ended up throwing up again. I'd never had an issue with flying before, but then I'd never traveled for so long at one time either. I'd have to pick up some medicine to deal with motion sickness before we went to Italy. No way in hell was I going to deal with this if I could avoid it.

I'd slept the rest of the way and when we landed back in Georgia, I excused myself to freshen up.

"Are you okay?" Holly asked, eyeing me as she washed her hands.

I looked at her in the mirror. "I think I'm having one of those flare ups I told you about." Her face fell. "Don't give me those puppy eyes. I didn't tell you so you can pity me."

She turned off the water. "I know. But I still feel bad."

We both dried our hands and walked out to the terminal lobby. Kova's forehead creased as he observed me, his eyes taking in the length of my body. I knew Holly was watching so I tried covertly to give him the look to stop.

He didn't catch on.

Men.

So stupid sometimes.

We retrieved our bags and got in Kova's car. I had Holly sit up front so I could sit in the back with the window rolled down, figuring it would help with the nausea. I slowly breathed in the salty air with my eyes closed. Home. I was home. Thank goodness the airport wasn't too far. Between the jet lag and the exhaustion of the meet, I wasn't feeling so hot.

"Bye, Holly," I said from the backseat.

"See you tomorrow!" she said, walking away. Kova stayed parked until she'd stepped through her front door.

"Want to jump in the front?" he asked.

I faked a groan. "I'm too tired. I'll just stay here if that's cool with you."

"It is cool with me," he said, and I chuckled. "What is so funny?"

"Sometimes you sound like a robot when you don't use contractions," I teased him.

He looked in the rearview mirror, grinning. "*It's* cool with me," he said again.

My stomach did a little flip and I smiled as he pulled up to a red light. Going with the urge in my heart, I unbuckled my seat belt and grabbed onto the seats in front of me to lean forward. Kova's gaze was on me as I stuck my head into the front and reached around to pull his face to mine to give him a quick, little kiss. He responded immediately, his hand to the back of my head while he kissed me deeply as he held me to him. A car honked behind us and I pulled away, our lips making a popping sound.

He shot me a quick glance before he refocused on the road, grinning from ear to ear.

"Minty. I am glad you brushed your teeth," he said, and I playfully slapped him. "What was that for?"

I shrugged and leaned against the side of the passenger seat watching him. "I just felt like kissing you."

Kova laced our fingers together and placed them on the console. My cheek rested on the fabric and I glanced down at our joined hands, feeling really good about us.

I thought about what Holly told me, how generous but discreet he'd been, and it made me swoon for Kova even more. My thumb rubbed the space between his thumb and forefinger in an effort to slow down my racing heart. I thought back to when he told me of his past and how he'd had so few opportunities growing up. It hadn't changed him, only reminded him of where he'd come from and what little he had. He was humble and it said a lot about his character.

"You did amazing this weekend," he said, watching the road. "Be proud of yourself. I know I am."

"You're always proud of yourself."

He grinned and I decided I would tell him my thoughts.

"It took a lot out of me. I'm so physically worn out, it kind of worries me."

His hand tightened. "I know it did."

"How?"

"I can tell by looking in your eyes, at your body. You are trying to stay strong, but your eyes are fighting a war inside and your body language suggests you are extremely tired."

"Yeah," was all I said. He was right. One could tell a lot by just paying attention. "It kind of knocked me down a little, but I'm okay. For once, I really feel okay. I want to give it all I've got right now because I know I'll never have this chance again. I want to know that I fought hard. The last thing I want is to wake up the next day with regret. I know it probably sounds silly, but I don't want to miss this moment."

Kova looked at me briefly. He brought our hands to his lips and kissed them before his gaze was back on the road. He held my hand the rest of the drive and stayed quiet until he pulled into my complex. The fresh air settled my stomach and my nerves subsided and all felt right in the world again. Like a peace fell over us where we finally reached a point in our relationship where we were good and nothing could ruin it. We were turning pages.

"Is everything okay?" I asked, concerned when he parked the car and stayed still.

"I simply do not want to say goodbye to you."

Bittersweet. That's what we were. Beautiful butterfly wings that disintegrated to ashes and floated away in the wind.

"Honestly, I want nothing more than to come inside and just be with you, and I cannot. I want to just drive around holding your hand, and I cannot. I want to wake up drinking coffee with you before the sun rises and then go to the gym together, and I cannot." He was quiet for a moment and I didn't interrupt his thoughts. Kova swallowed, his Adam's apple bobbing like it was a difficult pill to swallow.

"It is so unfair," he said, still looking ahead. "I am already missing you and you have not even left."

The defeat in his words caught me off guard. I was all too familiar with what he was feeling. Life was unfair. We were unfair. A war was raging inside Kova. He meant what he said and my heart ached for this moment when he was true to himself and his feelings.

"Come on," I said, urging him. "Come with me."

He shook his head. "I cannot. I have to go home."

Softly, I said, "Stay with me. Even if it's just for an hour. We can watch the sun set on the beach." Somehow, I knew he didn't want to sit inside, and somehow, I knew he wasn't looking for sex.

He studied me. I didn't falter under his gaze. The emotion in his green eyes was so thick with misery I thought he was going to tell me everything on his mind.

"Okay," was all he said.

That longing tension grew stronger in the confinement of his car. Our chests rose and fell, mimicking each other's, as we tried to steady our breathing. Whatever this was, he felt it too. I couldn't explain why, but after this moment, I knew it would never be the same for us.

We got out of his car and took my belongings upstairs. I grabbed a couple blankets and we made our way downstairs and onto the beach to one of the wooden lounge chairs offered to the tenants of the complex. Kova laid a blanket down. He took a seat first then tugged me to his lap. Chest to chest, I curled into his body, my legs tangling with his, and I used his shoulder as a pillow. I sighed in contentment and looked at the gently lapping waves. Kova draped the second blanket around us, then wrapped his arms around me and held me like he never wanted to let go. He pressed his lips to the top of my head, then nestled closer.

Kova instantly relaxed against me, like he could breathe again. Something was going on inside of him and if this was what he needed, then so be it. We both needed it.

It was only us on an ivory sand beach with the sun setting behind the calm waters. It was enough to lull me to sleep.

After a while, he spoke. "Why does this feel so natural?" he asked. "It is the most ordinary thing, something I have taken for granted living here, though I cannot imagine doing this or being this comfortable with anyone except you. I mean that, Adrianna."

I felt his confusion, how simple and easy this was, yet so hard to process. "I know. I'm trying to figure that out too. I never watch the sunset, but now that I am, it's so peaceful and relaxing." There was something about the whitecaps softly kissing the shore, the way the sun caused the waves to look like diamonds rippling in the distance, the peaceful sound of the vast ocean.

"I wish I could do this every day with you in my arms just like we are right now," he continued, like he was lost in his dark thoughts. I swallowed back my emotion and looked up. The green in his eyes was iridescent against the setting sun and it was startling with his dark lashes. Every time he blinked the hues of green shifted. "All we have is right now. This moment. Tomorrow I will not wake up with you, and tomorrow I will not go to bed with you. I will only have a few stolen hours of the day with you and that is just not enough for me. I want every waking minute to be with you."

I frowned, fear rising in me. I wondered where these feelings were coming from now. The last time he was deep in his feelings, my heart was shattered the following day.

"Kova?"

"Hmm?"

"The last time you were like this, you kept saying *prosti* over and over while we made love, and the very next day I found out you were married." I paused and licked my lips. "Please tell me it's not going to happen again tomorrow. Please tell me I'm not going to find out something shocking that's going to devastate me. I can't handle it right now."

The intensity in his eyes bore into mine. "I am hiding nothing from you. Nothing, Adrianna. I swear it."

I nodded subtly, accepting his answer. "I'm sorry I asked."

Kova shook his head. "Do not be sorry. I shaped that worry within you and it is my fault. But I swear I am not hiding anything. I am just bitter about the hand I was dealt, that is all. I wish I could change things."

Kova looked away, his gaze distant. "I am looking into how I can divorce her, if you want to know. I just have to be careful about the way I do it. It will take some time."

He glanced at me. All I could do was stare into his lonely eyes and know what he said was the truth, and it tore him up. Leaning toward me, he dipped his head and his lips captured mine.

My heart soared. This wasn't just any kiss, and it most definitely wasn't a sexual one. It was a kiss that could only be fortified with honest-to-God love that was bone deep. The kind dreams were made of. The kind we all searched for but rarely received.

It was a kiss that almost made me say I love you.

I clenched my hand around the fabric of his shirt and pulled him closer, breathing in the kiss like he was my life support. I opened my palm and slid it up his chest and around his shoulder to cup the back of his head. My fingers threaded his hair, our bodies flushed together as the passion between two people who had no right giving in to one another grew to a binding fever.

Kova rolled over me, his body half on mine as he deepened the kiss. He reached behind himself and pulled the blanket over his head to give us privacy. It was intimate without even having to try.

We stayed like that until well after the sun set, kissing away our fears and worries, and sealing any distance we'd had between us with a stroke of the tongue.

CHAPTER 55

I didn't challenge Kova when he told me to take the following day off.

For once I agreed, and I think it shocked him more than it did myself. His eyes filled with gratitude and it made me feel good seeing him like that. He kissed my forehead and said thank you before he left.

I shut the door and thought back to everything that had transpired since I'd come to World Cup and how we'd gotten to this point. We had our painful truths and lies, tried countless times to not admit our feelings, tried not to be together. But through it all, we were always there for each other because some force had compelled us to.

And even though he wasn't here, Kova was still all around me. Mixed with the scent of the salty sugary beach air, it was a heightened combo of sweet and dark wrapped in one. I could smell him in every room, and I took comfort in that warmth. It had physically hurt my heart to say goodbye and caused a deep melancholy in me, but I couldn't ask him to stay again.

My body needed the rest, and if I was going to be in this game for as long as I was physically able, then I needed to play my cards right. So I listened to my body, and my coach, and I decided to stay home.

IT WAS A GOOD THING I wasn't defiant for once. I woke up with terrible stomach cramps, and my boobs felt heavy and uncomfortable, so I skipped the coffee and made some peppermint tea hoping it would ease my upset stomach. I toasted a slice of bread, but I couldn't eat it.

A flare up. I'd need to make an appointment first thing with my doctor just to be sure everything was okay. This could really be the cause of a few things compiled together, but I had to make smart choices about my health. After all, I only had one life to live, and I sure as hell wanted to live it to the fullest.

After taking my medicine, I finished my tea and fell back asleep. I felt like crap. Three hours later I woke up and ran to the bathroom. I knew better than to take the medicine on an empty stomach, but the thought of eating made me feel sicker, so I'd skipped it. I figured the tea was fine. Clearly, I was wrong.

"I think I'm dying." I exaggerated a moan to Avery on the phone after I cleaned up and changed my clothes.

"Jesus, Aid, what the fuck time is it?"

I glanced at my clock and frowned. Had I gotten up in the middle of the night and not realized it? Jet lag was messing with me. "It's a quarter after seven."

"Go back to bed." She groaned, and I explained I'd already gotten up twice now. "You're so weird."

"I'm so tired. My period is all messed up and my stomach is eating itself. For once I have big boobs so I can't complain about that, but I'm having a stupid flare up and hating life."

"Your boobs get big during that?"

I thought about her question and palmed one. I winced and gasped.

"What happened?"

"I grabbed my boob to feel the size since I'm so happy they're not bee stings right now and it hurts so fucking bad. My nipples are sore."

"Has Kova been sucking on them?"

I laughed, curling up under the covers in my bed. "No."

"Pinching them?"

"No," I drawled out.

"Then it must've really hurt for you to curse. Are you sure this is normal for a flare up?"

I considered her question. "I mean, I've never really given it much thought, but now that I'm paying attention, I think?"

"What else?" she asked, sounding like she was awake.

"I keep vomiting, but I think that's because of traveling and shitty food I'm not used to eating. I fucked up all my medicine, got my period in the middle of the meet, which didn't help my nerves. Well, not in the middle of it, but right before I left the hotel. I told you, I'm dying. This is it."

"Shut the fuck up, you are not dying. You haven't even gotten my kidney yet. You are literally not allowed to die."

I chuckled. "I hate throwing up."

"I hate throwing up too. I'd much rather have a tooth filled than vomit." She paused. "Wait. Do you still have your period?"

"It's at the end of the cycle."

"So you had it for, like, three days?"

"Yeah, I guess."

"And that's normal?"

"Well, normal for me, I'd say."

"And your boobs hurt."

I was silent for a moment. All I could hear was the beating of my heart in my ears.

"What are you getting at?"

"Have you taken a pregnancy test?" she blurted it out.

Avery was crazy. "I'm not pregnant. Any time I've been with Kova I've used Plan B."

"I would take a test to be sure. Plan B isn't one hundred percent."

"I know that, but I'm not pregnant. What makes you think I am?" Just saying the word was making me tremble.

"Because your boobs hurt, dumbass. You're tired, and hello, you're vomiting." She basically spelled the words out for me and paused between them. "If that isn't a sign, then I don't know what is."

I rubbed my eyes with the heel of my hand. "So? All signs of a flare up and the effects. It's a lot shit it could and could not be, but not pregnant is one of them."

"All it takes is one resilient little fuck to slide on through. Ah, I take that back. An aggressive little Russian fuck to swim on by to the egg."

I couldn't stop the laugh from rolling out of me. "I hate you."

"Aid." I heard the plea in my name. "All jokes aside, humor me."

"I shouldn't have called."

"Don't be stupid. You're getting nervous because now you're actually thinking about it and it scares the shit out of you. I get it, trust me, I get it more than anyone. But the difference is, you have me with you. Get dressed and go to the pharmacy. If it's negative, then you go back to sleep and you don't have to worry."

She was right, and I didn't like it. My stomach was in knots. I threw the blanket off and kicked it away, feeling warmer than usual. Swallowing back the lump in my throat, I glanced down at my flat stomach. Pregnant? No, there wasn't a chance in hell.

"I think I'm having a panic attack," I said, panting into the phone. "I can't have a baby."

Avery sighed like she was annoyed. "Stop being dramatic. Get up and get dressed."

I was struggling to breathe. "I can't, Avery. I just can't." The back of my neck was damp and I felt sticky everywhere. I needed to shower.

"No one is saying you're having a baby, you lunatic. Just go get the test."

"What if I am?" I was only eighteen. Freshly turned eighteen. I couldn't get pregnant.

"I'd say I wouldn't be surprised. Kova is a freak in the sheets, and from what you've told me, you're just as bad."

"Avery! You're not helping."

"What? I'm being serious. It's kinda sexy and hot, but at the same time you guys are both nymphos. It's a good thing you don't live together. I think you'd guys fuck each other to death. Doesn't your vagina ever hurt?"

I shook my head. "What? No. I mean, at first, yes. Sometimes? If you're trying to take my mind off the terror that's consuming me, it's not working."

"I'm not. I was just curious."

I groaned and made sure she heard it. "I'm freaking out over the possibility that I could be pregnant, and you're asking about my vagina. Really, Ave?"

"Bad timing?"

"I know no form of birth control is one hundred percent, and considering how intense our sex is and how much we have at one time, maybe I didn't take the pills early eno—"

I froze mid-sentence. Had I taken them early enough? Had I taken enough? My mind raced through the brain fog back to the first time we had sex again. I blinked a few times trying to remember when it hit me… It was when I had carved an A into his chest during the hurricane, and again a couple of days later.

Tears instantly filled my eyes, but I pushed them back. No, I wouldn't get emotional just yet because I was fairly certain I took the pills within the correct time frame and I wasn't pregnant. Kova would've made sure of that.

Sitting up, I moved my hair off my neck and hunched over to hold my stomach. I was going to be sick and this time it was due to the reality of the situation and nothing else. There was an old wives tale that floated between the Florida-Georgia line that women got pregnant during hurricanes. Now my mind was overthinking stupid thoughts and actually considering them.

"Ria?" she joked, to which I actually chuckled sadly. I forgot she would pretend to say my nickname the way Kova did. "What is it?"

Deep breathing, I dropped my head into my palm. "What if I am pregnant? A baby, Avery? I could never admit Kova was the father—he'd go to jail. No, I take that back. He wouldn't make it to jail. My dad would slaughter him first and no one would find his body, then my child would grow up asking me who it's daddy is."

For once, Avery was quiet.

"Yeah, you're fucked. Let's hope it's negative."

CHAPTER 56

W hat the fuck do I buy?" I whispered into the phone. Wide eyes scanned the assortment of colorful boxes. "There's a million of them. Do they all work?"

"Yeah, they all work, but you can buy a few of them to be sure."

"Oh." I hadn't even thought of that. "There are two in a pack."

"Buy three of the two-packs."

"What? Why do I need six tests?"

"Because if you are pregnant, you're going to be in shock and think the test is broken. You'll end up peeing on all of them."

My eyes scanned the boxes. Some had an automatic reading, some detected a pregnancy in five days, some seven. "You're probably right. But let's not say the P word anymore."

"I honestly don't know how I'm friends with you."

"I had a period, though," I said, still in denial.

Trying to steady my nerves, I reached for one of the tests Avery named.

"You can still bleed and be pregnant in the beginning. It's called spotting. A lot of people mistake it for a period."

"Oh." I grabbed one more box and then turned out of the aisle. Head down, I counted the tiles as I walked quickly to the front to pay. "Would it be weird if I peed on one here?"

"I mean, is that where you want to learn you're carrying a future Olympian?"

"I'm hanging up on you."

She laughed. "It wouldn't be weird, but just do it at home. That way you can cry in peace."

"I just want to get it over with. I'm nervous." Heart racing a mile a minute, I paid at the self-checkout then hurried to my truck and jumped in. I threw off my sunglasses and said, "I feel like I'm going to be sick."

"That's because—"

"Shut up. I don't find this funny. My future is going to be ruined."

"Kova should've wrapped up his magic stick because pull out and pray doesn't work."

I fought the smile. "I keep taking deep breaths but I feel like I can't catch my breath. My hands are shaking and I can't stop thinking that I'm going to see a pink line."

"It's two lines, and it's normal. You know I'm just playing with you."

"I know. I just, I don't know." I stumbled over my words.

Sighing, my mind raced with a million different thoughts.

"I took the Plan B, but the more I think about it, the more I think I took it too late. But then I keep thinking about how the doctors said it's supposedly really difficult to get pregnant and I can't figure out how this happened. How are you so calm and cracking jokes?"

"Because I've already gone through this and sometimes jokes help lighten the mood."

I softened at her unmoved tone. She was right and I appreciated that. "I can't believe you did this alone. I feel so bad I wasn't there for you."

Turning into my complex, I was such a mess as I parked. I didn't know what I would've done if she hadn't stayed on the phone with me the entire time, coaxing me to get dressed and go to the store. Remorse reared its ugly head beneath the nerves. I'd been a terrible friend, I didn't deserve this, but I also didn't think I'd be able to do this alone, and I think she knew that. I'd handled everything thrown at me so far, some things better than others, but this, this was the icing on the cake.

"Don't apologize. It was my decision. It is what it is, and I won't think about the past. No good comes from holding onto regrets anyway."

While she had a point, I'd always live with the guilt of her having no one to talk to and the traumatic experience she'd gone through on her own. Letting go and moving forward was a harder pill to swallow.

Once inside my condo, Avery said, "Get a cup you can pee in then throw out."

"Are you going to stay on the phone with me even when I pee?" I asked as I reached into the kitchen cabinet with a trembling hand and pulled out a plastic cup. I looked into it.

"Ah, yeah? I need to know if I'm going to be an aunt or not."

My movements slowed. "Ave…" I couldn't process that thought right now.

"I know," she said, regrettably, and that was enough. She knew. "Just go in the bathroom so we can FaceTime."

Tears climbed my eyes and they immediately streamed down my cheeks. "How could I have been so fucking stupid?"

"I don't have an answer for you, not one that would be an acceptable answer anyway. We both were really stupid, but so were the guys. I hate saying you forget your responsibilities in the heat of the moment, but you kind of do. Still, it's not a good reason to be irresponsible."

Glancing down at my feet, I slipped off my flip flops. The cold tile shot chills up my spine while I stood there wondering how I got myself into this mess.

"Next time tell Kova he needs to tie down that dinosaur. Use some saran wrap."

A loud laugh erupted from me. I wiped away my tears and grabbed the plastic bag and walked to the bathroom.

"I seriously can't believe I'm doing this."

"I seriously can't believe you're going to pee as you're Face-Timing me."

Switching my phone so she could see me, I placed it on the counter and looked at the screen.

"Ave?"

"Hayyyy." She smiled when she saw my face. "God, you look like shit. You're almost transparent."

"I've had better days." I joked. "Okay, let me pee and then I'll be right back."

Turning the phone to face the wall, I grabbed the cup and relieved myself. I flushed, still in shock that I was taking pregnancy tests. I fixed the camera to face me. Avery's faced pinched up. "That's your pee?" she asked once I placed the clear cup on the counter to wash my hands. "It's really dark." She looked closer, squinting. "Is that blood?

I looked at it briefly. "Probably. My pee can range from the color of a banana to cranberry juice."

Her face twisted up. "Gross."

"How long does it take for the test to show results?" I asked, opening the first box. My fingers trembled as I pulled out both tests and placed them on a towel next to the cup.

I expelled a heavy breath. What happened next could change everything and I wasn't sure I was prepared for it.

"They're all different. Mine came up really quickly. Open two boxes. Do the early result one and the automatic. We'll save the seven-day one for like a week from now just to be sure."

I nodded and did what she said. When I had all the sticks lined up next to each other, I stared at them with a weird range of feelings. I most definitely did not want to be pregnant, but what if there was a baby already growing inside of me? Could I get rid of it? I'd always thought I could, but now that I was faced with the seriousness of the situation, I wasn't sure anymore. I had a plan, and that plan didn't include having a baby until I was married and at least twenty-six.

"What are you thinking?" Avery asked softly.

"That everything is fucked up and that my life is about to change. That I don't know what I'm supposed to feel right now. I'm giving myself a headache."

"This is what I want you to do. Dip the stick in the cup for a few seconds, then cap it and place it down. Don't wait, just move on to the next until you're done. Go get a drink of water or whatever it is you drink, and then go back and check the results. Don't hover. You're going to make yourself pass out waiting for the results with the way you're already hyperventilating."

I lifted my eyes to her and paused. Laughing, I hadn't realized I was panting so hard, but man, my nerves were shot. This was a moment of truth, and as eager as I was to find out, I was more terrified than anything.

"I'm scared," I said quietly.

Her eyes softened. "You can do two back flips with a bunch of crazy twists at the same time, run eighty miles an hour toward a table and flip over it, but this scares you?"

I shrugged one shoulder. "Yeah, a little."

Taking one last deep breath, I shook my fingers out and uncapped the first stick, dipping it in the urine for a few seconds. Recapping it, I moved on making sure I didn't look at the previous one until I was done with all four. Avery stayed quiet, watching me. Even though she was hundreds of miles away, I felt like she was right next to me, giving me strength. I needed that more than anything.

Once I finished the fourth one, I grabbed my phone as vomit climbed the back of my throat. I spewed into the toilet, dry heaving until I could barely catch my breath since there was nothing in my stomach to come up.

"This time I know it's your nerves," Avery said, slightly muffled.

Every so often her sassy southern belle side came out and gave me a good chuckle. I turned to look and realized I was covering the phone with my hand. Thank goodness. She didn't need to see me throwing up. Flushing the toilet, I wiped my face and crawled to sit against the bathtub. I brought my knees up and placed my arms on them.

"I don't want to look," I said in all honesty. And I didn't. Tears filled my eyes and I shook my head. "I don't want to look, Ave. I don't want to."

Her face fell, crippling with sadness. "I wish I was there with you," she said softly. "I'd look for you."

"I wish you could. How long has it been?"

"Like thirty seconds."

My jaw dropped. "That's it? It feels like forever."

She smiled sadly. "Yeah, that's how I felt too."

I looked above the phone at the counter and grimaced.

"What's wrong," she asked.

"My pee is more red than yellow from here. Do you think that could alter the test?"

"No, it shouldn't. It's looking for a specific hormone."

"Damn. I was hoping you would say yes."

"Wishful thinking." She paused. "Ready?"

I shook my head, eyeing the counter. My bathroom was so icy cold I started shivering. I held myself. It was the last thing I wanted to do.

"I can't remember a time when I've been so nervous. I'm terrified, Ave. I really don't want to look. I feel like I already know the answer."

I held my stomach. It was so flat.

Avery expressed her sorrow. "Just rip the Band-Aid off and do it."

"I can't believe I called to joke that I was dying and it turned into taking pregnancy tests."

"Definitely not what I expected, that's for sure."

Standing up, I tiptoed toward the counter.

"Pretend I'm there holding your hand," she said, and I swallowed and looked into the phone as I stopped in front of what could change my life forever. "Look at the counter, Aid," my best friend encouraged gently.

My lips were a thin, flat line as I shook my head. Tears spilled from the corners of my eyes into my mouth and I could taste the saltiness.

"Come on, bestie." She had tears in her eyes too.

Finally, I looked.

Chills racked my body as my eyes moved from one test to the other. My lungs ached with each result as I struggled to breathe. I was dizzy and lightheaded and staring with wide eyes in absolute shock until my vision blurred.

"Avery?" I said, my voice cracking.

Kidney disease wasn't going to kill me, a heart attack was.

I skimmed the row of tests again and all the lines in utter disbelief.

"What does it say?" she begged, but I couldn't find the words. I didn't want to say it out loud because then it would make it real. "Aid? Say something, please."

I told her.

"Christ on a fucking stick."

CHAPTER 57

I cried for an hour straight after I counted two sets of positive lines. I checked every few minutes hoping they would change. The parallel lines were solid and bright, except for the automatic two that clearly read pregnant.

Pregnant. How was I pregnant? More importantly, how did I let this happen?

Avery listened, and I loved her even more for it. She let me vent through the tears, even though I was a bawling mess of denial and heartbreak. She didn't try to hang up on me. She acted like she was right next to me as if I was crying on her shoulder. She was the perfect best friend, which made me feel even more like shit since I hadn't been there for her in her moment of need.

"How, Avery? How?" I asked for the millionth time and grabbed another tissue.

"I mean, I feel like you know how it happens at this point."

"What am I going to do? I can't tell my dad, and I definitely can't have a baby either. That leaves me with one option."

Avery was quiet for a little while. Gently, she said, "What do you want?"

"It's not that easy to answer."

"If you didn't need a kidney, what would you do?"

"I still can't have a baby. Kova would go to jail."

"What if he didn't go to jail?"

"My dad would never accept it."

"If he did?"

My face felt so swollen and the exhaustion from crying and the stress of the truth was a growing pressure on my chest. Her question wasn't cut and dry, and neither was my answer.

"I wish I could go back and change things. I wish I could go back and be smarter."

"Don't think about the past, it'll do you no good. Trust me. Think about the future and what you need to do."

Avery was right, but it was hard to do that when I was staring at all these tests telling me I was carrying a child.

Kova's child.

Our child.

Tears blurred my vision again and I started crying. In a rush, I scooped up the boxes and sticks and dumped them into the trash. The sticks stuck out of the garbage, but I didn't care. I took the last box and placed it between the towels in my bathroom closet. I couldn't stand to look at it any longer.

I rinsed my face with cool water, then dried it. Avery watched but didn't say anything, she just looked as sad as I felt. Lifting my shirt, I focused on my stomach, rubbing it in circles.

"How is there a baby in there?" I asked, more so speaking to myself.

"Technically it's a fetus."

"Whatever. Same thing, really."

"Yeah. Once the heart started beating, I viewed it differently."

I dropped my shirt, wishing I could reverse time. "When's that?"

"Six weeks."

I averted my gaze and thought back to when this could've happened. Staring at the bottles of perfume I never wore, I blindly read over the lush labels without really processing the words.

"How do I figure out how pregnant I am?"

Avery chuckled and covered her mouth. I glanced at her and saw regret fill her blue eyes.

"What? What's so funny?"

"It's how far along you are, not how pregnant you are. You're pregnant. That's it. Nothing more, nothing less. You're totally preggo. It's based on your last period, but since that's all messed up, when did you guys last have sex?"

My stomach knotted. I didn't want to think about that because there was a good chance the baby's heart was already beating, and remaining oblivious was just easier.

If I heard a heartbeat, would it change my mind?

The thought chilled me to the bone and a rush of emotions sucker punched me in my chest.

Licking my dry lips, I sniffled. "Never mind, I don't want to know. That'll just make it harder."

"You should call Kova," Avery suggested with a sugary tone.

"What? Why? No."

Her brows puckered together. "Aren't you going to tell him?"

"No. I think I'm just going to have an abortion."

The silence was earsplitting.

My heart dropped.

Reality set in and we were both still as we looked at each other, our expression mirroring each other's.

I'd already made my decision without processing it until just now.

I was eighteen, and I was going to have an abortion.

My chest deflated, lungs ached for air. The response was so fluid it caught me by surprise. The consequences for having unprotected sex and being irresponsible. Tears filled my eyes again, and my jaw trembled. I knew I'd regret this choice for the rest of my life. Yet the words spilled from my lips because I also knew what I had to do all along.

"I can't have a baby. I'm too young… right? I've come too far for that." A sob escaped me. "I know that's so selfish of me, but I just can't," I whispered, thinking it would lessen my decision. "I just can't," I paused, then told her how I really felt. "I can't imagine actually getting rid of it either."

"You have to tell him," she said softly.

"I don't want to. He's married, and he once said some harsh things about me getting pregnant and what he would do."

Avery groaned into the phone. She knew what I was talking about and she didn't like it.

"Stop thinking about the past. Think about how far you guys have come, how much you guys have grown. Regardless of what his choice is, he still needs to know. It's his right. Don't not tell him. You'll only regret it and then you'll have to live with that regret."

I sighed inwardly. Quietly, I said, "I know I need to tell him. Eventually I will."

"It sucks, Aid. Every day I blame myself for not pushing harder to talk things out with Xavier. It's horrible. Plus, you're going to need time to rest anyway. He has to know."

"Rest?"

"You'll need some time off for bed rest. When I miscarried, I had to rest for a good week or so. I had so much bleeding and my stomach killed me. The cramps are way worse than a period. There's no way you can practice like that."

"Bed rest?" My voice peaked. "But you were further along than me. Maybe I won't need that."

"I think after a specific number of weeks you have to have a procedure done. But I could be wrong. I couldn't just bleed everything out, I had to have it sucked out."

My lips parted in disbelief and I shook my head hastily. Sucked out sounded terrifying and dehumanizing. I wouldn't let it get that far. There was literally no time left in my schedule for bed rest, let alone a procedure. I had one international meet left where the team was selected, and then by some miracle, the Olympics. Two months max until it was all over. No time to rest. Not until after the Games, if I got to them.

"Two months until everything I've worked for is over. After that, I'll figure it out."

Her eyes widened. "Aid, that's a terrible idea. Probably the dumbest one you've had to date. You don't even know how far along you are. Maybe you can just take a pill or something—there are abortion pills—but waiting is not a good idea."

"I can't tell him," I panicked. "I'm not telling him. I'll just go to a clinic or something. I can't go to my regular doctor either. They'll have to tell my dad and he can't know. I'll search for a place online."

I swear she paled. Avery's face moved closer to the screen. "Listen to me. You're making a huge mistake. Tell him, Adrianna."

"I—"

"And you can't just go to some random clinic." Her voice rose, and I felt the alarm in her words. "Don't be stupid."

I rubbed my face, closing my eyes. "What a mess. I don't know what I'm going to do. I mean, I do, ugh. This really sucks."

"Start by telling him and go from there. He has a right to know," she urged softly. "Please, if you never listen to me again, make this the one time you do."

"He's going to be angry."

My stomach knotted tighter just thinking about telling him. I didn't even know where to begin, how to start the conversation, I couldn't fathom a response that would be less than negative. There was no right way to tell Kova I was pregnant with his child.

Avery's voice was strained. "You don't know that. And if you don't do this properly, you could risk having issues with future pregnancies. Don't be stupid."

I looked down. "Maybe that's a good thing," I said, my voice low. "It's what I deserve."

"Don't say that."

"It's true," I replied a little louder. "I fooled around with my coach, I slept with a married man, and I let it happen. I *wanted* it to happen. This is really my fault and what I get. It's Karma."

"You didn't make him do anything he didn't want."

"But I did. That's the thing. I pushed him since the beginning. Since the very first encounter, it was all me. I mean, he's obviously no saint, but I pursued him. In the back of my mind, I was making it so he couldn't say no. I went after him so many times, Ave." My chin quivered with guilt. I was a terrible, terrible person.

"Aid, listen to me. It's easy to blame yourself during a time like this, but it's not all you. Kova didn't do anything he didn't want to do. Even if you didn't make the choice easy on him, he still didn't have to keep it going. One time is a mistake. Two times is reckless. Three times is a choice. A conscious decision at that. He didn't have to keep it going, he chose to."

I looked at my best friend, thanking her for talking it out with me.

Taking a deep breath, I pulled myself upright from the floor of the bathroom and walked into the kitchen and placed my phone near my medicine bottles. I tied my hair up into a messy bun, then picked the bottles up one by one and uncapped them, pouring out the pills into a pile.

Avery was absolutely right, but I still held the fault for inviting it to happen and not stopping it from continuing. There was something too alluring about Kova I couldn't deny, and I didn't know why. He once told me I was the flame and he was the moth, but I couldn't help thinking it was the other way around. If we both felt that way, then a bigger, larger flame spread over time destroyed things in its path and was harder to put out.

I filled up a glass of water and placed it on the counter. Liquid splashed onto the marble. "I'm sure all these pills aren't good to take while pregnant. Maybe that's why I had my period, but it was actually a miscarriage and I didn't know."

"Only going to the doctor will tell you that. I think you would bleed heavily, like more than usual, and you would have severe cramping. You'd know the difference."

I sighed, filled with exhaustion. "What am I going to do? This is all so fucked." I scooped the pills up and swallowed them all at once.

One corner of her mouth tugged up to the side. "You know what you have to do," she said, and I nodded.

She was right, again. I couldn't not tell Kova, but how the hell did I even begin?

"I love you, Ave. I don't know what I'd do without you."

She fake flipped her hair. "Well, duh. That's because I'm the bestest friend ever. So when do you think you will? I hope sooner rather than later."

I shrugged. "I really don't know. Maybe after practice tomorrow."

Her brows rose. "You better text me ASAP the moment you do."

We said our goodbyes and I spent the rest of the afternoon agonizing over my current situation on the internet. It was a terrible idea, but I couldn't stop myself from looking things up, kind of how I did when I'd found out I had lupus and kidney disease. It made everything ten times worse but I couldn't help it.

I tossed and turned all night, sleep evading me, and when my alarm went off the next morning, I almost called in.

Instead, I got out of bed and went on with my normal routine. I was going to muster up the strength to tell Kova, but also make sure I stayed focused on my dream. He'd understand.

One day I'd have kids, just not now.

Until then, I would mourn the child I would soon give up with the man I loved.

CHAPTER 58

My first thought when I walked into World Cup and saw Kova was that he would be a hot-as-hell dad.

He had his hat on, this time facing in the right direction, and a heather gray and black baseball type tee that hugged his arms, and paired with his typical black shorts. It was hard not to stare at the cuts and curves of his biceps.

He made my heart pound so hard and a stupid number of butterflies in my stomach swirl ridiculously fast into each other. Kova lifted a folding mat and dragged it across the floor, creating rows for conditioning. I imagined a baby on his hip—not mine—and what he'd look like. He'd be so cute, probably insanely possessive, but deeply in love with his child who he'd teach gymnastics. I could see him explaining his actions and why he was always right, and how he was being a bossy coach with his child because he'd want the best for him.

Kova glanced up and our eyes locked. A different kind of smile pulled at his lips, one that said we were good, like he was happy for once. Go figure. The times that he's happy, I'm dying inside. I swallowed back my emotions and forced myself to return the smile.

He crossed the distance and my chest ached with each step that brought him closer to me. I could already smell his cologne, thanks to my heightened pregnancy senses that I'd learned about online, and it created a steady sensation of desire through me.

I wouldn't tell him today. I couldn't.

"How do you feel?" he asked. "You look a little tired. Did you want to stay home again?"

I shook my head and picked at my nails. I chewed on my lip, trying to fight the panic rising inside me. "Better. I slept all day yesterday."

He eyed me curiously, a shadow from his hat cast over half his face. "You are beautiful," he said softly, accepting my answer. A little smirk formed on his succulent mouth.

Before he could say another word, I stood on my tiptoes and reached for him. My emotions—probably the anxiety of needing to tell him—rose to the top before I realized what was happening. Palming his cheeks, I pulled his face to mine and smashed my mouth to his.

He lifted the lip of his hat and pushed it up, then wrapped his arms around my back and stepped closer to me. Kova let out a little moan as he returned the kiss. He always gave back even better. It was his way of showing me how he felt. His large hands roamed my back, skimming to my butt before he grabbed a chunk and held on. My fingers threaded the hair at the back of his neck as his tongue slipped past the seam of my lips and tangled around mine. He kissed me like he was hungry, like he couldn't get his fill. He was fighting for us and each lap of his tongue was a greater pull to what he wanted but ultimately may never have.

Still holding me, Kova broke the kiss, leaving my breathless. He glanced at my lips, then bit one. It was the little things like this that made me fall deeper for him, but it also helped me decide that today just wasn't the day to drop the ball.

"You're a lover, not a fighter."

He smirked, brows furrowed. "What made you think of that?"

"By the way you kiss. I can feel it."

He seemed content with my answer. "Life is too short to fight. Unless, of course, we fight during sex." His eyes heated with the thought. "Then, I am up to fighting."

My head fell back and a laugh rolled out of me before I could stop it. He dipped his head, his nose tickling my neck. I felt the outline of his smile under my ear. Kova pressed into me and I stepped back until I felt the wall against my back. Heat zoomed down my spine as his chest pushed into me, the warmth of his strong body brought a sense of security and love I so desperately needed.

"Like when we made love again for the first time after so long, when you were throwing things at me, when you tried to cut me…" He emphasized the last words and I laughed. "When you *did* cut me. As much as we both hurt that day, and as much as I loved every minute, I never want to fight with you again like that. So, yes, maybe I am a lover, but I am only a lover for you, and I am only a fighter for you." Kova looked down. "I thought I'd lost you for good during that horrible time. I never want it to happen again."

I swallowed. Yeah, definitely not telling him today.

Quietly, I said, "I don't think it's possible to lose me."

The corners of his eyes softened. "Same. Now, let me fuck you before practice starts."

A loud laugh burst from my chest. "No," rolled off my lips. He made me so happy and I wondered if he even knew that. "Way to ruin the moment with your quick fuck."

Kova whimpered. "You cannot come in like this and kiss me and expect me not to want more. I feel like I just woke up next to you, and you know how much I want that. To see you supple and soft like you are now, and be able to wake up balls deep inside you, to feel you squeeze around my dick, hear your soft little sighs… There is nothing I want more than that."

He made my heart pound wishing for that.

"You only want me for my pussy."

His eyes flared with desire. "Among other things."

I tried not to smile at his response. I knew he was teasing me, but it was doing the trick and making me not think about the larger issue at hand.

"You're such a smooth talker."

"I have my moments. So what do you say, yes? I can pull up your leg like this." His voice dropped as he got lower and hooked my thigh around his hip. "Then I can move your shorts aside and take you quick and fast like this," he said, pulling the material to one side and teasing my bare flesh with his fingers. I'd worn small shorts, a sports bra, and a tank top today. "Or I can lift you up and take you quick but slow right here in my gym." He groaned at the thought of his own words. "Slow because I need to feel every inch of your sweet body. You know I am already hard for you." He pushed one long finger inside and I gasped. "I feel you clenching around me," he said, kissing me. His tongue making me crazy with lust. "Come on, let me have you," he begged, and it was pretty cute.

"No." My response came out a little more breathless than I wanted. "But maybe before I leave tonight," I said, pushing my hips into his hand. Damn traitorous body.

His exaggerated groan was one of epic proportions. "You are going to kill me. How the fuck am I going to wait until then? You should just let me fuck you." He chuckled. "It will not take long."

I ignored his annoyingly right comment and reached between us, slipping my hand beneath the elastic of his shorts to find his bare cock rock solid. Kova grabbed my wrist.

I squeezed. "Still no boxers, I see."

"Never," he said between clenched teeth. "Plus, I like catching you checking out my dick. I will never wear them for that reason alone."

My cheeks flamed. "I do not."

"You do, and you know it makes me fucking hard every time." He tightened his hold. "You had your chance, now you have to wait until tonight."

Frustrated, I leaned in and bit his lip until I tasted blood. I moaned, lapping at the tiny crimson droplets. Kova's cock twitched in my hand and I felt a wave of pleasure roll through his body. I loved that he loved what I did.

"Tonight, I fuck you in here."

⁂

"I BAILED," I SAID QUIETLY into the phone.

I don't even know why I whispered when I was alone and no one else could hear me.

"On who?" Avery asked.

"Kova."

"Ohhh," she responded. "Why did you dip out on Fish Lips?"

"We were supposed to have sex after practice. When he wasn't looking, I ran."

Avery chuckled. "Let me guess, you didn't tell him about the spawn."

I shook my head, fighting a grin. I was almost home. "Nope."

"How was practice anyway now that you're carrying a little Russian hothead?"

This time I laughed. "Avery…" I groaned. "It was so stressful, and I don't know why. I'm not keeping the baby, so it shouldn't have bothered me, but I kept thinking I'm going to hurt it, so I hesitated a lot."

She was quiet for a moment. "I think that's normal. Do you think Kova noticed?"

"He notices everything, so I played it off and used my disease as an excuse."

"Who knew kidney disease would come in handy for once. So what are you going to do now when he goes looking for you and you're MIA?"

I sighed into the phone. "I don't know. I guess I'm just going to tell him I'm not feeling well."

"And you think he's going to buy it," she stated, clearly not sold on my lie.

"Yes, but that's only because he knows I'm sick and doesn't want anything to happen to me."

I pulled into my complex, grabbed my things, and made my way upstairs.

"You really need to just tell him, Aid," she said softly.

"I know. I really was going to when I got to practice, but then I saw him, Ave, and I imagined him with a baby. It fucked with my head."

She hummed under her breath. "He would look really good with a baby."

"Drool worthy. See? The words evaded me and I didn't know if I should just blurt it out or ease my way into the conversation, and then I decided to kiss him…"

She giggled. "I know it's easier said than done, but the longer you wait, the harder it will be. The anxiety will eat you away."

I already felt like that now. Once I was in my condo, I dropped my stuff to the floor and sat on the couch. I exhaled a sigh and listened to the silence for a second. "Yeah," I said a little out of breath.

I glanced down at my stomach, still in awe that I was pregnant. I placed my hand on my belly, fearing my next question. "Ave? What if this is the only time I can get pregnant?"

"You can't look at it like that. If it happened while you were training like a damn lunatic, then you should be able to in the future when you're a normal person again. Plus, there's a whole slew of drugs you can take to help you conceive."

I thought about what I had to do and how disheartened I was feeling over the choice I had made. It made me sick. I never really had a view on abortion, not until Avery told me she had one, and now that I was faced with the same decision myself, it was proving to be much harder than I thought. I could not have a baby, but I was quickly learning I didn't like the thought of having an abortion either. I was stuck in the worst predicament of my life with no right choice. Everyone was going to get hurt because of my recklessness.

I sighed inwardly. I felt myself starting to slip into a dark hole of depression and I fought it. There was no time in my schedule to climb my way out of that dingy hole. I'd just done it a few months ago.

"It's going to be really hard, and one of the most difficult moments of your life," she said sympathetically. "You'll feel better about it once you tell him. I can sit here and crack jokes, tell you what to say, but I know firsthand how difficult it really is. The anxiety of it alone will kill you. You're going to try a few times until one day it just comes out."

I wrapped a protective arm around my stomach. "He's going to be so mad."

"I have this really weird feeling he won't be, but even if he is mad, at least you told him. You'll feel better telling him in the long run. Then you can go ahead and schedule whatever you need, and I'll be there with you when it happens."

I swallowed. "You're going to drive over and come with me?"

"Of course, you dumbass. I love you."

My phone beeped and I pulled it away to see a text message come in from Kova. My heart dropped. I knew he'd look for me.

"I gotta go, Kova is texting me."

"Just so you know, I wouldn't recommend telling him over text."

I chuckled. Right before we hung up, I said. "Believe me, I wasn't planning on it."

COACH

Where did you disappear to?

I was looking for you.

I chewed my lip trying to conjure up a good lie that would suffice.

> **I'm not feeling well. I think I'm having a flare up and just needed to go home. I'm sorry.**

I held my breath and waited for him to respond. Hopefully he bought it, but I expected him not to.

COACH

> **Your health is more important. Get the rest you need, and if you need more time, just let me know. Can I bring you some dinner?**

I quickly replied with a no thank you and threw the phone down onto my couch. Rolling over onto my side, I cried myself to sleep over the things I had no ability to change.

CHAPTER 59

I purposely went into practice late so Kova couldn't talk to me.

Well, twenty minutes late, but it was enough to aggravate him for the rest of the day.

It didn't help that I was terribly nauseous. Either from the pregnancy or because I was nervous as hell to tell Kova, I wasn't sure. All the times I'd thrown up since the last meet could really be from either one. My stomach was all sorts of messed up.

Tonight I'd tell him I was pregnant.

His eyes found mine the moment I stepped into the gym, but I quickly averted my gaze and started stretching. My first thought was that I would play my lateness off since he had said if I needed extra time to rest I could take it, but I also knew I was required to tell him in advance if I was.

"Adrianna. Three miles," he ordered with a bite then turned away from me.

My jaw plummeted to my stomach but there was nothing I could say or do since he was my coach, so I got up, went into the locker room, got my clothes and running shoes on, then went outside. I did a few stretches so I wouldn't irritate my Achilles. It wasn't healed and it wouldn't be until I had surgery, but I would almost go as far as to say it was in remission with the pain and inflammation. No new tears thankfully, and while I hadn't needed a blading session recently, I knew Kova would want to do one before I went to Italy for the meet. It did give me a little pep in my step and Lord knew I could use that right now, and before the biggest gymnastics competition of my life.

The moment my feet hit the pavement, I forced myself to run the three miles straight without stopping. By the time I got back to World Cup, I was winded and in dire need of using the bathroom. I was all cool and collected until I noticed the toilet water was tinted pink.

My sad reality. Either it was just spotting, or I was miscarrying and I didn't know it. I padded myself with some toilet paper but there was no blood. Confused, I did it again with the same outcome when it hit me that it could actually be my kidneys causing the blood. It was a common symptom of chronic kidney disease.

Anger filled my eyes with tears but I inhaled them back and flushed the toilet. Shaking my head and fingers, I stepped out of the bathroom only to come face to face with a very annoyed Kova.

"Hey," I said, pulling back. I frowned. "Were you waiting for me?"

Kova's green eyes glared down at me and I recoiled. "Do not take advantage of my kindness, Adrianna. You will not walk all over me just because I am sympathetic to your health. If you need something, tell me, but do not show up late and assume you can do what you please without clearing it with me first."

My jaw bobbed. I was a little offended he thought I would take advantage like that, especially after everything. I tried to explain myself, but he cut me off and started speaking again. His Russian accent was thicker this time, and that only happened when he was furious.

"You have ten working days left and that is it. Two weeks until we board the plane." He emphasized the time. "And only one shot left. Let us make it count. We are going to be doing two-a-days until we leave, with the weekend to recoup. Unless you tell me otherwise, you will be here on time and ready to practice."

Mouth shut, I nodded. After all, he was right. I'd purposely showed up to practice late and it worked against me.

He dipped his head and stepped closer. "Inside these walls we are coach and gymnast. Outside, you are Adrianna Francesca Rossi and I am Konstantin Kournakova, and you are my life, but until the day comes when I can claim you in public, we cannot allow anything to deviate us from the goal."

Without saying a word, I stepped around him and walked right into the gym.

I loved him and hated him so much.

All week I'd worked my ass off. Kova and Madeline dished it out and then some. Neither coach went easy on me, which I loved. I hadn't felt that strain in so long, that soreness in all the hidden places. Sure, I'd been uncomfortable and tired and hardly able to walk by the time I got home. Mentally, it was exactly what I'd needed. I refused to allow my exhausting diseases that had the power to cripple me stand in my way. They wouldn't win. There were a few times I'd felt myself slipping and Kova was right there, talking it out of me, but making sure I was okay at the same time.

He'd been right. Now was my time and I had to make it count.

That didn't mean I wasn't dying by the end of the night and nearly crippled in the morning. A little dramatic, maybe, but Jesus, I felt bruised and battered. I soaked in Epsom baths, had Kova do deep tissue massages, and I even made sure to stay on the special diet for my illnesses. I never missed a dose of medicine either. By night, I welcomed my bed with open arms, and in the mornings I was greeted by the toilet. Morning sickness was no joke. One thing I was looking forward to being over was the constant vomiting that came with the sunrise. It was weird how the timing worked with that.

By Friday, I was counting down the hours until I got the next two days off. I'd looked into cupping, something that was supposed to be divine for sore muscles with lactic acid buildup. It pulled the skin from the underlying muscle to stimulate blood flow, which produced a faster recovery, but I wasn't sure I was ready for the little flaming cups of fire to be suctioned and dragged on me just yet. I'd ask Kova and see what he had to say. We could do a test run and see how it went.

"Hey," Kova said as I was eating lunch in the café. I felt his energy enter the room before I felt him.

I looked up, chewing an apple slice from my spinach salad. "What's up?"

He glanced over his shoulder then pulled out a chair to sit down. My brows furrowed and I eyed him curiously.

Kova leaned over and placed his elbows on his knees. "Come away with me this weekend."

My eyes popped and I almost choked on my food. "What?"

"There is this little town I want to take you to about an hour away."

The creases between my brows deepened and I slowly swallowed the bite I'd been chewing. "Is there something wrong with you?"

Kova released a full grin and dropped his head for a second. His back shook with a chuckle. He looked back up, smiling. "We already know I am not sane."

I tried not to laugh. "Isn't that the truth. But how are you going to slip away without Katja knowing?" I wanted to say Cuntja like Avery had, but I withheld.

He brushed it away like it was no issue. He didn't want to talk about her with me and I didn't blame him, but it was the first thing I thought of. I wondered how he was going to continue his infidelity on his day off if his wife was around.

"So what do you say? Stay tonight after everyone leaves and have dinner with me. I will order whatever you want, and then tomorrow, or Sunday," he offered, "we can go to this little town. Let me take you there. It is just for the day."

I placed my fork down and pushed my salad away. Kova slid it back in front of me. "Eat," he said.

We'd never gone anywhere together. "Why do you want to take me there?"

"You have been very distant with me this week and I do not want that."

"I've been a little busy working my ass off, you know…" I averted my gaze.

I had a reason to be distant, besides trying to keep my focus on gymnastics when the idea hit me.

Maybe I could finally tell him my secret tonight. He wouldn't want to take me anywhere after that, and it would give us a few days apart. There was no way he would receive the news of his child any other way but negative.

He continued, trying to drive his case home. "I know. This is the last weekend before the meet that you will be free for a long time. I am selfish enough to say I want you to myself. Think about it, but at least eat with me tonight. Can you give me that?"

Chewing my lip, I nodded. "Okay."

Kova's hand slapped the table and he bounced up. I smiled at his excitement, feeling a little good to see him so happy over something so miniscule, even though I was going to ruin everything tonight.

Leaning in, he cupped the back of my neck and dropped a kiss to my forehead. I froze with his lips on me, and so did he.

"You can't do that here, Kova," I whispered.

He dropped his hand and took one step back. "I know. I was not thinking. See you later," he said, then walked out of the café.

I watched him leave, wondering what had come over him and if he was serious when he'd said he wanted me to himself for my last free weekend. I knew what he was talking about—he was hopeful I'd be chosen for the Olympic team. If I was, I'd be shipped off to the training center for four weeks—with Kova—to train for the Games with the Olympic coaches.

Thinking about that made me realize I had two choices: Tell Kova tonight that I was pregnant, or keep it a secret until it was all over.

There were a total of seven weeks from today until I left the Games, if I got lucky. Seven weeks of anxiety I had to deal with, or get it over with tonight.

Glancing down at my flat stomach, fear furled inside my chest like a bad omen. I wasn't sure when bellies started to grow, but I prayed mine wouldn't anytime soon.

What was more distressing was I had no idea how far along I was to anticipate such a thing, but that was something I didn't want to know.

My only worry was I hoped the heart wasn't already beating.

CHAPTER 60

Why did you want to have dinner?" I asked after everyone left for the evening.

Yawning, I was sitting on the comfy couch in his office. I didn't have an appetite and I wasn't sure how I was going to eat to cover that up. All I wanted to do was go home and crash, not divulge the dirty little secret I was carrying. I glanced down at my stomach feeling a bit of remorse for calling it a dirty little secret.

"Why not?" he responded, as if my question was so odd.

I looked up, feeling defensive for reasons I couldn't explain. "I don't know, because we never do?"

"That is why I wanted to."

I frowned, watching as Kova placed the paper bag on his desk and removed the contents. When he'd asked what I was in the mood for, I'd told him whatever he wanted. Food was the last thing on my mind.

"What else?"

He paused and stood straight. Kova looked directly in my eyes, and said, "Because you have been working hard and I feel a little distant from you. That is why."

My shoulders relaxed. He was being honest and it wasn't fair of me to be rude. "Thank you," I said.

Kova carried over the containers and we sat face to face. There was nowhere to really eat in the gym besides the café, but that felt too sterile.

Once I took a bite, my appetite came roaring back. I didn't eat too much of the steamed vegetables and fresh salmon baked in an almond butter sauce, only until I felt the first hint at being full. We took pieces of each other's food until I was full and Kova polished off the rest of mine along with his.

"This office gets a lot of action," I joked.

I curled up into the corner of the couch and nestled my cheek into the cushions with a dreamy smile. All week I'd been on edge and stressed out. Tonight, I was at peace and I wasn't sure if it was because I knew I had no choice in what I was about to say, or because being around Kova settled my nerves.

Kova got up and placed me in his lap with my back to his chest. He let out a sigh as he wrapped his strong arms around me. He kissed my temple. My eyes closed and I settled into him.

"I have been waiting all day to do this," he said in a low voice, and I chuckled. "What is so funny?"

"I was thinking that same exact thing."

"Great minds think alike."

I smiled and relished in the simplicity of how easy we were, how I totally understood when Kova said he simply did not want to say goodbye, because when there were moments like this, I didn't want to either.

"You have been awfully quiet? What is on your mind?"

My throat tightened.

So much.

Everything.

I didn't know where to begin, but I knew this was it. This was when I would tell him that where his hands were currently on my stomach, there was a life growing inside that we'd created. A life that would never be able to live.

"Nothing, really. I'm fine."

"You said fine. Now I know you have something on your mind," he said with a mixture of playfulness and unease. "Are you nervous about the meet? Because I truly feel like you have nothing to be worried about. You are a shoo-in."

"No," I said quietly.

For once I wasn't panicked about a meet. I was confident. Just thinking about walking out with my coaches, and in my crystal-encrusted leotard, as a top-ranking competitor for one of the four coveted spots on the United States Women's Olympic Gymnastics team caused a flurry of anxious dragonflies to swarm my chest. I was beyond excited for next weekend and the days couldn't come fast enough.

"Did something happen at the doctor regarding your kidneys?"

"No."

He let out a whoosh. "Thank God. Did you have a fight with Avery?"

"No."

Silence filled the room. Kova gave me a little squeeze and settled in closer to me. He was trying to dissect what was going on in my head, but he'd never guess.

I remained quiet, searching for the right words to start the conversation. I wanted to blurt it out just to get it over with, but at the same time, I was terrified.

"Ria?" His voice was thick with worry. "What is wrong? You are worrying me?"

My entire body started shaking, my breathing intensified. Kova tried to turn to face me, but I stopped him and gave him more of my back. I couldn't look at him while I did this. I didn't want to see the look in his eyes when I told him I was pregnant. Would he be relieved I was going to get an abortion? Angry I was pregnant in the first place? Or shock me completely and be disappointed with my decision? My heart raced so fast, my dinner was as heavy as a concrete block in my stomach, threatening to come back up.

"I thought you forgot about that name," I said, my voice thick with emotion.

"Is that why you are so bothered? I can use it more. I worried it came with bad memories, and I was trying to avoid those."

"No," I said, this time tears filled my eyes.

"Why can you not look at me, Adrianna? You are scaring me."

I grew warm, heat bubbling over my entire body. Oh, God. There was no way I could do this. I just couldn't. Avery was wrong. Kova didn't need to know. There was no reason for him to know, it would only cause more unnecessary heartache.

"Please, look at me."

"I..." I started. "I need..."

"What do you need? I will give it to you."

My chest ached from the pounding it took from my heart. I shook my head and dragged in a taxing breath, trying to pull up even a sliver of courage to tell him, but I was struggling to find it. This had to be the hardest thing I'd ever had to do in my life.

"Do you remember when you asked me if my back was up against a wall with a decision that could change my life, what would I do?"

Kova was quiet before he answered in a low voice. "Yes."

"Well…" I began and swallowed as my body roasted with trepidation. "It's my turn to ask that. If you were backed up against a wall with a decision that could change your life, what would you do?"

Kova's body turned to stone under me.

"What do you need to tell me?"

"Answer the question."

Kova rambled in Russian.

"Answer the question, Kova," I said again with a little bite this time.

"No," he said, breathless. "I invented this game. Now tell me what you are hiding."

Tears spilled from my eyes and I shot up from his lap. A gush of air expelled from my lungs. I started pacing his office, staring at the floor wishing it would open up and remove me from this cruel world of anxiety that suffocated me. My chest was so tight, strict with lack of air, and my heart was such a mess I thought I was going to vomit.

Kova stood up and tried to come to me but I wouldn't allow it. I put up my hand to stop him.

Grabbing my keys and cell phone from his desk, I made a beeline for the door. He was quick, though, and slammed it shut. I held my breath and felt his chest to my back and his arm wrap possessively around my hips. There wasn't an ounce of anger coming from Kova and while that was relieving, it was also terrifying, because if he knew the truth, I don't think he'd touch me. I clenched my eyes shut, wishing I had the strength to tell him.

"Let me leave," I begged, barely above a whisper.

He forced me to turn around to face him, but I couldn't look. I stared at his chest, ashamed.

Kova lifted my chin, forcing me to meet his gaze. "What are you hiding?" he asked, his heart clearly holding those words. His frantic eyes searched mine for a clue. "Did you fuck Hayden again? Because I swear on my dead mother's grave…"

Shaking my head, I was offended he would think that, even though I knew he was still sleeping with his wife. "No, you lunatic."

"Then what is it?"

"What would you do?" I asked again, going back to my original question he'd avoided.

Kova exhaled. His gaze lifted above my head as his eyes searched for the right words. Then he looked back down. "I guess I would do exactly what you said to me when I asked you that. Now do you understand why I did what I did? Why I had no choice? Why I hid the unwanted marriage?"

I nodded, my lips a flat line coated with salty tears. Sorrow filled his green eyes. His words dripping like melting wax. I got it, even though I hated it more than anything.

"To tell the person you love that you are marrying someone else causes a stairway of turmoil so bad that no one could ever anticipate. I did not even realize I loved you then, but I could not stand to see you suffer, so I thought I could hide it. I thought I would find a way to divorce her before you could know, but I had nothing. In the end, I was not strong enough to admit it to you." He paused. "Is whatever you are holding in why you have been distant with me?"

My eyes searched his hoping he'd see the truth.

"Stop telling me you love me. I can't handle it."

He looked so wounded. His green eyes pierced me with immense grief and for a split second I felt bad I asked him that. Kova swallowed and his Adam's apple bobbed like he was struggling to breathe.

"No, I will not stop. I love you, and whatever you are scared to tell me, it will not make me love you any less. Just, please, Adrianna, what is it?"

"Stop it. You won't love me after this."

"Impossible. You are an integral part of me now and forever."

I slapped his chest, angry that I didn't have the courage to speak up. "I'm sorry."

I broke down inside. I hated that Avery had pushed me to do this. I knew I should've just handled it on my own.

Kova's face fell and it crushed me to see him like this. The last thing I wanted to do was hurt him.

"For what? Please, tell me. I cannot stand to see you suffer like this."

Shaking my head, it was my turn to apologize to him. I crumbled in his arms and cried until I didn't have any tears left. Until he finally let go and stopped pushing me to tell him.

Instead, he just held me the entire time.

CHAPTER 61

Knock. Knock. Knock.

Groaning, I dragged my feet across the living room to the rapid knocking that hadn't stopped. My eyes were heavy and drowsy from lack of sleep. Without looking through the peephole, I knew it could only be one person, and opened the door.

"Kova…" I said, and yawned. "What are you doing here?"

I opened the door wider so he could come in, then shut it. He turned to look at me with wide eyes like he was on the edge of something beautiful, but I was too tired to show any interest.

"I know I was not supposed to see you until tomorrow, but I had to come."

I frowned, rubbing my eyes with the heel of my hand. Before I left World Cup last night and my tears had dried, we'd agreed we would go to the little town together on Sunday. It was the perfect plan for me, strategic really. I'd planned to rest all day while mustering up the strength to tell him about the pregnancy tomorrow night after our day out. There was no way we would have another day like that anytime soon, or if ever, so I figured waiting until the end of the day was the best time to drop the bomb. I just had to figure out how I was going to.

I glanced at the clock and noted it was barely seven in the morning. I was beyond worn out physically, and needed to go back to bed.

"Kova, I didn't sleep at all last night. I'm really tired right now. Can this wait?"

"No, it cannot. I had to see you to tell you the news."

He was resolute in his decision and my shoulders dropped. I waved a hand, signaling him to go on and blinked. Kova regarded me, his eyes taking in the length of my body. I was only in a tank top and bikini underwear since I was so hot at night.

"I am filing for divorce."

My lips parted in shock. "What? What do you mean?"

"I found my way out," he said excitedly, almost as if I should know what he was talking about. "I am leaving Katja for good."

My heart raced a mile a minute trying to process the words Kova just delivered. I blinked hard, and blinked again.

"What did you just say?"

He was grinning like a fool. "I am getting a divorce and you will be all mine." He stalked toward me while I stood frozen in place.

His smile was so big and happy and I would've smiled in return if I wasn't in such a state of absolute shock. Kova pressed his body flush to mine and grabbed my face. I stumbled back and he stepped with me. Planting his lips on mine, Kova's kiss was filled with relief, like the restraints had been cut and he was finally free.

My hands were flat to his hard chest. He flexed under my touch and groaned in the back of his throat.

Breaking the kiss, I said, "What are you talking about? What happened?"

Kova gripped my hips and lifted me up. My legs automatically wrapped around his hips.

"Open your mouth and let me kiss you first."

"No—"

With his hand at my nape guiding me to him, he closed the distance. His tongue slid along my lips. A stream of desire roared through me and I kissed him back.

"I need you."

I pulled his hair and he arched his neck back. His eyes glistened with heat and I knew he had one thing on his mind. Sex.

"No, you don't. Tell me what happened first."

"Yes, I do," he said, walking with me in his arms toward my bedroom.

"You're confused."

He flipped on the light and quickly climbed on my bed with me in tow. "No. I am more awake than ever. I see clearly now."

I shook my head, baffled, as he dropped his weight to mine. I tried to move him away so I could get answers, but Kova was quick and pulled both my hands above my head and secured them to the bed in his grip. His other hand glided up my thigh to my ribs. In seconds, his mouth found my neck and his tongue licked a wet trail. All sensible thoughts left my mind when he pulled my tender skin into his mouth and suckled hard. My back arched and a gasp of bliss escaped my lips. His tongue was flat and moving in slow sensual circles. My body shivered and my eyes rolled shut as pleasure hummed through me. He feverously peppered kissed along my jaw until his lips met mine.

"I don't understand," I managed to get out.

But Kova didn't stop the torment when he said, "Katja. The marriage."

"What?" I asked, yanking away in breathless anticipation. "What changed? I don't understand."

"We had an argument and she slipped up. Do you remember when I told you I thought she was up to something? I found out everything she was hiding."

As selfish as that sounded, if I wouldn't give it up for my kidneys, then I wouldn't for Kova.

"You do not understand," he said. He pulled me to sit on his lap and I placed my hands on his chest, feeling the warmth come off him. "I am not asking you to give anything up. I will wait for however long it takes for you to be mine. I just wanted to tell you what happened and how this changes things for us.

I shook my head in disbelief. Tears clouded my vision. "But why? Why? What if we can never be?"

"I will not have to report to anyone. What we have is something people search their entire life for. You understand me, I understand you. Do you honestly think a coach and an athlete have never fallen in love? It has happened more times than you can imagine. A coach knows more about his athlete than anyone."

"But, Kova, I'm eighteen."

"I know," he said softly, brushing a lock of hair behind my ear. "And even though I am thirty-four, I will wait for you. However long it takes, I will wait because I love you and I want us to be together one day."

Stupid tears fell from the corners of my eyes. I didn't even know why I was crying, but I was, and they started coming out faster. A gentle smile formed on his full lips. His *kissable* lips.

Kova wiped my tears. I shook my head, staring at his chest. "This is all so confusing."

"Love does not ever makes sense. You just go with what your heart feels. The way you look at me, the pain of wanting something you cannot have, I know that look because I feel the same for you. I know it is there for you, even if you do not tell me."

I chewed on my bottom lip and glanced up to meet his eyes. The corner of my lips tugged up. "I may…"

His lips formed a huge smile. "Admitting you are in love with someone is much harder than it sounds. The most important things in our lives are the hardest to get out. Is this why you do not like to admit your love for me? Because I am important? I did not say I love you for you to say it back, but I can feel it in your touch, the way you grip my skin, the way you reach for me. I know what you feel in your beautiful heart without you having to say it."

I took a deep breath, and asked, "Can I ask what your argument was about?"

"Oh, so much. It was like a domino effect and it could not have pleased me more. After I learned she was pushing for the marriage to get her citizenship, I read an email between her and a friend. Her friend encouraged her to take what she can get out of me. I knew she loved money, just not that much. Even before you came around, I always gave her what she wanted without questioning her. Money is just money. But it hurt to see she was using me for both."

My brows bunched together. "She still doesn't have her citizenship? I assumed she did."

"No, she is on the faster track to receive one, but she still does not have it. Without marriage, it would take much longer for her. The last person we spoke to said she should have it in a year or so."

There had to be more. "What else?"

"I had the strangest feeling she had been cheating on me."

My eyes softened. I wrapped my arms around his shoulders and pulled him down to me. I kissed his lips and couldn't help it, but I smiled at him.

"You can't possibly be upset if she was cheating on you, Kova."

"I know what I do is wrong, and I feel bad about it, but I never, ever used her. I love her, Ria, I always will, but I will never love her the way I do you."

"So, let me get this straight. You're divorcing her because of the citizenship and because you think she cheated?"

Kova dragged his teeth over his bottom lip and averted his gaze. His hands skimmed my thighs and over my hips, the tips of his fingers slipped under my tank top. Leaning in, he pressed a kiss to my chest.

"What is it?" I asked, my voice shaky. My chest rose and fell faster and harder with anticipation.

"Do you recall the night I sent you to my office and she happened to be there?"

Unfortunately. "Yes."

"Do you recall the white envelope she shoved at me that I threw on my desk?" he asked, and I nodded blindly. "I never opened it. I actually placed it in my desk that night and never thought about it again."

Oh, God. Somehow I knew where this was going before he finished explaining himself. My heart was burning. I could feel it in my gut. I tried to scoot off Kova, but he held me in place. I didn't have the strength to fight his hands off.

"She's pregnant," I whispered, chills tightening down my spine.

Something inside me crumpled to dust and I let out a breath of defeat.

I'd never win when it came to him. I'd never be first.

CHAPTER 62

Yes," he said, dropping his head to my chest.

I cupped the back of his neck. The anguish in those three letters crushed my heart and I realized Kova now had two women pregnant. I was so glad I hadn't told him. This made my decision that much easier.

His hands tightened on me. "I drank a half bottle of vodka straight from the mouth after your father told me about your kidney disease. An hour later I finished it off. I blacked out."

"You had sex with Katja when you found out I was sick?" I stated in utter and complete disbelief.

Of all the things. Of all the things he could tell me, nothing could amount to this kind of devastation now consuming me. Numbness crowded me, sweeping everything else away.

His voice was low, quiet, and surprisingly remorseful. "I do not remember all of it. Just flashback moments of that night. I have tried so hard to remember but my memory is just not there. I woke up naked and disoriented. I could not believe it, and since then it has never happened once."

"You slept with your wife when you found out I basically had a death sentence," I said slowly, trying to wrap my head around it.

Kova didn't respond. His silence was his answer, and his truth would cause me to suffer considerably more.

He tightened his arms around my waist and dropped his chin onto my shoulder. He was warm, but I felt nothing. He was shaking, but I was still. I thought his marriage had been devastating. This was soul-crushing.

"I never planned to tell Katja about us. I was going to eventually leave, but Joy had other plans. She is a woman with vengeance, power, and money. I have yet to know why she is after me. I thought possibly because she was concerned about her name being ruined and the humiliation it would cause." He paused, running a hand over his jaw. "It was Joy who found my jacket in your room on New Year's Eve and shipped it to Katja. That was how it started, until Joy took it a step further and hired a private investigator to follow us. They have so much against us, Adrianna. So much damning evidence. Joy was able to retrieve all of our text messages from the cell phone carrier. She read every message, saw every image, including the video I sent to you while you were sleeping. They have photos of us at the gym, from meets, my home, your condo. She handed everything over to Katja, and from what I have gathered, used it as bait for your father to get what she wanted. I was cornered."

We were both quiet, lost to our heavy thoughts and the reality of our lives.

"I had no choice but to marry Katja. She had been begging me for years, but I could never bring myself to get down and ask her. After Joy gave her everything about us, she was devastated when I told her I would never marry her. I will never forget the way she looked at me, like she had revenge in her eyes. She was angry, saying I wasted her life and that I will get what is coming to me. She wanted me to expel you from training at World Cup. When I told her no, that was when Joy stepped in. I bargained with both over expelling you from my gym. There was no legitimate reason to kick you out, and you would never just leave on your own when there were coaches after you for the Olympic team. Too many questions would arise and bring unnecessary attention to all. Both of them knew this. It was either marry her, or your gymnastics career would be over, and I would be taken away in handcuffs."

"Joy isn't after you." My voice was hoarse. "She's after me for what my dad has done, and has continued to do. She's taking it out on me because I'm a replica of my biological mother, and because my dad is still talking to her after he promised Joy years ago he wouldn't. Why would Katja go through with this after she found out about the infidelity?"

"When she found out I was cheating, and with you, all she wanted was for me to kick you out because she knew you would go back to Palm Bay. After I refused to, and she spoke to Joy, she threatened to go to the police. She knew I would lose everything if she did that, but so would she because she had no legal tie to me. As the saying goes, money talks, and Joy paid her a large sum. Her heart grew hard from Joy whispering in her ear. Since then she has been just as bad, and it has been two against one."

Kova shook his head in defeat. I remembered my dad telling me Joy had something on me that she couldn't show him because she was actually worried it would give him a heart attack. He thought she was lying. Now that I knew the truth, it would kill him, and I was actually grateful she hadn't shown him, but I was also terrified if I did one more thing wrong, she'd show him everything.

"Dad said Joy's spiteful and jealous, but I find it difficult to believe she would be jealous of me. I think she sees me as the same as my dad, with you." My voice was quiet. "I wouldn't put it past Joy to tell my dad one day, but I don't see her going public with it."

I didn't recognize my own voice. It was as empty as my chest and as dead as my heart. I felt ruined. We were both pregnant, but the difference was that Kova and Katja would be able to raise their child.

For the first time in a long time, tears didn't fill my eyes. Rage didn't fill my blood. Hate didn't seal the wounds on my heart. I was just really sad inside.

I unwound my arms and placed my hands on his shoulders. Kova sensed what I was about to do and hugged me tighter, placing his face on my chest like he was holding on to me for dear life and didn't want to let go.

"Kova—" My voice was cold, distant.

He cut me off so he could rush out his next set of words. "Katja is pregnant, but it is not my child."

I lowered my eyes. Would he deny our baby too?

"Of course it's not your kid. You would say that."

He spoke faster, his eyes hard. "No, it is definitely *not* my child. I walked in on her taking a pregnancy test when she thought I was working out in the garage. The shock was written all over her face, and I know my sudden appearance flustered her. She started stammering and said since she never gave me the test stick as proof the first time she took one, she wanted to make up for that now. I had no idea what she was talking about. When I questioned her, she claimed to have told me she was pregnant, but I had no recollection of that.

A man does not forget that vice grip on his heart feeling when he finds out he will be a father. She said it was in the envelope she gave me in my office the night you were there. I was completely ruined when she told me that. So, I drove to World Cup and went through my drawers and found it. I tore it open and sat in silence for hours trying to figure out how it happened when I realized that none of the dates matched up. None of them.

"Maybe you got her pregnant the night you found out about my kidney disease," I spat out.

"Not possible."

My eyes widened. "You said you didn't remember."

He held up a finger. "Just listen to me. I logged on to her accounts and scoured her emails and went through her social media pages. I found conversations between her and multiple men, one of whom I expect is the father."

My brows shot to my forehead. "I didn't take Katja for a cheater."

"Neither did I, so I called her doctor's office and spoke to the nurse since Katja has me listed as an authorized person to receive medical information on all her files. While Katja is indeed pregnant, she is very early in her pregnancy. Just a few weeks actually. My conniving wife had given me someone else's ultrasound photo and was trying to play it off as ours because she knew I did not want her, but also knew a baby would tie us together forever."

"When did all of this happen?"

"Yesterday morning and today."

My heart pinched at his response. I asked, "Why didn't you tell me this last night?"

"I planned to after dinner, but then…"

But then I'd flipped out.

"I'm sorry."

I drew in a breath, feeling the blood drain from my cheeks. I couldn't believe how far she'd gone to keep Kova in her life. I had no words. All I could do was listen in silence.

"Adrianna, I did not have sex with her recently enough for her to be pregnant. I have only been with you. The night when your father called me with your diagnosis, yes, I fell into a state of mind I did not know how to climb out of. The thought of you not being in my life is not something I ever want to imagine, but I did not know how to deal with it either, especially since I could not talk to you. I had to stay quiet and it was killing me. So I fucked off with writing in the notebook, which I am trying to barter with her to get back, and pulled out my old anxiety medication my therapist had given me. I think the shit was expired. I took a couple anyway and opened a bottle of aged vodka. I am not making excuses, but I blacked out that night. Still, I do not think I ever had sex with her. What man forgets when they have sex?"

I stared up at him speechless.

"That is not my baby, but that baby is my way out," he said.

We were breathing heavily, our chests thrust together.

"You're lying," I whispered, my heart racing so fast. "You always lie to me."

He shook his head, his eyes pleading with me. "I told you I would not lie to you anymore. I am telling you the truth. Why do you think I ran over here so fast to tell you everything? I surrendered to the blackmail because I had no choice. Your future was at stake and I was not going to risk it, but there is no way I will put up with this too. Was she going to act like some stranger's baby is mine for the rest of my life and never tell me? That is cruel and heartless. What about the real father? Would he never know? Come Monday, I am filing for divorce. I want her off my hands and out of my life for good. This is… How do you say, the cake's icing?"

I chuckled a little at his words, understanding what he was trying to say. "You mean the icing on the cake?"

His lips twitch, and he continued. "I know what I have done with you is wrong, but this is… I have no words for it."

I had a lot going through my head and I didn't know what to start with first. My stomach was starting to toss, the usual morning sickness I had every day bubbling to the surface.

"Say something," Kova begged. "Please."

Exhaling through my nose, I said, "Get off me."

His face fell. I knew it wasn't what he wanted to hear, but I was about to throw up all over him if he didn't move. Kova released his hold on me and I shoved off the bed and ran to the bathroom, making sure I locked the door behind me. My knees slammed to the floor and I vomited the moment I looked at the toilet water.

God, I hated this. There was no way I could handle nine months of this. I'd wither away to nothing. My throat tasted like acid and my stomach was already empty to begin with, and now it felt like a dry sack of nothing. I washed my face and brushed my teeth, then stepped out to find Kova sitting on my bed with his head dropped between his shoulders. I could feel his guilt from where I stood and I felt terrible.

I walked over to him and placed a hand on his shoulder. He leaned his head into my stomach and wrapped an arm around my butt to pull me closer to him. He wouldn't meet my eyes, but I knew he needed me, was seeking support, and I was more than willing to give it to him. His pain was too overpowering to ignore, not that I could ever do that to him anyway.

Kova was suffering and it was bleeding into me. He looked up, and the vulnerability in his gaze was too much to handle.

CHAPTER 63

There was no way I could tell him about the baby when he looked utterly defenseless after learning how deceitful his wife had been.

I knew it was wrong, but he was a man devastated, torn, and at odds with his life, trying to find which door was the right one. I wasn't going to beat him down further.

"I'm sorry," I said. My fingers were in his hair. "Everything you told me just made me sick to my stomach and it was a lot to process." Not necessarily a lie, but it wasn't the full truth either. "I don't know what to think, okay? She's so deceitful it's appalling. It just got to me, especially hearing Joy was involved the way she was. I actually spoke to my dad about that a couple of weeks ago, but Joy hasn't told him any of it. I guess it's just really upsetting to see someone go to the lengths she has. I'm already a ball of nerves, you know?"

He nodded, his hand playing with my long hair against my back. "I did not mean to upset you."

"I know," I said softly. "I might have something that could help you. My dad told me whatever Joy has she won't go public with it. She never showed him, but he said she's too concerned about her image to ruin it, and he's right. She won't go to the police because she'll get dragged through the mud too, no matter how hard she'd try to prevent it."

"Why did you not tell me this sooner?"

I shrugged. "I didn't know what she had until you told me. My dad thought she was making it up, and I did too. We had nothing to go on. But now that I know exactly what she has, she'll never tell anyone besides my dad if she really wants to ruin me. It's too damaging to go to the authorities, and I really don't think she ever would."

Kova stared up at me with so much hope that I smiled. Placing my hand on his chest, my fingers spread out. "When will you tell her you're divorcing her?"

"I am not going to tell her, I am just going to file. Let her get served. I am fairly positive she will go back to Russia." He paused. "Although, she really wants her citizenship, so I am not entirely sure. I do not know what she will do about the baby. What I do know is that Katja is no longer my problem."

I swallowed hard, feeling my emotions rise, and threw my arms around his shoulders. I climbed over him, forcing him to lie back onto my bed. Our bodies pressed together and we both sighed like we'd been waiting for this moment, when he would no longer be tied to her. Kova's hands guided me, finding their place on my hips as I leaned down and kissed him hard. Fingers digging into my skin, his body fitted to mine as I melted at the touch of us joined.

I had to wonder if he would still wait for me after I told him about the baby.

"Where is Katja now?" I asked, breaking the kiss.

He blinked like he was trying to process my question.

"Home, I think. I am not sure now. After our second argument this morning, she told me to go fuck myself and that she would not be home tonight."

"Did you say anything else to her?"

"No. I wanted to, but I have already done enough damage and felt like walking out was enough." Kova grinned. "I did turn off access to my bank account and her credit cards. Let her use the money Joy gave her."

I gave him a little kiss. "I know you like to put on a strong front, but I think in here"—I tapped the left side of his chest—"you have a bigger heart than you let on. You care, you're just guarded a little more than others."

He looked at me with a puzzled smile on his face.

"I know what you did for Holly and I think it's the sweetest thing ever," I said, my voice low, and I swear his cheeks deepened in color. "She told me everything you did for her and Hayden, the stupid dating rule and all, the scholarship. Yes, she knows about us, but she will never say anything." Kova froze and I couldn't blame him. I continued. "She won't say anything. Trust me."

"Ria…" he warned, but I placed a finger over his lips. He tried to bite it.

"She was legitimately concerned. She told me what happened with her previous coach and was worried that was happening with me. I assured her it wasn't. I explained what I needed to, of course not going into detail, but she *will not* say a word," I reiterated. I kissed him again, then changed the subject. "Does this mean I get you to myself this weekend?"

Kova's eyes lit up with desire. Sliding his hand up my back and into my hair, his nose touched mine. He pulled the hair tie out, dropping it to the bed, and my hair enclosed us.

"When you are around me, please wear your hair down." He threaded his fingers through the hair at my nape and tugged, causing my back to arch and my chest to push into him. "You are breathtaking," he whispered, pressing a hand to the small of my back. A blast of desire shot down my spine and my body relaxed on his. "I do not know what to make of this, of us, but in my heart it is right. God, I sound like such a sentimental fuck." He chuckled, his breath tickling my neck.

My teeth dug into my lip. "You're totally sappy right now, but it's cute."

Grinning, Kova pressed his lips to mine. My heart felt full seeing him so happy and at peace. He flicked his jaw and slipped his tongue into my willing mouth and devoured me. He kissed me deeply, slowly, with hunger. I moaned, arching my back and pressing my chest to his. I needed to be closer, to feel him everywhere, even though I was already as close as I could be. I widened my hips, shifting to feel more of his erection. He groaned into my mouth and pressed his lips to mine harder, causing a flow of moisture between my thighs.

My hands slid down his shoulders and I dug my fingers into his rigid muscles. My blood was heating, and I suddenly felt like I was wearing too much clothing. Kova wrapped his tongue around mine and tugged on it. I whimpered, nearly crying out as need curled my toes. He ground his cock against me, provoking a response. Wetness coated my panties and I rolled my hips seductively into him. A groan vibrated deep in his throat. His body was warm to my touch, inviting me into his world. Pleasure bloomed through me, my need for him something fierce.

Fisting his shirt, I whispered for him to take it off. I sat up, straddling his hips as Kova arched his back and pulled off his shirt. His hands immediately found my hips, tugging off my panties. My gaze traveled the cut of his abs, loving how each muscle caused a shallow indent, down to that sexy dip by his hips to his groin. This man, with his honey-colored chest that led to strong, curved shoulders, and the letter I had carved into him, was the most beautiful man I'd ever seen. My eyes skimmed lower to the bulge in his pants as a seductive smile pulled at my lips. He was always hard for me and I loved that.

My fingers tentatively traced down his chest, down his sternum, and around his dark nipples. He flexed under me, sucking in a breath through his teeth, watching my every move. His green eyes were filled with desire. Our gazes stayed locked as my hand trailed lower, over his taut stomach to the elastic waistband of his shorts. I dipped my fingertips inside and rimmed the fabric, feeling the hair at his mound. His nostrils flared and he shifted his hips around, his Adam's apple bobbing slowly. Leaning forward, I licked my lips and pressed them to the carved A on his chest. My tongue slid out and lavishly licked the scar, feeling the grooves. Kova's hand came up and gently cupped the back of my head, I could feel him breathing heavily on me. Making my way up his body, I peppered him with kisses until I reached his mouth.

Without asking, I lifted my hips and reached between us to pull out his cock. He was already so thick and ready. He gripped my hips as I positioned his swollen tip at my wet entrance. Looking into his eyes, I sank down on his length slowly, feeling myself stretch wide to fit him. His fingers dug into my skin, his palms hot to the touch. Once he was fully inside me, he tugged off my shirt, his eyes fastening on my breasts. I was throbbing, needing to widen a little more before I could start moving or he was going to tear into me.

His brows bunched together, and he reached for my chest. "Your breasts are bigger." The pad of his thumb traced a circle around my areola and I purred in the back of my throat. My skin prickled with desire, my nipples hardening. "Even here, they are larger."

I glanced down, they did look a little bigger, but I knew why. Emotions clogged my throat and I sucked them back, wondering if we would have this after if he found out the truth.

Placing my hands on his stomach, I let the sensations take over and I began a slow ride, needing him so bad. "Oh," I sighed.

"Lean back and place your arms on my knees."

I did as he asked and let my head fall back as I rode his cock at my pace. It was hot and slow and sexy and just perfect, like a lazy Sunday morning.

"Yes, like that, Ria," he said through clenched teeth.

I glanced down. His finger found my clit and I shuddered, taking him how I knew he liked as I climbed higher from the orgasm that was already climbing. He carefully spread my pussy lips apart and watched as I took his cock. His eyes glowed with a craving so dark my clit throbbed.

"I'm very close," I said breathlessly.

His cock twitched and he grabbed my hips, speeding up the pace as he thrust into me hard. Our bodies slapped together. We moved faster, needing more, my breasts bouncing, my long hair falling over them. They were so tender and the loose strands grazing my nipples tickled a little.

"More," I begged, my eyes closing.

Kova lifted his hips slightly so my clit would hit the base of his cock. It was a different angle and it was exactly what I needed.

Little sounds escaped me and Kova growled. I orgasmed like it was the most amazing high of my life. I never held back when I was with him. Pleasure consumed me and I greedily took all he had to offer. His hand reached up and grabbed my neck. I panicked for a split second and grabbed his wrist until I remembered how much I loved when he did this. Kova took control and wrapped his fingers around my throat and shoved me down roughly, squeezing. Stars exploded in my vision, making me feel like I was coming out of my skin. He released, then squeezed again.

"Don't stop," I whispered.

"You are stunning like this. Take my cock for as long as you like. I am yours."

And I did. Even when our pleasure subsided and he pulled out, we stayed where we were. I rubbed my swollen pussy along his soft dick until I came once more. He loved it.

Kova secured me in his arms. My chest grew with hope and I thought maybe one day we could have more. What we had was more than love. This was a devout connection only two people could share.

I looked into Kova's green eyes and studied his gaze. To have someone behind me, pushing me, seeing and helping me achieve my dream, and more importantly, wanting to be there along the way was special.

But to have someone love me the way he did? There were not enough words in the dictionary to describe that feeling.

CHAPTER 64

A knot sat in the pit of my stomach as we exited Alligator Alley. Worry plagued me with impending dread as Kova drove us to the next town. Something wasn't right, but I couldn't quite place my finger on what it was that bothered me exactly.

The pregnancy was heavy on my mind, and I one hundred percent planned to finally tell him tonight. The conversation was a delicate one, but that wasn't it. This felt different. I think the unease came from the fact that I'd never been alone with Kova outside World Cup or our homes, and it stressed me out a little, especially since I knew Joy had hired a private investigator in the past. I had no idea if she was still using one after all the damning evidence she had, but I learned to put nothing past her. I never got the notion someone was following me, which only amped up the anxiety even more.

Kova parked his car, then leaned over to press a kiss to my lips. He stepped out and walked over to the passenger side as I rummaged through my purse for a pair of sunglasses. Opening the door, he offered me his hand. Kova looked utterly delectable. Dressed in a pair of distressed dark jeans that hugged his fine ass and a stark white plain T-shirt that accented his biceps, he was simple but insanely appealing. His aviator sunglasses held my reflection and his hair was styled back. He looked delicious. I stepped out and Kova laced his fingers through mine, then lifted his arm to wrap it around my shoulders and tugged me tightly to his side. I rested my cheek on his chest, and he dropped a kiss to the top of my head. We started walking side by side.

Too many emotions hit me all at once while we walked down the boardwalk taking in the salty air. Boats were docked, and people strolled aimlessly like we did. It was a cloudy day but luckily not too humid. We grabbed lunch by the water and chatted about gymnastics, then shopped in some of the small stores. Kova refused to let me buy anything. He paid for lunch and anytime I mentioned I liked something, he purchased it. I fought him tooth and nail on it.

"Stop," I urged, yanking a heavy candle from his hands.

"Stop what?" he looked at me, puzzled.

Kova reached for the glass jar but I pulled back, and said, "I broke it when I threw it at you. You're not replacing it."

He grinned, remembering our fight.

"You threw more than a candle at me, if I recall."

I pursed my lips together, fighting a smile because he looked so damn hot.

"Ria, do not be foolish. It is just a candle. I know how much you love them, so let me get it."

I angled my head to the side and pointed to his hand. He was holding three bags of items he'd bought me throughout the day.

"That Tommy Bahama bag has more than just a candle in it. So does the Sephora one."

"So?" He appeared truly confused.

"So? So stop buying me stuff. Just because I say I like something doesn't mean you have to buy it. That's a lot of money right there, and now you want to add more?"

His eyes softened and he gave me an amused smile. "Give me the candle, Ria."

"No."

"I like buying you things. It makes me happy, now give it to me," he said, but I stood my ground. "I will buy every single candle in this store if you do not give it to me." He waved his fingers for me to hand it over. His eyes glistened with humor.

I held it behind my back and Kova stepped toward me. "I don't even like it."

"You are such a damned liar—a horrible one at that." He chuckled, his eyes gleaming. I loved the playful look on his face. "Just give it to me."

Kova placed the bags on the floor then leaned in to me to reach around my back. I arched, trying to keep it out of his reach, and he pressed a kiss to my exposed neck. I tried to act firm on my decision, but my giggle gave me away.

"Don't be a dick, Kova. I don't like it—or you. Now go away."

"That is not what you said this morning…or last night," he growled in my ear, his hand on the glass jar.

I gave it to him willingly—more in fear that it'd fall on the tile floor and break—as he dropped a gentle kiss right under my ear again. His warm breath tickled my neck. Smiling, I curled into him. Kova hooked his arm around my neck and yanked me to him while his other hand was pressed to the small of my back. He laid a hard kiss to my mouth and just as I was about to give in, he looked up and froze in horror.

"Kova?" I tried to look over my shoulder to follow his gaze, but he swiftly spun around with me. I tried to look past him, but he blocked me.

"Adrianna," he said under his breath.

My smile faltered and my heart dropped at his grave tone. "What is it?"

Kova moved my sunglasses from the top of my head to sit on my nose. He corrected them, then said, "I need you to grab the bags, turn around, and go straight to my car with your head down. Do not turn back, just go and I will meet you there."

Alarm rang through my bones. I knew it. Something in my gut had warned me against coming here and now I knew why.

"What's going on, Kova?"

Kova stared down, begging me to adhere to his request. Reaching into his pocket, he handed me his keys. "Just listen to me, please. I will explain, just go to my car and wait for me."

Dipping my head slowly, I did as he asked. I reached down and grabbed the bags, then turned and quickly walked toward the exit. I could feel Kova's eyes burning on me the whole way, watching me. Just as I was about to leave, I pulled my sunglasses down just a fraction and drew to a stop to peek over my shoulder. I had to look. I needed to see what he saw, what made him go from teasing and fun to somber and serious. Carefully, I twisted around just enough to get a look.

My lips parted.

All sound faded around me.

I was numb, unable to move, unable to feel, unable to hear. I should've listened to him, because nothing could have prepared me for what I saw.

I could only stare at the couple embraced behind Kova. So in love and so…

My dad.

And my mom. My *real* mom.

I couldn't see her full face, but I'd met her once to know it was indeed Sophia. In my heart I knew it was. Her height and hair were similar to mine, and we had an almost identical body shape, only I was much thinner than her. Sophia turned to the side and Dad gave her a kiss on her cheek. They looked up at each other, so in love and so normal. I was stuck for a moment at the simplicity of them, and the blow of betrayal booming through me. I knew Dad was divorcing Joy, but I didn't expect him to be with anyone else, especially not my biological mother. I thought he only gave her updates about me. This was not that. There was a familiarity and understanding with her that came over time, not overnight.

My heart ached, shattered with lies and deceit. With Kova's subtle waving urging me to leave, I turned away and walked out.

It only took me a matter of minutes to get to his car. I sat slouched to the side, hiding in the shadows, silently begging for Kova to hurry up. My nerves were frayed, and my fear was sky high as my heart pounded viciously trying to analyze what I just saw. There were so many thoughts spinning through my head that when two knuckles tapped on the tinted glass, I nearly jumped out of my skin.

Kova got into the car and dropped a bag onto the floorboard by my feet. He'd still bought the dumb candle.

"I can't believe it," I said quietly once we were on the highway. "I can't believe he's with my mom."

"I had a feeling that was your mother."

I turned toward him. "How so?"

"She looks just like you," he stated, slamming on the accelerator. "I just never realized it until now how similar you guys look."

Dread filled my veins. "What the hell are you talking about?"

"I have known for a long time Frank is not a monogamous man."

"Back up. What do you mean you never realized that was my mom until now?" My heart was racing faster than the speed of his car. "Where have you seen her? How do you know her?" Terror filled my blood. "Oh my God. Do not tell me you've been with her."

CHAPTER 65

Kova's eyes widened like he was offended.

"No, I have never cheated on Katja except with you," he spat. "I am not a cheater, and I have never been with Sophia."

I let out a whoosh. Kova exited the highway and pulled up to a red light. I stared straight ahead in a daze.

"You knew he was a cheater," I whispered in understanding.

He shot me a fleeting glance and placed a hand on my knee. Remorse was written all over his face.

"Of course I knew." He lowered his voice, and said, "I have seen him with her before. I just never knew it was your mother until I saw her again just now. I forgot about her, to be honest."

My head spun. I felt like I was missing a huge piece of the story. Kova took note of the expression on my face and continued. "He has brought her to my home in the past for Christmas parties. We have had quick holiday weekends away with them here and there. It has not happened in a while, so I forgot about her."

My eyebrows shot up in anger. "You knew he was cheating and you were okay with it? I can't believe you went along with it like it was nothing. For how long? Didn't it bother you?"

"What he does in his spare time is none of my business. I know it bothers you but do not take that out on me."

I turned back in my seat and looked ahead. He was right. "I'm sorry. I just didn't think adultery was a casual thing."

Kova was quiet. "It is not a casual thing for everyone," he said low, like he was hurt.

I released a pent-up sigh. This day was going all wrong. "Do you think my dad saw you?"

"Oh, he saw me."

My lunch was going to come up. "I'm gonna throw up again," I said, holding my stomach. "What happened?"

He shrugged as if he wasn't fazed. "Nothing. I bought your candle and left."

"I don't understand. That was it?"

"I was not going to strike up a conversation while his daughter was hiding in my car, Adrianna. I said hello and left. What would you like for me to have done? Ask him to have a drink?"

I pursed my lips together but didn't respond. He had a point, so I let it go.

"Did they ask you who you were with?"

"Yes."

My heart stopped. Quietly, I asked, "What did you say?"

"I told them I was alone and that I'd come to pick up candles for Katja since I knew she loved that store."

Kova pulled into a parking spot and turned off the car and looked at me.

"Has she ever been there? With you?"

"Never."

I threw the door open and stepped out, but Kova was already moving toward me. He invaded my space and pressed his body flush to mine, making sure I felt all of him. He cupped the back of my neck and pressed his forehead to mine, breathing into me.

"While I get hard seeing you jealous, I just want to make it clear that I did not take you where I took Katja, you crazy little psychopath. I would never do that. I lied to your father," he admitted before smashing his mouth to mine.

I kissed him back because I couldn't not. He played me, but I let it go. Kova knew how to subdue me with his tongue, his touch, his hold, and that's exactly what he did. He shoved his tongue into my mouth, and I moaned and clenched his shirt in my hand, wanting to push him away, but all I did was tug him closer. He kissed me, his mouth bruising hard, and I sighed, melting into him.

"I really thought you took me where you'd taken her for a second," I said. "I was going to kill you."

Narrowed eyes pierced my heart. "Stop thinking I am always lying to you or trying to hurt you," he said against my lips. I felt the dejection in his words and immediately regretted how I acted. "I told you, full disclosure." Kova thrust his hands into my hair, tugging on the strands at my nape. My stomach tightened when he pulled hard, my body coming to life and aching for him.

Reaching between us, I cupped his swollen length and gave him a good, hard squeeze. His eyelids dropped, heavy with unchained lust. I unbuttoned then unzipped his pants and stuck my hand inside to pull out his hard length. He was bare as usual and rock hard. We were standing so close together no one could see what I was doing. I wrapped my fingers around his shaft and stroked him. Kova groaned, his jaw flexing in an effort to keep it together.

Hands on my neck, he angled my face to his. Goose bumps prickled down my arms as his seductive words circled round me, "Do you know how easy it would be to fuck you out here with no one to ever know?"

My cheeks burned with heat and I squeezed his length without realizing it. I just planned to work him up, not have sex here. He dropped a little kiss to my lips and looked down.

"Look around," he said. "No one will see us."

He was probably right. There were trees everywhere, and in front of the car was a cement wall surrounded by more bushes. There wasn't a person in sight. Leaning down, he nuzzled my neck, his unshaven jaw enticing me to agree.

"All I have to do is lift your dress and slide right in, and your clothes would hide everything," he whispered, drawing in a breath through his teeth. "Let me fuck you out here. No one would know, they would think we are just kissing." Kova was ridiculously hard in my hand, and throbbing. I felt a little moisture and used it to run my hand over his tip. "Let me show you how I barely need to move to make you come." Kova groaned and I knew he'd kill for it to happen. "Let me in that little pussy of yours. I will make it quick."

His hand skimmed up my thigh and under my dress to cup my ass. Cool air breezed past my skin and I shivered. Thankfully it was my thigh that was facing the wall, that way if anyone walked past us they still wouldn't see anything. Swiftly, he dipped his fingers into my panties.

"You're so confident it will happen quickly. No way," I said, my voice a little breathless. "You're not quick—you like to take your time."

"I am a man hell-bent on winning every challenge presented to me. Now stroke my cock, Ria, and do not go light. Do it hard. Use your wrist and twist and squeeze the head."

Heat zipped down my spine as I did exactly what he demanded. Taking me by complete surprise, he leaned forward and licked my lips like he was licking an ice cream cone. I gasped and automatically squeezed my legs together as his finger caressed my clit.

"You play dirty," I said.

"I play to get what I want. Now spread your legs for me, *malysh*."

I shook my head, but my stupid body complied with him once he started rubbing a finger in circles on my clit. I couldn't not. It was impossible. Kova grinned, then slid a finger down my wet crease.

On a lusty whisper, I said, "I'm sure there are cameras out here."

He raised a pointed brow and dipped a finger into my entrance. "Does it not make it that much better?"

My mouth fell open and I struggled to stay quiet, clutching his shirt, pushing and pulling him.

"You do not want to push me away," he teased, "someone might see what we are doing."

My heart was racing, my body on fire for this reckless man who made me do things that were not something I'd typically do. I loved it, though. His gaze was as dark as the devil's and filled me with cravings I wanted him to satisfy. I looked deep into his eyes, inviting him. He could have whatever he wanted. With one pull, he ripped my panties at the crotch. He bit my neck and lifted one leg so my ankle was inconspicuously hooked around his hip.

"I need to be deep in you. Do not deny me."

Bending his knees just slightly, Kova angled himself at my entrance. In one swift motion, he surged inside. We both groaned at the same time, falling into each other. He shoved my hips down and I clenched around him, throbbing from the tightness.

I exhaled a painful breath. "Fuck, Kova. This hurts."

"Eyes on me, Ria."

CHAPTER 66

Kova carefully dropped my leg so I could stand, then fluffed my dress on the other side to hide anything that may show.

I winced at the snugness, holding my breath. Little silver stars danced in my vision.

"What are you doing?" I asked, standing on my tiptoes. I glanced around, nervous that someone would see us. He was swollen and thick and it almost hurt to have him at this angle.

"Wrap your arms around my shoulders and fucking kiss me. Let me take care of the rest."

So I did.

I understood what he meant now. Kova barely had to pull out for pleasure to burst through me. It was a slow, hard fuck. This angle made his cock caress my clit with every move he made and hit me deep inside. Warm, powerful strokes, and I was soon trembling on the edge of desire. My nails scored his biceps. I moaned into his mouth, sucking on his tongue, not caring if anyone heard. We rocked into one another, and the hard and shallow drives of his hips worked exquisitely. I wanted to bite him, eat him, devour him until he fucked me senseless. I began panting, my breathing deepening as I felt an orgasm climb almost immediately.

"I told you," he said as breathless as I felt. "I fuck like a champ. Three minutes tops. Maybe less."

"Why… Why didn't you just tell me that from the beginning?" I joked.

Kova placed both hands on my hips and rolled his pelvis into mine. My eyes rolled shut, closing from the bliss strumming through me.

"I need more."

He clucked his tongue. "Always so greedy for my cock. You act like you do not want it and then you beg."

"Just shut up. I'm going to come any second."

"That is good. Because a couple is walking this way now."

My eyes flew open and locked with Kova's. I panicked, but a lazy grin spread across his handsome face like he was pleased with himself.

Dropping his voice, he said, "I am going to come deep inside your pussy when they walk past us." His grin was enough to push my orgasm closer to the brink of insanity. "Try not to make a sound now."

Lips parting, my heart beat rapidly against my ribs. My cheeks flushed as the sound of footsteps drew closer. I placed my hands on his shoulders and chest, hoping it would look like we were talking.

Without taking his eyes off me, he said, "They are getting closer."

Then he thrust two more times, pulling all the way out to where I truly thought we were going to get caught from the way his body surged back and drove in. He shoved my hips down so I couldn't move when I felt him spasm inside me. His jaw flexed and his nostrils flared, eyes a dark pit of euphoria. I started coming just as the elderly couple walked past us. I feigned a breezy smile in their direction as Kova dipped his chin to greet them. I came even harder, pulsing around his swollen cock. As soon as they passed us, Kova leaned in and devoured my mouth as he pushed in one last, hard time as far as he could go. He let out a deep, guttural moan from his chest. My nails dug into his skin and I sighed, taking his cock the way he liked.

"Holy fuck," I said, breaking the kiss.

"Slow and steady wins the race." He grinned, then looked at his watch. "Next time we time it," he said. "I bet I can have you finishing in two and a half minutes."

"You're such an ass. Why do you do this to me?" I teased, still out of breath.

"Do not even act like you regret it," he said, pulling out of me with a pop. He fixed my dress so I was covered again.

I clenched my thighs, hoping it wouldn't drip down my legs as we walked through the building.

Kova leaned down and dropped a soft kiss to my lips. I took a step away but Kova stopped me. "Let me grab your bags."

I'd completely forgotten. I watched as he reached inside the car to get our stuff. He slammed the door shut and engaged the alarm, then reached for my hand. He briefly looked at me with a simple smile. Hand in hand, we walked toward the sliding glass doors.

There was an energy buzzing, an excitement spreading inside me, and I wondered if he felt it too. I leaned on him as we went up the elevator in silence and mused over the day, what we'd talked about, what had happened between us.

As soon as the door shut and we were in my condo, Kova dropped everything and slammed me up against the wall. I gasped in shock, my breath lodging in my throat.

"The clock starts now."

"What—" I said but was quickly silenced by his devilish mouth.

"I am not through with you. What happened outside was only an appetizer compared to what I'm going to do to you. This day, being out with you like we were, has made me incredibly hungry for you."

His fingers were in my pussy, pushing his cum back inside me. My hips moved against his hand, desire roaring back through me. A little whimper escaped me.

"After today, you are getting on birth control," he ordered, almost out of breath. "I want you all the time and I do not want to worry about you getting pregnant. It will be better for both of us."

I swallowed hard, choking on his words. All day I'd forgotten I was pregnant until now. Melancholy belted me but before I could react, his mouth was on mine and I let it go. Soon he'd know the truth. Until then, I wasn't going to worry.

My cell phone rang in my purse and Kova pulled back. "Do not even think about it," he warned. His wild eyes holding me captive and I leaned into him, listening. "Take the dress off now or I will rip it to shreds."

It was off in seconds. He reached behind his head and pulled off his shirt, then dropped it to the floor. His mouth was back on mine as he kicked off his shoes and pants.

Both of us completely bare, Kova picked me up and consumed my mouth. I should've known he wasn't done with me. Passion engulfed the air surrounding us and we caved to our decadent desires. I wrapped my arms around his shoulders, my ankles locked around his hips as he carried us across my living room. My cell phone rang again, but I ignored it. Only Avery ever called me back-to-back like that. There was no way I was stopping now that I knew it was her.

Breaking the kiss, my lips moved across his jaw and followed his alluring cinnamon scent I loved, suckling his neck and biting down hard. Kova paused. A low guttural sigh rumbled in his throat and then his hand came down and slapped my ass hard. Sexy as hell, it made my skin tingle.

Kova slid the patio door open and stepped out, my heart racing a million miles a minute. I lived on the top floor and there were plenty of condos around that could see us through the white opened slats. I glanced over my shoulder and noticed some of the balconies were occupied. If I could see them, then they could see me. Which meant anyone could look up and see two naked people going at it like rabbits.

Kova stopped in front of the railing. Looking at me, he said with unyielding resolve, "You are going to be mine out here."

I shivered with steady agreement. The thought exhilarated me completely.

I unlocked my ankles and glided down his body to stand. His erection stood tall between us and the urge to look out to the opening to check if anyone could see us was strong. Grabbing a fistful of my hair, he wrapped it around his hand, then guided me to my knees, forcing me to look up. I was a little nervous, but without hesitation, I opened my mouth and took as much as I could of him. He moaned on contact, angling his hips and holding the back of my head for a good minute. I sucked, swirling my tongue around his length, tasting myself on him. A little salty, I quickly licked it away so I could taste only him. Kova guided my head to his hips, pushing all the way in. His other hand grasped the back of my neck. I couldn't move even if I wanted to.

"Oh, fuck," he breathed loudly. My heartrate skyrocketed, thinking that someone had heard him.

I remembered how he'd taught me to suck it like a Blow Pop so I did just that, making sure I showed attention to that long vein I loved.

"Put one hand on my balls and massage them, squeeze them. Use your other hand and play with your pussy."

Despite the sun shining on my back, anticipation steamrolled through me. I liked touching myself. I knew exactly how to get myself off, and since I was already on the edge, I planned to do just that.

Cupping his sack, I rolled his heavy balls in my hand. I surprisingly liked the way they felt as I tugged and twisted them. I could tell he did as well, especially when my fingers scraped past them. I felt him clench his cheeks as he pushed into my mouth and held still. My eyes watered as I struggled to breathe, and I pinched his sensitive sac between my fingers.

"Oh, fuck me." He moaned long and loud.

I looked up to see his head thrown back, the veins in his neck jutting out. What an angle to see Kova at. I was on the verge of an orgasm and began twirling my tongue around the head of his cock every time he pulled out.

"Keep sucking like that, work that throat."

Oh God, this view of him, my fingers, his balls… I was right there… Right… There. My breathing labored and I rubbed myself hard and fast, my blood rising and my insides quivering. I reached for him and gripped his balls in my palm and squeezed as I came on my fingers. Kova thrust in and hit the back of my throat. My stomach tightened for a second. I was lost on what to do.

"Ria," he yelled, unloading in my mouth. He was so loud I was sure if anyone was outside they heard. I wasn't expecting him to come and almost gagged at the initial stream of the warm, salty fluid. "Swallow it," he demanded, caressing my throat with his hand and fingers. There was so much I squeezed my eyes shut, swallowing it like he said.

Kova pulled out and stepped back, a stream of creamy white fluid dripping off him. "Tsk, tsk, Ria. I said play with yourself, not make yourself come. Get up and on the chair now."

Anticipation seized my chest. My gaze met his. I wiped my mouth with the back of my hand and stood on shaky knees. The beautiful swirls of black and obsessive green in his eyes intrigued me.

"On your hands and knees," he ordered. "Ass up."

I got into position and reared back, placing my chest to the lounge. Before I could blink, a hand came down and stung my ass with a slap.

I didn't cry out. Instead, I chewed my lip and stayed where I was. Kova leaned forward and grabbed my hair and yanked my head back, delivering another pleasure-filled smack. My skin pebbled with goose bumps. I was starting to wonder if there was something wrong with me. Shouldn't I have been repulsed by all the spanking, the biting, the roughness and blood? I was supposed to like it soft and gentle, yet here I was rearing back and wiggling myself in his face.

I loved everything he gave me, and that's what confused me. I could feel my blood climbing and the sensations pouring through me as my body desired more deviant touches and illicit whimpers.

CHAPTER 67

Kova let go of my hair.

He pushed on my shoulder blades and forced my face down. My nipples grazed the coarse material of the lounge and shot a zest of bliss down my spine. Grabbing the chair, he slid it closer to the railing. My balcony was enclosed with a screen, but if anyone walked by the building and looked up, they'd see us.

Kova dropped to his knees and grabbed my hips, rotating them upward. He spread my cheeks, and my back bowed, mortification roared through me.

"Your pussy is dripping," he said, his voice thick with desire and it excited me.

He leaned forward until I couldn't see his face. My eyes rolled shut as he ran his flat tongue along my wet lips, all the way to my ass where the tip of his tongue ran little circles.

A moan rolled off my lips and I rocked back into him. My eyes opened just as he swallowed, his throat bobbing. His heady gaze locked with mine. "Had to clean you up before I can play."

"You're such an ass man."

Palming both of my ass cheeks, his hands so large I knew they covered me, he leaned forward and I held my breath as he spread them wide to almost the point of pain. His green eyes were enthralled with me and it sent a shiver of power through my veins. A little sting, and I gasped. I'd never looked at my ass in the mirror, but the next time I was alone, I would. This position was slightly embarrassing, and I hoped I was shaven and cleaned for him.

Kova leaned forward and penetrated my pussy with his warm tongue. I sighed. My back bowed even more and my body relaxed, only for him to pull out and go straight for my ass.

I should've known.

"Arch more for me."

I did as he asked. His teeth clamped down on the skin as he tongued my hole, creating a suction around me. His fascination with that forbidden spot created a frenzy in my blood. I didn't get it, but I didn't question it either, because the truth was I loved it just as much as he did.

"Oh my God!" I screamed, not worried if anyone heard my breathless pants at this point.

Kova gripped my hips and held me to his mouth. My legs widened on their own and my backside pressed embarrassingly hard into his face.

"One day…" he said, his voice a deep husky.

I knew what he was referring to. Anal sex. It was a conversation we'd already had and something that will never happen.

"No, you're not. That's never going to happen."

"Yes, it will."

"No, it won't."

"Ah, but *malysh*," he drew out, his thumb running circles over the puckered little hole, "you have no idea what you're missing."

"There is no way you—or anyone else with a smaller dick—will fit in there. No thanks. Not happening. End of discussion."

Kova's grip tightened on me to the point I knew I'd have a bruise. "No one is ever getting this ass. Do you understand? I will personally strangle anyone who gets close to it. It is mine."

His thumb pressed the hidden spot while he inserted a finger into my pussy.

"I can make you like it, you know," he whispered, pulling out his finger and using the wetness to trace the tight hole.

He applied more pressure, pushing the tip of his finger in. This time he stuck two fingers in my pussy and slowly rubbed along my inner walls, eliciting a low moan from me as he stretched me. I fought back a groan at the double intrusion.

This man knew exactly what to do to my body and I was slightly startled by it because I never found myself saying no, only yes. Body manipulation at its finest. I watched as Kova spit onto his fingers then applied pressure to the tight bundle of nerves. I flinched but held still.

"Are you not worried someone can see you?" he asked.

It was hard to think clearly when my body was a blaze of heat and lust.

"I am, but no one can see my face. So I guess not."

"But those who live in the building can probably figure out what number your condo is."

He was probably right, but I didn't care. "Maybe."

"Take a deep breath," he ordered. My eyes widened, I knew what he was going to do. "A deep breath, Ria." Exhaling, my body softened, and he pressed a finger into my ass, then pulled out. I hope it was a pinky. "Breathe," he instructed, and I did. "Trust me, you will love it when I am done with you."

"It hurts," I said, but he pressed deeper, and when I realized he wasn't stopping, I closed my eyes and took a deep breath and focused on the pleasure. The way he played with my tender lips, working an orgasm up again, was quite remarkable. I was shocked my body was ready for another one.

"Bear down, push back, and relax. Focus on my fingers stroking your pussy."

Surprisingly, he placed a kiss to each cheek, then slid his finger farther into my ass. I clamped together, and my arms shot out in front of me for something to hold on to. My back arched and I rocked my butt into his face.

This hurt. This hurt worse than losing my virginity.

"Kova, please. It hurts," I whimpered somewhere between pain and pleasure as he used a finger to tease my clit and stroke my ass.

Little sparks went off inside of me and I shuddered in ecstasy. I didn't know if I was coming or going. I didn't know what I wanted or didn't want anymore. I was lost in a haze of sex and gratification. Kova was right. He could make me want it, because now I kind of did.

Kova groaned behind me, sliding his finger out but carefully pushing back in. He wasn't aggressive or harsh, but shockingly gentle. He let out a long breath of air and it hit my cheek.

"Just listen to what I say and you will thank me."

As Kova gently worked his finger in and out of me, I glanced between our bodies. His cock was erect and straining to the point it looked painful. The tip of his shaft was purple and almost angry looking. His stomach was rock hard like he was holding on tight to the last bit of his sanity he had left. But he was right. I think he could make me love it because this was better than I'd expected.

I felt myself spasm around him and just as I was about to come, he pulled out and stood.

"Kova… Please…"

With his cock in his hand, he looked at me then angled himself at my entrance, and slid into my warmth that was aching for another orgasm. We both groaned in unison from the sheer pleasure of it all.

Leaning down, he licked a wet trail up my spine to my shoulder and under my ear. He tugged on the lobe. I didn't even know it was possible to have goose bumps outside in this heat.

"I want to hear you scream," he whispered, his hot breath on my face, thrusting into me. "Let everyone hear me fucking you and wish it were them."

I nodded. I'd agree to almost anything at this point.

As he began thrusting in and out of me, my eyes rolled shut and I heard him spit. I cracked one eye open and watched as he rolled his saliva between his fingers and then dropped them behind me.

"Arch back," he ordered. "Exhale."

Then, one long finger slid back into my ass while he was deep inside of me. My body trembled in ecstasy and a raspy moan rolled off my lips. The pressure was almost too much to bear.

I let out a high-pitched moan as he worked me ever so slowly that it almost brought tears of pleasure to my eyes. Like he knew I could only handle so much and didn't want to hurt me. He was careful and attentive and I couldn't stop the sounds escaping me even if I tried. It was impossible.

"Kova…"

"Ria…"

"Why do I like this so much?" I nearly whined. My inner thighs were wet with my pleasure. "I never want you to stop. Can we do this all day?"

He chuckled and teased me. "Oh, *Malysh*. Now you know what I deal with on a daily basis. How I imagine taking you, how it can never be enough. Now you see."

"I do, good God, how I do…" I could barely find my words. "How… Why?"

My body was engulfed with dark desires, cheeks flushed with a tinge of pink, thighs trembling, and shaking from the hunger. I was floating on another level. My body was going to combust from the pressure of pleasure only Kova could give me.

"I don't think I can hold on much longer, Kova. Please, I need to…" I begged.

A dark chuckle enveloped me, and he reached around with his free hand to circle my clit. A loud purr escaped me and I slowly rocked back into him, loving this so much. I wasn't too embarrassed to beg at this point, and I could tell he was close as his dick twitched inside me and his thrusts became harder, deeper, more controlled for both of us.

Kova yanked me up so I had my back to his chest. We were both kneeling, a slave to each other's desires.

"Put your arms behind my neck."

I did as he asked, my breasts swollen and bouncing while he teased and taunted every erogenous area I had. My mind was misty, he took me to new heights. After spending the day with him and our conversations, our connection only grew stronger and it scared me a little. Now I understood what he meant. I wanted this all the time too and I didn't just mean the sex. My heart was his, just like I knew his was mine. I liked seeing his arm across my belly. The vascularity that oozed from him and the vein twirling down. He was strong and rough, and the pleasure so divine.

"Come, come now with me," he said, then sank his teeth into my shoulder, his tongue lapping my skin.

My body exploded with rapture on a throaty sigh, like a huge wave roared through me. I yelled out his name, driving my hips back into his. His pleasure trickled down my inner thighs and I felt tender everywhere, sated from this touch. Our orgasms receded but the content bliss that followed was sizzling between us. We were both panting, a sheen of sweat coating our bodies, but it didn't bother me. Kova reached up to cup my jaw and turn my face toward his. Our eyes locked for a split moment before he gave me a tender kiss that enclosed around my heart. His lips were soft and sweet, his tongue light, as if what he'd just done to my body was normal.

There was nothing normal about Konstantin Kournakova and Adrianna Rossi, but that's what I loved about us.

Breaking the kiss, Kova opened his eyes.

Heart thumping wildly in my chest, the setting sunlight flickered against his compelling green eyes that unveiled an openness with a love so deep my stomach tightened. I was trying to stay strong, I didn't want to say something and regret it, but in this moment, what I felt was love.

Love was a look. Love was a feeling. Love was a four-letter word that held more weight than gold.

Love was clarity.

CHAPTER 68

K ova," I whispered, like it was the word only he wanted to hear. His eyes glimmered with awareness and he carefully pulled out of me, then turned me over to lay me on my back on the lounger. His length, still warm and hard, pressed against my thigh. My heart was pounding. We should've been sensible about being so free with our carnality, but we never could control it. It was only us and that's all that mattered.

Our eyes were focused on each other's as he covered my body with his, his mouth with mine, his weight falling onto me. I loved when he did that, when he laid on top of me without abandon and gave me himself. It was one of the rare times I got just him without all the layers, like he was giving himself to me. My arms wound around his shoulders, my fingers through his hair. He kissed me so greedily I could barely keep up with him. Hands sliding down his back, he shook like he was in dire need. He passionately pushed his tongue in my mouth. His hands found my neck and applied pressure, and I went with it. My body unraveled under his. He unleashed on me and I took it all.

"I need to see your face when I make love to you," he said, leaving me speechless.

I didn't question it. I just nodded my head. It's what he needed, and I gave it to him. I knew deep down in my heart that after this weekend, when he found out my secret, it would most likely break the connection we'd worked so hard to rebuild, so I was going to savor it for as long as I could.

Without a second thought, he lifted his hips and pushed his cock into me again. A glaze swept over his eyes and he moaned. He began making love to me like a beast, pumping his hips with ardor. Hard and long strokes, holding himself in me before he was retreating and doing it again, building a maelstrom of desire. An erotic growl vibrated in his chest when he drove harder. My back bowed in response at how deep he was, my nails scoring his back. He shuddered against me and I locked my legs around his waist.

This was lovemaking.

"Kova…" I swallowed, quivering. "Oh, my God…" I moaned against his mouth. "It hurts." And it did. He was so enlarged and hitting all the way in the back.

"Shhh…"

"Kova." I dug my fingers into him, feeling his skin break under my nails.

"Take me. Take all of me," he gritted between clenched teeth. *"Mne nuzhno, chtoby ty byl bez sderzhannosit, bez osuzhdeniya."*

"Please…" I wasn't sure what I was begging him for.

"Ty nuzhna mnye. "

My heart ached at the sound of his cracked voice.

"Just hold on… I need this, I need you. I need to feel more of you."

"You're going to make me bleed, Kova."

He growled, reluctantly slowing his pace. The muscles in his shoulders relaxed, his body loosened, and he cupped my damp neck and held on like I was his salvation. His dominant kisses were almost careless, like he let himself go as he urgently thrust into me. He was getting closer. The little sounds in the back of his throat made me disentangle my feelings for him completely and it scared me a little.

Kova gave one good last stroke, held my jaw in his palms and kissed me so deeply and so desperately my heart contracted and my toes curled. I whimpered, my body shuddering with pleasure. His cock jerked, we gasped, then we were both falling into a blissful state of ecstasy at the same time. The way his tongue enveloped mine, how he used one hand to grip my hip to make sure we were joined perfectly, how I could feel him unloading inside me, made my chest hurt.

"Malysh," he whispered on a groan.

Pulling back, Kova looked down at me and licked his lips. We were nose to nose and breathing heavily. His gaze swept over my face. Sweat trickled the sides of his temples and I wiped it away. The way he looked at me made my heart ache for him with so much affection it was difficult to put into words. We were both sticky and hot. I threaded my hands through his wet hair and locked my fingers behind his head.

"You know that I love you, right?"

Swallowing thickly, I nodded. He was waiting for me to respond. I wanted so bad to tell him I loved him too, because I did. I wished I could give that to him, but something warned me to hold back.

"Ya vlyubilsya f tyebya s pyervava fsglyada."

I waited for him to translate it for me, but this time he didn't. Instead, he smiled, a little sad, but covered it up with a quick kiss.

Cradling me to him, he slid out and stood, taking me with him. I laid my head on his shoulder, a peaceful air settling around us as he walked toward the sliding glass door and stepped inside. I was ready to go to sleep, even though the sun hadn't set completely yet.

"I can walk, you know."

Kova leaned in and kissed my neck. "But I like having you in my arms. I never want to let you go."

"Who knew you could be so sweet."

He chuckled and said, "I am not sweet."

"It's okay to admit you're soft sometimes," I said, egging him on.

He paused right in front of my bathroom. I looked up, waiting. "Soft?" he responded with a confused grin. His hand skimmed over my hip and down my backside and settled over my leaking sex. He inserted two fingers and I clenched around them, drawing in a breath as he pushed his semen back inside me. "This is not from me being soft, *moya lyubov.*" He glanced at my lips. "My love," he translated, his voice low.

I blushed. My teeth dug into my bottom lip and I melted a little. I clenched again and his eyes flashed.

"Whatever you say, big boy. Now put me down so I can get cleaned up."

"I will clean you up."

I sighed loudly, faking annoyance. "Why do you have to act like a cave man all the time?"

"Why do you have to be so outspoken? Let me do what I want and we will have no issues," he responded.

I laughed. "You like my mouth."

He raised his brows, his eyes glittering with hunger. "I do *love* your mouth, especially when your lips are—"

I slapped his chest playfully. "Kova! Shut up!" I laughed, squirming in his arms as he walked into my bathroom and turned the shower on. "I need to wash my hair."

"I can wash it."

"You think you can wash it and hold me at the same time? You do realize you need two hands, right?"

He slapped one of his thighs and it echoed against the tile walls. "You underestimate me."

I chewed on my bottom lip. "I need to shave my legs."

"I will shave them for you."

I raised a brow. "Fine. If you can shave my legs, I can shave your balls."

Kova's eyes popped open wide in shock and his jaw dropped in horror. A fit of laughter burst from my lips at his expression.

"Never, ever going to happen," he said clearly.

"That's what I thought," I said. "Now let me down."

"Fine. But I want you back in my arms again right after."

Joining me under the warm spray, his soft tone raised a few flags. "Hey, what's going on?"

He shook his head, unable to meet my gaze.

"Tell me," I pressed, "please."

Kova let out a long sigh and his fingers danced along my shoulder. We stood a few inches apart and I could feel his emotions as if they were my own. We washed up quickly.

"Nothing is going on. I just want you back where you belong. We do not get much time like this together and I want to make the most of it while we can."

Be still my fucking heart. I made Kova meet my gaze and drew in a quiet breath. He was unguarded, water trickling down is face, but it was the pain in his eyes that sucker punched me. There was so much anguish it tore me up. I always thought I would never win with him, but now I wondered if he actually felt that way with me. He was trying and I was holding back.

Blood rushing through my chest, I was trying to stay strong and not cave and admit my love for him, but when it was so rare for him to be this candid with his feelings, I wanted to let go of that last wall I'd put up and run to him.

"We will not be able to have moments like this often," he said, like reality had dawned on him.

A half smile tugged at my lips. Kova picked up the shampoo and lathered up my hair. "I know. Maybe one day, though." I swallowed and decided to finally give a little piece of me that I knew he needed to hear. "I'm yours." I put emphasis into my words, hoping he'd see I meant it.

Without hesitation, he leaned down and wrapped his strong arms around me, pressing his lips to mine. His tongue swept along the seam, requesting access. I gave in willingly, falling into his emotional embrace.

Pulling back, he exhaled a heavy breath and pressed his forehead to mine. "God. How am I supposed to stay away from you when all I want is to be touching you, holding you, just fucking being next to you breathing the same air? I am going out of my mind trying to make this work and I do not know how without fucking it up. I am obsessed with every part of you and never want to let you go."

Breathless, I knew I needed to reassure him as much as I needed the reassurance for myself. "I wish I had an answer for you that was right. For us, nothing is supposed to be right. We just have to take each day as it comes. Always remember I feel the same way as you."

He nodded. "I know. You are correct. It fucking sucks," he said, almost angrily, but not toward me.

I felt bad. "Nothing worth having ever comes easy, remember? That's what makes it so much better." Just then my stomach grumbled embarrassingly loud. "You worked up an appetite in me."

He pinched my hip. "You could stand to lose a few pounds." My jaw dropped. "I am only joking." He chuckled. "Let us finish up and I will cook you something."

I held up my fingers and said, "I'm getting all pruney anyway."

Kova kissed my fingers and laughed. I turned off the shower and he slid open the curtain to step out. "You Americans and your strange descriptions. Where are your towels?"

I stared, riveted with his body the way water trickled over the dips and curves of his natural muscle. It was when he turned to the side that my lips parted and a sigh worked through me. He was physically perfect with a firm, round ass and hot-as-hell hips that led to powerful thighs. But it was the sexy V at his lower abdomen that twisted a need in me to reach out and touch. What this man did to me…

Kova snapped his fingers and my eyes shot up to him. I blushed, and he was grinning like a fool. He loved it.

"Towels?"

I had to think about it for a minute. "Ah, they're in the closet on the shelf."

I stood in the stall shivering as Kova stepped out and opened my linen closet. I glanced at his reflection in the mirror taking in his magnificent backside down to the floor when something caught my eye.

Sticking out of the garbage were the pregnancy test boxes and the four sticks I'd peed on.

CHAPTER 69

I tried to figure out how I could hide those when it hit me that the closet Kova was opening up contained the last box I'd yet to use. Oh God.

My heart was beating harder than it ever had before. There was a pounding in my ears, a ringing that shot a shrill of anxiety through me. I felt my emotions rising to the top threatening to break the barrier I'd carefully put up. I felt the tears forming before the words were ever spoken. I felt it all coming, the heated words, the pain that would follow, the accusations. I had no idea what to do. It was all happening in slow motion and I couldn't stop it no matter how badly I wanted to.

Taking deep breaths, I was trying not to choke, but my chest burned, and I couldn't find the words to stop him from going in there. I'd had my chance to tell him and I hadn't. I'd been a coward, too scared to tell him I was pregnant. My hands shook, and my jaw bobbed. I felt my lunch in my stomach slosh around.

I'd forgotten I'd stuffed the box between the towels. I'd been so upset that day I didn't want to look at it or think about the positive tests, so I'd hid it.

I held my stomach, fear crippling me as Kova handed me a towel, then took in my face. His eyes were suddenly filled with concern and he opened his beautiful mouth to speak when I heard the box hit the floor.

Blood drained from my face. I was going to be sick. The room started to spin, the chill filling my veins, making me shake.

I watched him turn back to look at the closet, then down at the floor. His brows furrowed and he bent down to retrieve the box. I pressed the towel to my face, still unable to speak while he picked it up and turned it over.

Kova froze and I felt his confusion pulsating around us. The silence was earsplitting as he stared in shock at the pregnancy test box. I couldn't even hear him breathing.

Droplets of water surrounded his feet. He still hadn't grabbed his towel.

"When were you going to tell me?" he asked so quietly, not looking at me.

Words were lost on me. Oh God, I was going to be sick. My stomach was clutched with pressure and my heart was about to explode.

"When?" His voice was grave, low.

He turned his head to look at me and I still couldn't say anything. His eyes were huge. Color drained from his face too and I felt a tremor of blame in his gaze. My lips parted but nothing came out, because I knew there was nothing I could say that could fix this or justify not telling him.

"When, Adrianna?" Tears filled my eyes. His voice, so severely hurt that I was rooted in place. "Or were you not going to?" I was so guilty, and he knew it. "When?" he asked again, this time his voice rose. His beautiful green eyes were heartbroken.

Somehow, I was able to wrap the towel around my body and rush to my room. I shifted through my drawers and grabbed a pair of bikini panties and a tank top. Dropping the towel, I slipped on my clothes just as Kova walked in wearing a pair of shorts, water still dripping down his body, and the box firm in his hand. He hadn't even dried off.

My heart was racing so hard and fast. I took a step back, scared of how he would react. There was only one way this could go, and that was south.

"I asked you a question, Adrianna."

I glanced at the now crushed box in his hand. That was all it took for me to break down. I started crying profusely, my breathing erratic. I was trying to catch my breath, knowing this was going to kill us both. We'd come so far and now everything was ruined.

"I'm sorry. I'm sorry. I'm sorry," I cried. I didn't know what else to say.

"How long?"

"I don't know."

"What do you mean you do not know?"

I jumped at his harsh tone. "I mean I don't know how far along I am."

I reached blindly behind me for my bed. I was going to fall if I didn't lean on something. I dropped my hips to sit, the sight of my carpet blurry from my tears. Shame filled me. I couldn't even look at him.

"Take the test."

I shook my head, my lips pressed tightly together. Fat tears flowed down my face. "Take it, Adrianna."

I glanced up and a gush of air rushed from me. "I already did."

Eyes hurt, he said, "When?"

"Last week."

Understanding resonated within him and he turned ash white. His eyes dropped to my stomach then met mine again.

"You are pregnant."

It wasn't a question but an assessment. Covering my mouth with my hand, I nodded silently. A strangled cry burst from my lips and I gasped, drawing in a loud breath. The dense air singed my lungs. The pain wracking my heart was unbearable, but it didn't compare to the torture I could see burning inside Kova. I felt it, God, did I feel it, and it was overwhelming. Like a black cloud of smoke slowly killing me. He didn't seem angry. He looked downright devastated, and I didn't know if it was because I didn't tell him sooner, or because I was pregnant. His entire face was that of grief and regret and it was suffocating me. He stared at me like he was reaching out, searching for an answer I was incapable of giving. His emotions were on display for me, so prevalent that I could barely stand to explain myself.

Inhaling a heavy breath, I finally spoke. My voice was very low. "I took four tests. They're in the garbage in my bathroom."

Kova spun around before I'd finished my sentence and I found the will in me to rush after him.

He picked up my garbage pail and turned it over, shaking it so all the contents fell out. One stick was turned up and I could see the two pink lines from where I was standing, so I knew he could too.

"I'm sorry," I said again. "I know I should've told you but I was scared and I didn't want you to blame me and think I planned it. I tried to tell you a few times but I just couldn't do it. I was too scared. Then you started talking about Katja's pregnancy and I didn't want you to think I was lying too."

Kova fell to his knees and picked up the tests, flipping them over. He didn't say anything, just studied them, reading the two that clearly showed I was pregnant.

"I know you probably hate me for this, but I really did try. I don't know what happened… I took the pills like I was supposed to. I didn't even know I was pregnant until we came back from the meet."

Holding the tests, he turned to face me. He squeezed his eyes shut, remorse filling his face. "I could never hate you," he said.

Another sob burst from me and I ran to where he was kneeling. I got down and looked into his eyes. "I'm so sorry."

"You were pregnant at the meet," he said.

"Yes, I just didn't know it."

His face fell. "What made you take the test?"

"Avery. I was so sick, and it was her idea. I just thought I was sick because of traveling and my stupid kidney issues and how it took so much out of me. It never occurred to me I could be pregnant."

He looked down at the tests, staring hard at them like he was looking for an answer.

"You have to be a few months. Two, close to three."

"No," I wept, my jaw quivering. "That means the heart is beating." Fresh, warm tears fell.

Kova looked up, but before he could say anything, I told him what I had already decided.

"I can't have a baby, Kova. I'm sorry but I just can't. I'm going to have an abortion. I've already made up my mind. It's my body and you can't force me to have a kid, not that I think you want one, but I'm not changing my mind. I'm sorry but it's what I have to do."

I don't think I even breathed through that.

"Were you even going to tell me?"

I blinked. I went for the truth because at this point I had nothing left to lose. "I honestly don't know. I was going to, then I didn't know how to tell you. I really don't know. I want to say yes, but I've been a mess and I couldn't find the words. There was never a right time."

Exhaling, I said, "No, I know I would've told you. I just don't know when I would have."

Recognition dawned on him. He held the stick up. "This is why you kept pushing me away?"

I nodded.

Kova grabbed all the sticks, then carried me to my room where he sat me down, then placed the throw blanket I had at the end of my bed around my shoulders. He rubbed my arms, trying to warm me up and sat down next to me.

This wasn't what I'd expected. I'd expected rage. I'd expected yelling. I'd expected the worst and yet there was nothing. But he wasn't saying anything, and that terrified me.

"How was I supposed to tell you I'm pregnant?"

Silence.

"I knew you would be mad. I knew it."

Silence.

"An abortion is the only option for us."

Silence.

"I can't have a baby."

Silence.

Silence.

"Say something!" I yelled, breathing heavily.

I could deal with Kova's anger. I could handle Kova's pain. What I couldn't handle was his heartbroken silence. My stomach was a pit of rocks and the fact that he was sitting there in utter silence did nothing to ease the stress I was under.

His eyes flared and he glared at me. "What do you want me to say, Adrianna!" he yelled. "You have already made up your mind. What is done is done," he spat. "That is it. There is nothing left for me to say."

I pulled back and gasped. "You're mad," I whispered, shocked. "You expected me to have this baby, didn't you?"

"No, I did not. If you wanted to, then I would have supported your decision. I would never force you to have a child or get rid of one. I am hurt that you did not come to me," he said, and I got fired up real quick from that. "But I know I have no right to be upset after what I have done to you, so I am dealing with this the best way I can right now." He was quiet for a moment and I started to cry again. "I just wish you would have told me sooner so I did not have to find out this way."

"I'm sorry," was all I could think of saying. I didn't know what to say.

He frowned, looking at the tests again then back to me. His eyes searched mine. There was nothing but sorrow in them.

"I am devastated for more reasons than one. I am mad because I did not ever want a child, but finding out you are pregnant, looking at you and imaging you with my child, it makes me think differently. It makes me want that with you now and it fucking kills me that you will have an abortion..." Kova trailed off and started mumbling in Russian. "What I am, is sorry that I got you pregnant." He looked down, almost as if he couldn't bear to say his next words. "And now you have to terminate our child."

He couldn't even finish the heartbreaking words. We were both paying the price and I wondered how we would ever persevere from this.

"Honestly, it kills me too," I whispered. I'd spoken those words from my heart. "This is going to ruin everything, isn't it?"

"It definitely changes things." He paused, and I held my breath. "If anything, it makes me love you even more than I thought was possible."

My lips parted, my heart shattering down the center. I got up and stood in front of Kova, palming his cheeks. He wrapped an arm around my shoulders and pulled me to him. I felt his breath on my neck, the way his body trembled against mine. I broke down, my heart emptying, and I cried with him. He pulled me tighter and put me on his lap. Kova tried to look at me, but I wouldn't let him and I kept my head down. I leaned in, breathing him in, needing him so desperately. Wrapping my arms around his neck, I placed my face against his chest, and I could hear his erratic heartbeat. I looked up at him just in time to see one lone tear fall down his beautiful face.

"You will never understand how truly sorry I am. For everything I have ever done. To you. To us. For all the pain I have caused you. You must know whatever you want to do, whatever you decide, I will support you. I love you so much, Adrianna, that at times it is hard for me to deal with. Damn the consequences. We are a team—but the truth is, when *you* exhale, *I* inhale. Not the other way around.

I might be the beast beneath your beauty pushing you to succeed, but you are the anchor that holds me steady in a churning ocean threatening to drown me. It is how it has been for me since day one, and it will continue to be that way. Always remember that. So whatever you decide, I will support you."

I cried harder than I'd ever cried in my life.

I cried for myself.

I cried for Kova.

I cried for our child we'd never get to meet.

I cried harder, feeling his sorrow as my own.

After a few moments when the tears subsided, I pulled back and took a deep breath. Kova wiped my face and we stared into each other's eyes without saying any more words.

There was nothing left to say. He was right. This would definitely change things.

Easing myself from his lap, I moved to use the bathroom. The emotional stress of this conversation was killing my stomach. I probably just needed to splash some water on my face.

I took one step, but Kova grabbed my wrist and pulled me between his legs. He placed both hands on my hips, then leaned forward and pressed a soft kiss to my stomach. I drew in a quiet gasp, trying to hold back the tears. Kova looked up at me with sorrow in his sad green eyes, almost like he was in mourning.

With his hand splayed on my stomach, he reached forward to press his lips to mine.

"Kiss me, damn it," he fucking begged.

Oh, God, my heart. His gravelly voice made my jaw tremble and the tears to surge again.

"I don't want this to change anything between us," I said against his lips. He started breathing heavily. "I'm scared."

"Kiss me, Ria, please," he begged, his voice completely shattered this time. "I need you to kiss me so I know you do not hate me. So I know you still love me as much as I love you."

And so I did. I kissed him while he kept his hand on my stomach as if he needed to remember this moment, us, and what was growing inside me that we had created. I kissed him back for not treating me the way I'd feared he would. I kissed him back for understanding that while this was our choice, I made the decision and he accepted it. I kissed him back for us and the hope he'd see from this moment on that I was still his and he was still mine and we would forever be Kova and Ria.

As Kova dragged me closer to him, a knock sounded at the door. Our kiss broke apart and our expressions mimicked each other's.

"Are you expecting someone?" he asked.

I shook my head and stepped back.

Puzzled, we both got up to answer the door. The only other person who knew where I lived that ever came over was Hayden, but after the discussion I'd just had with Kova, I prayed it wasn't him.

The rapid knocking persisted and I looked over my shoulder and saw Kova close behind, the pregnancy tests still in his hand. It crushed me to see that because I felt like it meant he was holding onto the only evidence he'd ever have of our baby.

Turning the lock, I didn't look through the peephole before I pulled it open. Hindsight is 20/20, and looking back, I should've never answered the door.

Maybe I'd prayed a little too hard, because right now, I would do anything for it to be Hayden.

CHAPTER 70

D ad?"

He didn't hear me.

He didn't see me.

The silence was deafening, the accusation clear. All he saw was Kova in my condo without a shirt on, fresh from the shower, the water from his hair dripping over the scarred letter I'd marked on his chest.

I was going to be sick. Dad tilted his head to the side, his harsh gaze taking in Kova. I was in nothing but a small shirt and underwear.

It felt like everything was happening in slow motion as my father stepped inside the condo and shut the door.

Dad glanced at Kova's bare chest, then his jaw locked. Nostrils flaring, he said, "Well, this is certainly a surprise. Care to tell me what you're doing in my daughter's condo, Konstantin?"

A chill of terror rolled down my spine. I held my stomach. This was far worse than telling Kova about the pregnancy.

Kova stood completely stone-faced. We both knew there was no legitimate reason for him to be here, and I kind of hoped he wouldn't try to make an excuse. Kova gave nothing away. His breathing was steady as he remained calm under pressure. The situation was fucked up, and even I knew there was nothing I could say to get us out of this. We were both caught red-handed.

"Do you have an answer for me?" Dad asked. He removed his navy blazer and folded it over one of the high-back chairs.

Kova's eyes shot to mine and the tension grew to a thickening level. His Adam's apple bobbed.

"No. Don't look at my daughter," my dad said casually, as he if was asking him to lunch. He uncuffed his sleeves and rolled them up. "I asked *you* a question and I expect an answer from *you.*"

Kova put his hands up. "Frank—"

"You know how this looks, right? A man, one I trusted with my teenage daughter—my sick daughter—to watch over her is in her condo. Both of you are wearing fucking scraps of clothing, not to mention, is that a fucking tattoo with the letter of her name?" His jaw flexed, and I thought he was going to pop a blood vessel in his eyes. "So, tell me, what the fuck are you doing in my condo with my fucking daughter?"

My stomach dropped. His cursing isn't what held me immobilized, it was his words spoken with such disgust that frightened me.

"Are you a sick fucking pervert preying on young girls?"

My jaw dropped. "Dad—"

Dad pointed a finger at me. "Shut your goddamned mouth, Adrianna. There is nothing you can say that will help you out of this. I've seen everything I need to. Go pack your clothes. Whatever the fuck this is, ends here."

Tears sprung to my eyes. "No," I gasped.

"Frank, please—"

"You can't be serious," I said, barely able to breathe. My heart was in my throat. "Just let me explain. It's not what it looks like, I swear."

Dad lowered his voice, his eyes narrowing to slits. "Does it look like I'm fucking kidding? I'm not playing games with you."

I took a step closer, but also kept a decent amount of distance. I could feel the heat and rage blistering around him, and it scared me.

"Dad, it's not what you think. It's really not." I tried to think of a lie he'd believe. "I wasn't feeling well. I got sick, and he was helping me."

A sardonic huff escaped him. "Joy was right. This whole time she was right about you and your coach, and I denied it. She showed me a photo of you guys I rejected it, saying she'd Photoshopped it for her own motive. I figured I'd give you the benefit of the doubt and show up for you to explain, but then I find this…" He eyed Kova with repugnance, then looked back to me. "I defended you. I thought you were smarter than this. I thought you were better." He scoffed under his breath. "What a fucking fool I was."

My face fell. I blinked and Dad was standing in front of me. I jumped backward, but he grabbed me in a rough hold and yanked. Pain shot through my shoulder and I yelped.

"Ow, you're hurting me!" I cried out and tried to pull away.

Dad's eyes bulged from his head. "This is what you wear around your coach! Do as I say and get your things now, Adrianna, or I will fucking lose it." He paused. "Now."

Kova stepped in. "You do not need to hurt her because of me. Let her go."

Dad's head whipped toward Kova. His gaze was deadly. "Do not tell me what to do with *my* daughter, you sick fuck. I asked you to watch over her and protect her. And this is how you do it? Get the fuck out of my face, you disgusting piece of shit." He paused, his face getting redder by the second, his grip thickening. "I trusted you! I'm calling the cops—I want you thrown in jail!"

"No! Dad, no!" I yanked away again, but it was a mistake because he only jerked me harder. A breath gushed from me. Something twisted in my arm and it made me weak in the knees. The pain made me lose my breath and I almost fell to the floor.

Kova calmly held his hands up in surrender. My eyes widened at the tests in his white-knuckled fist. Air lodged in my throat. He'd forgotten he was holding them. If there was a God, I would sell my soul for Dad not to see what he was holding. It would only escalate things and make them worse.

"Frank, please do not do this to her. I will leave."

Dad turned toward Kova with fire spewing from his eyes. "Is this what I've been paying for? For you to fuck my daughter?" Then he turned toward me. "Joy was right. I had no idea you were such a slut."

He pulled his phone out with his other hand and swiped it open. I needed to keep his attention on me and away from Kova now.

Kova took a step closer.

"Take another step toward me, Konstantin, and I won't hesitate."

My stomach was a knotted mess. I didn't want Dad to try and hit Kova because as much as I loved my dad, Kova was much bigger and stronger and I worried one punch would knock him out.

"Dad! Stop! Nothing is happening here. Why won't you believe me?" I bawled, but he pulled my arm so hard and high that it forced me to stand on my toes. He twisted it behind my head and a cry burst from my throat. I'd been luckily enough to have never broken a bone, but judging by the agony that took my breath away, I'd say it was fractured or dislocated.

"I'm done with your lies, Adrianna," Dad said.

Kova looked at me. I didn't see the tests in his hand anymore, he must've pocketed them. He was white as a ghost but riled and bursting with the impulse to protect me. I'd never once seen him as I did now, torn from trying to do the right thing and trying to not make it worse. He was holding back from stepping in with reason— he was wrong, we both were wrong—but he also couldn't take seeing me in such pain either.

"My arm, please, let go," I said breathlessly, tears streaming down my face again. "It hurts."

Swallowing, Kova raised his voice. "Do not call the cops. I will walk away from everything. I will sell my gym, I will go back to Russia if I must. You will never see me again, but this is not her fault. Do not ruin her career because of me. Just let her go and I will leave."

Dad's fingers dug into my skin, and my own fingers were numb from his tight hold on me.

Dad ignored Kova as he erratically pressed buttons on his phone. I watched, trying to see who he was calling. My heart was going to jump out of my chest. I was shocked that he'd call the police because it would affect the Rossi name as well as Kova's reputation.

I took one quick glance at Kova, then I turned toward the front of my dad and shoved at his chest with my free hand, pushing as hard as I could. My strength was weak, but I couldn't let this happen. I had to stop him.

Only, I didn't push hard enough.

Dad's eyes flared, a blackness overtaking them. I didn't recognize him. My stomach clenched with fear. He reacted, twisting my arm so hard that I felt another pop. Kova's eyes widened and he rushed to grab me. A scream erupted from my throat and my dad finally let go. The pain took my breath away and I clutched my arm to my chest, closing my eyes in agony as I fell into Kova.

"Adrianna," Kova said. The tone in his voice alarmed me.

I opened my eyes and saw that my dad was about to press the phone icon. Standing up, I lunged with my good hand and reached out, slapping his phone away. It tumbled to the floor and the screen cracked.

Relief coursed through me, but not for long.

The back of his hand flew toward my face.

My head whipped to the side and I flew, my body slamming to the floor with a crash so hard my head smacked it. Kova bent down immediately and tried to help me, but Dad threw him off me.

"Don't you dare touch my daughter!" he roared.

Holding my cheek, I opened my eyes just as Kova got up, but that was all Dad needed. In a fit of rage, he flew at Kova with his fist raised in the air. Kova ducked and swiftly moved to the side, but surprisingly he didn't retaliate. I glanced down, seeing that his hands were balled into fists and his knuckles were straining against his skin.

"Touch her again and I'll rip your head from your neck!"

"I'll tell the cops you hit me," I said hoarsely, trying to stop the fight. I blinked, trying to clear my blurry vision. I don't think I could ever do that to him, but I needed a diversion. My stomach was aching, and it was a struggle to stand. "Your hand print will still be across my face. Not to mention, I can't move my arm. You attacked me. I'll deny anything you say about us because there's nothing to admit."

"Who knew what a manipulating young lady you'd turn out to be. Did you forget you're a minor and have zero authority here? You're coming home with me, and Konstantin is leaving in handcuffs."

I shook my head. I tried to get up and whimpered from the throb in my arm. Tears streamed down my cheeks and my eye felt swollen already.

A meaty fist landed on Kova's jaw and his head flew to the side, blood spurting from the corner of his mouth. He picked himself up quickly and took a step toward my father, but he quickly stopped when he realized what he was going to do.

His skin was flushed, damp with perspiration. I could feel the fury in his blood simmering beneath the thin layer. I'd never seen Kova so restrained before. The veins twirling down his arms were protruding, and every time he made a fist they swelled larger. His jaw was locked as he stared at my dad.

"You won't hit me because you know I'm right. You're a fucking pervert," Dad accused, walking toward him. My heart slowed down as I watched. "But that won't stop me," he said, and hit him again.

Kova took another round to the face and my heart broke for him. He put his arms up, blocking a few swings, then he gave my dad one strong shove. Dad stumbled back, and Kova placed the back of his hand to his mouth and wiped the blood away, leaving a smear across his jaw.

I couldn't take Kova being hit again. I knew he was restraining himself for me—and maybe because they were friends—and he knew deep down he was wrong, but I couldn't handle it anymore. It was slowly killing me.

Pushing off the floor, I ran forward and shoved myself between them. Kova saw what I was aiming for and flung me to the side as my dad landed another blow to Kova. I hit the floor so hard my vision shifted to double.

"Stop," I screamed and got back up.

Kova saw, his frantic eyes wide as I pulled myself up. "Stop, Adrianna!" he ordered, but I couldn't.

Dad was in a blind rage and I had to break them up before something worse happened.

"Dad, please stop," I said and grabbed onto his bicep.

He reared back without looking and shoved me with such force that I tripped over my feet. My breath rushed from me as I slammed into the wooden coffee table and my head hit the corner of the couch. Everything went black for a split second as stars danced in my vision, and I crumbled to the floor.

I was suddenly too weak. My body was giving out.

I tried to push up, but I was struggling to find even an ounce of energy. I heard Kova yell something, then, a crunching sound.

I had to get back up.

I was so disoriented, I couldn't tell whose blood was on my dad's fist, and I was sure my arm was fractured. I sucked in a strangled breath and tried to pick myself up, cradling my midsection. A sharp pain lacerated my stomach. I drew in a gasp, feeling like I was going to vomit. Something warm glazed down my thighs, but I was too off balance and fell to the floor again.

"Please! Stop hurting each other," I cried out, and managed to stand on wobbly legs. I was afraid to walk.

I looked up. Dad's back was to me as he threw punches at Kova, who was still blocking them. I took a few steps to reach him, hoping he'd stop when he saw me.

I don't know who pushed me, but my attempt to break them up was foiled. In a blink, I was flying across the room again, this time over the couch and onto the wooden coffee table.

My head whipped back and slammed into the wood with a crack. I slid across the table, taking the décor with me. Glass shattered under my body as I crumbled to the floor in a dead heap. My head began pounding, and I felt warm, sticky liquid all around me.

This time I couldn't move.

This time, I wouldn't be getting back up.

Coldness seeped into me and a metallic taste filled my mouth. I wondered if I'd bitten my lip when I fell.

I tried drawing in a breath only to flinch and cry out in agony from the sharp, shooting pain. A cough erupted out of me that caused my ribs to ache. I whimpered and tears fell from my eyes. I struggled to draw in a lungful of air again without it feeling like I was suffocating.

I could hear them scuffling and I tried to push myself up one last time, only to fall to the floor again.

"She is pregnant." I heard Kova say.

"Pregnant! What do you mean pregnant!"

"Adrianna." I heard my name in the distance.

"Open your eyes!"

"She is bleeding everywhere!"

Their voices began to blend together.

"Oh, my God."

"What did you do!"

"Open your eyes."

"Call an ambulance. Hurry!"

I couldn't move my lips to respond. I couldn't lift myself to stop them from killing each other.

My vision was spotty. I tried to blink a few times, attempting to stay awake and fight the body-draining fatigue that was taking over me. I just wanted to go to sleep.

Sleep sounded like a good idea.

"*Malysh!* Stay with me!"

I couldn't.

All I could do was lay there in agony, my broken body trembling in a warm pool of blood as my eyes rolled shut and darkness consumed me.

TO BE CONTINUED ONE FINAL TIME...

ACKNOWLEDGMENTS

With each book that comes to an end, I find myself surrounded by the same incredible people again. These women are my team. The ones who keep my head screwed on straight and lift me up when I'm feeling down. They're my squad girls, my biggest cheerleaders. I wouldn't be able to do this without them in my corner.

Jill Mac, Nadine Winningham, Amber Hodge, Vashti Dawn.

Each of you have played an integral part of this journey with me. Whether it's being a shoulder to lean on, brainstorming a plot with me or beta reading, editing and proofreading, and being an incredible assistant who goes above and beyond, Twist would not be what it is. I'm grateful for the friendship, but also that I get to work with you professionally. Who wouldn't want to work with their best friend? I could never thank you enough for all the hard work you put in to help me bring another book to fruition. It doesn't go unnoticed. Love you gals!

Readers, you humble me. Your love and support for this series is what encourages me to write, and make every story better than the last. Between the messages and tags, I'm honestly blown away. Never did I expect you guys to ship a series the way you do this one. Thank you for being patient with me while I finish writing Adrianna's story. It's been a long and angsty ride—we're almost to the finish line!

To my fabulous street team members who jump at every chance to promote my books—you guys have rendered me speechless with your endless support. Thank you for showing me that my words matter. I love you guys so much!

A huge thank you to my family for dealing with me. I spend a lot of time in my little office, and there is never a complaint from anyone. If anything, I'm being pushed to do more, and I love that. Thank you for talking about my books to friends any chance you get since I'm too shy to, and for just being a pretty rad family.

ABOUT LUCIA FRANCO

Lucia Franco resides in South Florida with her husband and two sons. She was a competitive athlete for over ten years – a gymnast and cheerleader – which heavily inspired the Off Balance series.

Her novel Hush Hush was a finalist in the 2019 Stiletto Contest hosted by Contemporary Romance Writers, a chapter of Romance Writers of America. Her novels are being translated into several languages.

She's written over a dozen books and plans many more for the future. When she's not writing, she can be found swimming in the ocean or getting lost in her butterfly garden.

Find out more at authorluciafranco.com